Nina Singh lives just outside Boston, USA, with her husband, children, and a very rambunctious Yorkie. After several years in the corporate world she finally followed the advice of family and friends to 'give the writing a go, already'. She's oh-so-happy she did. When not at her keyboard she likes to spend time on the tennis court or golf course. Or immersed in a good read.

Though her name is frequently on bestseller lists, **Allison Leigh**'s high point as a writer is hearing from readers that they laughed, cried or lost sleep while reading her books. She credits her family with great patience for the time she's parked at her computer, and for blessing her with the kind of love she wants her readers to share with the characters living in the pages of her books. Contact her at allisonleigh.com

Also by Nina Singh

The Marriage of Inconvenience
Snowed in with Her Reluctant Tycoon
Reunited with Her Italian Billionaire
Tempted by Her Island Millionaire
Christmas with Her Secret Prince
Captivated by the Millionaire
Swept Away by the Venetian Millionaire
Their Festive Island Escape
Her Billionaire Protector
Spanish Tycoon's Convenient Bride

Also by Allison Leigh

A Weaver Christmas Gift
One Night in Weaver...
The BFF Bride
A Child Under His Tree
Yuletide Baby Bargain
Show Me a Hero
The Rancher's Christmas Promise
A Promise to Keep
Lawfully Unwed
Fortune's Texas Reunion

Discover more at millsandboon.co.uk

HER INCONVENIENT CHRISTMAS REUNION

NINA SINGH

SOMETHING ABOUT THE SEASON

ALLISON LEIGH

MILLS & BOON

First Published in Great Britain 2020
by Mills & Boon, an imprint of HarperCollinsPublishers,
1 London Bridge Street, London, SE1 9GF

Her Inconvenient Christmas Reunion © 2020 Nilay Nina Singh
Something About the Season © 2020 Allison Lee Johnson

ISBN: 978-0-263-27903-0

1120

MIX
Paper from
responsible sources
FSC
www.fsc.org
FSC™ C007454

This book is produced from independently certified FSC™
paper to ensure responsible forest management.

For more information visit: www.harpercollins.co.uk/green

Printed and bound in Spain
by CPI, Barcelona

HER INCONVENIENT
CHRISTMAS REUNION

NINA SINGH

To my mum and dad.
For all the hard work and sacrifices.
And for your continual support.

CHAPTER ONE

You two need each other.

ZAYN JOFFMAN READ the words once more, holding the official document in his hand so tightly, he felt the ache in his knuckles. The solicitor's envelope had contained a personal letter imploring him to understand.

He didn't. Not at all.

Why was he surprised?

He answered his own silent question. Because he was foolish, that was why. Foolish enough to believe that the one member of his family whom he thought to be decent, accepting and kind, was enough of all those things to do right by him in the end. Well, he'd been wrong. And she hadn't done right by him at all. In fact, his late great-aunt had pretty much stabbed him in the back with her last official act as sole owner of Stackhouse Winery in the heart of Napa Valley.

Outside his window, the Manhattan skyline darkened with threatening storm clouds. The forecasted blizzard couldn't be too far behind. A late-night storm—a harbinger of the mess that was about to come his way.

How very appropriate.

Tossing the letter on the mahogany desk in his study, Zayn rubbed his eyes and tried to take a calming breath.

It was bad luck to think ill of the dead, wasn't it? Though, truth be told, he was more disappointed in himself than he was in Great-Aunt Myrna. He should have never for one moment believed that any one of them would deem him worthy enough to be sole heir to any of their holdings. Not even the sole relative who had taken him in. To add insult to injury, he'd have to share his inheritance with someone who wasn't even blood. Of course, Myrna considered the other inheritor family. She always had.

Well, he would figure it out; find a way around this. It would be simple enough to buy the other party out. He certainly had the resources. Despite his family's utter dismissal of him as anyone of any worth, he'd built quite a successful empire all on his own. Nevertheless, people had been underestimating him all his life. If he were honest, he would have to admit he'd given them good reason to do so in his earlier days. Still.

Their total brush-off stung just a bit. Okay. It stung a lot. Surely, they'd all seen how much he'd accomplished over the years, all that he'd achieved for himself. Shouldn't that have been enough to alter their view somewhat?

Turned out the answer was a resounding no—as clearly evidenced by the letter currently lying on his desktop.

Despite his success, his great-aunt's bequest came with a tremendous caveat. He would have to share everything fifty-fifty.

Rubbing his eyes on a weary sigh, Zayn walked around his desk to plop down on the ergonomic leather chair. What's done was done; he would have to move quickly to fix it all. He already had enough on his plate and would have to take care of this matter to move on to more pressing matters.

No, there was no doubt he would have to deal with the current scenario directly and by himself. He had a lot to discuss and negotiate with the other inheritor, and he couldn't trust others to do this for him.

You two need each other.

The written words echoed in his head in Great-Aunt Myrna's voice. He had no idea what she could have meant by that. He certainly didn't need anyone's help to run the place. In fact, he already had a vision for the winery that would be completely at odds with anyone who'd been involved with running it so far.

Stackhouse Winery was too small, too quaint. It didn't even accommodate online orders, for heaven's sake. That meant only mostly locals and a handful of seasonal tourists as customers. Such a setup made no sense at all and was completely unacceptable in today's global economy. The place was way overdue for a massive expansion.

Zayn wouldn't need a business loan to implement his ideas. He had ample resources. Perhaps that was why Myrna had made such an inexplicable decision. She'd probably figured Zayn would be the cash cow that kept the winery running completely as is without tampering with the status quo.

Well, if that was her thinking, she'd been terribly mistaken. And she'd greatly misjudged him.

Pulling over his tablet, he called up his assistant's number in the contact list. She answered before the first ring concluded, despite it being a Saturday morning.

"Clara, I know it's going to be a pain this close to the holidays, but please clear my schedule for the next two weeks. I have to make an unexpected trip to California."

Initially met with a long, silent pause, he realized how totally uncharacteristic his request had sounded.

"Is this regarding the recent passing of your great-aunt?"

Equally uncharacteristic of Clara to ask any kind of personal question.

Zayn supposed it was a rather unconventional time. "In a way," he answered. "The will has finally been revealed."

"I see."

This time Clara's question went unasked, though Zayn could guess what she was wondering. She probably couldn't fathom why he wouldn't just send a corporate representative to deal with the legalities and establishment of his latest acquired asset—or partial asset, as the case may be. He had plenty of qualified MBAs and attorneys on staff who could attend to such matters. And as tempting as it was, Zayn knew sending someone else would simply be the coward's way out. He may have been many things, but he'd never be credibly accused of cowardice.

"We'll be adding another winery to the corporate holdings, it turns out," he told Clara. No need to get into details regarding how he didn't quite own the entire property just yet.

"I see. I'll start the paperwork."

"Thank you. I'm afraid I'll have to personally go see about the acquisition. For various reasons…" He finally answered her unspoken question.

More silence. His assistant would never understand why he had to deal with this himself. How could she? She didn't know the history behind it all. The property wasn't even that large, as she was well aware. Not, at least, when compared to his other holdings.

Clara didn't realize this inheritance was part of his legacy—one final yet slim entry into the world he'd been born to but that had never wanted him.

There was no doubt he would have to deal with the other inheritor directly. The whole situation was one big, sensitive, complicated mess.

Made all the more complicated by the fact that he'd been in love with the other inheritor once long ago.

Santa Claus was most definitely drunk.

Izadora Veracruz had no doubt about it. She just had no idea what she was going to do about it. One thing was certain, she couldn't let Mr. Reyes go through with handing out presents in his current state. Why had he been "in his cups" already? It was barely noon. Though, she knew, day drinking was hardly an unheard-of custom in the heart of Napa Valley.

Still, did he have to be inebriated on this of all days? There was a line of kids in the tasting room at this very moment waiting to sit on Santa's lap for a photo and a small, token gift.

"Why, he's drunker than a rat in a whiskey barrel," Paula said, coming up to stand next to her. They both watched in horror as Mr. Reyes bent to tie his bootlace and nearly toppled over in the process. "He can't go out there, Izzy."

"I know," she responded on a deep sigh. "I can practically smell the fumes on his breath all the way over here."

"You certainly can't let him interact with the children in the state he's in," Paula added, once again telling her what was obviously clear as day.

"I know," Izzy repeated.

"Well, do we have a plan B?" Paula asked.

Not yet. But Izzy would have to come up with one.

With Myrna now gone, she was general manager of the winery, and all the responsibility fell squarely on her shoulders.

Correction: she was officially more than general manager now; she was part owner. Not that she expected any kind of help from her "partner." Zayn Joffman couldn't care less about this place. He hadn't been around the winery in years. No doubt he'd assume the role of silent partner and interfere just enough to rub against her nerves.

He'd always been good at doing that.

"I guess I'll have to take care of it myself," she said in answer to Paula's question.

Paula scoffed. "No offense, but you don't exactly fit the description. You'd make a lousy Santa."

She had a point. "Maybe. But I think I can pull off the role of helpful elf." She took her friend/employee by the forearm. "You go tend to Mr. Reyes. Take him to the kitchen and brew some coffee. Strong coffee."

"What are you going to do?"

"I'll go get dressed. I know there's at least one elf costume back there among the plethora of holiday decorations and knickknacks."

Paula gave her a brisk nod and went to do as instructed. Though it didn't appear that a pot of coffee would do much good—Reyes was three sheets to the wind. The man was sure to suffer one monster of a headache in a few hours.

By the time Izzy located and squeezed herself into the elf outfit, she was feeling much less generous toward her irresponsible Santa. For one, the green-felt costume was at least two sizes too small. She'd never been what one would consider petite and her generous curves screamed in protest at the tight confines. Playing Santa's helper had so not been on her agenda for the day.

This event was an annual holiday tradition at Stackhouse Winery. And Reyes had been playing the role of Santa Claus for several years. Why had he picked this day to indulge?

Sighing in frustration—and uttering a silent prayer that the cheap costume material held up for the next couple of hours—Izzy went out to address the children who would almost certainly be disappointed about Santa Claus's absence.

She was right. When she got to the tasting room and greeted the first child, she was met with a resounding frown. No one wanted to have their picture taken with an elf in a too small costume. The token gift would only do so much to tamper the disappointment. More than one parent could be heard grumbling about the waste of time and how they would have to make a trip to the mall.

Izzy could guess what they were all thinking. This was the first event she'd been responsible for since Myrna's passing. And somehow she'd utterly, embarrassingly, failed to pull it off. By the time the last child begrudgingly grabbed his gift and left, it was taking all Izzy had to keep from crying. Not one bottle of wine sold.

She missed her. Myrna had been so much more to Izzy than an employer. She'd been a trusted and solid friend since Izzy was a child, a parental figure who she'd miss forever.

Tearing the elfin cap off her head, she used it as a tissue to wipe her eyes and nose. Damn costume. She could hardly breathe in it. It was going straight into the trash bin as soon as she peeled it off.

The door opened suddenly, letting in a wave of cold air. What now? The tasting room still hadn't been set up, she had to go see about Reyes, and, if she had to spend one more minute in this sausage case of an outfit, she didn't think she could bear it.

"I'm afraid we're all out of toys," she told the newcomer, not bothering to look. "And you probably won't want a picture."

"On the contrary," replied a deep, masculine, and all-too-familiar voice. "I would love a photo. You have got to be the most adorable elf I've ever seen."

Izzy froze in place, at a complete loss for words. She had no question as to who that voice belonged to. She'd know it anywhere despite all the years that had passed since she'd last heard it. Zayn Joffman. As if this day hadn't been bad enough already.

Why in the world had he said that?

Zayn wanted to swallow back the words the moment they left his mouth. Of course, she looked adorable. She always had. So inappropriate for him to say so, however. There was no excuse for it. He'd just been so thrown off kilter when he'd walked in to find her clad head-to-toe in green felt with pointy-toed slippers. The material hugged her tightly in all the right places. Her dark, wavy hair fell in luxurious waves to frame her heart-shaped face. If anything, she'd grown even more beautiful with time. Though he'd thought he'd been prepared, seeing her again in such an unexpected getup had served to figuratively punch him in the gut. Who knew elves could be so fetchingly sexy?

Still, he should have been much more professional. Past history aside, the fact that they were currently business partners precluded flirtatious banter. For better or worse.

Judging by the glaring look of disdain currently shooting his way, this particular moment definitely fell into the latter category.

He cleared his throat, aiming for a do-over. "Hey, Izzy."

Now that he could clearly see her face, he felt like even more of a heel for the way he'd greeted her. She was clearly upset. Heaven help him, it looked like she'd been crying.

She sniffled. "Zayn."

"Is this a bad time?"

She didn't bother answering but asked a question of her own instead. "What brings you back around these parts?"

He couldn't tell if she was being sarcastic. Surely, she had an idea what had brought him home.

"I'm thinking you can guess the answer to that."

She shook her head. "I don't have a clue."

Still, Zayn couldn't be sure of her angle. She was one of the smartest people he knew. "I'd say we have some business to discuss, wouldn't you? Considering the contents of Myrna's will."

Izzy tapped a finger to her chin, as if contemplating what he'd just said. "Surely the CEO of a multinational corporation doesn't have to fly across the country himself for such a matter. Don't you usually send representatives and proxies to handle your business affairs?"

He shrugged, stepping farther into the room as he removed his gloves and shrugged off his coat. December in Napa was considerably warmer than the Northeast but still held enough of a bite to warrant such winter gear.

"I figured I'd handle this one personally." Again, she could certainly guess why. "First things first, however. Why are you in that ridiculous getup?"

Izzy made a show of rubbing her hands down her sides

and did a little twirl. "Oh, just something I threw on. Besides, I thought you said I looked adorable."

So she wasn't going to let him slide on that. He should have known. "Nevertheless, is there a particular reason one of Santa's elves is playing hooky in Napa during the busy holiday season?"

"There is. It's because Santa himself decided he needed something more festive than java this morning. The same morning he was due to meet and greet kids for our annual Take Your Picture with Santa event."

"So you had to step in as his loyal helper."

She pointed a finger at him. "Bingo."

"Good thing you happened to have a handy elf costume lying around."

She looked down at her midsection. "If only it fit better."

From where he was standing, it looked like it fit just fine.

"Not that it mattered what I looked like," Izzy continued. "The kids were disappointed to get an elf when they were expecting Santa. They didn't seem to think I was all that adorable."

"That bad, huh?"

She nodded, her eyes clouding. "Myrna would have never let this happen. She probably would have called Mr. Reyes last night to make sure he confirmed and that he showed up sober."

"Ah, yes. Myrna Tabor was perfect. I'd forgotten."

Izzy's eyes snapped up to glare at him. "What's that supposed to mean?"

"Nothing. Forget I said it." Izzy had been one of Myrna's biggest fans. And as far as he could recall, the feeling had been mutual.

In many ways, Izzy had been the daughter his childless great-aunt had never had. He, on the other hand, had been the reckless, draining child she hadn't been able to handle.

"Look…" Izzy began, her voice laced with ice. "I know you've had your issues with your family, but Myrna, for one, always tried to do right by you."

That statement was laughable given their current predicament. In all fairness, his great-aunt had indeed done the right thing where he was concerned. Myrna had taken him in and given him a permanent home after years of his being bounced from one to another. But she certainly had *not* done right by him in death. "Let's agree to disagree."

"Fine. I don't have the energy to argue with you anyway. Not after this colossal failure."

Zayn sighed. Such events were exactly the types of things he wanted to eliminate. Myrna and Izzy had thought it important for their role in the community to hold such lighthearted so-called family gatherings.

He couldn't disagree more.

His vision for Stackhouse was much different. He wanted the winery to be a major player in the high-end wine market. His personal brand, known the world over, was exclusive and luxury-oriented for the most particular sort of customer. Frivolous activities meant for kids had no business in a winery that was now part of such a portfolio.

Izzy and his great-aunt had always wanted to run this place like a small mom-and-pop establishment. Cozy and familiar.

He had bigger ideas for it. Ideas his great-aunt had subtly and gently, yet firmly, shot down over the years.

No need to get into all that now.

Izzy reached down to remove the pointy-toed slippers from her feet. Zayn had to force himself to look away from the shapely, feminine calves. In another lifetime, he'd run his hands down those very same legs. Back when they'd both been barely more than kids. They were very different people now. The whole world was different.

"Where are you staying?" Izzy asked when she straightened.

He gave her a shrug. "I thought I'd stay right here, on the estate."

"That's your right I suppose. Considering it's partly yours." She didn't sound happy about it.

"Don't worry, I don't intend to be in town for long."

She narrowed her eyes on him. "Now, why am I not surprised?"

CHAPTER TWO

WHO KNEW SHE was such a good actress? The very fact that her knees hadn't buckled yet was a true testament to thespian skills she wasn't aware she had.

It hurt to look at him. Zayn was handsome in a way that was striking. Dark hair and piercing black eyes. He wore his hair much shorter now, though he still sported the barest hint of facial hair along his jawline. How often had she teased him all those years ago about his constant and perpetual five-o'clock shadow? The tailored gray suit he wore fit him like a glove, accentuating a toned physique and muscular arms. The overall look was comparable to a model's for an exclusive men's cologne ad. He looked like the international success that he was. Much more polished than the teen she'd fallen in love with, he was the man he had left her to become.

Izzy swallowed the lump of emotion at the base of her throat and willed her pulse under control. She was doing fine on the outside. Calm and collected. All the while inside… Well, her insides were shaking. He was really here, standing before her. Her first love, the one who'd crushed her heart when he'd just up and left town on a sudden whim. She hadn't been enough to keep him nearby.

And despite all of that, every cell in her body wanted

to fling herself into his arms, tell him she'd missed him, pretend the last five years had never happened.

How foolish of her. To feel that way when it was clear he was only back because of Myrna's passing. To want his arms around her once more when some of the first words out of his mouth involved leaving yet again...

All this time, she'd thought she'd gotten over him. That he was a large part of her history she'd managed to bury in the past. How very mistaken she'd been. Only fooling herself. It had only taken one look. Just the sight of him brought all those buried feelings of loss and hurt sky-rocketing to the surface. But damn if she'd let him know. Especially considering how utterly unaffected he looked himself. While she stood there a roiling ball of emotion.

He was glaring at her after what she'd just said. So she repeated it. "It doesn't surprise me the least bit that you're already talking about leaving when you've only just arrived."

Here it comes, Zayn thought. The recrimination, the accusatory blame.

Izzy squared her shoulders. "I'm not sure exactly why you're here, Zayn. But I'm guessing you don't want to be. You haven't so much as set foot in Stackhouse since you stormed out five years ago."

Zayn hadn't intended their first interaction to be argumentative, but things appeared to be heading in that direction. Par for the course when it came to Izzy Veracruz. Well, if she was looking for a fight, he wasn't about to back down from one.

"I didn't 'storm out,' as you put it. And I hardly had a choice in leaving."

"That's where we disagree."

If she only knew. But this was not the time for enlightenment. Zayn had had his reasons for leaving Napa. And they involved her family just as much as they involved his. Perhaps even more so. It may very well be the one thing they had most in common. A complicated history with their respective families. Only in her case, it had been born of love and concern for her well-being. Whereas his situation had been forged from derision and unacceptance. But he wouldn't be the one to tell her the truth of it all. He'd given his word and he would keep it. As much as it pained him.

He'd have to bear the brunt of Izzy's ire and disappointment to protect the man who'd triggered it five years ago. For the truth of it was, that man had been right to do so.

Izzy gave her head a shake. "Let's not get into all this now. I have to get the tasting room ready for the first visitors scheduled for today. And I can't wait to get out of this confounded costume—which might take a while."

He couldn't even help where his mind went. Zayn had to bite his lip to keep from offering to help her undress. The images traveling through his mind of him doing just that weren't exactly helpful. He had to shift his focus.

"So you're still doing tastings via reservation only, then?" he asked her.

"Yes. That's how we've always done it."

Therein lay the problem. When was the last time this place had any kind of improvement or change? Even the décor was as he remembered it.

A deep, red-hued Oriental carpet lay in the center of the room, the large mahogany table centered atop it. There were still twelve burgundy-velvet chairs placed neatly around the table, though they did appear to have been reupholstered. One wall was lined from floor to ceiling with wine racks, and a black-leather armchair commanded every corner. The various paintings on the walls had changed. But that was to be expected. Myrna had loved to showcase pieces from local artists and to sell their work to interested visitors.

"What of it?" Izzy pressed.

"Let's just say I don't agree with every aspect of how this place is run."

"Is that why you're here? To tell me all the things I'm doing wrong?"

Not so much. He was here to take it off her hands with an offer she couldn't refuse. The idea of the two of them running a winery together was preposterous. He'd tried too hard to forget her. Being her business partner would only pick at the scabs of old wounds. They'd been lovers once. But the past was the past.

Though, she was right about one thing. This wasn't the time or place to discuss all that. He'd just arrived in town, after all.

"Not quite."

Her gaze on him narrowed even further; he felt like a specimen being examined in a science lab. "Then what?"

"Let me buy you lunch when you're done with the tasting. We can discuss some things when we both have time. Does the culinary place still make those rustic sandwiches?"

"As a matter of fact, they do."

"What do you say? Can I buy you a gourmet smoked turkey with soft Brie?"

Her lips tilted to the side. "On a baguette?"

As if he'd forget that's the only kind of sandwich she liked. "Absolutely."

She released a sigh. "All right. Why not?"

"It's a date, then." He flinched as soon as he said the word. It most certainly was not a date. Not like when they were kids and stole every opportunity to sneak off together, either to go to movies, to share a greasy burger from Sal's, or to just lie around the mountainside behind the vines.

She looked down, away from his face. Was she remembering all those times, as well?

"I suppose we do have a lot to go over."

"That, we do," he agreed.

When she looked back up at him, her eyes were sharp and focused. "Why do I get the sense I'm not going to like what you have to say?"

She held a hand up before he could respond, a habit of hers. "Rhetorical question. I'll see you in a couple of hours for lunch." With that, she turned on her heel and walked out, her shapely bottom swaying in the beckon of the tight elf pants. Not that he had any business noticing that kind of thing.

Zayn stood where he was, trying to gather his thoughts. Seeing her again had been as much a punch in the chest as he'd anticipated. Somehow, she'd grown even more beautiful. Or maybe he'd just missed her.

On that disquieting thought, he made his way outside. By the time he grabbed his bags from the rental car and headed for the house, the morning had already grown late.

Going upstairs was like stepping back in time. A large pine loaded with delicate ornaments and tinsel loomed in the foyer by the spiral staircase. Thin garland interwoven with silver tinsel wrapped evenly on the railing and banister. Poinsettias the size of small trees decorated every corner. Just as he remembered from his childhood when his mother had deposited him here with Great-Aunt Myrna before taking off on one of her many holiday excursions.

Her trips abroad grew longer and longer, and consistently became more frequent, until the time she never bothered to show up at all. His father had never been a presence in his life to begin with. Until very recently, Zayn hadn't even heard from the man. The memories resurfaced in his mind like barracuda jumping from choppy waters. His breath caught in his throat and the familiar chill ran up his spine.

Not now. Not here.

Closing his eyes once he got to the top of the stairs, he forced himself to concentrate on the darkness behind his lids and count backward from one hundred. Nausea churned his stomach as his chest pounded. Ninety-eight, ninety-seven…

Blessedly, though it took a while, his breathing resumed to an even, steady pace and his heart rate gradually slowed. The roiling in his gut quieted. That had been close, but luckily short-lived this time. He made himself focus on the afternoon that lay ahead of him. Lunch with Izzy. Their upcoming conversation wasn't going to be the easiest one he'd ever had.

Her parting question echoed in his head. *Why do I get the sense I'm not going to like what you have to say?*

Because she'd always been whip-smart, Zayn answered silently in his head.

And because she knew him all too well.

Get a grip, already.

How many times had she uttered those words to herself since the events of this morning when he'd arrived? Countless. So far, the mantra didn't seem to be working. It had taken everything she'd had to appear calm and unaffected. Cool as a cucumber on the surface.

All the while, inside, she'd been quaking with the shock of seeing him again after all these years.

She'd had no warning. But she had ignored the two emails in her inbox that he'd sent, not ready to deal with the ramifications of Myrna's will. Izzy sighed and smoothed down the skirt of her business suit. The truth was, she hadn't been ready to deal with him. Served her right. She'd have been prepared to face him if she'd known he'd be coming. Bad enough, he'd had to appear during the fiasco with the children and an absent Santa.

Now she had to go out there and commence the wine tasting. But that was good. Her work was like a balm to her soul. Focusing on the wines and presenting them to potential customers would take her mind off her frazzled nerves. She loved introducing Stackhouse wines to visitors. Her job as winery manager was all she could have hoped for.

Heaven knew, she'd given up enough for it. One could effectively argue that she'd given up everything. Her father still wouldn't return her calls. He made himself scarce whenever she visited her parents' home.

Ernesto Veracruz couldn't seem to forgive his daughter for working at a winery other than the one he'd established.

Now, as she made her way back downstairs and to the tasting room, she felt eternally grateful that she had such a job. And for Myrna for giving her the opportunity. Though she would have never guessed in a million years that, in death, the woman would actually bequeath her half of the winery itself. No, that had definitely come as a surprise. Several days had passed since the estate attorney had announced the news and Izzy still hadn't quite processed the ramifications. Perhaps she never really would.

When she reached the tasting room, Paula was already there setting up. Gone were the scraps of wrapping paper the children had haphazardly thrown around. The Santa chair had been moved back to its spot by the wide stone fireplace. Only a few random bits of glitter remained.

"You're a miracle worker, Paula," Izzy told her, full of yet more gratitude for the woman's sheer competence.

"I'd say you worked quite a miracle yourself earlier," Paula responded. "Averting the crisis that could have been with no Santa to greet the children."

Izzy rolled her eyes. "Hardly—that went about as poorly as it could have."

Her friend gave her a wink and a mischievous smile. "Oh, I'd say it could have gone much worse."

The thought made her shudder. "I suppose."

"And who was that? The tall, dark, handsome looker who showed up? You two seemed very…cordial…"

Paula had no idea about their past history. She'd only been hired a couple of years ago. As far as Izzy knew, the name Zayn Joffman was only one she'd seen on various emails occasionally throughout the years.

Oh, to be so lucky.

"That was Myrna's nephew," Izzy answered.

Paula's jaw dropped. "You mean the one who inherited this place along with you?"

Izzy gave her a nod. "The one and only."

"Huh. I'd seen pictures of him in the past. But, yowzah. That man looks like he could seduce the habit off a nun. No doubt he charms women wherever he goes."

Izzy winced at the description. She knew firsthand just how seductive Zayn could be. And she certainly didn't want to think about just how well he could turn on the charm.

"He grew up in this house, right?" Paula continued. "You must know him well."

Something in her facial expression must have betrayed her emotions judging by Paula's reaction. Her friend clasped her hands in front of her chest with a gasp. "You two were a thing, weren't you? It's written all over your face!"

Izzy did her best to feign an indifference she didn't feel. "Yes, if you must know. Zayn and I were 'a thing.' That was a long time ago, however."

"Well, what happened? Why didn't you two keep in touch all these years?"

"We just didn't."

She knew Paula wasn't going to be satisfied with that kind of an answer.

"Why did you two break up? I mean, you must want to talk about it, seeing as he's back and all."

Did she want to talk about it? Did she want to tell Paula how Zayn had been her first and only love? Or how he'd simply walked away one day never to look back? The way he'd shattered her heart into pieces without so much as an explanation as to why he was leaving?

Zayn had arrived at his great-aunt's house one sunny afternoon when she was twelve and Izzy's life had never been the same. They'd worked the fields together, pelting each other with fat, juicy grapes when the adults weren't looking.

And one day, as she grew older, the playfulness between them had turned into something deeper. It had all come to a head when Izzy had been stood up for her high school prom. Her date had dumped her for the captain of the cheerleading squad after said cheerleader's original date had broken his leg and she'd found herself in need of another one.

So Izzy had turned to her best friend. And Zayn had stepped up to accompany her. Izzy had been the talk of the prom that night, showing up as she had with an older, devastatingly handsome young man.

He'd kissed her for the first time that night and there'd been no going back. Not for her, anyway. Her affection for him had only grown stronger over the years. By the time she was a sophomore in college, she'd been head-over-heels in love.

She'd had her whole future in front of her and was wholly besotted with someone she'd thought had felt the same way about her.

Before it had all come crumbling down around her shoulders.

She shook off the memories to find Paula staring at her, still awaiting an answer. "Zayn decided he wanted something different than what he had living in Napa."

Paula lifted an eyebrow. "Simple as that?"

Izzy nodded. "And then we just sort of lost touch."

In fact, the full truth wasn't simple at all. Not in a way that Izzy had ever understood. For Zayn had left after barely saying goodbye. Totally unexpectedly. He'd given her nothing but a short speech about how he didn't fit in, had never belonged in Napa. How he needed to make his own way far from Stackhouse.

And then he was gone.

A shudder racked through her at the memory of those first few weeks after he'd left. She never wanted to feel such loss again. The loneliness she'd endured without him had nearly broken her.

"Just like that?" Paula asked.

"Just like that."

"Well, it's no wonder you don't date. That man would be a tough act for any man to follow."

Izzy figured Paula might be due for a taste of her own medicine. "And what about you?"

Paula scrunched her eyes. "What about me?"

"I don't exactly see you with a full social calendar. Why aren't you dating anyone?"

"I haven't really thought about it."

Izzy couldn't resist teasing her. "Oh, you haven't? Or is it more because you've been thinking about a certain handsome GP?" Izzy knew for a fact that her friend had a heavy crush on the town's handsome young doctor who'd recently opened his own practice. From what she could tell, the feeling was mutual. Neither one seemed to be doing anything about it, however.

Paula refused take the bait. "We're not talking about me. We are talking about you. Now, I have some more questions about my new boss. Or half boss, as the case may be."

Izzy didn't get a chance to respond as the reserved party of tasters arrived through the front door. She uttered a small prayer of thanks to the timing gods. She didn't really want to answer any more questions about Zayn right now. Not even for Paula, trusted friend and colleague that she was. As it was, she'd had about enough of meandering down memory lane for one morning.

With a wide smile plastered on her face, she greeted her guests and showed them to their seats. The door opened once again, letting in a slight breeze and signaling yet another arrival. That didn't make sense. There were five people reserved for this time slot. And all five were already in place. Two couples and a solitary man who appeared to be in his early thirties.

When Izzy looked up to see who the latest arrival was, she realized she'd thanked the gods much too early. Apparently they weren't quite done playing with her today.

Again, she should have known she wouldn't get off that easily. So much for letting work take her mind off her troubles.

Zayn walked into the room and straight to the tasting table. He'd changed into a black collared shirt and pressed khakis. His dark hair was combed neatly back, though a wayward curl fell lazily over his right eye. Izzy ignored the twitch in her finger signaling a desire to reach for that curl and smooth it back into place.

Pulling out a chair, Zayn nodded to the others in greeting. Then he flashed her a brilliant smile that almost had her knees buckling. "I thought I'd join in. Dying to get a taste of the latest harvest products."

If looks could kill, Zayn figured he'd be good and buried by now. Izzy looked like she was ready to throttle him. In fact, he could have sworn he saw her fingers twitch. Probably itching to wrap around his neck.

"Zayn, what a surprise." Izzy's voice was full of warmth and welcome. If he didn't know her so well, he would have never guessed that she was less than pleased about his presence. He just knew that she was seething under the cool exterior.

"We're only set up for five people," she added.

"Would setting up another spot pose too much trouble?"

The petite blonde next to her with the too tight ponytail seemed to hesitate, her eyes traveling to Izzy's face as if seeking approval.

Izzy responded with a subtle shrug.

"I can set up another spot for him," the blonde said. "It will only take me a sec." She ran to the bar and disappeared behind it. The sound of glasses clinking echoed through the air.

Izzy's eyes flashed with irritation but, to her credit, the smile never wavered.

The blonde returned within moments and efficiently set up a place for Zayn where he sat.

Izzy cleared her throat and began pouring from the first bottle. A deep amber chardonnay fizzed ever so slightly with effervescence as it filled the bottom third of the goblet.

The slender man with the thin wire spectacles was definitely trying to catch Izzy's eye, silently flirting with her. Zayn could hardly blame the poor fool. Izzy was beautiful, graceful and naturally vivacious. And at the moment, she was completely in her element. She was a true professional who knew her craft well. No wonder the guy was looking at her with heart-filled eyes. Even the coupled gentlemen shot her appreciative glances as she spoke. Still, annoyance with the besotted spectacled stranger prickled like thorns under Zayn's skin.

Not that he had any kind of business feeling what could only be described as jealousy. He'd be a fool to deny that's exactly what the tightening in his chest was about. All these years and his subconscious still figured he had some sort of claim to her. As if he could walk into her life and pick up where he'd left off.

Yeah, right.

One of the women asked Izzy a question. Something about how she'd gotten into this line of work. He hadn't heard the exact words. He'd been too busy focusing on the striking hue of Izzy's eyes that went from dark chocolate to a rich shade of caramel when the sunlight hit her face just so.

Izzy answered right away, almost without thought. As if she was used to receiving the inquiry. She told them her history, of growing up in a family hired to work the vines of a large, established winery, and how she'd fallen in love with every part of the winemaking business. Hardworking and dedicated, she'd gone to school to learn the business end.

She'd been a stellar, accomplished student. Too good for the likes of him. He'd done her a favor all those years ago when he'd left her alone to pursue her dreams. Not that it had been his choice exactly. No. The choice had been her father's.

But the old man had been right when he'd asked Zayn to leave town and leave Izzy alone. He'd been right that it would be for the best if Zayn stopped seeing his daughter and got far away from her. The old man hadn't been nasty or mean about it. Just straightforward with the clear facts. Izzy was doing great at university; she had a bright future ahead of her. Zayn was spinning his wheels, working odd jobs, and getting arrested for bar fights and other troublesome behavior. He hadn't been in a good place back then. The underlying message hadn't been mean-spirited. But it had been clear. *You're not good enough for her.*

Just like he hadn't been good enough for the parents who'd abandoned him and all the families that had come after. Families ready to get rid of him as soon as they could.

Now, as Izzy reached the part about her college years, she glanced his way ever so swiftly. He caught her eye for the briefest flash. It was enough to send a surge of painful guilt through his core. There was no denying the hurt behind her eyes.

Damn it.

What was the use in feeling guilty? That wouldn't do either of them any good. It was all water under the bridge, anyway. She may not know it but he'd done right by her.

The proof was the accomplished, savvy businesswoman standing before him now.

And he'd done right by her old man for keeping that long-ago conversation a secret from Izzy all these years.

She really knew her stuff. And was clearly excited about what she did for a living. All in all, Zayn figured he could have done much worse for a business partner. Too bad the status quo was unsustainable. Never mind the fact that it would drive him insane to try to behave as if they were nothing more than business partners, Izzy would never go along with his vision for the future of this place. And he owed it to himself to pursue that vision. When it came to the one small piece of legacy his family bequeathed him, he wasn't up for negotiating.

One more reason to give Izzy to hate him. As if she didn't have enough already. His hope was that her reaction wouldn't be so bad if he made her a once-in-a-lifetime offer. One she'd be foolish to refuse.

He watched her now as she moved on to the reds. Her hair was done up in a tight chignon, her suit a dark steel-gray—serious, with a sharp collar and high waist, yet somehow feminine at the same time. Still, he had to admit he preferred her in the elf outfit, her hair in disarray under a floppy hat that sported a bell at the pointed tip. Go figure.

"All our wines are aged in red oak barrels," she was saying. "This particular cabernet is especially nuanced by the influence of the oak flavors."

One of the women took a small sip and actually groaned in pleasure as Izzy continued. "Unfortunately, this particular vintage has sold out already. We have a wait list for those who are interested."

"Oh, no!" the groaning woman exclaimed. Other rumblings of disappointment sounded around the table. It all served to prove his point exactly. Exclusivity was one thing. But such a loss of potential sales had to be addressed. As far as he was concerned, there was a failure in the overall process somewhere if a popular wine wasn't available for interested customers. Once he had full control of winery operations, he would definitely address these exact shortcomings.

"We'll make sure to put all your names on the wait list," Izzy assured them, presupposing the future sale. That was something, at least. "In the meantime, please allow me to pour you our pinot noir." She pulled the stopper off another bottle. The reaction to this wine was just as enthusiastic after she poured.

All right. He had to give her that. She had recovered pretty well from what he considered to be a large flaw in their system.

He would be sure to point that out to her right before he told her how he planned to change it all from top to bottom.

CHAPTER THREE

WHY IN THE WORLD had she agreed to this?

Izzy climbed up the makeshift wooden stairs alongside the mountain behind the rows of grapevines. She was still having trouble wrapping her head around the fact that Zayn was actually back in town. She'd fully expected him to dispose of all this with a simple phone call. To tell her what he wanted done now that he was partner, to wish her well and then tell her to send him an occasional email to keep him up-to-date. Then he would leave her alone. Wishful thinking.

He certainly had better things to do, one would think. He'd turned his back on this place years ago, after all.

So her curiosity had gotten the best of her and she'd agreed to this meeting. But why here of all places? If she was smart, she would have insisted on a different location. This spot held too many memories. For her, anyway. Zayn probably couldn't even care to remember the stolen moments they'd spent on this mountainside. Away from the world, away from all those who frowned upon their even being together in the first place. No, he'd probably forgotten all the stolen kisses and gentle touches. That was doubtlessly why he could suggest they have their lunch meeting here of all places, while she was trembling at the thought of being alone with him in this spot.

She found him already setting up at the wooden picnic table when she got there. To anyone observing them, the picture would look like the perfect romantic scene, straight out of some kind of movie about a couple on the verge of falling in love. Zayn had centered a bottle of wine resting in a frosty silver bucket and two goblets at one end of the wooden table. A glass bowl full of some kind of green salad occupied the middle of the table, along with what appeared to be deli-wrapped baguettes. The man sure knew how to treat a woman to a picnic lunch.

Steady, girl. She'd best be sure to remember this was nothing more than a business meeting.

Izzy slowed her gait and forced away the smile that had crept onto her face when she hadn't been paying attention.

"You're here," he announced, flashing her a grin. He hadn't changed his clothes, unlike her. She'd swapped out the stifling business suit for a comfortable pair of jeans and a thick, velour sweater. But Zayn remained in khakis and the same shirt. Only he'd undone the top two buttons, exposing just enough of the golden skin beneath that she wished she hadn't noticed.

"This looks like quite the spread."

The grin grew wider. "Guess it beats all the wheat toast and soggy hot dogs we used to sneak out here. Back when that was all we could afford."

Did he have to bring up such pleasant memories of their shared past? They surfaced on their own quite well enough without his help. And remembering any of it was the absolute last thing she needed. She'd tried hard all these years to forget.

He'd only been in town a few hours and already her focus was completely shot.

"Yes, well…this definitely beats hot dogs," she said as she sat. "Thanks for running out and getting all this."

"You're welcome. I hope you're hungry."

"Famished," Izzy assured him as she took hold of a napkin and draped it on her lap.

"And thirsty, too, I hope." He grabbed the goblet in front of her and began pouring the wine. A rich, deep sauvignon blanc with a flowery scent she could detect from across the table.

Her stomach rumbled and her mouth watered as she unwrapped the paper from her sandwich.

A girl could get used to this. Delicious food and fresh air in the company of a handsome, attentive man. After the morning she'd had, she deserved to ignore the reality of the situation. Simply enjoying the moment didn't have to mean anything of high consequence. Zayn had gone to a lot of trouble to put all this together, after all. The least she could do was savor the moment.

"Care to sniff the cork?" he asked her before sitting on the bench across the table from her.

"That won't be necessary." She took a bite of the baguette and nearly moaned out loud at the burst of flavor along her tongue. Homemade French bread would always be her great weakness. These days, lunch usually consisted of a granola bar eaten hurriedly at her desk as she ran over numbers or processed orders. This was definitely a treat by comparison.

He really did appear to be trying here.

Whatever was to happen with their partnership, she had to give Zayn the benefit of the doubt. They'd been barely more than kids when he'd left; they were both older and wiser now. And what he'd done by bringing her this meal was clearly an olive branch of sorts. They could approach the upcoming days as two mature and reasonable professionals who only wanted what was best for Stackhouse.

"Thanks again, Zayn. This sandwich is to die for. It almost makes up for the morning I had."

He took a small sip of wine. "You're welcome."

"Mr. Reyes was deeply apologetic, by the way," she began by way of conversation. "Swore it wouldn't happen again. Next year, he'll be completely dry and properly sober. Downright Santa-like."

Something shifted in his eyes right before he cleared his throat. "Next year, huh?"

She nodded, took another bite, this time making sure to get a good chunk of avocado along with the bread. "Yes. There's always a Santa visit just as there's always the annual light show through the vines."

"That's part of the reason I wanted to have this discussion," Zayn said, putting his sandwich down to methodically run his fingers along the stem of his wine goblet.

Something stirred in the lower pit of Izzy's stomach. Her libido resurfacing after many dormant years. So very inconvenient. She forced herself to focus on the conversation.

"What? About Mr. Reyes not getting drunk next year? He assured me he won't." She braced herself, ready to go to the mat to fight for the older man if need be.

"About all of it, Izzy."

Izzy swallowed the morsel in her mouth. The tone of Zayn's voice and his granite expression suddenly had apprehension fluttering in the center of her chest.

"All of what?" She put her food down and wiped the corners of her mouth with the paper napkin. "Maybe you should just come right out and tell me, Zayn. Why are you really here? Why have you come all this way?"

He tilted his head. "All right. I came to make you an offer."

"What kind of offer?"

Before she could process what he was doing, he slid his smartphone across the table toward her. The screen showed a series of numbers with a dollar sign.

"That's a lot of zeros. What do they mean?"

"It's my starting point. We can negotiate, but I think it's more than fair."

"Fair?" Her mind had somehow gone numb. Was she really hearing and understanding him right? His next words confirmed that she was.

"I'd be willing to write you a check right now with that amount on it. For your half of Stackhouse."

All thoughts of civility and mature discourse fled her mind and the blood chilled in her veins. What a fool she was. This lunch, the picnic table, the wine. She thought he'd gone out of his way to do something nice for her. Ha! What a joke. It was all just a way to butter her up before he dropped the bomb.

She should have known better.

He would never understand her. Not in a million years. Her whole expression went from calmly serene to hardened and angry. She looked ready to fling the wine in his face. Or to throw her sandwich at him. Probably both.

He'd known she wasn't going to be thrilled with the idea. But she could have bothered to at least listen to him for a minute or so.

"You have got to be kidding me." Her tone held a glacier's worth of ice.

He held a hand up. "Iz, just hear me out."

"Don't call me that!"

He hadn't even consciously thought to revert to his pet

nickname for her. He took a deep breath. "Fine. I won't. But can you just take a minute and listen to reason?"

"Reason? Is that what you call it?" She threw her arms wide and gestured around. "Is that why you went to the trouble of doing all this? The expensive wine, picking up a gourmet lunch the exact way I like, setting up a picnic."

Heaven help him. Were her eyes growing shiny? She was so mad at him, she was tearing up.

"Is that why you did all this?" she demanded to know. "So you could set up the scene to try to sweet-talk me out of my job?"

Out of her job? He had no intention of asking her to leave. The place would be lost without her. She was jumping to all sorts of conclusions. In all fairness, he probably could have handled the delivery of the message a bit better. Usually, he prided himself on being a master communicator, one who could negotiate and barter with outstanding results. But he was totally off his game here. Between seeing Izzy again and being thrust back into the memory trap that was his childhood home, he was completely off balance.

"Look, no one said anything about your job being in question. No matter what happens, you know you have a spot here. In fact, I'd love for you to continue on in your role."

Her lips thinned into a slim line before she spoke.

"Oh, you would, huh? Last I checked, you weren't the sole decision maker."

"That's the problem, Iz—" he caught himself "—zy." The elongation only served to make her name sound even more endearing.

She bristled some more. "What's that supposed to mean?"

"You and I both know we have very different ideas

about how this place should be run. You and Myrna ran it like a community social center that happened to sell some wine through some very narrow channels. That's no way to run a winery. Or any business, for that matter."

"I find that highly offensive. That way happens to work for us. It has been working for us."

He shrugged. "It isn't meant to be. I'm simply stating the facts. We are going to keep butting heads if we remain co-owners."

"What if I was the one who said I wanted to buy you out?"

He tried not to give anything away of his reaction to that so-called threat. They both knew Izzy didn't have those kinds of resources. He remained silent, figuring that was answer enough.

She waited several beats before continuing. "So, your brilliant scheme to address our differences is to buy me out. Is that it?"

"I think it's a very sound, reasonable plan."

"But you'd have me remain on board as a voiceless employee who has no say in operations and is there simply to follow your directives? Do I have all that straight?"

When she put it that way... "Izzy, of course you'd have a say. You'd still be vineyard manager."

"Only by your good graces. And I can just guess how much weight my actual opinions would hold." She shook her head. "Why?"

He thought he'd explained his reasoning pretty well. Though clearly she didn't agree with it. "Why what?"

"Why did I think you might have changed?"

So now she was going to bring up past history? He didn't have to defend himself to her or to anyone else. The truth was, he had indeed changed. But no one back here would ever see that. Not Izzy. And most certainly not her father.

Well, he was done explaining himself to anyone. He'd made that decision years ago. Fighting to redeem himself in others' eyes had led to nothing but frustration and futility. Despite all his professional success, everyone in his past refused to see him as anything more than the angry, punk teen who constantly found himself in trouble. Such an embarrassment. Why would he think Izzy would be any different?

Her next words confirmed all the thoughts running through his head.

"You're still the same selfish man who thinks of no one but himself."

Stupid. Stupid. Stupid.

To think, she'd felt touched that Zayn had gone out of his way to treat her to a pleasant lunch. For a second there, she'd thought he might have actually been interested in catching up. That he might have been curious about how she'd fared since he'd left. All the while, he'd had the most crushing of ulterior motives. Well, it was her fault for feeling even one iota of hurt. How often could she be so foolish and deluded when it came to one man?

Five years ago, he couldn't wait to get away from her. Now he couldn't wait to get rid of her. This winery and the estate it sat on was her home, her refuge. What did he think she was going to do with her life if she walked away from it? And he had to know she would have no choice but to walk away if she took any of his money for her half of it.

Now, as she made her way to the cellars, she had to consider the possibility that his intention all along was to get her to leave and pretend he'd given her any kind of option.

She wasn't surprised when she heard footsteps behind her as she inserted the glass testing tube into one of the barrels.

"Look, I didn't mean to blurt my intentions out so bluntly that way. It was wrong of me to just throw it at you. I apologize." A bag of lavender candy materialized in her line of vision. "A peace offering. I picked it up for dessert from the culinary school shop. I hope you still like these things?"

Oh, no. She wasn't falling for that again. Tokens from the past were not going to work anymore. Fool her once and all that.

"I have a lot of work to do, Zayn."

She ignored the candy and heard his deep sigh behind her. He pulled his arm back when she didn't take the peace offering. "We have to address all this, Izzy."

Izzy gripped the tube so tight her fingers ached. He was right. As much as she wanted to slam the proverbial door in his face and walk away, logic dictated that she couldn't ignore him. Myrna had really put her in such a hard predicament. She'd known the woman her whole life. Myrna had never made any kind of decision without thinking it through completely. She must have had her reasons for setting up her will the way she had.

You two need each other.

Those words had been the end note of the letter she'd included for Izzy in her will. Izzy had no idea what she might have meant by them. Why would she need the man who'd left her high and dry with a broken heart? It had to be a reference to Zayn's business acumen combined with her own intimate knowledge of Stackhouse. Myrna must have thought the two of them could work together in her absence. Or maybe Izzy was just grasping at straws. One thing was for certain—she had to deal with Zayn until they settled all this. One way or another.

Sighing, she turned to face him.

"I'm really sorry, Izzy. I didn't mean to upset you." He sounded sincere enough. He held out the bag of candy once more. This time, she reluctantly took it. But she refused to thank him. "I'm usually better at bringing up negotiations. It's just, you started talking about the Santa Claus winery visit and then the light show, and I figured it was a good segue."

"And you have an issue with such events?" she asked rhetorically.

He shrugged. "I don't see how they would work as any kind of marketing strategy to drive up sales. But I should have stated my point better. I know Myrna enjoyed such get-togethers."

"Look, this isn't exactly easy on me, either," she began, trying to keep her voice steady yet firm. "But Myrna wanted me to have half this place. She must have had her reasons." Probably because the older woman had guessed that her great-nephew would swoop in and lay roughshod waste to all that Stackhouse represented and stood for in Napa Valley. It was so much more than just a winery, but Zayn would never see it that way. All he saw were dollar signs.

"You are so focused on the numbers," she added.

"We can talk about the amount I'm offering you."

He'd misunderstood her. She resisted the urge to fling the candy bag in his direction. "This has nothing to do with your offer!" How could he possibly be so obtuse?

Zayn gave a slight shake of his head. Heaven help them both, he really didn't see it. "Then what?"

"Think about it. Myrna could have just given me a monetary amount as her operations manager. And stipulated as part of your inheritance that you keep me on board. But she didn't do that."

He lifted a shoulder. "And? What's your point?"

"Her decision to do things this way was about more than just making sure I'm taken care of." Izzy felt a tightness in her throat as she said the words. For there was no doubt Myrna would have done just that: made sure Izzy was well taken care of after she was gone. But the way the older woman had drawn up her will, Izzy knew she was asking for something from her, as well. To make sure the winery stayed the way it was, numbers be damned.

"She'd had a vision for this place since the moment she'd taken it over once your uncle passed."

He crossed his arms in front of his chest, studied her. "And she knew you would guard that vision."

Izzy nodded. Maybe there was some hope that he could understand.

"Then why did she even bother leaving part of Stackhouse to me?"

Wow. Izzy felt torn between shaking him and the sudden unexpected urge to hug him. For Zayn to even ask that question was downright heartbreaking. Just went to show that he really hadn't come to grips with his past despite all the years that had gone by.

"Because you were her great-nephew, Zayn. And because she loved you."

His only answer was to scoff at her words before silently turning around and walking away. She knew better than to try to go after him.

CHAPTER FOUR

WELL, THAT HAD gone about as poorly as it could have.

Zayn made his way back to his suite completely unaware of his surroundings. Somehow it was afternoon already, but it felt like weeks since he'd arrived. The familiar pounding in his chest taunted him, but he figured if he got back to his room in time and shut the door behind him, he'd be able to keep it at bay.

Izzy had no idea what she was talking about. Aunt Myrna may have given him a home, but any notion of love or affection was definitely a stretch of the imagination.

Izzy had always seen the best in his great-aunt. The admiration had been mutual. Myrna'd had a soft spot for Izzy since the day her family had started working this vineyard. The little girl had skipped right into his aunt's heart upon arrival. Eventually, Myrna had become Izzy's mentor. And Izzy had been an eager protégé.

Izzy was the bright spot in their lives back then. Whereas he'd been nothing but a dark cloud looming overhead.

Ninety-six...ninety-five...

By the time he reached fifty, to his relief, his breathing started to steady and his heart rate gradually slowed as he finally reached his room. Within moments, his cell phone alerted him to an incoming call. The screen told him it was Clara, his assistant in New York. She'd left several messages. He hadn't had a chance to call her back.

Begrudgingly, he answered the call, though more talking was the last thing he wanted to do at the moment.

"Hey, Clara."

"Hello," came her crisp, efficient voice from the other side of the country.

"Sorry I haven't been able to call back. Things haven't gone quite the way I'd planned."

"Oh? In what way?"

He could just picture her eyebrows raised clear to her hairline. "The negotiation isn't going well."

"I see. The other party is driving a hard bargain, then?"

"Yes." *And no*, he added silently. Izzy wasn't interested in any kind of bargain whatsoever.

"At the risk of sounding indelicate," Clara began, "she isn't family, is that correct?"

The question threw him off. Izzy wasn't family by blood. But in every other sense she was. "Not technically. Why do you ask?"

"Well, there may be other avenues we can pursue to acquire the entire property."

He had a feeling where she might be going with this. Clara could be like a pit bull with a bone when it came to business. Such a trait was one of the reasons he'd hired her three years ago. But her instincts were highly misplaced in this case.

"I don't think we need to go there, Clara."

Still, she pled her case. "Your great-aunt was old and frail. Perhaps not in her right mind. Someone close to her could have easily taken advantage of her frailty and old age."

Zayn had to bite his tongue to keep from laughing out loud at the suggestion. As if anyone could have taken advantage of his great-aunt. As for Clara, she was simply doing what she was paid to do: figure out what was best for the company and determine how best to achieve it.

"Not an avenue I'm willing to pursue."

"Are you certain, Mr. Joffman? It probably wouldn't even have to go to court. Usually such matters are settled outside of a courtroom."

"Not an option, Clara," he said with more steel in his voice than he'd meant to. Such an idea was out of the question. He wouldn't even entertain it for a moment. Izzy was the last person in the world who would have taken advantage of anyone, let alone his aunt. She'd worked hard at Stackhouse over the years and deserved what Myrna had bequeathed her. It was simply pure, rotten luck that they had such different ideas about how the winery should be run.

He began to explain. "It just so happens that the other inheritor happens to be an honest and valued member of the community. She doesn't have a manipulative bone in her body. I've never seen her so much as tell a fib. And I've known her a long time."

Clara didn't speak for several beats. When she did, she sounded surprised. "I apologize. I didn't realize you knew the other person so well."

Zayn couldn't help but wince at the last word. If Clara only knew how accurate a statement she'd just made. He and Izzy had known each other intimately, all right. Though that seemed like another lifetime ago. Especially now.

"No need for apologies," he assured his assistant. "Trust me when I say a resolution is forthcoming. We just happen to be in a holding pattern at the moment."

Luckily, she didn't press further or ask for any more information. "Then I will await further instruction and file the matter away for now."

He thanked her then powered off the phone. He needed some quiet time to think things through. What he'd said to Clara just now was the absolute truth. Izzy didn't have a manipulative bone in her body. In fact, the only character flaw of Izzy's he could even think of was that she could run a little hot-headed. Other than that, she was near perfect.

Izzy was the full package. Smart, hardworking, attractive as a siren. An image of her wearing the sexy elf costume flashed in his mind and he had to mentally swat it away. When she smiled, it was like a mini sun rising to brighten any place she happened to be. Was she seeing anyone? he had to wonder. Not the first time he'd pondered that particular question. She had to be. She was too good a catch. Any man on earth would be lucky to have her.

Damn. He didn't need to pursue that train of thought. Zayn rubbed his forehead and plopped down on the bed behind him. He had it bad still, didn't he? He'd managed to avoid facing it all this time, thanks to the physical distance between them. But his feelings for Izzy had never diminished. All it took was setting eyes on her again to bring them all to the surface.

He hadn't the slightest idea what to do about it.

"I don't see why these aren't lighting up."

Izzy stared up at Ethan Greaves, MD, as he stood on the stepladder in front of an animated Frosty the Snowman. The winery light display was almost complete. But there appeared to be a glitch in this particular section. Frosty was completely dark.

"Well, what's your professional diagnosis, Doc?" she asked him. Ethan was a true and loyal friend who took a day off every year from his busy practice to help Izzy and Myrna set up the mile-long display through the main part of the winery past the estate and down to the vines. All he accepted in payment was a case of cabernet and a homemade lunch. Izzy was grateful for his Christmas spirit. Particularly this year with Myrna gone and the return of the prodigal son.

Ethan draped the wires he was holding over the top of the ladder and stepped down. He answered her question with mock seriousness. "I'm afraid it's not looking good."

"Just give it to me straight. I can take it." Her reply was delivered in an equally solemn voice.

Ethan shook his head, his features cut in stone. "All right. But brace yourself."

She nodded fervently. "I'm ready."

He took a deep breath. "We're going to have to replace all the bulbs and restring the snowman."

Izzy gasped with exaggerated flourish and clasped a hand to her chest. "Is there really no other way?"

Ethan took her by the shoulders, continuing the playful charade. "I'm afraid not."

"Oh, no!"

His grip on her shoulders tightened ever so slightly. "I know this is hard. But you have to be strong, Izzy. For him. For Frosty."

That did it, the sheer gravity in his voice served to undo her playacting. She burst out in laughter, unable to hold it in any longer. Ethan chuckled along with her.

She felt Zayn behind them before she saw or heard him. A sensation of awareness had shivered along her skin, alerting her to his presence.

"Am I interrupting?" Zayn wanted to know.

Ethan turned to him, his hand extended. "Z-man! I'd heard rumors you were back in the valley."

Izzy watched as the two men shook hands. Zayn appeared cordial enough, said all the right words to the town doctor he'd been casually acquainted with before leaving Napa. But she could sense an undercurrent within him. He was displeased. She could just guess why.

He was unhappy about the light display. No doubt, he saw it as yet another unnecessary holiday feature the winery put forth every year at this time.

Had the man always been such an insufferable Grinch?

"No, you're not interrupting." She answered his earlier question, adding, "We were just working on reviving good old Frosty here. It appears he needs some new equipment."

Zayn quirked an eyebrow at her. "Maybe that's a sign?"

She decided to play devil's advocate. "What kind of sign do you think it might be?"

Zayn released a weary sigh and plunged his hands into his pants' pockets. "Is all this really necessary, Izzy? What does a winery in California need with a holiday light show? It has nothing to do with selling wine."

She knew it! "You can't be sure of that. At the least, it drives more traffic to the winery. This time of year isn't exactly hopping with tourists." She glanced at Ethan for some backup. But he simply stood there, glancing from her to Zayn, as if watching an entertaining tennis match. A small, amused smile hovered along his lips.

Clearly, there would no assistance forthcoming from that corner.

"You may have a point. But it's not the kind of traffic we need, I would gather. Families with small children are typically not big buyers. A bottle here and there."

She crossed her arms in front of her chest. He really wanted to argue this here and now. "It's better than nothing," she countered.

"Is it? Compared to the cost, I'd say it's not much better at all. The electricity bill alone is probably a non-starter."

Izzy gritted her teeth. "The entire community loves that we do this. It's the only light display of its kind within miles. There's no way we're canceling it." Not as far as she had a say.

Ethan cleared his throat. "I guess I should head out, then."

So now he was abandoning her altogether? Izzy thought. Men! They were all frustrating, undependable creatures. "Where are you going?" she demanded, her tone unintentionally vehement.

Ethan raised his hands. "I was going to try to locate some replacement bulbs. To see if we can find the dead spot in these lights."

Zayn tilted his head, stared up at the sky. He appeared every bit the part of a man trying to wrangle the last of his patience. "Fine. If you insist on doing this, let me have a look. I took a couple of electrical engineering classes in college."

She hadn't known that about him. Why would a businessman have taken engineering classes? "You did?" she asked, unable to mask the curiosity.

Zayn shrugged. "Elective. I've always been interested." He stepped over to Frosty to study the frame. "I'll just take a look."

Ethan stepped aside. "Go ahead, if you wish, but I've been trying for the better part of half an hour. It's not lighting up."

Zayn climbed a couple of steps and grasped the wires,

examining them. He unscrewed one of the bulbs and examined it, as well. "Nothing appears to be broken."

He climbed all the way to the top of the ladder, still holding the wires. "I think I see the problem. It might be—"

Nothing could have prepared her for what happened next. Zayn suddenly went still, as if frozen in time. She could only watch in horror as his body rocked head to toe with a sudden shudder. In the next instant, he toppled off the ladder and landed with a thud on the dirt.

CHAPTER FIVE

BAH, HUMBUG.

Zayn awakened to a beam of light flashing in his eyes. First the right, then the left. When the light lowered, he saw Ethan Greaves's face hovering near his. And he could detect the scent of lavender. That must mean Izzy was nearby. She always smelled of lavender. Or was it vinegar? No, that didn't sound right. It must have been *lavender*; that had to be the correct word. It seemed to sound better.

Clearly, he'd hit his head.

"What happened?"

"Must have been a faulty wire," Ethan answered. "You took some current through your body."

"Huh."

"The electric shock had to have been minor," the other man added, "but you hit your head in the fall."

Bingo. He'd been right. As if to confirm, the pounding behind his forehead chose that moment to register. A small groan of agony escaped his lips.

"Oh my God, Zayn! Are you all right?" He fought past the pain to turn and focus on Izzy's concerned, worried face. She sat next to him on her haunches, her arm around his shoulders.

"Sure, I am." He sniffed the area at her neck. "You smell like vinegar."

Her eyebrows scrunched together. "Huh?"

He must have said the wrong word. "Never mind."

"At least you had the presence of mind to fall where there was a doctor standing near you," Ethan told him.

"Lucky for me." It seemed Zayn's talent for sarcasm superseded head trauma.

"I think you'll be okay. Can you stand? Nice and easy."

With help from both of them, Zayn managed to get to his feet. Aside from a seesaw effect where the scenery in front of him tilted first one way then the other, he didn't feel too off balance. The pounding remained, however, and Zayn's vision was slightly out of focus.

"How're your eyes?" Ethan asked.

"Fine," he lied.

"Let's get you inside the house."

"Zayn, I'm so sorry," Izzy was saying under his left ear. "I will never forgive myself for this."

It wasn't her fault Frosty had taken offense to the way Zayn had manhandled him. He heard Ethan chuckle next to him and realized he'd said the words out loud.

"So glad your sense of humor wasn't damaged in your fall."

Several moments later, Zayn found himself semicarried into the front foyer of the house and settled on the large circular sofa.

Ethan stood with his hands on his hips as Izzy hovered over Zayn, adjusting the pillow behind his head. "Does it hurt very badly?" she asked.

"Don't worry, Izzy. It's fine." Another lie. The pounding was wreaking havoc behind his skull. He wasn't about to tell her the truth, however. His masculine pride had taken enough of a hit for one day.

The concern in her eyes didn't fade. She realized he was being dishonest; she knew him too well.

"Take something over-the-counter for the pain," Ethan instructed him. "I don't think you have a concussion, just a little jostled. Still, I'd like you to follow concussion protocol for the next forty-eight hours."

"What's that mean, exactly?" Izzy asked.

"No screens whatsoever. No reading. A dark room if you can."

Great. There went any hope of getting any work done while he was here in Napa. He was already behind on more than one major project. Maybe he should have never come. His Manhattan penthouse suited him much better than a sprawling estate mansion on any given day. He should have known nothing good would ever come from his coming back home. Now he was laid up with a huge goose egg on his head. Things couldn't possibly get any worse.

"You have to keep an eye on him, Izzy."

"I do?" she asked the exact moment Zayn asked, "She does?"

Correction: things had definitely just gotten worse. As if toppling off a ladder in front of her hadn't been bad enough, now he'd be beholden to Izzy.

Ethan shrugged. "Someone does. To monitor his pain and note if it gets any worse. And to make sure he doesn't have any balance issues when he does need to get up. The last thing he needs is another tumble."

Izzy nodded. "Of course." She'd said it without hesitation but Zayn had noticed the apprehensive swallow before she'd answered.

This all served him right. The only reason he was here laid up on this couch was that he'd behaved like a heartsick teenager filled with envy. He'd been in the middle of attending to some urgent emails when he'd foolishly looked out his window and seen her and Ethan working on that blasted display. He'd tried to ignore them, but it had proved futile. He'd finally given in to the urge and opened the window to hear snippets of their conversation. Lots of banter, plenty of laughing. Clearly, she enjoyed Ethan's company, unlike his own. Like a fool, he'd made his way downstairs and outside before he'd had a chance to think about why exactly he was doing so.

Then, to top it off, he'd tried to play the hero who could fix the electrical issue. Only to land on his back on the hard, stony ground. Not his finest moment. And Izzy had been witness to it all.

"I don't need a babysitter," he argued now. "I know how busy Izzy is. The last thing she needs is to hang around here and nurse after me like I'm some kind of invalid."

Ethan shook his head. "That's not how this works, buddy. I remember you being hardheaded, but not quite that hard. Someone needs to be by your side at all times for the next two days. Doctor's orders." His voice was firm.

Zayn opened his mouth to try to argue some more but Izzy held a hand up to stop him in that signature way of hers that he found both endearing and maddening at the same time. "I'll do it. It won't be a problem. I can take a day off of barreling. I'll just have Hector come by and help tomorrow when he's back in town. He's been away on business."

Hector was her brother. The same brother who had good-naturedly but relentlessly teased him when they were all youths. Zayn had given back in equal measure, but Hector was truly talented at leveling bona fide A-plus insults. He'd have a field day once he got a load of how Zayn had ended up in his current predicament.

Yep, things were just getting better and better by the minute.

* * *

Zayn could hear their muted conversation when Izzy walked Ethan out several moments later. The other man seemed to reassure her, his voice low and calming. His bedside manner was certainly not lacking.

She returned with a couple of painkillers for Zayn. "He's going to call one of his patients who happens to be an electrician to come fix whatever's wrong. A real electrician," she added after a beat and then handed him the pills.

Good ol' Ethan to the rescue. Again. "Ouch."

She startled. "What? Is it the pain?"

"No. Just another blow to my pride."

A smile appeared to tickle her lips. "Sorry. Couldn't resist. What were you thinking, anyway? Handling a live wire."

I was thinking how much I hated seeing you enjoying yourself basking in another man's charm and had to make a fool of myself as a result.

"Thought I could help," he said instead. "Not like I knew it was live."

"Hmm. Despite all those electrical engineering classes."

Harsh teasing apparently ran in the Veracruz family. "You know this is hardly necessary," he told her now that the doctor had left and the two of them were alone. "You certainly don't have to stick around and play nursemaid. I'm feeling better already."

To prove it to her, he lifted the quilted cover she'd thrown over him and made a move to stand. Only to discover he wasn't as steady on his feet as he'd hoped. The floor seemed to give out from underneath him and he stumbled backward.

Izzy rushed to his side and threw her arms around him in some kind of effort to stop the mishap. The end result was that both of them ending up haphazardly on the couch, Izzy sprawled on top of him. It took all his will not to reach his arms around her and pull her tight up against him. She felt so right where she was, like she belonged right there on his lap. Her soft skin radiated warmth in every spot their bodies were in contact. The smell of her shampoo, a light delicate scent of vanilla, tickled his nose and made him want to nuzzle his face into her thick, luscious hair.

Lavender and vanilla, the combination was delectable and oh so familiar.

All too soon, she scrambled off him and stood, before backing away several steps. "Would you stop being so stubborn?" she demanded. "You could have hit your head again on the back of the sofa."

"Aw, you sound like you might care what happens to me." He couldn't resist the taunt.

She gave a small shrug of her shoulders. "I would hate to have to explain it if my newly minted business partner up and died on my watch. Too many questions."

"Right. That would indeed look suspicious, especially given the topic of our last business discussion." Hard to believe they were joking about the very thing that threatened to further strain their already complicated relationship. But there it was.

"My point exactly. Now, would you please try to get some rest?"

"I can't. Too fidgety. I'm not used to sitting around."

"You can watch me bake cookies, I suppose. Though I guess I'll have to do it in the dark, given how you're concussed."

"You're baking cookies?" It occurred to him that he didn't normally date the type of women who baked cookies. Not that he particularly cared about that sort of thing.

"Dozens and dozens. I was going to stay up all night to do it, but looks like I don't have to now."

"Why so many?"

"The light display goes live tomorrow. We always have fresh-baked sugar cookies to accompany the hot cocoa the first night."

Zayn couldn't help his snort. "Still insist on going through with that, do you? Despite...you know, this." He gestured to himself and then pointed to the goose egg on his head.

"If the electrician gives us the okay. Why not?"

"I could give you several reasons why not."

"You can sit out there and greet everyone with me. The main tent is heated. Who knows? You might even enjoy some yuletide cheer."

He laughed at that. "Highly unlikely."

She slammed her hands on her hips. "What exactly do you have against the holidays, anyway? I know you were never particularly excited about Christmas, but now you seem to have reached a Grinch-like level of disdain for all of it."

"Come on, Izzy. You know we never really celebrated the way you did with your family."

Something flashed behind her eyes that he couldn't quite place. But it was gone in an instant. Perhaps he had imagined it.

He continued. "First of all, it was usually only me and Myrna. And she was always much too tired this time of year to do anything more than hand me the present she'd picked out for me. Then she went off to rest and I watched cheesy Christmas movies for about twelve hours straight." To Aunt Myrna's credit though, she'd been the only one who'd even tried to celebrate any kind of holiday with him.

Izzy knew all this—why had she insisted on bringing it up?

"You know you were always welcome to spend the holidays with us."

"I know. Believe me, the times I did that were the only pleasant memories of Christmas I can recall whatsoever. So, thanks for that. And thanks to your mama and papa, too. How are they, by the way? I've been meaning to ask."

The same dark shadow crossed her eyes before she looked away again. "Fine. They're both fine."

The hint of a waver in her voice kept him from asking anything more. Something was off about the way the conversation had turned and he didn't have it in him to try to speculate, the pounding in his head having not quite subsided enough.

In any case, it appeared the conversation was over, anyway. She suddenly reached her arm out and waited for him to take it. Then she helped him stand. For one insane moment, he wanted to pull her down onto the sofa with him instead.

"Well, if you're not going to try to get any rest, you may as well come with me to the kitchen. I have some baking to do."

CHAPTER SIX

IF SOMEONE HAD told her a week ago that Zayn Joffman would be sitting in the kitchen watching her as she baked her annual batch of Christmas cookies, she would have accused that person of heavily dipping into the eggnog. In fact, perhaps she could use a nip of something like eggnog herself. Maybe something stronger.

Why was she so jittery? Her sugar cookie recipe called for precision and care, or the dough turned too sticky and was impossible to work with. She didn't have time for that kind of complication. Her nerves seemed to not want to cooperate. There was no excuse for it. After all, she'd had an audience while baking in the past. Myrna had always kept her company in the kitchen during this annual tradition.

Granted, Zayn was most definitely not Myrna.

Izzy stole a glance at him now as he pulled out one of the wooden stools and sat at the counter. The collar of his white dress shirt was undone, exposing just a triangle of toned skin; again that wayward dark curl fell over his forehead above his eye. The man had taken a spill and gotten hurt less than an hour ago. How did he still manage to look so sexy and attractive? He'd rolled up his sleeves and she couldn't help but notice the muscular contours of his arms. An unbidden image of the last time those arms were around her waist sprang into her mind.

She gave a shake to her head. Thoughts such as those were not going to do anything to steady her nerves.

"Can I help in any way?" he asked from his perched position. "Not that I've baked anything in the recent past."

She quirked an eyebrow at him. "Or ever?"

"Or ever."

She grabbed an apron where it hung on the wall by the sink, put it over her head and tied the straps behind her back. "You can definitely help me cut out the dough later. This first part is all me, I'm afraid."

"Sounds serious."

She nodded solemnly. "You can't take any chances with sugar cookie dough. Only a true expert can be trusted to craft its creation."

"Then I promise not to get in your way, Master Dough Expert."

She chuckled. "Thank you. But start summoning your creative side. You'll need it for the cutting out part."

"Not like I have anything else I can do." He didn't sound happy about it. No doubt he hated this development. Having to spend time sitting here in his aunt's old kitchen. This scene was much too bland for him, much too domesticated. She knew from tabloids and papers—not that she sought them out, but he was featured just often enough as to be unavoidable—that the life he led now was much more worldly.

Those arms she'd been admiring earlier had been around some of the most attractive women in the world, from models to actresses to rock stars. Yep, Zayn Joffman had done quite well for himself since leaving town. He'd achieved professional success at a level most people could only dream of. He had wealth, no small amount of fame, and a fantasy lifestyle. And all he'd had to do was leave his old life behind. Including her.

"And where did you just drift off to?" he asked from across the counter. She realized she'd been staring off into space for a considerable amount of time.

Pull it together.

"Just mentally recalling the recipe." She turned to the pantry to retrieve the pastry flour, powdered sugar and the rest of the dry ingredients.

Measuring out the various amounts, she stole another glance at Zayn. He was fidgeting to the point of barely sitting on the stool. The poor man really wasn't used to sitting still. Izzy could tell he was going stir-crazy. She had to give him something to do.

Why had she thought he could just sit there and do nothing? She knew him better than that.

"Actually, there is something you can do right now. Please grab the cookie cutters and give them a rinse. They've been sitting in the cupboard since last year."

He looked relieved. "Sure thing. Where are they?"

She pointed to a cupboard on the other side of the kitchen. "Take your time, though. You still need to be careful with that head wound."

He turned to her. "You don't really need my help here, do you? You just remembered what a nuisance I am when I have pent-up energy."

He'd caught her. "Busted. I know things can go badly when you're standing still."

She hadn't meant to say it that way. Zayn stilled in the process of shutting the cupboard door. His reaction told her the words had landed exactly as she hadn't wanted them to.

"Those days are past me, Izzy. You have to know that."

"Zayn, that's not what I intended at all. The words were wrong."

"I haven't so much as had a traffic violation in the past five years." His eyes rested heavy on her face.

"Not even a speeding ticket?" She said it jokingly to try to lighten the suddenly heavy mood between them. It didn't work.

"I'm not that kid anymore."

Izzy set the measuring cup down with a sigh. "Neither of us is exactly a kid now. We're not the same people."

He raised an eyebrow. "You know what I mean. I'm not the angry, confused kid I once was. The one always ready for a fight, physical or otherwise. The one who stayed out too late and fought against all the rules."

"I'm well aware of that." How could she not be? Look how far he'd come, with virtually no help from anyone else. His success was solely a result of his hard work, determination and sheer will. But he was wrong about the fighter part. That was the reason he had been able to achieve all that he had. Zayn had always been a fighter when it came to what he wanted.

He hadn't wanted *her*. Izzy forced away the sharp pain that landed in the vicinity of her heart at the thought.

He studied her face before continuing. "Besides, you seem like your usual previous self."

Yow. Now it was her turn to be somewhat offended. "What's that supposed to mean?"

"Nothing derogatory. You're still a hard worker, loyal, with a large, loving family who adores you."

Izzy's spine stiffened. He was so wrong about that last part. So much had happened since he'd left. It would take too much emotional effort to explain all of it to him.

And this wasn't the time. So why did she want so badly to confide in him? He was the one man who'd torn her heart to shreds and left her without a backward glance. Without so much as an explanation as to his motives. She'd deserved at least an explanation.

But before all that, he'd been a close confidant. A friend. Someone she could turn to. A shoulder to cry on, an ear to bend. She'd missed having that. Especially this past year when everything had gone down between her and her father. She could have used a good friend to lean on during that time. More than a lover, she simply could have used someone to turn to.

Truth be told, when it came to Zayn Joffman, she missed so much more.

He would have known to simply listen, without trying to tell her what to do about disappointing Papa the way she had. He would have simply held her and soothed her when she'd explained that the choice she'd made was best for all involved. She'd chosen to continue working for Myrna rather than join her father's new winery because her and Papa were too alike, too intractable, and they would have butted heads constantly. She'd had no doubt her working for the family business would have resulted in permanent, irreparable damage to her relationship with her father.

Additionally, Papa had had her brother, numerous cousins, and Mama to help him get his winery up and running. Myrna had had no one. Not with Zayn gone.

Their respective pasts were the proverbial elephant in the room. So far, they'd been tiptoeing around it, but it would be naïve to think they could avoid confronting it altogether.

Zayn walked around the kitchen island and behind Izzy to the sink. The comfortable camaraderie they'd been enjoying just moments ago had evaporated like the top layer of wine in a barrel.

He turned on the water and held the various cookie cutters under the stream, one by one.

He'd often thought of this moment, what exactly he would say to her. Saying sorry seemed wholly inadequate. And, technically, he'd already done that years ago. Though back then, the timing had been way off. It seemed timing had been the root of all their problems so often in the past.

He grabbed the folded towel sitting on the counter next to the sink and went back to his stool to dry the cutters. The frowning expression on Izzy's face made him wince as he sat. She noticed.

"What's the matter? Does your head hurt?"

"No. I feel fine." He did physically, anyway.

There had to be a way to resume the easy flow of conversation. "So, will Christmas dinner be the usual boisterous, extravagant affair at the Veracruz house? With enough food and drink to feed a neighborhood?"

She didn't look up at him as she answered. "Always is. What about you? What are your plans for Christmas?"

Funny. It sounded, for all intents and purposes, like she was trying to change the subject. She clearly looked uncomfortable. But why would discussing her plans for the holidays with her family be a source of discomfort?

"I'll just be getting back from the Food and Wine Expo in Paris. So probably just a low-key couple of days at home to try to unwind." No need to elaborate on the rest of it. He didn't have to tell her that his dinner would consist of a catered meal for one, delivered from the bistro housed on the bottom floor of his Manhattan apartment building. Or how he'd probably just study spreadsheets, sitting alone on his sofa, a cheesy movie playing on his wide-screen TV until he fell asleep.

Same as it always had been.

"Sounds exciting." Again, her words were delivered tightly, flatly.

Curious. He got the impression there were things she wasn't saying, as well. So both of them were keeping secrets.

An hour later, when the dough was ready, they'd managed to avoid discussing anything of any substance whatsoever. Izzy washed her hands and dried them off. "That needs to chill. Let's get started on the frosting, then." She pointed to the plastic bag on the counter she'd pulled out earlier. "Pass me the powdered sugar, would you?"

Zayn shifted and pushed the bag over to her. Unfortunately, what he hadn't realized until that moment was that the bag had been opened already. A cloud of white powder erupted from the top and spread through the air.

"Uh-oh."

Izzy clasped a hand to her mouth. Through the cloud of white dust, she looked like a vision in some kind of late-night dream. Then she sneezed. And sneezed twice more.

He couldn't help himself. The sheer ridiculousness of the moment made him chuckle.

"Oh, you think that's funny, huh?" Izzy's voice held a hint of mischief that immediately had him on guard.

He was right. But he wasn't fast enough. In the next instant, she'd grabbed a handful of the sugar and flung it in his direction. It landed on his face, in his hair, all over him.

Now Izzy was laughing with abandon.

He made an elaborate show of brushing powder off his

left shoulder. An utterly useless action, there was simply too much of it. Izzy laughed harder.

"Did you honestly think you were going to get away with that?"

Heeding the warning in his voice, she turned on her heel to get away. But the only exit from the kitchen was to pass by him. He didn't let her. Grabbing her from behind as she tried to run past the counter, he grabbed a small amount of the sugar and flung it in the air above them both. In a matter of seconds, they resembled eerie ghosts straight out of one of those old-fashioned black-and-white horror movies. Like the first film version of Scrooge.

Still, he didn't let her go. His arms tightened their hold of their own volition, her back snug against his chest. The smell of her hair tickled his nose, the fruity shampoo now mixed with the sweet scent of sugar. He was oh so tempted to run his tongue along the back of her neck, to taste her skin and breathe in her scent. Somehow, he resisted, though he thought he might die from the strain and the effort.

They both stopped laughing. The moment hung heavy between them; neither one moved for several beats. Finally, all too soon, Izzy pulled out of his embrace and stepped away. Then she turned to face him.

She looked utterly adorable, good enough to kiss. And lick.

He clenched his fists to keep from pulling her back into his embrace. It wasn't easy.

It took forever for all the dust to settle. When it finally did, the entire kitchen looked like a sugar bomb had exploded in the center. They both stood staring at the collateral damage.

"What a mess." He stated the obvious.

Izzy agreed with a nod and a sigh. "This will take forever to clean up."

She wasn't wrong. "Guess we'd better get started."

She went to grab the vacuum and Zayn took the moment to try to forget the way it had felt to hold her once again. His arms still tingled with the warm current of her skin against his.

A warmth that didn't diminish in all the time it took them to vacuum and mop the mess they'd had so much fun making together.

What had just happened?

Izzy tried hard to ignore the pounding in her chest. Her body felt aflame from head to toe after being in Zayn's arms. She'd set out to bake some Christmas cookies while she kept an eye on Zayn, like Ethan had instructed.

Somehow, she'd ended up pressed against him, her back tight against the length of his body. His breath tickling the back of her neck. She'd been oh so tempted to simply turn her head. His lips would no doubt have been close enough to touch hers if she'd done just that. Then who knew where things may have led. She shuddered at the thought.

Her life was messy enough right now. She didn't need the added complication of falling again for the ex that had left her without a thought, alone and desperately longing for him. That longing had resurfaced much too easily. She knew he'd felt it, too. There was no doubt they were still attracted to each other. He'd hardly been in town for a couple of days and she'd fallen into his arms not once but twice already.

No more. It couldn't happen again. Her heart couldn't take it.

"Uh, we should probably go get cleaned up," she ventured, not quite meeting Zayn's eyes. She was too afraid of what she'd see in their depths. So help her, if he showed any signs that he wanted her as much as she wanted him, she'd be tempted all over again.

What a fool she was.

"I guess I could use a shower," he answered.

A nagging thought struck her. She was supposed to be keeping a steady watch on him. Could she even leave him alone to shower? What if he got dizzy? Or lost his balance?

"I don't know about you showering alone, Zayn."

She wanted to kick herself for the way the words had just come out of her mouth.

The corners of Zayn's lips lifted. "Oh? Are you suggesting we shower together, then?"

Her mouth went dry at the thought. The two of them, under a hot and steamy spray, squeezed tight against each other in the stall. She shook the image off. "That's not what I meant and you know it."

He slowly shook his head. "What a shame, then. It would have conserved water."

"I commend your sudden concern for environmental issues. What about your head? What exactly is the concussion protocol when it comes to showers?"

He shrugged. "Damned if I know."

"We probably shouldn't risk it."

He gestured to his upper body. "I can't stay covered in powdered sugar."

"I know that!"

"Well, I'm out of ideas."

There was only one way she could think of. And it was going to be torture. "I'll stand outside the door while you shower."

The grin that appeared on his face was downright wolfish. "Yeah? You want to supervise?"

"Stop, Zayn. This isn't funny. I'm just trying to be responsible here." She should have asked Ethan to be more specific with his instructions.

"Sorry," he answered. "Between the painkillers and the goose egg, I'm saying things I probably shouldn't say."

Izzy's breath hitched. He probably shouldn't have said that bit, either. The moment was getting much too heated for comfort. "I just don't want you to get hurt again."

He crossed his arms in front of his chest. "Huh. One might venture to guess that you're worried about my well-being."

"One would be mistaken. I simply don't want blood on my hands. Or on your head, for that matter."

"Because you care about me?"

"Let's just say it would put a damper on the festivities for our light display opening night if you took another spill."

In a move that sent a shiver down her spine, he reached over and tapped a finger to her nose. Then he licked the sugar off his finger. "If you say so, Iz."

He'd used her shortened name again. This time, she didn't have the wherewithal to protest. Instead, she gently took him by the elbow. "Let's go. The sooner you get in and out of the shower, the sooner I can take a long, relaxing one myself."

"I must repeat myself. It's a pity you won't entertain the idea of taking one together."

She ignored that as they made their way upstairs to his suite of rooms. Zayn grabbed a towel from the linen closet and went in to take his shower. Izzy sat on the edge of the bed, cursing herself for not having thought to bring

a book or a magazine. Anything to occupy her brain.
For the only thing she could think of right now was how
Zayn was only a few feet away. Without any clothes on.

With a huff, she shot up off the bed and paced around
the room. He really hadn't brought much with him. His
laptop sat open on the antique wooden desk; several file
folders lay strewed about the bed. He hadn't yet emptied his suitcase.

Clearly, he didn't plan on staying long. For all she
knew, he would have been out of here already if she'd
only agreed to sell and signed his blasted paperwork.

The recollection of the real reason he was there was
like a splash of cold water down her back. What was she
thinking? Relishing being in his arms. Laughing with
him as they played food fight with powdered sugar. Ban-
tering with him as he teased her about showering together. The man was essentially here for a business deal.
One that meant to oust her out of the winery she considered home.

Right now, it was the only true home she had.

His cell phone suddenly lit up and vibrated on the desk
with an incoming call. She stole a glance at the display.
The contact info of the caller had her doing a double
take. Lovely Clara.

Izzy felt her hands clench at her sides. Whoever this
Clara was, she apparently warranted an affectionate mis-
nomer. Who would have thought Zayn had turned into
the type of man who entered endearing nicknames into
the contact list of his phone? Then again, she didn't really know this new Zayn, did she? Perhaps she'd never
known the man at all.

The sound of running water shut off and she stepped
away from the desk as if caught in a clandestine, sneaky

act. A minute after, the cell phone dinged the signal of a voice message.

"Lovely Clara" had certainly left a long-winded voice mail. Probably full of kissy noises and telling him she missed him and yearned for him to come back already.

As if Izzy needed yet another reminder that she had no business being attracted to Zayn Joffman in any way. Those days were long over.

The smell of vanilla and cinnamon gently roused him awake the next morning. Certainly it beat the stale, dry scent he woke up to in his own apartment most mornings. Or the standard bland air of an overscrubbed room in a high-rise hotel. The aroma was mouthwatering by comparison.

Zayn rolled over onto his back and slowly opened his eyes. The ache behind his forehead was there just enough to make itself known. Not wanting to take any chances to exacerbate it, he took his time sitting up.

The scent continued to beckon him. His nostrils registered the additional subtle aroma of fresh-brewed coffee.

Izzy must have made her usual strong Hawaiian roast and started on the cookies. Perhaps she'd been baking all night, for all he knew. He'd stepped out of his shower to be greeted by disappointment when he'd walked back into the room last night to find she'd left.

Then he'd finally fallen asleep after waiting with futile hope that perhaps she might return. Simply so that they could talk some more.

She hadn't.

The neon-green digital clock on his bedside table read 8:00 a.m. He couldn't recall the last time he'd slept in so late. Or so restfully. Maybe a good and solid hit to the old noggin did that to a guy. He threw on a T-shirt and the pair of sweats he'd packed and made his way downstairs.

He had to pause in the kitchen doorway to take a breath when he saw her.

Izzy had pulled her hair back into a high ponytail with a headband at the crown of her head to catch any wayward strands. She wore sweats herself, the leg cuffs rolled up to right below her knees. On her feet were the thickest socks he'd ever seen. The tank she had on hugged her in all the right places.

How did a woman look so sexy wearing fuzzy, thick socks, ratty sweats and a plain red tank top?

Zayn swallowed and stepped into the room, making sure not to stare. It wasn't at all easy.

"You're awake," she said just as a timer beeped loudly behind her. Grabbing a comically large oven mitt, she pulled a tray of fresh-baked cookies out of the oven. Several more trays sat on cooling racks strewed across various surfaces of the kitchen.

"I am. And apparently you've been awake for quite a while yourself."

She nodded. "I wanted to get a head start." She pointed to the coffee maker on the breakfast island in the corner by the pantry. "Just brewed another pot. Help yourself. The mugs are where they've always been."

"You've certainly gotten a head start, all right." He grabbed one of the larger mugs—stein-size—and poured himself a generous cup. "How long have you been up?"

"Since dawn," she answered. "Didn't have time to spare. We never did get around to making the frosting last night."

He'd forgotten that part. Amusement bubbled in his chest when he thought of the reason they had been way-laid. The sensation turned to heat when he thought about what had happened after. The shower he'd taken last night, knowing she was only a few feet away, had been one of the most testing experiences of his life.

"Sorry, I wasn't much help."

"Don't worry about it. How do you feel?" she asked him, pulling off another hunk of dough from the massive ball that sat in a big silver bowl in the middle of her workspace.

"Fine. I had a great nursemaid taking care of me. I owe you one."

She shrugged. "I figured letting you get a good night's sleep was the best thing I could do for you after the day you'd had. Though I did check on you a couple times during the night. You were sleeping soundly and seemed to be shifting position." Her tone was very matter-of-fact.

She was different this morning. Distant. Fully focused on the task at hand. Zayn felt like an intrusive pest who was hindering her progress and distracting her needlessly.

"I see. Thanks." *I guess*, he added silently. If he were being honest, he'd have told her he would have preferred some company after the day he'd had. Her company.

Maybe he should have just come clean last night and told her so. He could have blamed it on the moment of levity they'd shared, the moment some of the ice between them had cracked. He could have even conveniently used the head injury as an excuse. For one brief moment, he'd had an opportunity to ask her to stay with him. Simply to talk. To catch up on each other's lives. He'd blown it by missing the opportunity to do so.

It occurred to him he may never get another chance.

CHAPTER SEVEN

IZZY WANTED TO forget all her concerns and troubles and all the questions plaguing her about Zayn and his reasons for being at Stackhouse. She just wanted to enjoy the evening. This night always brought out her holiday cheer, though it was all rather bittersweet this year with Myrna gone. She just knew her mentor was there in spirit. Izzy would like to think she'd be impressed. She'd worked hard to get everything just right.

Tomorrow morning, she would return to worrying about what she was going to do about Zayn, or the mess that was currently her family life. Tonight she just wanted to enjoy the fruits of her labor.

The day spent baking and cleaning and setting up had given her time to think and come to her senses. Zayn might be visiting right now, but he was no longer a fixture in her life. He was only planning to stay for a few more days. And once they resolved the whole issue of ownership, she most likely would hardly hear from him. She had to move on, go forward with her life, just as he clearly had done with Lovely Clara.

She wondered if he'd even bother to come out and join in the festivities. He didn't seem at all interested and she knew he disagreed with the concept overall. And he probably still had a headache.

Izzy took a deep breath and pushed the useless thoughts away. Tonight was about tonight.

A familiar voice shouted out from behind her, "There's my beautiful, talented sister."

A smile immediately found her lips. "Hey, Hector. You're back in town."

He wrapped her in a bear hug, as was his customary greeting when he saw her these days. Izzy knew he was trying to compensate and she appreciated it. Still, it just made things all the more awkward. Poor Hector was just caught in the middle of the drama between her and her father. She knew Papa loved her. He just had a funny way of showing it.

"Got in this afternoon. Took an earlier flight just so I wouldn't miss all this." He looked around appreciatively. "You did a great job."

He landed a small, affectionate peck on her cheek. "I'm gonna go fix myself a plate. I'm starving."

She had to laugh. Hector was always starving. At a little over six feet, with the general frame of a bean pole, she had no idea where he put it all. Whereas all her calories seemed to land in the general vicinity of her hips. They'd definitely inherited a different set of genes from their parents.

"Help yourself," she told him. "I'm sure I'll see you around later at some point."

As her brother walked away, she found herself scanning the rapidly growing crowd. All the regulars were already here. Mr. Reyes, his wife and two of their grandchildren mingled in the smaller tent across the pathway. Izzy spotted Ethan and Paula standing over by the vines. They appeared to be in the middle of what had to be a depthless, innocuous conversation. She knew they were both insanely attracted to each other but were too shy to do anything about it.

No sign of Zayn. Not that she'd been specifically looking for him.

The swell of disappointment in her chest made her a hopeless fool. There was no reason to think Zayn would attend. And absolutely no reason for her to want him to so badly.

Zayn supposed there were worse ways to spend the evening. Izzy's light display opening night was like one big outdoor party. He found himself being pulled into the spirit of it all, despite his general disdain for the entire affair. Maybe Izzy was right. Maybe he was simply being a Grinch. Or a money-focused businessman the likes of Ebenezer Scrooge himself.

In his defense, he was only thinking about the bottom line. And he just didn't see what all this did to contribute to that end. Still, he could see why Izzy and Myrna had enjoyed the tradition so much.

Outdoor speakers set up around the grounds and along the perimeter of the vines filled the air with bouncy Christmas music. A mountain of cookies sat piled on a center table already loaded with other munchies and snacks. Wine was being poured generously in every corner and several large thermos pumps had been set up to dispense hot chocolate to those underage.

All in all, he was impressed. Izzy had put all this together, mostly herself. Not that he should be surprised. She'd always been a study in efficiency and competence. And she managed to do it all with grace and style.

She approached him, dressed in a festive red-and-green wrap dress, a pointy Santa hat flopped over her head. Lace-up red boots with springy pom-poms on the laces rounded out the outfit. She looked like a fetching, sexy Mrs. Claus. Santa should be so lucky.

People were slowly starting to trickle in. Izzy had told him earlier that she'd planned to flip the switch and turn every display on in about an hour or so, just as the sky turned dark.

"I'm glad you decided to join us," she said with a smile, speaking loudly over the music—some lively Latin version of "Jingle Bells."

"I managed to summon some holiday cheer, after all." That was partially true. The fact was he'd spent the day working and had found himself counting down the minutes until he had an excuse to come out here to see her again.

"It's a Christmas miracle." She nudged him with her shoulder playfully. The warmth and good humor of last night was back. He was glad for it. Though it probably had less to do with him than the fact that Izzy was in her element right now. She'd worked hard to make this night a success and she'd done a great job. They already had a good number of visitors even though it was still rather early.

How she managed to look so fresh and energetic after working all day to put this together, he couldn't begin to guess.

The smile grew wider. "You've gone quiet. What are you thinking?"

"I'm thinking you're pretty darn miraculous yourself."

Her eyes flashed with surprise. He hadn't meant to say that; she'd caught him off guard.

"Oh?"

He gave what he hoped was an unaffected smile. First, he'd shamelessly joked about showering together last night—he should probably find a way to apologize for that. And now he was throwing unguarded compliments her way. As if they were a couple again.

"I just mean to say it's pretty incredible what you've managed to put together out here. I'm impressed."

She wiggled her eyebrows at him. "Even though you don't agree with the general idea?"

He stifled a groan. "Let's not get into all that right now. Just take the compliment, why don't you?"

"I will, then," she answered with a small bow. "So, thank you. For the compliment."

"You're welcome… I could have come down and helped you. You only needed to ask." It stung a bit that she hadn't.

"I had it under control. Besides, you don't do well being bossed around."

She had a point there. "Never did well with authority, did I? As the local sheriff's office can attest."

He'd had so much anger back in those days, such a chip on his shoulder. It's why he'd agreed to get out of town before he destroyed himself, as well as everyone in his general orbit. Including his great-aunt. And Izzy.

"If those cops could see you now. A self-made international success story."

Her words served to send a flush of pleasure through his system. Like he was a puppy and she'd just thrown him a chew treat.

"They'd probably find an excuse to arrest me again. Zayn the Troublemaker back in town," he retorted with a chuckle.

"Not like you didn't give them cause."

"Yeah, thankfully that's all behind me. These days, there'd be no one to bail me out." His aunt had given up on doing so after about the fourth or fifth time.

"Really? There isn't anyone?"

It sounded like a serious question. Somehow, he'd apparently lost the scope of the conversation. They were talking hypotheticals and joking around. Weren't they? So why was she staring at him so intently as she waited for an answer? She had to know he had no intention of doing anything that might land him in any kind of cell. He hadn't been in one for a long time.

"There has to be somebody," she persisted.

He gave a small shrug. Whatever this little wordplay game was, he supposed he'd go along with it. "I guess Clara might. She's my admin assistant."

She blinked up at him, confusion and some unknown emotion clouding her eyes. "You're dating your admin assistant?"

He nearly choked on the sip of wine he'd just taken. "What? Good God, no. Where'd you get that idea?"

She looked away, studied her fingertips. "I was just guessing."

"You've guessed so far wrong you've almost committed a crime yourself."

"I did?"

He turned to her then. "What's this about? Are you trying to ask me if I'm involved with someone, Iz?"

Her head flung up. "What? No! Of course not."

Right. That didn't sound convincing at all. Zayn found himself ridiculously pleased that she was inquiring about his personal life. Comically, she was doing a rather poor job of it. He decided to throw her a bone.

"I date occasionally." As she must know if she glanced at any kind of social media or business/entertainment website. "Very casual dating. Nothing has panned out into any kind of serious relationship. And I'm certainly not dating any of my employees." He shuddered at the thought and the potential complications of such behavior. "Clara Lovely happens to be my very efficient, very experienced assistant." The thought of him dating the nearly retired grandmother of five had him chuckling.

"I see. Well, I just assumed…" She paused suddenly. "Wait, what did you just say? She's lovely?"

"That's her name. Clara Lovely. Dutch. Or perhaps Swedish. I'm not quite sure."

She must have found the name incredibly funny for she bent over with laughter. There were times he didn't understand women at all. He certainly had trouble understanding this one more often than not.

In any case, two could play at this game. "What about you?" he asked once she'd straightened.

"Me?"

He nodded. "You must be seeing someone." His gaze landed on the edge of the line of vines where Ethan stood with Stackhouse's product manager, Paula. The blonde with the ponytail. "Doc Ethan seemed very eager to assist you with the display setup."

She snorted a laugh. "Trust me, that was not for my benefit."

"No?"

She shook her head with vehemence. "Not at all." She lifted her chin in Ethan's direction. "He's mostly doing it out of the kindness of his heart. But also to impress and hang out near Paula. Those two have the hots for each other and have had for years. Neither one is doing anything about it, though. Who knows why?"

Zayn felt a sudden empathy and unexpected kinship with the charismatic doctor he'd been so annoyed with just a few seconds ago. He could relate to the poor soul. He would have to buy the man an ale at some point.

Izzy continued, her gaze focused on the ever-growing

crowd. She wasn't meeting his eye. "I'm not involved with anyone. Certainly not Ethan."

The breath of relief Zayn released was audible. If Izzy noticed, she didn't comment on it.

He didn't get a chance to probe further as Izzy was approached by several newcomers. The crowd around them had grown considerably during the course of their conversation. Zayn watched her as she greeted her guests with characteristic warmth and friendliness. She really was something. He'd missed her. He had to admit that to himself once and for all.

If he was the sort to flatter himself, he might have even thought she'd been acting jealous when she'd asked about Clara earlier. Zayn took another sip of his wine, pleased beyond words at the overall direction the conversation had taken.

Izzy could feel Zayn's eyes on her two hours later as the celebrations were in full swing. She knew he'd been eyeing her for most of the night. When she thought about how foolish she'd been…assuming he was dating someone when the whole thing was a complete misunderstanding. Not that it was any of her business. Zayn Joffman could date anyone he pleased.

The lighting of the displays had gone off without a hitch and so far the night was a complete success. Ethan's electrician friend had come through and the weather was cooperating nicely. All in all, things were running along quite well. So why did it feel like her stomach was tied in knots? Every time she glanced up to find Zayn watching her, the knots grew a little tighter. This was right around the time of the night when she should be beginning to relax. Instead, she felt like a teenager at a school dance wondering if her crush had noticed her.

Snap out of it. You're a professional adult.

But her mind ignored the directive as she noticed Zayn was walking toward her.

"Now you've gone and done it," he told her, his voice loaded and serious.

What on earth was he referring to? "Done what?"

He pointed to a spot above her head. "You're standing under mistletoe."

She looked up to confirm he was indeed right. One of the beams along the ceiling of the tent had a dangling mistletoe plant right above where she stood. She had no idea who might have put it there. If she'd known, she might have taken care not to get caught under the darn thing. But here she was, right in the line of fire.

As if it was some sort of sign.

Her breath caught in her chest when she looked back at Zayn. His gaze was fixated squarely on her lips. His eyes had grown impossibly dark. Slowly, dreamily, he lowered his face to hers. Out of pure instinct, she bit down on her lower lip.

Heaven help her, she had no doubt what he was about to do. And she had no doubt that she wanted him to. Very much.

Her mind cried out that it would be all wrong. She shouldn't want this, couldn't want it. This was the man who had left her after breaking her heart. He was the one who'd replied with nonanswers when she'd emailed and called and texted to ask why. He was only here now because he wanted to oust her out of her very position as part owner of the winery she called home.

He'd be gone again in a matter of days.

What treacherous manner of heart did she have beating in her chest that she was ready to forget all that and long for him to kiss her?

She swallowed past the dryness that suddenly coated her tongue. "I have no idea how that got there. It's not part of the decorations."

"How lucky for me that it is." He leaned toward her then, reaching his arm behind her along her waist.

With the touch of his lips against hers, all the doubts and trepidation seemed to vanish into thin air. The crowd around them no longer existed. All that mattered was the taste of him, the warmth of skin against hers.

She felt as if time had reversed herself and she was catapulted back to the young woman she'd been all those years ago, being held and kissed by the only man she'd ever fallen in love with. The only one she'd loved since.

The moment was over all too soon. When he pulled away, she felt the loss like a physical ache. "We'll have to figure out who's responsible for the mistletoe," he whispered against her cheek, his breath hot on her skin. "So that I can properly thank them."

Before she could summon a response, she heard her brother's voice. "Zayn? Is that you, my man?"

Hector, she realized, clearly hadn't seen what had just transpired between the two of them.

Zayn immediately dropped his arm from around her middle and pulled away.

When her brother reached them, he and Zayn did some version of a complicated handshake before bumping shoulders. For an insane moment, Izzy felt a twinge of disappointment toward her only sibling. She'd always considered it somewhat disloyal that Hector still considered Zayn a close friend. That made absolutely no sense given she was her own person and so was Hector. He and Zayn had been close friends in high school and had played on the same baseball team. Not to mention, she'd been locking lips with Zayn only moments ago.

Suffice it to say, her feelings for her ex were rather complicated. Kissing him in a crowd of people certainly did not help matters.

"I heard you were back in town," her brother was saying.

"Not for long, I'm afraid," Zayn answered, once more dousing her with a good splash of reality. "Just here on some business." He gave Izzy a pointed look.

Business that involved her. Issues they were nowhere near resolving.

Hector stuck a finger out at him. "Let me tell you, bro. You could have done worse as a business partner. I bet she didn't even tell you." He turned to her. "Did you, Izzy? About the award?"

Izzy drew a deep breath. She really didn't need to get into that particular topic with Zayn. There was no need.

"She didn't tell me anything about any award," Zayn answered for her. He lifted an inquisitive eyebrow. "Care to do so now?"

"There's really no need."

"Sure there is, sis," Hector argued. "One of her cabernets from last year is up for an award from the editors at *World Vintner* magazine. She's just being her usual humble self."

Zayn studied her. "Is that so?"

"It's not a big deal. A French restaurateur who was out here for a tasting submitted it as a nominee upon returning to Paris. I highly doubt it will win."

"You don't know that," Hector countered. "She's not even going out there for the ceremony. Can you believe it?"

The eyebrow lifted even higher. "Why not?"

She shrugged her shoulder. "I hadn't really thought about it. There's been quite a bit going on, between the

holidays, rounding out the end of harvest season and…"
She knew she didn't need to say the rest out loud. Losing Myrna had been an unexpected and heartbreaking shock. The last thing on her mind had been some pretentious award everyone would forget about a year from now.

Her brother had other ideas about it, however. Ideas she had no intention of entertaining in Zayn's presence.

CHAPTER EIGHT

ZAYN WASN'T SURE if he was following the conversation fully. He felt a little loopy and it had nothing to do with the two glasses of wine he'd had—though that certainly wasn't helping matters. No, the real issue was what had just happened between him and Izzy. He was still experiencing the aftereffects of that mind-blowing kiss. Neither his body nor his soul had been prepared to taste her again. Now that he had, he knew he needed more. Whatever had happened between them up until now, however badly he'd messed up in the past, the spark they'd shared still burned as bright and powerful as it had ever had. He knew she'd felt it, too. How could she not?

He couldn't wait to taste her again, would have succumbed to the urge to retake her lips in his if it hadn't been for Hector. The arrival of her brother had thrown a proverbial bucket of cold water over the hottest of moments. Now the two siblings were arguing about some award Izzy was up for. Zayn had heard of it, of course. The magazine she'd referenced was well-known. She may not be terribly impressed with the accolade, but very well should have been. The honor she was up for was a fairly prestigious one.

"Come on, sis…" Hector was saying. "You know this might be a way to break through to him once and for all."

Who was this *him* they were talking about? Was it a high-end buyer? Or an industry influencer perhaps? It didn't sound like Hector was referring to any kind of romantic interest. Or maybe that was just wishful thinking on Zayn's part. Either way, it was just one more mystery.

Hector continued. "You know how much credence he gives to things like that."

Izzy laid a hand on his forearm. "I appreciate what you're trying to do, Hector. And I love you for it. I really do. But I don't want to talk about this right now. I just want to enjoy the evening and pour my first glass of wine. Things are finally at a point where I can relax and enjoy the night."

Hector looked ready to argue, but must have thought better of it. He deflated like a pricked balloon before speaking again. "Fine. But we're not done. This conversation isn't over. We can stop for now because you've earned a little rest and relaxation."

"Thank you."

"I'll go get you your wine," Hector said.

She patted him affectionately on the shoulder. "That's what a good sibling is for."

Hector didn't return her smile, merely rolled his eyes at her.

"Please don't ask," she said as her brother left them, giving Zayn the full-on side-eye. Right. Like he'd be able to help himself.

"I find that I must. What was that all about? Did I hear correctly that you're up for the *World Vintner*'s award in the cabernet category? That's a highly regarded magazine."

How had he not known about this? What he did know was that the ceremony was to be held during the Food and Wine Expo in Paris, precisely where he was headed next.

Izzy blew out a puff of air that lifted the bangs off her forehead. "Not a big deal. I was nominated for an award I have no interest in receiving."

"Why not?"

"Because it's not that important."

"I think it's pretty important. Clearly, Hector does, too."

"Yeah, well, his reasoning leaves a lot to be desired as far as I'm concerned."

"Reasons like prestige, attention, exposure? Sounds like pretty solid reasoning to me."

She didn't respond, just continued to study the crowd.

"Who was Hector referring to just now?"

She was silent so long, Zayn figured she wasn't going to answer at all. Finally, she spoke. "My father. We've been at odds. Hector thinks me being nominated might somehow break the stalemate between us."

"What kind of stalemate?"

Her body seemed to tense from head to toe and a slight sheen appeared in her eyes. When she answered, the hurt behind her words was as clear as the light surrounding them. "My father hasn't spoken to me in about thirteen months. Doesn't return my calls or pretends he hasn't received them. He makes himself scarce when I visit the house." Her voice quivered as she delivered the last word.

That didn't sound like Ernesto Veracruz at all. And it certainly didn't sound like the father who'd been so concerned about his daughter's future that he'd asked Zayn to leave town.

"Why would he—" Zayn didn't bother to finish asking the question as understanding began to dawn. Thirteen months. That was right around the time her family had officially opened their own winery. Aunt Myrna had mentioned that Ernesto hadn't been happy that Izzy had remained a Stackhouse employee rather than join her family in their endeavor. He hadn't realized her decision had caused such a rift.

Ernesto had always been so protective of his daughter, so proud of how smart she was, how hard she worked. And now they weren't even speaking. The reality of it seemed terribly wrong.

"I'm sorry, Izzy." He meant it, more than she might ever realize. "I have no doubt he'll eventually come around." He meant that, too. Everything he knew about Izzy and the man who was her father told Zayn this was a temporary bump in their relationship.

Still, there was no mistaking the toll the estrangement was having on Izzy. He wanted to ease her hurt, to help her soothe the pain. He knew firsthand the gaping wounds that came of absentee parents. It would be especially hard for Izzy. Her family had always been so close, with such a tight bond between them all. He'd been witness to their affection for each other through the years over countless dinners at the Veracruz house.

"He can't see why I chose to stay at Stackhouse," Izzy began, her voice low and strained. "I tried to explain that Myrna needed me more. She had no one really to help and she was at an age where she couldn't do as much. Paula hasn't been employed at Stackhouse very long… He's just being stubborn," she added after a pause.

Zayn didn't bother to point out that her father probably felt the same way about her.

"I find myself agreeing with your brother," he declared. "I think you should go to Paris. Not for Ernesto. Not to try to prove anything to him. But for yourself."

Izzy released a deep sigh. "The timing is just off, that's all. How can I drop everything here and go to Paris right now?"

"Why can't you? You said yourself that the season has wrapped up. Hector offered to help with the cleanup and maintenance. And I thought you said the barreling would only take another day or two."

"I just can't, Zayn. I haven't made any kind of plans to travel. The ceremony is in three days. I have no hotel, no itinerary, no plane ticket."

"Logistics," he told her, "which can easily be addressed. In fact, you can leave all that to me."

She scoffed at that. "Are you taking up travel agent as your next career?"

No, but an idea had begun to spark in his head and wouldn't stop niggling at him. It made no sense. Or it made all the sense in the world. He could just guess how Izzy would react when he told her. On the surface, his reasoning was solid. They were partners, they co-owned a winery and she was up for an award for that winery's cabernet. He'd made some spur-of-the-moment decisions in the past that had worked out pretty well for him.

None of this had anything whatsoever to do with that kiss.

"Come with me when I leave for Paris, Izzy."

Her eyes grew wide with astonishment. "What? Zayn, no."

"Why not? We could attend the expo together, make it to your ceremony, and maybe get up to speed on the latest trade developments."

"I don't…"

"Think about it," he urged at her pause. "You can hop onto my itinerary. We could do some sightseeing. At the least, we may even have a little fun."

Her tongue darted out to worry her bottom lip. "I'm going to stick to my original answer, Zayn. No."

Maybe he should have asked her after she'd had the

glass of wine. The more he thought about it, the more it made sense for them to make the trip together. She couldn't just ignore the honor she'd been nominated for. What if she did in fact win and she wasn't even there to accept the trophy? And if it was in fact an opportunity to crack the tension between her and Ernesto, wasn't it worth taking?

He pressed further. "You still haven't given me a reason. Not any kind of real one."

"There are too many reasons to count. Our past history being one."

"We'd only be going as business partners. Nothing more. You have to agree we have a lot to discuss and negotiate. What better time and place to make decisions about our mutual winery than at the French wine expo during a year you happen to be up for an award?"

She shook her head, still not moved by his urging. It stung a little bit that she was so doggedly turning down an offer to travel with him, even as simply his business partner.

"You don't have to stay the whole week. I'll have my crew bring you back right after the ceremony, if that's what you wish."

She sucked in her bottom lip, deep in thought. Maybe he was getting to her finally.

Her next words had hope blossoming in his chest. "Let me sleep on it."

He could deal with that. That gave him all night to work on her. He could be very convincing when he wanted something badly enough.

And he hadn't wanted anything this badly in as long as he could remember.

He'd kissed her.

Close to twelve hours had gone by since it had happened and she could still feel the tingle on her lips. The taste of him still lingered on her tongue. Izzy turned up the hot water of the shower spray as far as she could without scalding her skin.

Damn the man. He'd had her tossing and turning all night. If she wasn't thinking about his lips on hers, she was recalling the heat she'd seen behind his eyes when he'd pointed out the mistletoe and leaned in to take her lips with his own.

She'd found out later that one of the hands who was aware of Paula's crush on Ethan had placed the plants strategically around the vineyard and grounds, hoping they would prompt one of the besotted yet shy lovebirds to finally make the first move.

Only, Izzy had been the one caught in the trap instead. And she truly did feel trapped.

Zayn wanted her to travel with him to Paris. Another thought that had kept her up all night. She couldn't seriously consider going, could she?

She really did feel indifferent about the award nomination. She didn't need a miniature statue to tell her worth as a vintner. Hector, on the other hand, thought it was a golden opportunity—in more ways than one. Her brother saw this nomination as a channel for a way for Izzy to get back into her father's good graces. But she wasn't so sure.

Ernesto Veracruz could be a very stubborn man, particularly when it came to his only daughter. The daughter who'd had the nerve to turn him down last year when he'd asked her to help manage the winery her family had established. In many ways, given where he came from, her father had viewed her refusal as a rejection and sign of disrespect. Nothing could have been further from the truth. Izzy had more respect for her parents and all they'd accomplished than they would ever guess.

Papa had asked her to make an impossible decision—to choose between loyalty to him and *family* versus Stackhouse Winery and Myrna.

Grabbing the lavender body wash from the stall shelf, she lathered her bath sponge and inhaled deeply of the soothing, calming scent. She owed Zayn an answer today. Technically her answer should be obvious. She knew exactly what she should do: turn him down with the clear understanding that the subject was closed.

So why was she stalling in the shower? This was the third time she'd sponged herself down. At this rate, she was going to run out of hot water and emerge wrinkled and shivering. She had no business traveling anywhere with the likes of Zayn Joffman.

The question had to be asked. Would she even be considering his offer if it hadn't been for that kiss? She had to have been oblivious to not have noticed the mistletoe plants around the property. Almost comical, really. Someone had been trying to nudge Ethan and Paula along but had ended up forcing her hand instead.

If only those two could finally confront their feelings for each other once and for all. Izzy stilled in the act of scrubbing her shoulder. Of all the hypocritical takes. She was one to talk. She should have done some confronting herself. The moment Zayn had kissed her last night, she should have demanded some answers. A man didn't kiss a woman like that unless he was affected, too. The heat that she'd seen swimming behind his eyes bespoke an attraction that he'd be hard pressed to deny if pushed. It was high time she got some answers.

He owed it to her to tell her why he'd fled five years ago. And the answers had to be better than the unsatisfactory ones he'd been giving so far. He'd been committed to her and then he'd simply left. Judging from his behavior and the way they'd fallen into each other's arms within hours of him coming back was proof that neither one of them had gotten over each other. He was the one who had to explain why he'd felt the need to end it.

But she couldn't go at him with guns blazing. That hadn't worked five years ago, had only driven him further and further away. Maybe they did need to spend some time together. Maybe they needed to be somewhere far away from where the past had all gone down.

Or maybe her mind was simply making excuses for where her heart wanted to lead.

CHAPTER NINE

HAD HE DONE the right thing?

Zayn had the same thought that had plagued him for the past several hours as he escorted Izzy into the waiting limo after their flight landed.

It had seemed like such a good idea at the time, offering to have Izzy join him on this trip. As thrilled as he was that she'd agreed, he couldn't help now but wonder if he'd been caught up in the moment, in the headiness of that kiss they'd shared. Surrounded by jazzy music during a balmy evening with couples dancing all around them and wine flowing freely, he'd hadn't even questioned his instincts.

But reality was now staring him right in the face. He had three full days with Izzy in one of the most romantic cities in the world.

An awkward silence hung in the air between them as the driver eased into traffic to take them to the hotel. Izzy had slept for most of the flight, fallen asleep right after takeoff. He'd always envied that about her. The woman could sleep through anything, even turbulent jet flights.

So inviting her along on this trip had been something of an impulsive, spur-of-the-moment decision. Though not a conscious thought at the time, Zayn realized now that he'd been dreading yet another European visit by himself. Being here alone, particularly around the holidays, had always left him with a cold, hollow emptiness. So he'd been selfish, pretending the invite was a favor to Izzy when, at least on some level, he'd only been thinking of himself. Some things never changed.

Izzy hadn't been too far off track when she'd called him selfish his first day back in Napa.

"This is stunning," Izzy said across the seat from him. She had her forehead pressed against the glass of the car window. "I didn't realize how lovely Paris was during the Christmas season."

Outside, the city was decorated to within an inch of itself—festive mini Christmas trees, wreaths on light poles, and brightly colored window displays.

This! She was proving him right. This was why he had wanted her here. He wouldn't have even bothered to take the time to notice sidewalk decorations, choosing rather to focus on answering emails or updating project spreadsheets.

"Wait till you see it at night," he told her. "The Champs-Élysées has a spectacular light display." He gave her a teasing smile. "It might even compete with the one you put forth yourself at Stackhouse."

"I'd love to see that," she answered, not looking away from the scenery as they drove down the city streets.

"We can head there tonight if you're up for it. Gets chilly, though. Mild compared to the US east coast but still rather frosty. I hope you brought some outerwear."

"A few sweaters," she replied. "I don't really have anything winter worthy, living in Napa."

That wouldn't do. He would have to see about keeping her warm. That thought brought forth mental images he had no business thinking given that they were here on...well, business.

"Maybe we can visit some of the shops. They do a rather excellent job of Christmas window displays. Or we could visit one of the Christmas markets that are put up around the city this time of year." That was a much safer idea than what had run through his mind earlier.

Izzy turned to face him then and the smile on her face sent a surge of pleasure through his core. "That sounds lovely, Zayn. I've never been to a Christmas market in Europe. I can't wait to experience it."

Surprisingly, neither could he. He wouldn't have even entertained visiting the shops or markets during the busy Christmas season. But with Izzy here, the concept held a distinct appeal.

About half an hour later, he helped her out of the car once they got to their destination. A bellhop immediately appeared to handle their luggage while Zayn led her through the front door so that they could check in.

Izzy gasped in pleasure when they stepped inside the hotel. The lobby looked like the North Pole had exploded on the first floor of one of Paris's deluxe luxury hotels. An immensely tall, white-pine Christmas tree reached the high ceiling, fake presents with large red bows surrounding its base. By the entrance, eight reindeer statues were strapped to a wood sleigh that held a smiling mechanical Santa whose hand waved to and fro.

Had this hotel always done such an elaborate setup for the holidays? He probably hadn't even noticed. Now that he was seeing it all through Izzy's eyes, he felt like a child on Christmas morning. Any other child perhaps; his own childhood hadn't held many happy memories of the holidays. Or none at all, to be more accurate.

"Oh, my!" Izzy exclaimed, pausing next to him to admire the distinctively French-looking Santa. He was actually wearing a bright red beret and his short beard resembled more of a white goatee. Zayn had to chuckle. "Let's get to checking in, shall we?"

Izzy nodded and followed him to the front desk. Where they were immediately met with a snafu.

"Your room is all ready, *monsieur*. The bellman will take you right up," the attendant announced in perfect English with a heavy French accent.

"You mean room*s*?" Zayn corrected. "There are two of us traveling. The arrangements should have been made two days ago."

The man's brow furrowed as his perfectly manicured fingers flew across his computer keyboard. "I'm afraid there is only the one room under your name, sir."

That didn't make any sense. Clara had to have registered Izzy under her own room. "Try Izadora Veracruz."

The man shook his head. "I'm afraid there is nothing here for that individual, either."

Izzy stiffened next to him. "There must be some kind of mistake."

"My administrative assistant would have called to make an additional reservation. Could you recheck the spelling?"

The attendant did so, only to look back up at him worriedly. "I have nothing but the one room in your name, sir. Perhaps there was a language issue."

Zayn rubbed his chin. This didn't bode well. "Perhaps. May we simply add an additional room to the reservation, then?"

The man audibly scoffed. "We have been booked months in advance due to the expo, sir. I'm afraid there is nothing available. I'd be happy to give you each a separate key."

Izzy stepped over to the desk, her face ashen. "But

it's not like that. We…aren't…you know…we aren't together or anything."

Izzy most definitely did not want to share a room with him. Not that he could really blame her under the circumstances. Still, his ego took a bit of a bruising at her reaction.

She turned to him, mild panic in her eyes. "Maybe another hotel nearby."

The attendant shot that idea down before Zayn could answer in kind. "The entire city is at capacity. You are welcome to call around, however."

Zayn took her gently by the elbow and pulled her aside. "These are very large suites, Izzy. I'll just sleep on the couch. We'll only have to share a bathroom. Like roomies. It will be fine."

She hardly looked convinced.

Well, this was a mistake. An unmitigated, full-blown disaster of a mistake. Izzy stepped into the hotel room behind Zayn and took in the luxurious surroundings as she stood in the doorway.

The place looked like something right out of a romantic movie, exactly what a honeymoon suite would look like. They did say Paris was the city for lovers. Obviously, the hotel industry took that reputation to heart when choosing their décor.

Plush, thick carpeting the color of desert sand, with gold-tone paint on the walls. Subtle hues of deep burgundy and rose-pink adorned the bed and furniture. A huge painting of a cherub hung on the wall above the wide-screen television.

Honestly, it all bordered on cliché, complete with the Eiffel Tower in view outside a glass door that led to a charming balcony.

This is what she got for ignoring her instincts and blindly following her impulsive heart. How in the world was she going to spend the next few days sharing this space with Zayn, her ex-lover?

"It won't be so bad," he said from across the room, as if reading her thoughts. "There's plenty of space. I promise I'll be a perfect gentleman."

Ha! As if she'd believe that. "Unless I happen to come to stand under some mistletoe?"

The smile he gave her was downright wolfish. "Well, I'm not made of stone."

She chose to ignore that. His eyes fell to the sofa in the center of the room just as hers did. The problem was immediately obvious. Far from any kind of comfortable place to sleep, the piece looked like it would barely fit a man of Zayn's stature. Given its size, the ornate armrests and a curved cushioned back would no doubt have him rolling off onto the floor in the middle of the night.

"I'll sleep on the sofa," she declared, stating what was clearly the only option.

Zayn grabbed his luggage and began unpacking. "You can't seriously think I'll allow that."

Why had she hoped he would just accept her wishes? Honestly, it was as if she didn't know him at all. "And I can't allow you to try to contort yourself into a pretzel shape in the very hotel room you booked and are paying for."

"You'll have to. Like I said, I am a true gentleman. One who would never let a lady spend a night on—" he pointed to the sofa in question "—that thing."

"Then we are clearly at an impasse."

He shrugged. "Let's discuss it over dinner. I'm famished."

Another thing they were going to put off addressing

until later. But her stomach grumbled in response to the mention of food, so she decided not to push it. "I insist that it be my treat. You're paying for the hotel room. I'll pay for the meals." Only as the words left her mouth did she begin to question them. Knowing Zayn, he was probably used to eating in the finest, top-star restaurants. A place like that would probably cost her a pretty penny. She lived a comfortable life, but she was trying to stick to a budget. The winery always needed some equipment repair or upkeep and she desperately wanted to renovate the tasting room.

"It's a deal," Zayn agreed, surprising her by not arguing.

Looked like she would have to budget harder when she got back to California.

When they made it outside, the air had definitely grown chillier. A frosty breeze bit at her and she shivered in the too thin sweater. Zayn noticed. He shrugged off his scarf and handed it to her.

"Thanks. You weren't kidding about the nip in the air."

Inhaling deeply as she wrapped the scarf around her shoulders, she sank into its warmth. The scent of him filled her nostrils—sandalwood combined with a hint of lemon citrus and a distinctive tinge that was purely male and purely Zayn.

The scent flooded her senses, reminding her of the times he'd sneaked into her bedroom in the middle of the night and left his scent behind when he'd sneaked back out. Her father had been furious when he'd found out.

Shaking off the nostalgic memories, Izzy stepped to the curb. But Zayn took her by the elbow and kept walking down the sidewalk.

"Aren't we hailing a cab?"

He shook his head. "Nope. What I have in mind is within walking distance."

In no time, they approached what Izzy could only describe as a makeshift Christmas town. Mini wooden chalets lined the walkway, along with stall after stall selling everything from hand-made ornaments to small watercolor paintings.

"Welcome to the Élysées Christmas market," Zayn said, gesturing to the magnificence that surrounded them. "These started out in Germany, but they pop up all over Europe during December."

Izzy found herself at a loss for words. "Oh, my!" was all she could manage.

"What are you in the mood for?" he asked her. "You can pick from all sorts of treats—everything from cheese to biscuits to crêpes."

"It all sounds heavenly."

"Which one?"

She laughed, her senses on overload with complete delight. "All of it. I'd like to try everything."

He winked at her. "That's my girl. Let's start with crêpes."

They spent two hours simply browsing and munching on one treat after another. By the time Zayn led her to the stall of fine chocolates, she could swear she'd never be hungry again. But then she couldn't resist and bit the head off a tiny milk-chocolate soldier.

"That's it," she declared once the soldier's feet were devoured. "Not one more bite."

"Giving up so soon, are you?"

"I'm afraid so. 'Uncle' and all that."

"Wait here," he told her. "There's one more stall I'd like to visit. I'll be right back."

He strode off without giving her a chance to respond.

Just as well, Izzy thought as she waited for him to return, admiring the knit shawls in the next cart over from the chocolate vendor.

She needed a minute to process all she'd just experienced. And to come to terms with the knowledge that she'd just spent the most enjoyable evening of her past five years.

Since Zayn had left.

He'd wanted to get it for her as soon as he'd seen it. Zayn discreetly placed the matchbox-size ornament in his pocket as he rejoined Izzy where she stood waiting for him. He'd give it to her later, when they weren't in a crowded shopping bazaar. Maybe he'd even wait and give it to her when they were back in Napa on Christmas morning, a true holiday gift.

That thought gave him pause. He'd fully intended to fly right back to Manhattan from Paris. Turned out his subconscious had made other plans while he hadn't been paying attention.

Would Izzy even want to spend Christmas with him? He probably shouldn't make assumptions. Was he even ready to ask her? For someone who prided himself on being decisive and action-oriented, he sure seemed to be all over the place when it came to his ex.

They made their way slowly back in the direction of the hotel, walking along the Seine. The city's lights burned bright around them, holiday bulbs adding to the luminescence. In the distance, the Eiffel Tower glowed like a decorative monument to the holiday.

He didn't want the night to end, wanted to somehow capture this moment in time and hold on to it tight. So he paused at the next empty bench, silently led her to it and waited for Izzy to sit. She didn't protest.

Several moments passed in comfortable silence as they both sat watching the river and others strolling along the path. It was like spiraling back in time, the comfort between them, the pure familiarity.

Izzy was the first to break the silence. "This was one of the places we always talked about visiting together."

They'd had any number of dreams back then. Visiting Paris had been one of many.

Izzy chuckled. "How many hours do you suppose we spent talking about all the places we wanted to travel to as soon as we could?"

"Too many to count. It didn't help that my mother would show up occasionally, promising to take me on her next adventure with her. Only to come up with an excuse about why she couldn't."

He hadn't meant to bring up such a somber memory, didn't realize how close to the surface it had been all this time.

Izzy leaned her shoulder against his. No one knew better than her the sheer number of times he'd been disappointed by the mother who'd given birth to him. Izzy had witnessed many of the occasions firsthand. They sat together in silence, Zayn didn't even know for how long, content just to bask in the comfort of having her there beside him. Finally, as the evening grew chillier, he stood and took her hand, pulling her up, too. They resumed walking.

"I don't know why I believed her every time," he found himself admitting. "How did I not learn after being bounced from one home to another each time she promised to pull me out only to not show up?"

He'd lived the life of a nomad, discarded from various relatives and foster guardians, some of them cruelly mean and completely unfit to take care of a child. Finally, his great-aunt Myrna had stepped in once and for all. It had almost been too late. By the time he became a resident of Stackhouse, Zayn had already harbored a level of anger and resentment that no kid should have experienced. Unfortunately, he'd found release in ways that had often landed him in trouble.

"Do you ever hear from your mother?" Izzy asked.

He shrugged. "The occasional birthday card. Or postcard from her latest destination." He tried to recollect her most recent correspondence. It must have come a while ago for he couldn't seem to remember. "I got a wedding invite once. I believe she's married to some sheikh in a small Middle Eastern province. Or maybe she's divorced him since then. I don't really know."

"A sheikh? Huh."

Zayn rubbed his jaw. "Come to think of it, I don't even know my own mother's full name at the moment. If she is indeed remarried, I have no clue what surname she may be carrying."

Then there was his father. A man whose existence Zayn hadn't even thought of until he'd received a strange phone call a few months back. But that was the last thing he wanted to be thinking of right now.

He realized just how much he'd missed Izzy just as a trusted confidante. Someone who listened without judgment, a rarity in his life. Someone who knew him better than anyone else on this earth. And somehow she'd cared for him anyway.

His hand moved toward hers of its own volition. He stopped it just in time, began to clench his fist, only to notice that she'd reached for him, too. Gently, slowly, she wrapped her gloved fingers around his. Holding her hand felt so right and so familiar; the sensation flowed over him like a warm wave.

In the next instant, as if the magic between them had somehow conjured it, large snowflakes began to gently float down from the sky. He couldn't recall a time he'd been in Paris and had it snow. Izzy nudged him and lifted her eyes to the sky, letting the snow fall across her face. A large, fat flake landed on her nose and instantly melted.

Zayn couldn't seem to help himself, he leaned over and kissed the moisture off her skin. She tasted fresh and welcoming and like home.

"Zayn," she whispered his name against his cheek. Part question, part demand. Full of desire.

Heaven help him, he was going to need a cold shower when they made it back to the hotel. Suddenly, he wasn't feeling quite so blasé about the shared suite. As it was, he was ready to pull her into his arms and plunge her mouth, trail kisses along her neck and pull her close against him until he could feel her very breath. Right here, along the path of the river, with crowds of people surrounding them.

The magic and romance of Paris.

He shuddered to think how bad his desire might get when they found themselves alone in the privacy of the suite. Or maybe the shudder had everything to do with how much he wanted her.

Somehow, he managed to pull away and forced his feet to move. Izzy pressed closer against his side.

"I'd forgotten how romantic this city is," she said on a breathless whisper.

He had to acknowledge the implication in her words. Whether she meant it as such or not, there was the possibility that she was simply overcome with the novelty of being in Paris. Her attraction could be nothing more than the effects of being in this city during the most festive time of the year. Izzy could simply be getting carried away, without a clear thought about what was happening between them.

He should be the responsible one, the one making the right decisions.

And none of that seemed to matter once they made it back to the suite and walked through the door. He'd resolved to bid her good-night then leave the room until she fell asleep. He could try to get some work done in the lobby downstairs. Heck, he could even wander the city aimlessly until all this pent-up emotion within him had a chance to settle.

There was so much to consider—the physical distance between them now that he'd made his home across the country in Manhattan, the sins of the past that he would never be able to tell her, the very real possibility that he'd only end up hurting her again the way he had before. He should know better than to want her.

All those good intentions flew out the window once the door closed behind them. Rather than tell her he was going out for a while, he motioned to the coffee table where housekeeping had left a complimentary bottle of bordeaux.

"Any interest in a nightcap?"

She held his gaze for several moments before answering, heat swimming in her eyes. "I am a little thirsty after all that food and chocolate."

Zayn shrugged off his coat and made his way farther into the room. Izzy curled up on the couch and tucked her feet underneath her. She hadn't taken off his scarf. Her hair draped in glorious waves over where she'd wrapped it around her neck. He wanted to reach for her, remove the scarf, then continue disrobing her until she was bare and trembling in his arms. His breath caught at the image and he forced himself to look away and grab the wine.

But when he looked over at her again after uncorking the bottle, her lids were closed and she was breathing evenly. She'd fallen asleep.

Zayn didn't know whether he was more disappointed or relieved.

Izzy felt herself being lifted off the couch and carried by a set of solid, strong arms.

"I'm not asleep," she protested. "Just closed my eyes for a bit."

"If you weren't asleep, you were fast approaching getting there," Zayn's deep, rich voice answered.

"Besides, I thought we'd established that I'd be sleeping on the couch." Though now that she said it, she found the notion held absolutely no appeal. Heaven help her, she didn't want to be across the room from Zayn on a hard, antique sofa. She wanted to be where he was. In his bed.

"We established no such thing."

They'd reached the bed. Izzy met his eyes and her breath caught in her throat at the heat that swam in them. Desire flooded their depths. Desire for her. He wanted her. It was as clear as the bright lights shining outside their balcony door. Her own need burned just as strong.

Her gaze fell to his lips. So close, his mouth was a shallow breath away from hers. "Zayn?" She could only say his name.

His hold on her tightened. She could feel every beat of his heart against the skin of her cheek. Her own heartbeat echoed in her ears. She slid down until her feet touched the floor, her body full against the length of him. Wrapping her arms around his neck, she stood on tiptoe to even their height difference. He swallowed. "Iz, I'm not so—"

She pressed her fingers to his lips to stop him from

going further. She didn't need to hear any words right now. She only needed one thing.

"Sweetheart…" he began. "I'm trying really hard here to stay true to what I said earlier about being a gentleman. You're not exactly making it easy."

"I think I'd be sorely disappointed if you were finding it easy."

Then she couldn't think at all as he pulled her tighter against his chest. Her body was crushed against his and it felt exquisite. His hands moved down her back, lower, until he cupped her bottom, pulling her up until she could clearly feel the strength of his desire.

It made her heady to know how much he wanted her, how powerful his need for her was. His hands roamed over her body, burning a trail of fire wherever he touched her.

It had been so long. And she'd missed him so much.

Consequences be damned. She would worry about those later.

CHAPTER TEN

HE'D DREAMED ABOUT THIS, thought about it more often than he should have over the years. Holding her again, tasting her, feeling her luscious curves against him. In his imaginings, he managed to go slow, take his time, start with a small and gentle kiss then trail further kisses along her chin and down her neck. Fully in control of himself. How naïve of him.

Reality turned out to be very different. He'd thought he'd have more restraint if he ever got to touch her again. But he was barely hanging on to any semblance of restraint at the moment.

This is how things had always been between them. Passion and fire and pure want combusting in a powerful force until neither one of them could think straight. In fact, he didn't think he could form another coherent thought for as long as he lived.

He none-too-gently nudged her onto the bed beneath him, limbs intertwined. Her breath gasped against his chin and then her hands began torturing him. She ran her fingers up his chest, palmed over his shoulders then moved back down, lower and lower until he thought he'd stop breathing. All the while, he couldn't get enough of her mouth on his. When she cried out his name again against his mouth, he thought he might die from need.

It took seconds for their clothes to end up in a haphazard pile on the floor. One of her buttons tore free and rolled off the bed. How could he have ever thought he could resist her when he saw her again?

He wanted to slow things down, but it was all out of his control. He was mere clay in her skilled, capable hands. Izzy was solidly at the helm. And he was going to let her lead.

Tonight, he would follow anywhere she took him.

She woke up exhausted and mildly achy the next morning, albeit in an entirely pleasurable way. It also appeared she'd woken up alone.

Bolting upright on the bed, Izzy glanced around for any sign of Zayn. She'd had dreams of rousing out of sleep embraced in his arms, proceeding to take up where they'd last left things.

Her cell phone lit up on the bedside table with a text message. Ran out to get you pastries and fresh rolls for breakfast. Don't go anywhere. He'd added several emojis at the end, some of them rather naughty. Definitely not the standard set that came already loaded on the smartphone. A couple at the end brought a blush to her cheeks and reminded her of the previous night. Those thoughts only led to further blushing.

Zayn certainly seemed to bring out a side of her that she didn't usually let loose. She felt comfortable with him. He'd been her first real boyfriend and anyone she'd dated in between hadn't stood a chance against what she felt for him.

Izzy swore and plopped over onto her back. Now that morning light was shedding some clarity on things, nagging thoughts bordered the edges of her mind. Did she really know what she was getting herself into here?

She'd been crushed when he'd left. Her heart had been irreparably damaged. It had taken her months to begin to feel like herself again. And years to so much as start dating other men. None of those relationships had taken root.

Now she was lying in a warm bed in Paris and Zayn was sending her sexy text messages. They'd spent all night in each other's arms. As if the last five years had never happened.

But they had.

And she still didn't have any answers.

Or perhaps she did. Maybe what he'd told her the day he'd left really was all there was to it. Maybe his silence all the time since then was answer enough.

That he'd left because Napa was too small for him, the town held too many bad memories.

Maybe he had left her to become the global professional success that he was today. And maybe their relationship had always meant more to her than it had ever meant to him.

So what did all those possibilities mean for where they stood today? More specifically, what did it mean for her that she'd fallen into Zayn's bed within a week of seeing him again? The charms and enchantments of Paris during Christmas were no excuse.

The truth was she didn't have any kind of excuse. She had to accept that. Had to accept the reality that she hadn't gotten over the man despite all the time that had passed. She probably never would get over him.

Suddenly her appetite for pastries or anything else had completely disintegrated. Despite Zayn's directive to stay put, she got up to shower and get dressed. It was time to be brutally honest with herself. When it came to this particular man, she would always lead with her heart. Even if it ultimately meant getting it torn to shreds. It was high time for her to decide, once and for all, what she planned to do about it.

Could she be the type of woman who could take whatever was offered by the man she loved? Because she did love him; there was no denying that anymore. Another thing she had to come to terms with: Zayn's reappearance in her life was temporary. After this trip, she may never see him again.

You could be a big girl and take what life...and Zayn... have to offer. Try to enjoy what you can have rather than wallow about all that you can't.

She'd never been the type of woman who could do relationships without emotional involvement. But if there was anyone on earth who might tempt her to do just that, he was the one whose toiletries lay strewed all over the bathroom she'd just entered.

When she emerged half an hour later, the suite was still empty. Except there was a cardboard box tied with pastry string sitting on the coffee table. No sign of Zayn.

She went to check her phone and, sure enough, there was a message.

Sorry, got called away on an emergency conference call that I decided to take in the hotel's VIP business lounge. Let's meet for lunch at the Eiffel Tower. Can't wait to see you!

No playful emojis this time. See, maybe this was some kind of sign. The morning after they'd fallen back into bed together and they couldn't even connect in person. Quickly typing an affirmative reply, she pushed away her disappointment at the delay.

The phone pinged again before she could even set it down.

Still stuck on this call but wanted to send you this. I'm so proud of you!

The text had an attachment from the expo brochure. They'd highlighted her cabernet in a write-up about the awards ceremony.

A completely unwelcome pang of longing settled in her chest. He was proud of her. His accolade shouldn't have meant as much as it did. She knew her wine's nomination was a fluky thing akin to winning the state lottery. Not that she wasn't proud of her work, she absolutely took great pride in it. But her pride and dedication weren't dependent on some industry award she'd randomly been selected for because a tourist to her tasting room happened to work for a beverage magazine. Stackhouse wasn't the type of winery that normally warranted that kind of attention. And that was fine with her. She liked that it was relatively a nonplayer, with visits by appointment only and cases that sold out every year because their entire operation was small. All the qualities that had driven Zayn to want to buy her out in the first place.

She stared at his words again on her screen. Did he mean he was proud of her as a business partner? Or as the woman he… She didn't even know how to categorize what she might mean to him. For all she knew, her feelings were completely one-sided and there was nothing more than physical attraction where Zayn was concerned. She might have thought to ask him before sleeping with the man last night.

Well, she was done wallowing in self-pity and drowning in questions. She was here for an expo and there were panels to attend and wines to taste. She was a professional vintner on a business trip and she needed to act like it.

She picked up the hotel phone to order a pot of hot

French roast to go alongside the pastries. Then, putting her hair up in a tight bun and pulling out a pencil skirt business suit, she dressed and began preparing for her day.

Heaven help her, she had no idea what she intended to say to Zayn when she saw him in a few hours. Or how she would resist running into his arms the moment she laid eyes on him.

He shouldn't have even bothered with that conference call. The emergency turned out to be an overblown crisis spurned by a panicked employee. And it wasn't as if he'd been able to pay any kind of close attention to what was being said. That's why he'd opted to take the call in the lounge in the first place; he'd known being in the same room with Izzy would have proved much too distracting.

What a shameful waste of time. He would have much preferred to spend the morning the same way he'd spent most of the night, with Izzy snuggled up close to him in bed. Not that that's what they'd been doing for most of the time.

He could hardly wait to see her again.

Though he was starting to rethink this plan of his to meet her for lunch at the Eiffel Tower. What had he been thinking this morning when he'd sent her that text? He should have told her to take off every article of clothing and wait for him in the hotel room wearing nothing but the scarf he'd let her borrow yesterday. The scarf and nothing else. Perhaps he could ask her for a rain check on that score.

Hastening his pace, he glanced at his watch. He was running a few minutes late, hated the thought that he might be keeping her waiting. But when he reached the square, he realized he'd been harried for no reason.

Izzy was nowhere to be found. Had she forgotten? She was one of the most prompt and time-conscious people he knew. Or at least, she had been. What did he really know anymore about her? People changed a lot in five years. Look at all the changes he'd made for himself. One could argue he was a completely different person.

It was foolish of him to think that Izzy was the same loyal, unaffected person she'd been when he'd walked away. For all he knew, she'd turned into the kind of woman who forgot lunch dates she'd made the next day with men she'd spent the night with.

The thoughts scurrying through his brain had him gripping his phone so tight, he actually felt the screen bend.

Get hold of yourself. She was probably just running late, the same as he had been. It was only about fifteen minutes past their agreed-upon time. She'd probably been distracted at a panel back at the conference center or on the way here doing some impromptu window-shopping. Paris boutiques could have that sort of effect on women; he'd witnessed it firsthand on some of his previous visits with others.

He fished his phone out of his pocket to check for last-minute messages. Nothing. Not from her, anyway.

Looking around the square proved futile. She wasn't there. The familiar quickening of his breath sent a surge of annoyance through him. This was no time to have one of those damn episodes—or whatever they were. They'd been plaguing him for the better part of two years now and they'd grown more frequent and more bothersome.

He refused to be distracted by one right now. This was so not the time.

Loosening his grip on the phone, he started to pull up Izzy's contact info. There was also the possibility to consider that she may have gotten lost. Paris wasn't exactly a familiar city for her. He should have made sure to tell her to take the car and driver he had on standby with the hotel. Some parts of the city were definitely seedier than others. He clicked on her number and waited, his breath hitching in near panic. He'd never forgive himself if harm had happened to come to her.

The call immediately went to her voice mail. Zayn bit out a curse. He should never have left her alone in an unfamiliar city. What had he been thinking?

A familiar voice sounded from behind him before he could dial her again.

"Zayn, here I am." She ran up to him, rosy-cheeked and near huffing for air. "Were you waiting long? I'm so sorry. I was doing some shopping." She held up a parcel. "The French salesladies definitely make it a leisurely affair. They serve cookies and everything as they wait on you. Took forever to try on dresses and find one I liked."

She stopped to study his face. "What's the matter? You look a little pale."

The relief he felt surging through his system kept him from answering right away. Now that the scare was over, he felt rather foolish for jumping to so many erroneous and perilous scenarios in his mind.

"I thought you might have gotten lost. Wasn't sure whether I should start looking for you."

"I'm so sorry," she repeated. "I didn't realize the shopping would take so long. And then I underestimated the time it would take to walk over here. I'm not terribly familiar with the city."

Zayn closed his eyes and took a calming breath. "It's okay, Iz. I just started to worry. Then when you didn't answer your phone..."

Her face brightened once more and she hooked her arm through his elbow. "You were worried about me, huh?"

He forced a smile through the tense muscles around his mouth. "Maybe a little." He took the bag from her hand and led her toward the opposite side of the square and the small bistro he had in mind for lunch. He could use a sit-down with a nice cold glass of chardonnay.

Izzy paused before the second step. "Wait. Do you mind if we do a quick climb of the tower first? I haven't been here since they debuted the glass floor and I've been so looking forward to seeing it. I'm not terribly hungry just yet."

He took a moment too long to answer.

"Unless you're hungry right now," she hastily added at his hesitation.

Zayn forced some air into his lungs and wrangled some calm. "Of course, we can visit the tower. Anything you wish."

What he really needed was to sit and gather himself in a quiet, peaceful spot like the bistro. But the smile Izzy flashed him made it hard to deny her.

"We're lucky it's not terribly crowded today," Zayn said next to her. He'd taken her hand and still carried her package.

Given the rather cloudy day, there weren't as many tourists visiting the tower. Izzy let Zayn lead her into the small crowd of other visitors. The line moved slowly but pretty steadily. She stole a sideways glance at his profile. There was something off about him; he didn't seem his usual, assured self. He appeared distracted, anxious.

Must have been something to do with his emergency call earlier. She felt guilty for having alarmed him at all by being late. The truth was she'd had no intention of doing any shopping. She'd packed everything she'd needed, including a sensible, casual black wrap dress to wear to the awards ceremony. But that text had made her rethink her options. Zayn had said he was proud of her. He'd be with her at the dinner event as they announced the winner. Suddenly, she'd cared about dressing up for it, wanted something more than the boring outfit she'd purchased off the discount rack at a department store back home. She was in the fashion mecca of the world, surely it was worth a look.

But she'd ended up alarming Zayn. Though why he'd been worked up over her being a few minutes late was something of a mystery. It took about ten minutes for them to reach the base of the tower. They bustled into the elevator and got off on the first level.

"The last time I was in France, I didn't get a chance to do much sightseeing," she explained. "Thank you for indulging me."

"You're welcome, Iz."

Izzy squealed in delight as she walked out onto the deck. This first level was the one with the see-through glass floor panels. They were about two hundred feet off the ground and the people below looked like little ants. Izzy felt like she was walking on air.

The feeling of standing on the glass was a little disconcerting. She gingerly stepped closer to the edge, staring at the view below her feet. Though confident it was safe, her lizard brain cried out a warning that she shouldn't be this high off the ground and be able to see the world below.

Something fell to the floor behind her. She looked over to see that Zayn had dropped her package. He was as white as a bedsheet. Rushing to his side, she grabbed him by the arm.

"Zayn? What's the matter?"

He swallowed hard. "Nothing. I'm fine."

He clearly wasn't. A smile spread over his lips that appeared forced and fake.

"You've gone very pale," she told him, concern flooding her chest.

"Have I?" He appeared to be studying her as he spoke, hyperfocused on her face. As if he were afraid to let his eyes travel anywhere else. "The glass floor just threw me off, that's all. Feeling a bit dizzy."

She could only nod. He certainly wasn't the only person here who appeared to be experiencing a touch of vertigo. But a nagging voice was telling her there was more going on. Zayn's pallor had started turning a concerning hue of green. She thought she might have heard him muttering numbers under his breath.

"Perhaps you're coming down with something?" she ventured.

He gave a small nod. "Hope not. I have a rather busy couple of weeks ahead of me. Don't have time to catch a cold." He tried to uphold the fake smile but the effect came off as more of a grimace.

"Have you had breakfast?"

He shook his head. "No, I haven't eaten yet today. I'm sure that isn't helping."

Her guilt multiplied by several factors. First, she'd had him worried by making him wait, then she'd ask to delay lunch even longer. This after the man had hand-delivered breakfast to her and then made reservations for lunch.

"Oh, Zayn. I wish you'd told me you were starving. We could have gone straight to eat." Leaning down, she picked up the package he'd dropped. Zayn stared at it as if seeing it for the first time. He didn't even seem to be aware that it had slipped out of his hand.

Alarm bells began ringing in Izzy's head. She nudged him gently ahead of her toward the elevator.

Looked like their Eiffel Tower visit was over.

"Let's get you back on solid ground."

He immediately began to protest. "No, I don't want

to be the reason you don't get to tour the Eiffel Tower, Izzy. I'm fine to go on to the top."

Was he serious? He appeared to be in no condition to continue standing, let alone do any more sightseeing with her. "We have a couple more days in Paris," she reassured him. "I'll make you come back with me when you're up for it. After you've eaten something."

Izzy swallowed past the concern rising in her chest. Zayn was one of the strongest, most virile, men she knew. It was unsettling to see him the way he was right now. But her main focus at the moment was to get him out of the bustle of tower visitors and back to the first floor. It seemed to take forever, but finally they made it outside and onto a bench. She quickly stopped to purchase a bottle of water from a vendor along the way.

By the time they were seated, she was relieved to see some of the color return to his face. He appeared less ashen, less shaky. She handed him the water.

Izzy blew out the breath she'd been holding as he took a sip. "Are you feeling better?"

He gave her a wry smile. "Nothing hurts now but my pride. Who knew I suffered from vertigo?"

"Is that what that was?"

"Had to be. I'm otherwise fit as a fiddle. Let's go eat, shall we?" With that, he stood and reached his hand out for her to take. He certainly seemed to be feeling better. And the recovery had happened so quickly that she supposed it must have been a temporary touch of vertigo. It made sense based on the fact that they had been literally standing on glass several floors above the ground. Not everyone was cut out for such a visual. Right now, he appeared recovered and energetic.

She took Zayn's hand and stood.

CHAPTER ELEVEN

How mortifying.

So much for being the dashing and suave gentleman who had whisked his ex-girlfriend to Paris. Zayn waited for Izzy to sit at the corner table the greeter had led them to before taking a chair himself. He hadn't had an episode that bad in as long as he could remember. Just his luck it had to happen in front of Izzy. She was still watching him with guarded scrutiny.

"You look adorable when you're worried. Particularly, when it's me you're worried about." It was a rather lame attempt to lighten the moment, which didn't seem to work judging by the concern still clouding her eyes.

"I can't help it, Zayn. Are you sure you're all right? Is this because of the mishap with Frosty?"

That question was so preposterous he almost had to laugh. "No. Definitely not."

He had to give her something, he supposed. "Nothing to fret about, Iz. It's just something that happens occasionally."

Her eyes grew wide. Rather than placating her, his words appeared to have further edged her concern. "You mean this has happened before?"

He nodded. "Started a couple of years ago."

"Why haven't you had it checked?" she wanted to know.

She should give him more credit than that. "I have. In fact, I went in for a complete workup before I flew to Napa."

"And?"

"Nothing out of the ordinary. Was told to try to relax more. Cut down on stress and take more vacations." He didn't have to tell her he could pinpoint exactly when the episodes had started. She didn't have to know that the very first one had been triggered by a phone call he'd received out of the blue one fateful day. A call he would have never imagined getting. From a man he'd never expected to hear from. His absentee father who'd apparently suddenly had a change of heart.

No, he didn't want to get into all of that with Izzy. He didn't even want to think about it. Or the myriad reasons he'd clicked off the call before the old man could finish saying whatever it was he'd had to say. Nor why Zayn had ignored his repeated attempts to reach him again afterward. He'd eventually blocked the number. Only to have a different one call his phone a few weeks after he'd done so.

She reached across the table. "Zayn, I think you've been having anxiety attacks."

The waiter chose that moment to hand them their menus and fill their glasses with ice water. Izzy didn't let go of his hand.

He waved off the suggestion. His own doctor had tried to tell him something similar. What difference did it make what the clinical term was? He'd been burning the proverbial candle at both ends for years now and those blasted phone calls had simply tipped things over the edge.

In any case, he didn't have time to deal with it. "Nah, I just need to slow down."

She didn't seem convinced. "Maybe when we get back you can go see Ethan—"

He held a hand up to stop her before she could go any further. No way in the world he was going to discuss his shortcomings with anyone from his past. And especially not Izzy.

"No," he stated simply.

"Why not?" she pressed. "It's not something to be ashamed of."

Zayn pulled his hand out of her grip. "Honestly, Izzy. You don't have to concern yourself with this." His tone sounded sharper than he'd intended. But he really was tired of discussing it. If the episodes didn't stop on their own eventually, he would deal with it when he had time.

She pursed her lips before speaking. "In other words, it's none of my business."

"That's not what I said, Iz. Let's just enjoy our lunch for now." He opened up the cloth-covered menu. "This place is known for its duck à l'orange. I'll get a bottle of champagne to go with it."

She didn't make a move to look at her own menu. She just wasn't going to let this go.

Zayn sighed and rubbed his forehead. "Would it make you feel better if I promise to take a vacation when I get back to the States?"

"Maybe." She shrugged an elegant shoulder. "It would be a start, I suppose," she added begrudgingly.

"Then I promise to do just that."

"I'm not so sure you know how to relax, Zayn. How do I know you wouldn't just work through your vacation?"

She knew him too well, probably better than anyone else on the planet. He chuckled. "Would you like me to sign a contract?"

She leaned over the table. "This is not a laughing matter, Zayn. I wish you would take it more seriously."

He wanted to put her mind at ease. He really did. He could only think of one way that might appease her for the short term.

"How about I prove to you that I can take it easy and take time off?"

She lifted her chin, silently scrutinizing his words. "How do you propose to do that exactly?"

"After your ceremony tonight, I say we beg off the rest of this expo. We have two more days in Paris. Let's turn it into a vacation of sorts. Then I can show you firsthand that I'm taking time off."

He certainly seemed to have her attention. "Go on. I'm listening."

Now that he was saying the words out loud, he was growing keener and keener on the idea. "For the next two days we become full-blown, bona fide tourists. Nothing but sightseeing, fun and frivolity."

Finally, a small smile seemed to creep onto her face. "How do I know this isn't simply a shameless attempt to get me to spend more time in hotel rooms with you?"

"Not shameless at all," he teased. "I fully admit to being guilty on that count—that thought had indeed crossed my mind."

She steepled her fingers on the table, considering. Zayn actually caught himself moving to the edge of his seat awaiting her answer. Finally she blew out a puff of air. "All right. Let's do it. Why not?"

Clasping a hand to his chest in mock despair, he grinned at her. "Not the most enthusiastic acceptance, but I'll have to take it."

He was ridiculously pleased at the unexpected turn

of events. For the next two days, he'd have Izzy all to himself in one of the loveliest countries on the planet.

A man couldn't ask for much more.

For an awards ceremony she didn't particularly feel invested in, Izzy found herself spending quite some time standing in front of a mirror to get ready.

What exactly had she agreed to at lunch?

She'd been so concerned about Zayn, she probably would have agreed to anything. If he really did need a break that badly—and, judging by the severity of the panic attack she'd witnessed, he clearly did—then she would see to it that he took a couple of days off. Besides, a girl could do worse than to spend two days playing tourist throughout France.

First, they had to get through this ceremony tonight. She didn't get many opportunities to dress up in a formal evening gown. This was a bit of a novelty. The dress she'd bought on impulse this afternoon hung on the back of the bathroom door as she toyed with her hair.

What in the world would she say if she happened to win? From what she'd been told, the winner was expected to go up on stage to accept the trophy. Like the Oscars. Or Grammys.

There was a possibility, albeit she believed it to be slim, that it very well could be her.

Ha! Fat chance. There were at least a dozen nominees altogether. The chances of her coming out on top were slim to none. Some of the wines she was up against were masterpieces from some of the most renowned vineyards in Europe.

Okay. So maybe she was more nervous about this ceremony than she was allowing herself to believe. When she'd first been notified of the honor, she'd been too busy with all her new responsibilities and reeling in the middle of grieving the loss of Myrna. Now that the time was here and reality stared her in the face, she had to acknowledge that this was actually a pretty big deal.

I'm so proud of you.

Win or not, Zayn was impressed with her. The thought shouldn't thrill her as much as it did. But he had her worried. Whatever was going on with him, she planned to do her best to get to the bottom of it. It wouldn't be easy; she could guess he wasn't going to let her in. All the more reason to believe he wasn't after anything serious as far as the two of them were concerned.

Yet she wanted to make sure he was okay. And she'd have two days to observe and take notice if he had another episode. She'd work on convincing him to seek better treatment, as well.

But tonight…tonight was another matter. Tonight she was going to dress up and attend a fancy ceremony on the arm of a handsome and charming entrepreneur while she sipped fancy champagne and enjoyed herself.

Almost like some kind of date.

Stop it. She was being silly. That's what happened when you hadn't gone out in ages with anyone resembling a romantic interest. Still, would it be so wrong of her to play pretend? She glanced at the dress once more. Strapless, with tiny hints of glitter intertwined in the silly fabric. The color was a rich midnight-blue that shouldn't have worked with her coloring but somehow did. Just as the saleslady had assured her it would. Paula had loaned her a pair of stilettos as she'd never owned a pair in her life. Black-leather straps with two-inch heels she'd be lucky not to trip in.

Between the dress and the shoes, the outfit was so unlike anything she would normally wear.

Like the saying went, when in France and all that.

Zayn adjusted his collar and clipped on the gold cuff links he'd brought along specifically for this event. Normally, black tie affairs bored him to tears, but he found himself looking forward to this one. That feeling had everything to do with the company he'd be keeping.

A twinge of guilt made him wince when he thought about all that had happened earlier that afternoon at the tower. He'd given Izzy quite a scare. He owed it to her to try to make that right. Part of the reason he'd wanted to whisk her away for some fun and sightseeing while they were here.

The shower had gone off a while ago but Izzy was still in the bathroom. He'd been tempted to knock on the door, in the hope of catching her as she toweled off. He could help her get dry, running the Turkish towel over every inch of her before lifting her and carrying her to the bed.

He shut his eyes to force out the images. They had an awards ceremony to get to. He couldn't make her late when she was one of the nominees, as appealing as that idea was.

He found himself surprised at how long it was taking her to get ready. It wasn't like Izzy to spend too much time prepping and fussing. Though, admittedly, this was a rather special occasion.

When they'd been kids, Izzy had always leaned toward an understated style of dress, bordering on tomboy. She'd still always managed to look feminine and alluring. Torn jeans or black yoga pants with baggy shirts or tanks. It would be interesting to see her in anything formal.

Only "interesting" didn't even begin to cover it when

she revealed herself. He wasn't prepared for what he saw when she finally stepped out. His mouth went dry at the sight of her.

The dress existed to be on her skin, as if it had been created for her and her alone. Deep, dark blue, the color reminded him of a starless night in the height of summer. There was a slit that went up her leg several inches above her knee. Heaven help him, his hand itched to run his palm up the gap and then go higher. Her hair—she'd done something complicated with it. It was piled high atop her head with delicate tendrils loose around her face. And heels. He was pretty sure he'd never seen her in heels before.

She looked sexy as hell.

"I'm sorry if that took a while. I'm not used to getting dolled up. Don't really know what I'm doing."

She was clearly a fast learner. He could only nod in response.

She rubbed a hand down her middle and did a little twirl. "Well, what do you think? Will this work?"

He remained silent so long, she started to fidget. But he couldn't seem to get his mouth to work. Finally, he found his tongue and managed to answer.

"Oh, yeah. It works, all right. It works very, very well."

She hardly recognized herself. Who was this person so effortlessly mingling among the stars of the international wine community? It was almost as if she actually belonged among them.

Much of the credit for her confidence went to Zayn. He kept feeding her positive reinforcement as they moved along the crowd to their assigned table. She introduced herself to a couple of the magazine editors, one fellow vintner from Spain and an American distributor. She even threw in some high school French while speaking and managed to stay balanced on the stiletto heels that felt totally alien on her feet.

The reception was being held in the banquet room of a deluxe restaurant in the heart of Paris. Christmas decorations adorned the walls and mini decorated trees served as centerpieces on the tables. Two wine fountains had been set up in opposite corners of the room, one for white and one for red. Hovering servers, dressed in tuxedo vests and pressed slacks, carried trays of hors d'oeuvres among the crowd.

"This is the fanciest dinner I've ever attended," she admitted to Zayn as they took their seats.

He sat next to her after helping her into her own chair. "Just think, you're one of the guests of honor."

A nervous flutter tickled the center of her stomach. She'd have to apologize to her brother when she returned home. If it wasn't for Hector, she would have completely missed all this. She owed him a debt of gratitude for his persistence. As she did with Zayn. He'd played no small role in getting her here.

She stole a glance at him now for what must have been the hundredth time since they'd left the hotel. The man looked like he could be featured in a yacht ad or in a Billionaire Bachelor calendar spread. The formal tuxedo he wore must have been custom made for him. It fit him perfectly, accentuating his toned physique and wide shoulders. While such extravagant surroundings were so new to her, he was clearly in his element. This was a whole different world for her, but there was no question a man like Zayn belonged with a crowd such as the one they were in. If anything, he commanded the room with his presence.

Now, with the barest nod of his head, he summoned

one of the servers who brought over a tray of bubbly champagne. Taking two flutes off the tray, he handed her one then lifted his.

"A toast, to you and the cabernet you've created."

"Don't toast me yet," she protested. "I haven't actually won anything."

"You're already a winner as far as I'm concerned."

Their tablemates arrived at that very moment. An older couple impeccably dressed.

"Oh, how romantic," the silver-haired woman said in perfect English as her husband pulled out her chair. "If you don't mind my saying," she continued, taking her seat, "you two are quite a charming couple."

Izzy didn't get a chance to form a response before Zayn immediately corrected the statement.

"Thank you, ma'am. But we happen to be business partners, nothing more." He went on to tell her where they were from and bragged about her nomination.

Izzy couldn't help the bristle that skimmed over her skin. He was so quick to set the record straight, even to a couple of strangers they would most likely never see again after tonight.

"I beg your pardon for the misunderstanding, then," the woman said with a smile. "But I stand by what I said," she added rather cheekily.

Izzy took another sip of champagne. Silly, really, to feel out of sorts at the exchange. Zayn hadn't said anything incorrect. It was nothing but foolishness on her part that she let it bother her in the least.

The lights dimmed ever so slightly as the ceremony began.

There were so many different categories, Izzy found it hard to pay attention. Everything from best barrel maker to adherence to organic practices was considered for an award.

Finally, when time came to announce the cabernet winner, she thought her heart might pound right out of her chest.

But it wasn't her name that was called. Someone else, a rather plump man from Argentina was the lucky recipient. Izzy tried to clamp down on her disappointment. She hadn't really expected to win; the competition was too stiff. Still, it would have been nice to bring the miniature glass bottle trophy home. This was exactly why she hadn't dared to hope. Except that it turned out she actually had.

She felt Zayn give her knee a squeeze under the table. His support was something of a buffer, one she did appreciate.

He leaned over to whisper in her ear. "You'll get 'em next time, Iz."

The chance of being nominated again was not something she was going to hang her hat on. One day she'd be able to appreciate the honor of simply being nominated. Right now, she just wanted to wallow in disappointment for a while.

Two hours later, when the ceremony was over and the lights returned to full brightness, she was more than ready to leave.

What had started out as an exciting night full of potential had turned into nothing more than a major letdown.

She couldn't even be sure if she was referring to the loss or to Zayn's abject dismissal of them being described as any kind of couple.

Though truth be told, one definitely stung more than the other.

CHAPTER TWELVE

SHE PRETENDED TO SLEEP in the car on the ride back to the hotel. She was in no mood to talk. The day felt like it had gone on hours too long. Had it really been just this afternoon when they'd attempted to tour the Eiffel Tower?

If Zayn knew she was faking, to his credit, he wasn't calling her on it. Probably thought she was crushed by her defeat. Little did he know, that was only part of her disappointment this evening.

She fully intended to continue the charade until she heard him say something in French to the driver. *"Arrêtez, si'l vous plaît."* He was asking him to stop the car.

Izzy opened her eyes.

"Sleeping Beauty awakens," Zayn said with a soft smile.

Hadn't she required a kiss first? She probably shouldn't bring that up. "Just resting my eyes. It's been a long day. Why are we stopping?"

He pointed outside her window. "We happen to be driving by the Champs-Élysées."

"Why would we want to stop here?" The question was answered as soon as she turned to look behind her. The sight was breathtaking—an extravaganza of lights. There had to be millions of tiny bulbs set up like works of art. She gasped as the color theme changed from blue to red then a brilliant green.

Zayn shifted in the seat to move closer to her. "I figured we might start our minivacation here and now. If you're up for it."

Despite her aching feet—how did women wear such pointy heels on the regular?—and despite her general tiredness, she suddenly felt a surge of energy. She had to see it up close.

Zayn led her out of the car and over to the display. Despite the late hour and the December chill, there was a good number of people admiring it along with her. It was easy to see the draw. The effect was like watching fireworks suspended right there on the ground.

"This is a masterpiece," she said on a breathless sigh.

"I thought you'd like to see it. Every year they seem to outdo themselves from the year before."

It was hard to decide where to look. Orbs and spirals and geometric shapes presented like a visual banquet. Though it would never capture the true magic on display, Izzy fished out the smartphone from her clutch purse and snapped a picture. "No wonder you weren't impressed with my light-up snowman."

He chuckled. "In my defense, the snowman did try to kill me."

"I'm terribly sorry about that," she apologized, though it sounded rather insincere considering the words were muffled by a giggle she couldn't help. "He's been reformed."

"Then I can relate." His words held a wealth of meaning, she knew. Zayn's history of getting into trouble ran the gamut with everything from disorderly conduct to disturbing the peace. As well as a few bar fights in between. He really had turned himself around as an adult.

"You're a true American success story, Zayn. Resident bad boy turned billionaire entrepreneur. The stuff of legends."

He scoffed at that. "I made some smart business decisions after working my behind off for a few years."

She wondered if the sheer tenacity required for such a transformation had had anything to do with the bouts of anxiety that were now plaguing him. But he'd made it clear at lunch he didn't want to talk about his episode. And she didn't want to ruin this moment by pressing.

Besides, as he'd made very clear to their tablemates earlier tonight, there was nothing between them but a business partnership. So it was clearly none of her business.

Never mind that they'd spent their first night in Paris in the deepest throes of passion, unable to get enough of each other.

"Were you terribly disappointed? About losing tonight?" he asked.

Zayn had a tendency to change the subject when it veered toward him for too long.

"More so than I would have thought," she admitted. "But I'm slowly getting over it."

"There'll be other awards, Izzy. This nomination put you on the map. You're an internationally recognized name now."

"Are you saying that as my business partner?" she couldn't resist asking.

The lights before them changed color again, this time transforming into a brilliant shade of silver. Izzy felt as if she were standing in the middle of a constellation of stars.

"Did that bother you? My saying that?"

She simply raised a shoulder.

"We were at an event thrown by a magazine. There

were at least three photographers there. I didn't want the attention and gossip that any innuendo of a relationship between the two owners of Stackhouse Winery might lead to."

Well, when he put it that way, she supposed he had a point. A spark of hope began to heat in her chest. So he'd had a good reason for shooting down the older lady's assessment of them as a romantic couple.

His next words were like a bucket of cold water thrown over the flame. "But you bring up a good point. The fact is we are still business partners."

And apparently that was the part of their relationship Zayn wanted to focus on. Despite the fact that they'd slept together last night. "And we have very different ideas about how to run things."

"You're not telling me anything I don't know."

He crossed his arms in front of his chest. "You know as well as I do that, at some point, we are going to have to figure out how to reconcile those differences, Izzy. For the sake of the winery and it's bottom line."

Of course, she knew that. What she had no idea about was how she was going to reconcile her heart when Zayn walked away from her again once the business affairs were finally put in order.

They were both too tired and spent to do much more than take turns brushing their teeth then collapsing onto the bed when they returned to the suite close to midnight.

As much as he wanted her, and as much a temptation as she was curled up on the mattress next to him, Zayn was more than content just to be able to watch her sleep.

In hindsight, he knew he should have never touched her. He should have kept a tight rein on his control the night before, despite the strong desire that had clearly never waned over the past five years.

He'd just missed her so much.

Still, he should have slept on the damn couch. Or, better yet, in the marble bathtub in the bathroom, with the door securely locked to keep from succumbing to temptation.

There was too much baggage between them, too much unresolved. They still hadn't figured out how they were going to move forward as co-owners of Stackhouse. He had no doubt now that Izzy would never agree to sell her share. In hindsight, it had been foolish of him to ever think otherwise. And this past week, after seeing her in action, he had to admit Stackhouse needed her at the helm. But he still disagreed with the general business model the winery operated under. That meant they would have to somehow find a way to compromise. Not exactly a history of success between them in that regard.

Then there was the matter of her father. If Zayn had ever been tempted to tell her the truth about why he'd left Napa and the part Ernesto had played in his decision, there was absolutely no way he could give in to that temptation now. There was already a rift between father and daughter that was clearly hurting Izzy. He would never forgive himself for having any part in widening that rift any further.

It was all so messy. Sleeping together had only complicated things further. He had no idea what to do about it now.

Water under the bridge. What's done was done. And a million other clichés that could also apply.

He had two more days with Izzy before reality came back to retrieve him like the ghost of Christmas Present from that play featured in every metropolitan city theater during the holiday season. He vowed to make the most of these two days. After that, he needed to leave her alone to live the rewarding, peaceful life she deserved.

A life that included friends, family and career fulfillment. One that unfortunately couldn't include him.

Because, unlike the character in that play, he'd never fully been able to get away from his own ghosts of the past.

The next morning, he had the driver drop them off at the gold-colored gates of Château de Versailles. He'd promised her two full days of tourist excursions and Zayn figured the palace was the perfect place to start. Though seeing Versailles in the middle of winter wasn't ideal—one couldn't truly appreciate the gardens or the statues outside—the château itself was as grand as it ever was during the year.

He would have to bring Izzy back during the warmer months.

Whoa. Where had that thought come from? He had no business making any future plans that involved her. Hadn't he settled all that last night?

He led her through the entrance and Izzy gasped when they moved into the front garden. "Oh, my."

"It's lovely, isn't it? In summer, it's even more of a sight to behold." The fountain wasn't running and tarp covered many of the statues and bushes.

"It's spectacular." Her fingers covered her mouth as she looked on in awe. He loved seeing that look of wonder in her eyes. She'd always been very visual. He'd always wondered why she'd never taken up art.

Perhaps the creativity that went into producing a good bottle of wine served as all the outlet she needed.

Within moments they had entered the palace itself and

he took her straight to the hall of mirrors, the part of the tour he considered to be the highlight by far. Judging by Izzy's reaction, she appeared to agree.

"I don't even have the words to describe this," she declared.

Chandeliers hung from the ceiling as far as the eye could see. Gold and marble statues lined the hallway atop a shiny polished wood floor.

"Royalty sure knew how to live back then."

Every part of the hall they entered was more spectacular than the last. Izzy turned on the audio guide for the tour, using the headphones they'd been handed when purchasing their tickets.

Zayn was content just to watch her as she took in all the sights, occasionally nodding to whatever she'd heard in the audio. They'd reached the princess rooms, the section of the palace that could only be described as a true testament to insane wealth and extravagance.

"Louis XV's daughters sure knew how to live in style," Izzy declared, taking off her headphones.

Zayn followed her gaze to a particularly elaborate bed in the corner of the room—Marie Antoinette's "Pink Chambers." It looked like a cotton-candy machine might have exploded in the center. A large pink bed with a draping pink canopy surrounded by pink chairs and pink furniture.

Pink. Pink. Pink.

Marie certainly had a color preference.

Izzy interrupted his musings. "This looks nothing like the room I grew up in as a teen."

Her statement brought forth myriad memories. Most of them good. Until the end.

Zayn recalled her room well; he'd sneaked in more times than he could count. Until Señor Veracruz had opened her door without knocking one fateful evening. Zayn had been in the process of crawling in through her window. She would draw her lace curtains open to indicate if she'd unlocked the windowsill for him.

Her father finally catching them had been the beginning of the end, the catalyst that had started the sequence of events that would change Zayn's life. He couldn't really blame the man—Ernesto had simply been looking out for his child. What responsible and caring father wouldn't try to intervene when he found out the town's resident troublemaker had been sneaking into the house to visit his only daughter?

Now, years later, Zayn considered himself lucky to have left her house that evening with only a tongue-lashing and a warning of dire consequences if he ever tried such a stunt again.

Aunt Myrna's reaction when she'd found out had only been slightly less turbulent. He'd received an hours-long lecture about morals and decency and honorable behavior.

That night had been one of the moments in Zayn's life that served as a metaphorical kick in the pants. Though Ernesto had certainly looked like he was barely restraining himself, he probably would have loved to have landed some actual physical kicks, as well.

"It was the best of times, it was the worst of times…" Zayn shook off the thought as they moved to the next room on the tour. Luckily for his eyes, this one's color scheme was a bit more subdued. The Princess Adelaide's chamber sported rich hues of hunter green and calming beige. And yet another intricately designed crystal chandelier hung from the ceiling, one that gave the illusion of floating candles.

Izzy trailed her fingers along the wall as she stepped

farther inside. "Wow," he heard her whisper under her breath.

By the time they reached the outdoor part of the visit to tour the gardens, Zayn figured he could have done worse for his first choice of touristy destinations. The enchantment on Izzy's face was nearly tangible.

As was his ever-growing enchantment with her.

Whoever was calling her phone apparently refused to leave a voice mail and was just going to simply keep dialing until Izzy picked up. She'd been trying to ignore it, unwilling to let the outside world intrude on her fantasy outing. On a frustrated sigh, Izzy finally fished the phone out of her pocket and glanced at the screen. Zayn was across the museum's restaurant, ordering them some lunch. He said he would pick out something she would love to eat. He was fully committed to maintaining the surprise element.

Izzy felt immediately guilty when she saw the profile pic of the caller on her screen. Paula had been trying to get hold of her since yesterday.

"Hey, Paula."

Hearing her friend's familiar voice had Izzy feeling homesick all of a sudden. As much fun as she was having, she missed her beloved vineyards. She missed the harvest workers and ranch hands she considered family, the warmth of the cozy kitchen. Walking out to the mountain and inhaling the fresh air that always held the sweet aroma of the grapes was like a daily meditation for her, regardless of the weather.

But she knew once she returned, she would miss being here. And she would miss Zayn.

Izzy blinked away the thoughts and focused on her friend's familiar, soothing voice.

However, Paula sounded rather salty when she responded. "You know, Izzy... You don't call. You don't answer *my* calls. We are so going to have a chat about responsible girlfriend etiquette when you get back to the States."

There was a layer of sarcasm laced in her words, but Izzy felt guilty all the same. "Sorry, things have been rather busy."

"I forgive you," Paula immediately responded without hesitation.

"You're a gem."

"So don't keep me in suspense any longer. Did you win? Ethan and Hector looked it up, but I made them swear not to give anything away. I wanted to hear it straight from you."

It took Izzy a moment to register what she was referring to. Then it dawned on her. The awards ceremony. It felt like last night had been years ago. So much was happening so quickly.

"I'm afraid not. I lost out to a charming Argentinean farmer who only took up winemaking as a hobby just a few years ago. I'm looking forward to purchasing a bottle from his collection at the first opportunity, in fact."

Paula's heavy sigh could be heard over the tiny speaker. "Are you upset?"

Izzy had been, but she'd gotten over it. Just as she'd suspected she would. There had been other things to keep her mind occupied in the meantime. Speaking of which, she spotted Zayn off in the café queue waiting to pay for their lunch. "I'm in France, surrounded by holiday cheer and delicious food. I have nothing to complain about." She meant the words wholeheartedly, but even to her own ears her voice sounded flat and forced.

True to form, her friend picked up on the subtlety.

Something in her tone must have alerted Paula's friend sensor alerts. "Uh-oh. What's going on?" she asked.

"Nothing. Everything's fine."

"Sure it is. Don't tell me, then. I'll find out eventually."

That was probably the truth, Izzy had to admit.

"Wholly unfair that you didn't win. I'm sure our cabernet could run circles around that other wine."

Izzy had to smile. "You're just being a dedicated employee and a loyal friend."

"Always. How's everything else? I want to hear all about the delicious French food. Are you enjoying the expo?"

Izzy chewed on her bottom lip, contemplating how much she should divulge. There was a fine balance between confiding in your dear friend and divulging just enough to avoid a third-degree level of questioning.

"I'm actually begging off the rest of it. We're doing some sightseeing instead." Izzy cringed as the words left her mouth. She'd slipped with the use of the one word she should have avoided.

Her friend immediately picked up on the slip-up. "*We?* Either you've met a dashing Frenchman within days of arriving or you mean to tell me that you and Zayn are traipsing around the city of romance together. Either way, I want details and I want them ASAP."

If Paula only knew. Her friend would have a field day if she ever found out she and Zayn had ended up having to share a hotel room. And all that it had led to as a result. Someday, Izzy would have to tell her. Where would she even begin?

"You can start now, by the way," Paula prompted.

Izzy didn't get a chance to respond as Zayn finished up and returned to their table with plates of food and two cups of steaming hot tea, a welcome surprise. The outside tour had definitely settled a chill into her bones. Next time she visited France in December, she'd be sure to pack something thicker than a long sweater. Zayn had clearly noticed her shivering. Hot tea would definitely hit the spot. She was thankful for it.

"We'll have to rain check, Paula. It's lunchtime here and we're about to eat," Izzy said into the phone. After saying their mutual goodbyes, she clicked off the call.

"Thought you could use this," he said, handing her one of the cups.

The man sure knew how to guess what she needed.

CHAPTER THIRTEEN

THEIR CAR HAD to circle back to pick them up once the tour was over.

Izzy stood shivering in the cold. Zayn had given her his scarf again, but it could only do so much.

"Our ride will be here soon," he reassured her, wrapping his arm around her shoulders and pulling her close against him. "Here, we'll share body heat."

They'd fallen asleep last night, worn out after a long and tiring day. She'd woken up nestled in his arms. Somehow, she'd made herself resist running her hands along his jawline, down to his shoulders, and lower and lower until he could awaken. She'd gotten up and jumped into a near scalding shower instead.

Now, with his arms around her and her pressed close to his side, desire for him shot through her body once more.

She wasn't going to be able to resist him the next time they were alone together. It was a fact that had to be accepted. She had no willpower when it came to this man. She'd never had, had simply been fooling herself.

A glance over her shoulder and she caught his eye. The intensity in his gaze as he watched her face made her breath hitch. He wanted her, too.

Her heart thudded hard within her chest. A slow-burning ache formed in the pit of her belly and moved lower and lower still. They were out in public, for heaven's sake. A crowd of tourists hovered around them. She had to get a grip on her emotions and on her wanton desire.

Something vibrated against her hip. Zayn's cell phone in his pocket alerting an incoming call.

She had to laugh. "Saved by the bell."

But there was no hint of amusement in Zayn's eyes when he pulled out the phone and glanced at the screen. He swore a stunning curse under his breath and dropped his arm from around her.

"I have to take this. I promise it's not business. I know we're supposed to be vacationing, so to speak."

Izzy merely nodded as he stepped away to take the call. She watched as his shoulders slumped and a tightness settled over his features.

Whatever he was being told had to be some doozy of a message.

He was trembling when he returned. Alarm bells rang through her head. Was he about to have another attack? They were in the middle of the street, strangers milling all around them. Not that Zayn had actually lost control so much as his balance that day at the Eiffel Tower. Still, it had been disconcerting and frightening to watch.

That phone call he'd just received had triggered all of it.

"Penny for your thoughts," she ventured, hoping beyond hope that he might open up and tell her whatever disturbing thing he'd just heard. "It might help to talk about it."

Zayn didn't respond as their driver pulled up at that moment. He silently helped her into the backseat then waited as she scooched over before getting in himself.

As they pulled away from the curb, he slid off his coat

and undid his collar. A thin sheen of perspiration slowly appeared on his forehead above his brow line.

Izzy could do nothing but take his hand in hers. He responded by squeezing her fingers tight, as if he were holding on for dear life. They sat that way in silence for what seemed to be the longest, most disquieting, ride of her life.

When they finally made it back to their suite, she couldn't contain her questions any longer. "Zayn, please tell me what's going on. What was that phone call?"

"Nothing—it's not important." His denial wasn't even remotely believable.

"It's clearly more than nothing. Please just talk to me."

He threw his coat on the sofa and walked over to the wet bar by the side of the room near the balcony wall. He poured himself a generous helping of an amber liquid and tossed it back in one gulp. Then he poured some more.

Things really weren't looking good. Zayn appeared slightly calmer and less shaky now that they were in the privacy of their hotel room, but not by much.

Desperate for a way to help, Izzy did the only thing she could think of. She walked over, stepped up behind him and wrapped her arms around his waist.

"You can talk to me. It might help."

He slouched back against her, sending relief through her core that at least he was taking comfort in her being there next to him.

It gave her the courage and impetus to press further. He had to get this off his chest, whatever was bothering him so badly. Once she knew what was happening with him, she might have a chance to help him deal with it. She so badly wanted to give him some kind of relief, anything to take away the anguish currently flooding his face.

"What was that phone call, Zayn?" she repeated.

He took another sip of his drink and she felt him heave a deep breath against her chest. Several weighted moments passed with neither one so much as moving a hair. Gently, he eventually stepped out of her embrace and turned to face her.

"One I should have ignored."

That told her absolutely nothing. She summoned all her patience as she waited for clarification. It wasn't easy, but she felt like she was walking on broken glass here. One bad step might result in disastrous results. Finally, he spoke again after several tense moments. "That was a medical clinic located in San Antonio."

"I don't understand."

"It seems I'm the sole contact listed for one Keenan Manu Joffman."

It took a moment to process what he'd just said. When she did, Izzy felt genuine surprise clear to the bottom of her feet.

"Your father."

Zayn watched Izzy's features as the shock slowly registered on her face.

"He began trying to contact me about two years ago." He glanced at the calendar window on his watch. "Twenty-three months ago today to be exact."

She blinked up at him. "But why? After all these years?" Then it must have registered. "You said a clinic called you. I see."

She'd always been smart and observant. He should have guessed she'd put two and two together.

"He's sick. They don't know how much longer he has. Apparently, he took another bad turn overnight. They just moved him to palliative care."

"Two years ago his calls started... You said that's right

around the time your anxiety attacks began." She really was sharp as a whip. Still, he wished she wouldn't use that term. He just got a little worked up when news of his father reached him. The man had done nothing for Zayn, had been utterly useless as a parent. Now, he suddenly wanted to see his only son. Now that it was much too late for either of them.

"That's neither here nor there," he told her. "The point is I'm tired of hearing from him, tired of his attempts to contact me when it's much too late. I have better things to do with my time."

Her eyes grew wide. "I don't understand. Don't you even want to hear what he has to say? Aren't you the least bit curious about him?"

He had to laugh. Hearing from his father was so low on his list of priorities, it barely made the list at all. He gave her a small shrug before answering. "Not even a little."

"Zayn, the man is sick."

He felt his fingers tighten on the tumbler and lifted the glass for another burning sip.

"And?" Did she have a point here? Why were they even talking about it? He wanted to push it out of his mind once and for all and take up where he and Izzy had left off back outside the château while they'd been waiting for their driver at Versailles. He hadn't imagined the desire in her eyes, nor the way her cheeks had flushed rose-red when he'd put his arm around her.

Before that blasted phone call had interrupted them and ruined what had been a perfectly enjoyable day up until then. And the evening full of passionate promise it might have led to.

All laid to waste now. Pity.

Izzy's tongue darted over her lower lip before she answered. "And you might be running out of time."

A roaring had begun to sound behind his ears. He could feel his heart rate zigzagging—slowing down then speeding up. "Time to do what, exactly?"

"If there's even the slightest possibility that you'll regret—"

He didn't let her finish. Slamming his tumbler onto the bar so harshly half the liquid spilled out, he spun away and paced to the other side of the room. "I won't."

She looked ready to protest. Something in his expression must have given her pause. "That's absolutely your decision."

"Damn right it is."

"But it's one you should really think over carefully before arriving at any kind of conclusion."

He actually had to chuckle at her words. He spread his arms out wide. "What exactly am I supposed to weigh here? How he left when I was a toddler? How he never contacted me until he wanted to reach some kind of redemption? Or how about the way my mom took off, too, because she'd never gotten over her anger at him. Neither one of them cared that I was tossed from one relative's household to another in between foster homes until I was saddled with an elderly great-aunt who hardly knew what to do with a confused, abandoned little boy."

Even from across the room he could see the sheen of unshed tears in her eyes. She was ready to cry on his behalf. *Damn it.* This was exactly what he didn't want or need. Rehashing the past and invoking sympathy. She was the last person on earth whose pity he would want.

"I don't even know the man, Izzy."

Her lips tightened; she appeared to be chewing her words. "Zayn, what if he's dying?"

Of course, he'd thought about that possibility. In the end, what did it really change in the current scenario? In every possible way, the man was nothing more than a stranger. Zayn wouldn't even recognize him if he met him on the street.

"I don't owe him anything, Izzy. I certainly don't owe him an opportunity to redeem himself at my expense."

She swallowed. Her voice was thick and heavy with emotion when she answered. "I know you don't. But you might owe it to yourself."

Zayn stalked to the balcony door and slid it open with enough force that the windowpane next to it rattled.

"I need some air." He stepped outside, not bothering to slide the door closed behind him. A small breeze drifted in and gently rustled the curtains.

Izzy wanted nothing more than to go to him, to pull him into her arms and gently plant a row of caressing kisses over his face and down his neck. She resisted the urge and made her feet remain planted firmly where they were. Something told her Zayn wouldn't want anything that resembled coddling or sympathy. She figured what he probably needed most right now was some space as well as the fresh air he was out there seeking.

Outside, the sound of afternoon in Paris echoed in the air. Car horns beeped, motors roared and laughter floated up from the street below. A magnificent view of the Eiffel Tower in the distance added to what should have been a charming scene straight out of a postcard.

But her heart was breaking in her chest. The man she loved was confused and angry. And he was in pain.

She ached for the unwanted little boy Zayn had been. He'd never let on back when they were together just how badly the abandonment of his parents had hurt him. And he'd never mentioned having been placed in foster homes before arriving permanently to reside with Myrna. Myrna had never wanted to talk about it, either.

What he must have experienced in those other households, she didn't want to hazard a guess. The anguish in his face when he'd talked about them just now told her more than he might have meant to.

After staring at his back for close to twenty minutes, she decided it was time. She walked over to the mini-fridge, pulled two frosty bottles of sparkling lemon water from the upper shelf and made her way to the balcony.

He didn't so much as move a muscle when she joined him.

Zayn stood bent and leaning over the railing, his forearms resting on the metal top rail. His head was bowed, his shoulders stumped. The entire posture was a picture of a man weary with defeat.

She held the bottle near his face in his line of vision. "I come with a peace offering."

He took it without looking at her, his gaze remaining focused on the street below. Taking the cap off with one hand, he took a long swallow. "Thanks. All that brandy was starting to burn a hole in my gut."

"Perhaps you should have drank it slower," she admonished in a clear, teasing voice. "I've been told brandy is meant to be sipped."

"I guess wealth and professional success don't necessarily lead to refinement."

"Refined is boring," she scoffed. "I've never found you to be boring, Zayn. That's meant as a compliment, by the way," she added after a pause.

He took another long swallow of his drink. "Anyone ever tell you that you're lousy at giving compliments?"

She laughed. "We all have our flaws."

"Go on then," he prompted her. "Get it all off your chest. Say what you came out here to tell me. I'll warn you, though, that I've made my decision."

She dipped her head, weighing her words. "Are you sure you've made the right one?"

He didn't hesitate with his reply. "I'm sure."

"You don't even want to hear what he might have to say?"

He shrugged, still staring off into the distance. "There's nothing he can say. Nothing will ever change the past."

"That doesn't mean you can't look to the future."

He jeered at that, his shoulders stiffening. "Hardly likely."

"And seeing him might help you to come to terms with your past. Once and for all."

"Why are you pushing this so hard?" he asked. "Why does it even matter to you?"

Ouch. Zayn didn't seem to think matters that involved him were any of her concern. Even after what they'd shared years ago. Even after their time thus far in Paris. The knowledge felt like a dagger to her midsection. One that would sting for a good while.

She made herself push past the hurt.

"I just don't want you to regret this later. You might have to live with this decision for the rest of your life."

"Are you sure that's all there is to it?"

The question gave her pause. Zayn was implying she had alternative intentions. Personal ones. Did she? Was the current situation with her own father playing any kind of role in her desire to make Zayn reconsider his decision?

Well, so what if it was? It didn't make her intent any less valid. Zayn was clearly suffering. That had to mean some kind of ambiguity. His anxiety attacks were a clear sign of that.

"Maybe you need to examine your own current predicament with Ernesto before trying to offer any kind of advice."

Bingo. She knew that's what he'd been getting at this whole time. But her temporary estrangement with her father was completely different than what Zayn was currently grappling with. "We are talking about you, Zayn. This isn't about me."

"Isn't it?" His hands clenched into fists. "Nevertheless. You grew up with a father who stuck around and cared so much for you that—" Whatever he was about to say, he stopped abruptly.

It took a moment before he continued. "You have no idea what it's like to grow up without a dad, only to hear from a stranger decades later because he suddenly wants some kind of redemption."

"Maybe all he wants is a chance to apologize. Or to explain." And maybe a part of Zayn wanted to hear that apology. Needed to.

"I don't expect you to understand," he told her on a deep sigh.

"I'm trying to. I really am."

He shrugged. "There's no need. As far as I'm concerned, it's a moot point. No need to even talk about it." He turned then, ready to walk away and end any further discussion.

She halted him with a hand on his forearm. She'd never forgive herself if she didn't try to at least get him to see how conflicted he was.

"Zayn, don't you think there might be signs that you're not as certain as you seem? That, at the very least, you're torn about whether to see your father?"

He gave his head a shake. "I don't follow. What exactly are you getting at?"

She took a deep, fortifying breath before answering. "Your body is physically reacting to your choice with these anxiety attacks you've been having."

He suddenly went completely still. Izzy could practically feel the tension and turmoil emanating through his body. She'd said the wrong thing.

An uncomfortable silence hung in the air between them until he finally broke it. "Please don't play at being some kind of psychoanalyst with me here, Izzy. You may think you do, but you don't know me that well."

A flinch shook through her from head to toe. He was lashing out, which wasn't surprising. The knowledge didn't do much to lessen the sting of his words, however.

He delivered yet another blow before she could respond. "Why in the world would I trust you regarding this matter?" The words weren't said but she heard them all the same—he was referring to her own troubles with her father. "It's none of your concern even," he added, delivering another strike.

She wasn't strong enough to resist the innate desire to counter attack; his words simply hurt too much. She lashed out with a strike of her own.

"Somewhat hypocritical of you to bring out matters of trust, don't you think? The man who left without a word to his lover and didn't bother to ever explain himself."

His eyes clouded with disappointment. Izzy felt awash with shame as soon as she finished speaking. She should have tried harder to stay quiet, should have physically bit her lip to keep from hurling out such hurtful words. The man was in pain, and she'd just added to his suffering in a selfish fit of anger. Not that she'd said anything false.

So much remained unresolved between them, no wonder the issues rose like leviathans at unguarded moments.

She'd forgotten the lessons of the past when it came to the two of them. When things were good between them, they were very, very good. But when things turned sour, they could wound each other like no one else.

He slowly shook his head, grunted an ironic laugh that held zero hint of amusement. "I should have never come back to Napa," he declared, adding another stab and proving her point. "All I wanted was to help grow that winery to its full potential. I should have known better."

She had no desire to further hurt him. But she'd be damned if she wasn't going to defend herself.

"Stackhouse is fine the way it is."

"It's stagnant, too small. Too inaccessible to scores of customers. Stackhouse could be so much more."

Izzy tried not to react to the hit her pride was taking. The implication was clear: she didn't have the kind of vision Zayn had when it came to the winery she'd devoted most of her life to.

"I've earned what Myrna bequeathed me, Zayn."

He straightened finally. "Yes, you've earned your share of Stackhouse. But you're too stuck to see it's true potential and you're too scared to try to look."

Stuck. Scared.

He'd really just used those words to describe her? And here she thought he might have some respect for her, both as a vintner and as a lover. The ugly truth now stared her down. She wasn't important enough to him in any way that mattered.

This whole week had been nothing more than a tryst, a nostalgic trip down memory lane for him.

Whereas she'd fallen in love with him all over again.

Foolish and blind to the last when it came to this man.

Well, no more. It was over. She wasn't going to try to make him care for her.

Zayn Joffman was a loner and he wanted to stay that way. But she had to get one more thing off her chest before letting it go for good.

"I will tell you this. I don't think your anxiety attacks are going to get better if your father doesn't recover."

He visibly recoiled. "Please don't call them that. They're not any kind of 'attack.' I get a little shaky when I'm worked up, is all. I'm sure it happens to a lot of people."

She sucked in a deep, calming breath. She wasn't going to argue terminology or semantics with a man clearly in denial about what his physical body was trying to tell him. She'd been in some pretty deep denial herself, about so many things.

"However you refer to them, I think you need to consider that, rather than improving, they might get worse if you lose your father."

His eyes narrowed on her, a bitter smile tightening his lips. "How can I lose something I never really had?"

His words echoed through her mind like he'd shouted them from a mountaintop.

She could ask herself the same question.

She knew he was gone before opening her eyes upon awakening. The morning sun cast long shadows throughout the room. Coffee. There had to be a carafe of it nearby. The aroma tempted her nose and roused her further out of sleep. Not that she'd done much sleeping last night.

The whole evening had been an agonizing exercise in mental endurance, with her and Zayn both trying to ignore the awkward silence hanging between them. Izzy had pretended to watch an old French film with subtitles before crawling into bed early and feigning sleep. Zayn had pounded away on his laptop before slamming it shut and getting under the covers himself.

They'd stayed as far as possible on their respective sides of the bed with several feet of mattress between them.

Now she had no doubt that he was gone. For good.

She could feel it in her soul. And she felt the empty darkness his absence left behind. Her eyes began to sting and she willed away the tears. What was the point in letting them fall? Unfortunately, she hadn't learned her lesson not to play with fire the first time she'd been burned.

Rather than turning to her in his time of despair, Zayn had lashed out and pushed her away instead.

She was right, Izzy realized once she got out of bed. There was no sign of Zayn anywhere. He must have waited to make sure she'd fallen asleep then packed quietly and left. He'd bothered to bring her up a tray of coffee and croissants. One last act of indulgence right before he'd walked out of her life again.

Gingerly, she made her way over to the table and the breakfast tray. The carafe was cold now, so he must have been gone for hours. Not that it mattered; she wouldn't be able to enjoy it anyway.

A small note was propped up against the mug.

Izzy,
I'm sorry, honey. I had to leave.
    You deserve so much more. And you deserve Stackhouse. All of it.
    I've already instructed my attorneys to turn over my part of the inheritance and grant you full ownership.

Izzy had to put the note down before continuing. He was trying to wash his hands of her completely. Was even willing to give up his inheritance to do so. He wanted nothing more to do with her. Not as a partner. And certainly not as a lover. She'd lost him completely.

Hard to believe, but this time somehow hurt even worse than the first. For now she knew without a doubt she had never stopped loving him. And she never would.

With shaky hands, she lifted the note back up to continue reading. The words blurred before her tear-filled eyes.

Enjoy the rest of your stay in France. The car and driver are at your disposal. Your flight itinerary is in your inbox.

Take care of yourself,
Z

He'd given no explanation of his actions or any indication of where he was headed. His words from yesterday sounded in her head. That made sense. After all, he'd told her that his affairs were "none of her concern."

She sat slowly, the note still cradled in her hand. Her eyes fell to the other two objects on the surface of the table. She'd been so focused on the note, she hadn't noticed them until now. Folded in a neat square was the scarf he'd let her borrow so often to ward off the chill over the past few days. He'd left it for her. On top of the scarf there was a small cardboard box with a satin ribbon tied around the center. Her hand trembling, she reached for it and loosened the bow.

Her breath caught when she lifted the lid.

Inside, wrapped in delicate tissue paper, was a small, handcrafted tree ornament made of clay. A miniature elf complete with floppy hat and pointy shoes—reminiscent of the ridiculous costume she'd been wearing when he'd first walked into the winery a few days ago. He must have gotten it their first night here when they'd visited the Christmas market.

The whimsical expression painted on the little guy's face wrangled a small laugh out of her.

"Oh, Zayn," she whispered aloud, her breath shaky. Emotion and loss threatened to shatter her heart. She gripped the ornament in the palm of her hand and held it close against her chest.

When had he planned to give this to her? She would never know.

If she could, she would turn back time. Find a better way to talk to him about all he was dealing with. Offer to be there to help him deal with the difficult situation with his father. Offer to be a shoulder to lean on whenever he needed. That had been all he'd needed.

She'd only been trying to help but, truthfully, she'd been so arrogant. Izzy had her own set of issues with her own dad. She hadn't spoken to or heard from him in over a year. How did she think she had the right to try to lecture or guide Zayn about his own paternal relationship?

None of it mattered. The way he'd left in the middle of the night, with only a short, perfunctory note, was a clear indication that he was finished with her. He was turning over his half of the winery. He was completely done with her and he'd been able to walk away so easily—while she was shattering to pieces inside.

She would have to accept the loss and move on, as painful as it was. They were still business partners, but he had a slew of employees and representatives who would likely be assigned to deal with Stackhouse in his stead. He, personally, wouldn't have to deal with her.

With a cry of anguish, she unfolded the scarf and held

it to her face, sinking her skin into the soft fabric and breathing in the scent of him.

She didn't know how long she sat there. The morning grew brighter before she finally rose and started packing. There was no way she was going to stay here. She wanted to be home among those that she loved and in familiar surroundings while she licked her wounds.

And then it became impossible to keep the tears at bay any longer. She let them fall freely while she gathered her things.

CHAPTER FOURTEEN

"COME IN." ZAYN answered the knock on his office door without looking up from his computer screen.

Clara stepped into his office and dropped a file on his desk. "The figures you asked for."

"Thank you." He nodded to his assistant, marveling at her outfit once more. The normally stoic, serious secretary always seemed to transform into a completely different person the third week of December. She was currently wearing what could only be described as an ugly Christmas sweater complemented by flashing lightbulb earrings.

He found himself smiling at the getup.

"If there's nothing else then…" Clara began, "I was hoping to leave a little early today to get a head start on the holiday break."

That was his sign. Clara leaving from now until after New Year's day was Zayn's cue that the holidays were here and unavoidable.

The rest of his staff had already checked out. Clara was always the last. He stopped typing and leaned back in his chair.

"You're free to go. Merry Christmas, Clara. I will see you in the new year."

"Merry Christmas, Zayn." She turned to leave then hesitated in the doorway and pivoted to face him.

"Was there something else?" he asked her.

"As a matter of fact… I was wondering what you were doing for the holidays."

Zayn couldn't hide his surprise. It had to be the most personal question Clara had ever asked him.

He quirked an eyebrow at her. "Why do you ask?"

Clara crossed her arms in front of her chest. "May I be honest?"

This sounds ominous. "Go ahead."

"Well, you typically get a bit sulky around the holidays, but this year you seem more out of sorts than usual."

Wow. Things were definitely getting serious. And here he thought he'd been hiding his sour mood since returning from Paris.

"I appreciate the honesty," he lied. "As for the holidays, I'm looking forward to some nice downtime to relax and catch up on things."

She nodded knowingly. "Like work?"

"Some work, yes. And other things."

Now that he thought about it, maybe he'd go through his contact list and recruit some female company to join him. But he squelched that idea the second it popped into his head. There was only one woman he'd even hope to enjoy this time of year with. But he'd blown any chance he may have had with her, when all she'd been trying to do was help him. How many times in his life could he hurt the one person who deserved it the least from him?

Clara still stood in the doorway, studying him from across the room. He waited patiently for her to continue.

"I think maybe you're working too hard already. And if we're still being honest…" She let the words drift off, as if weighing them.

This was a side of the woman Zayn had never seen before. Clearly, she was concerned about him. Go figure.

"Yes?"

"You also seem a bit more on edge. Like you're waiting for the other shoe to drop."

Zayn pinched the bridge of his nose. So he'd been acting edgy on top of the sulkiness. Great. His professionalism was always something he'd prided himself on. Now even that was evidently slipping.

He should have seen this coming. Clara had always been observant and aware. "I appreciate the candor, Clara. The truth is, I haven't been sleeping well."

"Care to talk about it?"

For one insane moment, he actually considered taking her up on the offer, to reach for the opportunity to get some of the turmoil of the past few weeks off his chest. To allow someone else to help him with the burden of it all, if only for a few moments. But Clara wasn't the woman he wanted to confide in.

The person who'd been there for him all along was Izzy. She was the woman he wanted to turn to right now. But he'd missed the chance to do so. A chance he'd never get again thanks to his foolishness when it came to her.

"Just have a lot on my mind."

"I see." Clara studied him a little longer and then surprised him again with her next question. "Would you like to come to my house for Christmas dinner? I'm hosting, like I do every year."

Zayn could only blink at her. Exactly how sulky and on edge had he been these past few days?

"Fairly small crowd," Clara continued. "Me, my husband, my daughter and the twins—they just turned three over Thanksgiving. And my son will be bringing his new girlfriend and her preschool-aged daughter."

Zayn didn't want to think about what her definition of a large crowd might be.

"I appreciate the offer, Clara. I'll think about it."

Another lie. It was bad enough that he'd invoked a pity invite from his assistant. The thought of actually taking Clara up on it was just too much to bear.

For a while back there, while in Paris with Izzy, he'd actually entertained notions of Christmas the way others celebrated it. With loved ones, sharing presents, eating a holiday meal together.

But he'd blown that, too.

Normal Christmases were for other people. He couldn't recall ever looking forward to the day. There certainly wasn't anything about it to look forward to now. Nothing had changed. As far as he was concerned, it was just another ordinary day. Followed by another ordinary week.

"It's an open invite," Clara told him, breaking through his dismal thoughts. She added over her shoulder as she walked out the door, "Don't stay too late. It's almost Christmas Eve."

He wasn't going to lie to her yet again, so he didn't bother answering with anything more than a nod and a smile as he watched her leave, shutting the door behind her.

No. He hadn't told her that he actually planned to stay late. The fact was he would be here until about midnight or so. Then he'd head home, heat up some leftovers and pick at the food before falling asleep. Since last week, he'd taken to falling asleep on the couch with the television blaring. Having woken in the middle of the night in a cold sweat, his heart pounding, had made the thought of crawling into bed less than appealing.

He'd told Clara the truth just now about his restless nights. For the first time ever, after returning from Paris, he'd experienced one of the episodes while asleep. And it had happened more than once since then.

Nothing like a panic attack during sleep to jolt you out of bed and have you pacing the hallways till dawn. He'd finally stopped being stubborn and acknowledged to himself that Izzy had been right to call them as such.

He couldn't ignore them any longer.

He'd been mulish about so many things while Izzy had been right about all of it. She had simply been unfortunate enough to be standing in the line of fire that was Zayn Joffman.

Your body is physically reacting to your choice.

He'd resented her in that moment for saying those words. When all she'd done was hold a mirror up for him to look at. All in an effort to ease his pain. What had she gotten for her efforts? His scorn and dismissal.

For the umpteenth time since arriving back in New York, he thought about calling her then stopped himself. The decision whether they ever spoke again was her call to make. He'd done enough damage.

Had she liked the ornament he'd bought for her their first night in Paris? Was it hanging off one of the branches of the decorated pine in the front foyer at the winery?

Maybe she'd flung it into the waste bin. She'd have every right. When he thought about the things he'd said to her… How he'd mocked her about her lack of ambition simply because she had a different vision for Stackhouse than he did. A vision his great-aunt had shared and encouraged.

Zayn threw his pen down onto his desk so hard, it splotched ink on the wooden surface. He was going to make himself crazy wondering about her.

The truth of the matter was that *he* was the one who was stuck. He was the one who was scared. All the things he'd accused her of… And holding on to anger and hurt that did nothing for him other than make him…well, sulky. He'd been in a holding pattern for so long, he hadn't even noticed he'd stalled.

No more.

Izzy had a point: he could no longer ignore things he didn't want to face. And there was one aspect in his life he had to address before anything else. Yet another thing Izzy had been right about.

Clicking the icon for the search engine on his browser, he called up contact info for Ethan Greaves, MD, and proceeded to draft an email to his old friend.

The problem with holding patterns was that they kept you spinning around in circles.

Izzy pulled into the long circular driveway that led to the entrance to the Pestaña Winery in southern Napa, the winery founded and owned by her family. The name meant *eyelash* in Spanish.

Her father liked to explain that he'd chosen the name because he'd fallen head over heels in love with Izzy's mother after she'd batted her eyelashes at him at the open market in Mexico City.

Mama always denied she'd done any such thing.

Her parents had built the winery from the ground up and had been expanding it ever since. The place had been a source of contention between Izzy and her father pretty much since its inception. It was high time to finally put a stop to that.

She hadn't announced her visit, simply because she hadn't been certain she was actually going to go through with it. Not until she clicked on her turn signal and pulled into the parking lot.

Pleased that the lot was rather full, she got out of her

car and walked to the front gate. Hector and two other employees were running a tasting outside. Papa liked to do most of the tastings on picnic tables on a veranda by the vines as long as the weather cooperated. It was certainly doing so today.

Her brother poured a rosé for the six people at his table then quickly put the bottle down. Spotting her by the gate, he gave her a wave.

"Excuse me," he told his party. "My pesky sister is here. We have to watch out for her—she's the competition." He winked after making the outrageous statement. The women sitting at his table laughed dutifully at his joke, lame as it was. Hector had the type of look a lot of women fell for. Tall and dark, though rather lanky, he somehow pulled it off. He was one of the major draws at the winery.

He strode over to her and gave her a brotherly peck on the cheek.

"Hey, sis. What brings you out here? Mama's out at the organic farm picking up ingredients for the munchies." He pointed to the picnic tables. "And I'm in the middle of a tasting."

"I actually came to see Papa. Is he here?"

Hector couldn't hide his surprise. Then his grin grew wider. "It's about time. You two are both too damn stubborn."

She ignored that. "Is he in the house?"

"He's out back, testing soil."

Izzy thanked him and took a deep, steadying breath before making her way behind the tasting area to the vines. She found her father crouched over a large silver bucket with a spade in his hand.

He looked tired. And so much older than when she'd last seen him. He worked too hard and rested too little.

The kind of impressive work ethic that one would need to move from being a hired field hand from a foreign country to owning one of the most successful wineries in Napa.

She was so damn proud of him. But she would never understand him. And they would probably never see eye to eye on how to make and sell wine.

She cleared her throat by way of announcing her arrival. His eyes shot up and he did a double take when he saw her. He quickly hid his surprise.

"Hi, Papa."

"Izadora." He stuck the spade in the dirt and dug up another mound of soil.

"Isn't it kind of late to be bringing up soil samples?"

"I like to see what it's doing throughout the year. Is there something you need?"

This was it. She was here for one reason and it was too late to back out now. This was not the time for restraint. He had to know how she felt.

"Yes," she answered. "I need my father back, Papa."

His eyes shot up to glare at her. "Is that so?"

Izzy forced herself to continue. In for a penny and all that. "You have to forgive me for the decisions I've made. And you have to let me live my life."

Dropping the spade, her father pulled a handkerchief from his back pocket and wiped his brow. Suddenly he looked weary and defeated. More tired than she'd ever seen him. The silly discord between them had to have taken a toll on him, too. She, for one, was tired of it.

With a sigh, he upended two empty buckets and motioned her over. "Have a seat."

Izzy smoothed the skirt of her sundress and did her best to sit on the too small bucket bottom. Her father sat on the other.

"Hector told me why you went to Paris. You should be proud of yourself."

With those simple words, he was telling her he'd forgiven her. Izzy felt the sting of tears behind her eyes. Her father wasn't terribly forthcoming when it came to praise.

"I didn't win in the end."

He grunted. "Nevertheless. Being nominated is quite an honor."

She sniffled, a wealth of emotion forming a brick at the base of her throat. "Thanks, Papa."

"Your brother also told me you were accompanied by Zayn Joffman on your trip."

Izzy's heart lurched at the mention of his name. Not that she hadn't been thinking about him every minute that she was awake. And when she wasn't awake. The man invaded her dreams at night.

Papa had never exactly been a fan of Zayn's. In fact, he had made it quite clear he'd wholly disapproved of the young man back when they'd been dating. In her father's defense, Zayn had not been the type of boy most fathers would have approved of.

"You don't have to worry about that," she reassured him. "We're just partners in Stackhouse. It was simply a business trip."

She prayed a punishing bolt of lightning didn't come down from the sky and strike her on the spot for such a colossal lie. The rest of her statement was true enough. She had no intention of signing and returning the paperwork Zayn's solicitor had rushed through to grant her full ownership. Myrna had left her great-nephew half of Stackhouse and that half would stay rightfully his.

But Papa had nothing to worry about if he thought Zayn was back in her life.

Her father rubbed his brow, suddenly looking tense

174 HER INCONVENIENT CHRISTMAS REUNION

and uncomfortable. "Well, there's something you should know when it comes to Zayn. Something I should have told you years ago."

Izzy studied her father's face. Where in the world was he going with this line of talk? The conversation had taken a turn she would have never seen coming. She'd come here to make peace with her father once and for all, to ask that he simply accept her for who she was. Yet, somehow, they were discussing Zayn.

The pieces began to fall into place with her father's next words.

"I'm the reason he left Napa, *mi niña*. I told him to go."

CHAPTER FIFTEEN

THE SHOCK OF her father's revelation reverberated in Izzy's mind the entire drive back to Stackhouse.

When she finally reached the house, she had still not fully processed the enormity of what he'd told her. That was no doubt going to take some time.

In hindsight, she really should have known. It was the only thing that made sense. Papa's interference. How could she not have guessed?

Flinging her key fob onto the side table in the foyer, she stormed off toward the tasting room. The quietest and most peaceful room on the estate, she knew being there would help to calm her. She needed to pull her thoughts together, to somehow try to think through what she'd just learned.

Zayn hadn't left her. Not really. He'd simply done her father's bidding.

Slamming the door behind her, she kicked at a chair at the tasting table. The resounding thud of wood hitting wood echoed through the air.

"Watch it—behavior like that might lead to a lump of coal in your Christmas stocking."

She jumped at the sound of Paula's voice as her friend suddenly materialized from behind the bar.

Pulling out the offending chair, Izzy flopped herself down onto it.

"White or red?" Paula asked.

"White to start with."

Within moments, Paula had pulled out the seat next to her and produced two wineglasses and a frosty chardonnay.

"Spill," Paula ordered as she began to pour. "Does this have anything to do with your tall, dark and handsome business partner?"

Izzy sniffled. "Why do you ask?"

"You haven't been the same since you got back from Paris last week."

"It's that obvious, huh?"

Paula shrugged. "As obvious as Mr. Reyes's fake Santa beard when he drunkenly tugged at it." She comically demonstrated and earned a chuckle for her efforts. "So tell me what happened."

Izzy took a long sip of her wine, trying to gather her thoughts and put them into coherent sentences. It wasn't easy but, before she knew it, the whole sordid tale was spilling out of her.

When she finally stopped, most of the bottle of wine was gone and Paula sat staring at her, a stunned look on her face.

Izzy pushed her wineglass away, suddenly regretting the indulgence on an empty stomach. A tinge of nausea had started to whirl in the pit of her belly. "I don't know how I'll forgive him," she stated, not even sure which man she was talking about.

"You have every right to be hurt," Paula told her. "That's a lot to take in."

"And angry. So very angry," Izzy found herself admitting. The rage was making her shake inside. So much lost time.

"What exactly is making you so mad?"

Did she really have to ask? "The way I was kept in the dark... The decisions that were taken away from me... How I had no say in any of it."

"What else?"

A flash of annoyance sparked in her chest at the question, the answer was so clearly obvious. "Mostly for all the years that were wasted."

Paula took another sip of her wine. "So maybe you shouldn't waste any more time, then."

Izzy couldn't come up with a counter to that. Resignation quickly replaced irritation.

After several silent seconds passed between them, Paula sighed long and deep. "In the end, I think there's one underlying factor you shouldn't lose sight of."

"What's that?"

"They both love you, Izzy. Your father did what he did because he wanted to keep you safe." Her friend set her glass down on the shiny, heavily polished table then turned to face her. "And Zayn loved you enough to let you go."

Izzy let her friend's words fully sink in.

A flurry of conflicting emotions churned through her core.

Anger at her father for keeping the truth from her until just now. Yet she couldn't help but feel moved at the knowledge that Papa had simply been trying to look out for her.

Relief that she finally had the answer that had so long eluded her about Zayn's sudden departure five years ago.

Admiration for Zayn in that he'd never betrayed her father's trust and divulged the truth. Though heaven knew how badly she wanted to throttle him for doing just that.

And then there was Myrna's clear attempt to once more bring them together through her last will and testament. Izzy bit back the sob at the base of her throat. Even in her final act, Myrna had managed to look out for her.

You two need each other.

Myrna's written words echoed through Izzy's head. She knew what she had to do. After all, her mentor had never led her astray yet.

Zayn figured he had to be seeing things.

He must be missing Izzy so much he was imagining her standing in the lobby of his apartment building. Wearing the elf costume, no less.

No way any of this could be real. He was definitely daydreaming or something. He had to be.

He gave a shake of his head and blinked before pulling the door open and stepping inside.

The elf was still there. An elf with Izzy's thick, dark hair and chocolate-brown eyes. And the same curves.

"Iz?"

She'd been staring at her phone screen and glanced up when he spoke her name.

"Zayn. Where have you been? I thought you'd never get home."

"I was working," Zayn answered, still not completely sure he was processing accurately exactly what was happening.

"It's Christmas Eve," she announced and then glanced at her watch. "Around ten o'clock."

He didn't know what to say to that.

She stepped toward him with hesitation. "Um, well... surprise!"

Zayn gave his head a shake to try to clear it. He didn't

recall having any eggnog at the office earlier. That left only one real possibility. Izzy really was here.

"You traveled across the country to surprise me? Wearing an elf costume?"

She waved her hand dismissively. "Don't be silly. I put the costume on after I got here. I didn't board the plane wearing it or anything."

He nodded his head slowly. "Well, then it all makes perfect sense."

She looked down at the floor with a grimace. "A bit impulsive, huh?"

"I'd say."

"It seemed like a good idea when Paula and I were discussing it the other day."

Clearly, they'd been the ones having eggnog.

And then it hit him, the full-blown reality of what was happening. Izzy was here. She'd flown across the country to see him.

He didn't give himself a chance to think. Rushing across the lobby, he took her in his arms and lifted her off her feet.

"I missed you," he whispered against her hair.

Her laughter was like a healing balm to his soul. "See, this is definitely more the reaction I'd hoped for."

An older woman entered through the doors, carrying a purse, a small, furry dog poking its head out the top. She gave Izzy a look from head to toe then shrugged and walked past them.

Zayn put her down and punched the penthouse button on the elevator panel, still holding her hand. He was half afraid to let her go and risk her disappearing like a mirage.

The doors slid open a few seconds later and carried them into the hallway of his unit. Izzy stepped out before him and he flicked the main switch on the wall. Soft light flooded the apartment and the ambient fireplace at the far end of the room came to life.

Izzy pulled the elf cap off her head and squeezed it between her fingers. "I figured we needed to talk." She gestured toward her midsection. "The costume was an attempt to be playful. A way to break the ice."

She really had no idea how sexy she looked in that outfit. The look was playful, all right. But in all the wrong ways.

All that mattered was that she was here.

In a somewhat surreal moment, they both spoke at the same time, only to say the very same thing.

"I'm so sorry." Their combined apologies echoed through the air.

He stepped closer to her, took her hands in his. The elf hat fell to the floor. "I don't know what you're apologizing for. As for me, I'm so sorry about our last night in Paris. I should have never said those things to you. Please forgive me."

Her eyes grew wide. "Oh, Zayn. Don't apologize. You saying all those things gave me the push I needed to make some hard decisions, to finally move forward with things I'd been putting off."

He could hardly believe what he was hearing. He could say the exact same words to her.

Izzy continued. "I thought my father would never forgive me. And I was too afraid to find out once and for all." She bit her lip before going on. "It's okay now. We've come to an understanding."

Zayn decided to stay quiet, as hard as it was. Talking about her father was a risky subject. He'd given his word years ago to the older man.

Izzy's next words told him the secret was out. "I know,

Zayn. My father told me everything. He told me he asked you to leave because he was worried about me. Because he didn't think you were a good influence."

He pulled her hand to his lips, kissed her fingertips. Relief surged through his bloodstream. Izzy finally knew the full truth.

"I never wanted to be the cause of any kind of friction between you and your family, Iz. That's why I walked away when he asked." Also, he'd known her father had been right to want him gone. He'd been trouble back then. Ernesto had given him the push he'd needed to take a good, hard look at the direction his life was headed.

"My father and I don't seem to need any help in the friction department," Izzy was saying. "We seem to butt heads just fine without outside help. I don't think that will ever change."

She took a deep breath before continuing. "But I know you both did what you thought was best for me. I've come to terms with that, though I have to admit it took some time and meditation."

Zayn rubbed his thumb along her bottom lip.

"There were so many times I wanted to call you after I left," he admitted. "Just to hear your voice. And to try to explain."

"Why didn't you?"

He sucked in a breath. "Because Ernesto was right. I had to get my act together before I deserved you. And I was too worried I'd be tempted to tell you the truth and break my word to him. So I put it off." He pulled her closer. "Until it felt much too late and I couldn't even figure out where I'd begin. I regret that now. I so regret not having tried."

Her eyes swam with emotion. "Then promise me there'll be no more secrets between us."

"I promise. This time I'm giving *you* my word. I'll never risk losing you again."

Izzy actually chuckled. "Well, I certainly know you're good for it."

She was so pure, so selfless. He couldn't believe he was lucky enough to be getting a second chance with her. Heaven knew, he didn't deserve it.

"I think we have a lot of lost time to make up for," she said, her breath hot against his finger at her lip. "A wise friend told me just the other day I shouldn't waste any more of it."

He nodded and pulled her closer. "Wise indeed. I agree—I think we should get started right away."

And then he didn't bother to try to think at all. Just took her lips with his own. He was panting with need by the time Izzy finally pulled away. He felt the loss like a physical blow.

Her top had crawled up several inches to reveal the luscious, tempting skin at her midriff. She adjusted the waist of the shirt and laughed. "Silly costume is just too darn small."

He gave her a wicked smile and wiggled his eyebrows. "Then we should definitely get it off you. The sooner, the better."

The next morning, Izzy woke in Zayn's sunlight-filled bedroom to the smell of hearty, rich-brewed coffee and a perfectly toasted sesame bagel smothered in cream cheese waiting for her by her bedside. She could definitely get used to the way the man she loved made sure she woke up to a delicious breakfast in the mornings. After taking a few bites and lingering in bed, she figured she should probably find him and thank him. She had all sorts of ideas about how to go about doing so.

He sat perched on the kitchen counter when she located him, his phone to his ear. He gave her a brilliant smile in greeting when he noticed her presence. She approached gingerly so as to not interrupt his call and placed a small kiss along his jawline.

"I can make it out there day after next," he was telling whoever was on the other end.

Izzy's heart sank. She was hoping they could spend the days between Christmas and New Year's with each other. But it sounded as if Zayn was making business plans. The perils of falling for a workaholic.

He clicked off the phone and reciprocated her chaste kiss with a much more passionate one. Her breath was heavy when he pulled away.

"Merry Christmas," she said when she managed to find her voice.

He grinned at her. "It certainly is."

"Who was that on the phone? Sounds like you're going somewhere."

He set the phone down with a long, weary sigh. "You're right. That was the clinic in San Antonio. I'm going to make a trip out there for a couple of days."

The ramifications of what he was saying dawned on her slowly. He'd just made arrangements to go see his sick father. A wealth of emotion swelled in her chest and she threw her arms around him.

"What made you reconsider?" she asked, still tight in his embrace.

He planted a gentle kiss to her temple. "Because you were right. The panic attacks did get worse. I couldn't ignore them or what they might mean. I couldn't risk making another bad decision that I might not want to live with for the rest of my life."

Her chest heaved against his. "Oh, Zayn."

"Any chance you're free to come to Texas with me?"

He had to know she would, that she would be with him for every step of this journey for as long as he needed her.

She hugged him tighter. "I would go anywhere with you, my love. All you ever need to do is ask."

He must have liked her response. He proceeded to show her just how much without using any words at all.

CHAPTER SIXTEEN

One year later

SHE WAS DEFINITELY better prepared for the chill this time. On this visit, she'd made sure to pack a solid, warm winter coat. Good thing, too; this year appeared to be much colder than last.

Izzy clasped Zayn's gloved hand as they walked through the square to get to the Eiffel Tower. He'd promised her he'd bring her back and he'd been true to his word.

Several moments later, when they reached the top, it had already grown dark. Slowly, gradually, lights began to come on throughout the city. They stood staring at the majestic skyline, her back to Zayn's front. Below them, Paris's lights sparkled like millions of brilliant diamonds against a dark velvet backdrop. Adding to the view, the slew of Christmas decorations all around the city and dotting the banks of the Seine.

She felt a tremble of pleasure move through her body. How had she become so lucky? She had a career she loved, lived in a gorgeous part of the world and had the love of a man she'd more than once thought was lost to her forever.

"Cold?" he asked beneath her ear from behind, misinterpreting her shiver of delight.

She didn't correct his assumption. "A little."

"I'll have to try to fix that," he said playfully and nestled closer against her. His hot breath sent trickles of pleasure over her skin.

Their trip to France this year was so much more relaxing. None of the pressures that had existed last year had followed them this time.

Zayn had made a visit to his father just before their flight. The man was still quite ill but his condition was considered to be stable for now. Izzy knew it hadn't been easy for him, but Zayn was making a true effort to forgive and understand his father's mistakes. He made her so proud.

Now they were in Paris strictly for pleasure. No expo. No awards ceremony. No angst. Just the two of them enjoying each other's company.

Izzy released a contented sigh and nestled further into Zayn's warmth. His arms tightened around her midsection.

"I don't think I've ever seen anything more beautiful," she whispered, taking in the majestic scene below. She found herself wishing she was an artist who could somehow capture the visual on canvas, preserve it for all time. Not that it would ever leave her memory.

"I have," Zayn said pointedly, studying her profile. The way he was looking at her sent a surge of pleasure through Izzy's core. She'd been in love with him since she was a young girl, had somehow grown to love him even more since Fate had thrown them together again last December. She decided Fate had done pretty well by her for this lifetime.

"I'm hoping you'll think this is beautiful, too," Zayn said, gently turning her around to face him. In a movement that sent shock waves through her center, he pulled a small velvet box out of his pocket and knelt on his knee.

Izzy thought she'd forgotten how to breathe. Doubted she may ever remember again.

"I love you, Iz," he told her, taking her hand in his and gently removing her leather glove. "And I'd love it if you'd do me the honor of being my wife."

The ring he slipped on her finger shone as brilliantly as the magnificent lights sparkling along the skyline.

Izzy's vision grew blurry as tears of joy clouded her eyes. "Yes!" she managed to blurt out, pulling him up to stand and flinging herself into his arms. She repeated the one happy word over and over, in case there was any doubt whatsoever.

A family of tourists nearby began clapping and cheering.

Izzy couldn't help but think that Myrna was somehow watching them now, witnessing their happiness. Izzy offered up a silent thanks to the woman who had been so right to try to bring them together. Her wise words echoed through Izzy's head as they so often did. *You two need each other.*

"Merry Christmas!" someone shouted from behind them in perfect English.

It certainly is, Izzy thought, her heart near to bursting with joy in her chest. She couldn't have wished for a better holiday.

* * * * *

SOMETHING ABOUT THE SEASON

ALLISON LEIGH

For Greg, who can always make me laugh,
even when we're social distancing

Chapter One

"What fresh hell is this?"

Gage Stanton ignored his brother's question as they rolled to a stop in front of the entrance to Angel River Ranch. It had taken hours to reach what was just a tiny map dot near the Wyoming/Montana border.

Noah sat forward in his seat, raking his fingers through his hair as he surveyed the landscape beyond the windows of Gage's BMW. "This blows," he muttered, not for the first time since they'd left the courthouse in Denver that morning.

"Would you rather be sitting in jail for the next few months?"

Noah's lips thinned. He was twenty-two years old. Spoiled. Selfish.

Rich, except that Gage had managed to secure the bulk of Noah's inheritance so he couldn't squander it. Still, he consistently blew through his extremely generous allowance.

"I wouldn't be in jail," he muttered after Gage had rounded another curve. "Archer would have gotten me off."

"Kid, the only reason you're not in jail is because I convinced the judge that working for me would put you back on the straight and narrow." Not that Noah had *ever* walked the straight and narrow path. Before she'd died, it had been one of their mother's greatest regrets. "And Archer Templeton is my attorney. Not yours." He wouldn't admit how many times his lawyer had already intervened on his brother's behalf. But even Archer was fed up.

Noah drew himself up tight. "Don't call me *kid*."

"Then stop acting like one," Gage snapped. He turned onto the dirt road and drove through the guest ranch entrance marked by a forged iron sign.

He should have taken time to get an SUV. Something more suited to driving in this backwater than his M8.

Considering the rates Angel River commanded, he was surprised by the primitive road. He made a mental note to check about the roads getting in and out of the Rambling Rad Ranch.

He still wasn't sure what had prompted him to become the majority partner in the guest ranch development in the first place. He built luxury resorts.

Master planned communities. Industrial complexes. Not places where people went to pretend they were cowboys. And he didn't work with partners—even when they happened to be former employees that he trusted.

It wasn't that it was a *bad* plan. The Rad was located—literally—right on the edge of Rambling Mountain. The Wyoming mountain had, until earlier that year, been privately owned by an old man who'd never shared an acre of his property with anyone. Now, Otis Lambert was gone and Gage had won an expensive bidding war to purchase the decrepit cattle ranch. Because of Gage's new partnership with April Dalloway and her husband, Jed, the stakes to turn it into something successful were even higher. It wasn't only Gage's investment on the line. Aside from the expensive—but relatively simple—purchase of the ranch itself, use of the remainder of the mountain remained uncertain.

In his will, Otis Lambert had stipulated that the mountain beyond the ranch borders be for public use—ideally a state park—but so far nothing was set. As the matter languished on the vine because of politics and budget constraints, Archer had been bugging Gage to get involved at the local level— namely the town of Weaver, located closest to the mountain. Because if the land didn't become a state park, it would fall under Weaver control. But Gage preferred keeping his distance from Weaver for reasons that had nothing to do with getting into the guest ranch business or who ended up in control of the pristine mountain wilderness that surrounded it.

Gage had always believed that good business trumped personal business. It's what had gotten him this far in life. But in this case, Weaver was way too close to personal.

"Doesn't look like much." Noah's morose voice brought Gage's thoughts back to the present.

He had to agree. The curving road bisected one side of nothing and the other side of nothing. There were no trees to speak of. There wasn't anything particularly green. The fields had bypassed gold and headed straight into brown.

He couldn't blame that on anything other than the time of year, though. It was the end of October. Back home in Denver, it had already snowed once that month before temperatures soared back up again. When he'd spoken with Sean McAdams, the owner at Angel River, Sean had told him they probably wouldn't see snow until after Thanksgiving. But Gage should pack for it. Just in case.

Since he hadn't really planned to make this jaunt to Nowhere, Wyoming, in the first place, he hadn't put a lot of advance thought into what he'd thrown into his suitcase. He traveled a lot. He'd grabbed the usual stuff and pitched it in.

His lawyer had told him about the Angel River property a few months ago. It had plenty of travel and leisure awards to its credit and was one of the most well-regarded guest ranches in the Western United

States. Based on Archer's research, Gage had arranged to send Wade Jenkins from his office to find out what did and didn't work for Angel River. Gage had been ready to pay the price for that research, too. Not just the cost of lodging Wade for a couple weeks, but compensation to Angel River for behind-the-scenes information that would be used by the Rad, which—in time—would be their competitor. Sean had agreed to the plan.

Then the situation with Noah had reared its ugly head.

Gage damn sure hadn't planned on coming here himself, much less with his spoiled half brother in tow. But during court that morning he'd felt forced to act.

Because before she died, Gage had made an impossible promise to his mother that he'd always watch out for him.

Noah's latest stunt to land him in front of a judge again had been crashing his car through the plate-glass window of a Denver high-rise. A high-rise that Gage owned.

Thankfully, Noah hadn't hurt anyone. Not even himself.

Of course, he'd been drunk, despite just spending weeks in a rehab facility.

He'd also been pissed at Gage for finally telling him his allowance was being cut off. For telling him that he needed to find a job. Go to work and be a productive member of society.

Needless to say, Noah hadn't been happy. He was the only heir of a pharmaceutical magnate. He didn't "do" work.

Gage's choice that morning had been to either let his brother see serious jail time for this latest escapade or personally guarantee that Noah would stay sober and productive.

He'd called the owner of Angel River yet again with a change in plans. Squirreling Noah away at the ranch for a month and a half would either be Gage's best idea ever or one of his very worst.

He squelched a sigh and continued following the dirt road until it took a sharp turn. Suddenly they were overlooking a verdant strip of land. Autumn-hued trees clung to the banks of a glittering river that flowed past a large lodge situated on a hill. Several other smaller buildings were scattered on both sides of the river.

Horses grazed in a pen some distance away from the lodge, and even farther beyond that, Gage could see cattle milling around and a few figures on horseback. It looked as picture-perfect as it did on the ranch's slick website.

"What am I supposed to be doing here, anyway?" Noah's sulky tone raked on Gage's patience.

He pulled up to a glorified shack bearing a stop-here sign. "It's a ranch," he said flatly. "I'm pretty sure there'll be plenty of things to keep you busy."

Noah started muttering what he thought about that, but he broke off and rolled down his window when the young woman who'd stepped out of the shack approached his side of the car.

She leaned down to look through the window, wearing a smile that spread all the way to her sparkling eyes. "Welcome to Angel River. You must be Mr. Stanton."

"*He* is," Noah said with a jerk of his head.

Despite Noah's sullen tone, her smile didn't waver. "I'm Marni. If you'll pull up to the main lodge, they've been expecting you." She gestured toward the log building situated on the knoll, her bright gaze skipping from Gage's face to Noah's and then back again. "You'll have a chance to settle in, but don't take too long. Everyone's already gathering at the barn for the afternoon activity. Here's a map of the property." She thrust a black-and-white brochure through the window at Noah then stepped back from the car. "Enjoy your stay!"

Gage watched her practically skip back toward the shed, her spiky pink hair bouncing. "Cute."

Noah just made a grunting sound. If he appreciated the girl's cheerful friendliness or gamine prettiness, he obviously wasn't going to say.

Gage was damned if he knew what qualities actually interested Noah. He'd never seemed to date a girl more than a few times.

But then, the same thing could be said about himself. He'd been married once. Briefly and a long time ago. As exes, he and Jane were a lot happier with each other than they'd ever been when they'd been married. Now she was married to a decent guy who gave her the sort of time a man should give his wife. Should *want* to give his wife. They even had kids.

But Gage had learned his lesson. He liked playing to his strengths. Relationships weren't one of them.

He continued on to the lodge while Noah looked at the map.

The closer they got, the more rutted the road became. By the time Gage parked between a couple of muddy vehicles, he'd decided that *all* the access roads to the Rad would be paved. Just because the place wouldn't be one of his typical luxury resorts, guests still shouldn't have to worry about taking out an axel before they even reached their destination.

As Noah just sat there, Gage climbed out of the car with relief and pulled out his cell phone. There was barely any signal. Regardless of the reasons that had brought him here, Gage still had a business to run. He hoped the ranch at least had decent Wi-Fi.

"Come on," he told his brother. "Sitting there sulking isn't going to change anything."

From inside the vehicle, Noah told Gage what he could go and do with himself.

Gage almost smiled.

His brother was nothing if not consistent.

Inside the lodge's office, Rory McAdams stood at the window and watched the tall man climb from his low-slung black vehicle. He was too far away to see his face, but everything about him looked impatient.

From the fingers he thrust through his dark hair to the way he looked at his cell phone and wristwatch.

On top of everything else, he was going to be one of *those*.

The kind of guest who arrived all tensed up and would stay that way once he realized that all of his fancy little tech devices didn't count for squat here. The ranch provided wireless internet, but it wasn't exactly the lightning-fast variety. The phones were connected by that old-fashioned thing called wire. There weren't even televisions inside the guest rooms, and the newspaper that her father still insisted on subscribing to was always delivered several days late.

She glanced over her shoulder at him. Despite the latest tests that said Sean McAdams's cancer hadn't returned after two years, the battle had left its mark. He looked a fraction of the man who had been at the helm of Angel River for nearly all of her life.

"He's here," she said.

Her father nodded. "I told you he would come." He gave her a pointed look that was reminiscent of his precancer days. "No matter how much you hoped he wouldn't."

Rory swallowed the denial on the tip of her tongue. What her father said was true.

"Better go and greet him," her dad prompted. "He's a paying guest."

"Gage Stanton's a competitor," she muttered. One who wanted to pick their brains for every secret to their success just so he could turn around and use that information against them.

Aware of the way her dad was watching her, she tightened the ponytail at the back of her head, picked up two of the gift bags they always presented to incoming guests and left the office. Maybe her steps were a little more like stomps, but she couldn't help it.

Aside from the arrangement he'd made with Stanton, her dad hadn't made a single decision where the ranch was concerned since he'd gotten sick. What other things might he be planning without telling her?

The office had once been on the third floor with windows that afforded its occupants a near-panoramic view of the main ranch. Since her dad's health had declined, they'd relocated it to the main floor, taking over a guest suite. It was convenient for him since there was a fully equipped bedroom. It meant he could rest whenever he'd needed to without returning to his cabin located a few miles away.

Now that he was feeling better, they could have moved the office back to its original location, freeing up the room for bookings again.

Only there'd been no need.

Right now, the lodge was quiet, but its peacefulness didn't soothe her like it usually did.

The lunch hour had passed. Bart had cleared everything away, and the guests were off on their afternoon activities. Frannie, she hoped, was cleaning the guest rooms while they were empty.

Rory reached the lodge entrance and pushed her lips into a smile she didn't feel before pulling open the heavy door. The wind whipped at her ponytail as she stepped outside. She gathered it over one shoulder, trying to keep it under control as she walked along the wide porch toward a set of stairs that led down to the driveway.

Most guests preferred to fly. Wymon, the nearest town, had an airstrip the ranch paid to maintain just so their guests would have an easier time reaching them. The fact that Stanton had chosen to drive such an impractical vehicle here only underscored the fact that he wasn't a typical guest.

She still couldn't see the man's face. He was too busy with his cell phone.

This time she deliberately clomped her boots just to get his attention. Finally he lifted his head and looked her way.

Rory was immediately glad that she'd already reached the bottom of the steps, or she might have fallen over her feet.

Gage Stanton—assuming the new arrival *was* Gage Stanton and not the other guest he'd told her dad he was bringing—was gorgeous. Seriously, studly gorgeous.

So gorgeous that it was an effort to get her mouth to work in conjunction with her brain. Her mouth wanted to drool. Her brain wanted to get him moving on his way as quickly as possible. She was a thirty-three-year-old single mom trying to keep the family business afloat and did *not* have time to be drooling over anyone. Least of all someone who'd paid them a fortune to learn their so-called secrets of success.

The last time she'd drooled over someone, she'd ended up with Killian. And though she wouldn't trade her son for the world—he *was* her world after all—she wasn't prepared for a repeat.

Not that the gorgeous black-haired man looking back at her with meltingly beautiful brown eyes would ever drool over *her*.

Undoubtedly, his last-minute guest was one of the female variety. He wouldn't be the first of her guests with "companions" they preferred to keep discreet.

If they paid their fees and didn't cause any damage to the property or her staff, who was Rory to judge?

Anyway, she never got involved with guests. Not that way. Especially guests who brokered deals with her father behind her back.

As she closed the distance between them, she made an effort to put on her usual greet-the-guests smile. "Good afternoon. Welcome to the Angel River Ranch." She extended one of the tote bags fashioned with the ranch's logo of unfurled wings superimposed over a curving river. "I'm Rory McAdams. I manage the property here. You must be—"

"Gage Stanton," he said in a deep voice. The kind

of voice that made shivers dance across a woman's shoulders before slipping down her spine to points beyond.

Her practiced smile didn't waver. "I'm glad you made it safely. Much longer and we would have been sending out a search party for you." She wasn't joking, though she said it lightly.

His perfectly molded lips tilted slightly. "Sorry about that." He lifted his phone. "Would have called to let you know we'd be arriving later than planned, but—" A faint line appeared in his lean cheek as his smile deepened. "I keep forgetting that there are still places in the world where these barely work."

The self-deprecating smile was almost enough to throw her.

Almost.

"You're here now, so that's what counts." She looked toward the car. The front window was almost as heavily tinted as the side windows, and she could barely make out a slender figure with dark hair in the passenger seat. "Now let's get you settled so you both can begin enjoying your stay."

The developer opened his door and angled his head to look in at his companion. "Get moving." His voice was short to the point of rude before he shut the door again with a decisive click.

Oh. Kay. Then.

She would be discreet about this guest if it choked her, but it would be even harder if the guy turned out to be a total jerk. No matter *how* much money he was paying them. On the other hand, if he *was* a jerk, he could learn all of Angel River's secrets and he'd still fail, because nobody liked visiting a guest ranch that was being run by a jerk.

As if it were a weather vane, she felt her sympathy suddenly swing around in the direction of the man's companion.

Stanton stepped forward and took the tote bag from her. His fingers barely grazed hers as he took the strap, but it was enough to make her shiver yet again.

Dang it all.

She deliberately moved away from him and crossed to the other side of the luxurious car.

"Good afternoon," she said brightly as she pulled open the door for the poor woman inside. "Welcome to Angel River."

But it wasn't a woman who uncoiled herself from the seat.

It was a man.

Young.

Painfully thin.

He was almost as handsome as Gage, but in a less-finished way. And his face also had a distinctive pallor that reminded her of her father's.

She felt her practiced smile soften, feeling even more sympathy. Man. Woman. What did it matter? Suffering was suffering.

"I'm Rory." She extended her hand to him. "If

there is anything I can do to make your stay here more enjoyable, all you have to do is say the word."

He suddenly smiled. His eyes were blue. Set off by all that dark hair and stubbled jaw, they were quite striking. "Word," he said and clasped her hand.

His fingers were cool. They did *not* send shivers down her spine.

"Give the woman back her hand, Noah." Gage had moved around to open the trunk and was lifting out a small suitcase that looked brand-new and a second bag that looked anything but. "You'll have to excuse my brother, Rory." He pushed the trunk closed. "He obviously doesn't know how to behave around a pretty woman."

Chapter Two

*B*rother?

Pretty?

Rory wasn't sure which word surprised her more.

There was no way he meant the "pretty" thing. She was under no delusions when it came to her own looks. Thirty-three-year-old single mothers like her had more pressing things to do with their time than regularly sit themselves down in a chair at the beauty salon. Her hair needed a good five-inch trim, and she couldn't remember the last time she'd filed—much less polished—her fingernails.

Stanton probably tossed that phrase around whenever he was in the vicinity of a woman.

Her friend Megan would've objected that his words were hardly politically correct in this day and age and that Rory was a ninny for not pointing it out to him.

Fortunately, Megan, who was also the ranch's head wrangler, wasn't here. So Rory, whether she believed Gage or not, could secretly enjoy hearing the word *pretty* being applied to her.

Particularly since his unnamed guest turned out to be his *brother, not a mistress.*

Maybe she was getting cynical. Painting guests with too broad a brush.

She ignored the fact that her step felt springier as she began walking them to their lodgings. She had a job to do—get them settled—and a limited amount of time in which to do it because of their late arrival.

She gestured to the cabins situated on the other side of the gravel road. "We had the original reservation assigned to a room in the lodge. But considering how long you're planning to stay, I've moved you instead to the Brown cabin. As you can see, it's almost as close to the river as the lodge. You'll have more privacy and space. But if you prefer more interaction with other guests, I can move you back to a room in the lodge."

"Rooms," Gage and Noah both said at the same time.

She glanced at them. The two seemed to be making a point of not looking at each other.

Aside from the espresso-dark hair the two men shared, Rory didn't see much of a physical resemblance between them. When it came to surveying everything around them as they crossed the road, though, the expressions on their faces could have belonged to twins.

Neither one looked enthusiastic about being there. Which made her wonder why Gage had not only taken the place of his employee and lengthened the original reservation, but brought Noah along as well.

They reached the cabin and she unlocked the door, dropped the key into Gage's palm without any contact and led the way inside.

She turned to watch them enter, gauging their reaction. The two-story, two-bedroom unit was spotless and had been carefully maintained. However, the Western-style furnishings were more than a decade old and in her opinion could stand some updating.

If it weren't for her father's medical bills, she'd have worked some needed renovations into the budget by now.

"The kitchen is stocked, but you're welcome to join us for meals. Breakfast is always in the breakfast room, but the location for lunch and dinner can change from day to day. You'll find a brochure with menus, locations and times in your welcome totes. As you know, we're all-inclusive here. No hidden fees are going to be sprung on you. It's entirely up to you how much or how little you want to do while you're here, and that includes satisfying your appetites. In terms of activities, all you have to do is show up at the activity barn on time. Every outing begins there." She glanced at her watch. "It's too late to participate in one this afternoon, but since you missed the lunch hour, I can get something prepared for you both."

"That won't be—" Gage started to say.

"That sounds great," Noah said over him.

She hesitated, looking from one to the other.

Gage dropped the suitcase and the battered bag on the floor inside the door. His dark brown gaze slid from his brother to her. "Guess we'll take you up on that, Rory."

Shivers again.

Darn it.

It was safer focusing on his right ear than getting trapped in his deep brown gaze. "I'll let you settle in, then," she said. "Head on back up to the lodge whenever you're ready. If I'm not there, Chef Bart will take good care of you."

Without waiting for a response, she hurried out the door, pulling it closed behind her.

Gravel scraped under her boots as she crossed the road that wove between the cabins and the lodge before branching out toward the activity barn in one direction and the river in the other.

Typically at this time of year—when the autumn colors were on full display and the weather still allowed for lots of outdoor activities—all of their units would be occupied. That included the ones here in the main camp as well as those near Angel's Lookout. Even the Uptown Camp didn't go more than a week without a booking. Maybe there'd be a room or two open in the lodge, but never had they had more vacancies than occupancies.

Except this year.

It was an unpalatable truth that the fees Gage Stanton had paid—in advance, no less—were more welcome than ever.

She glanced at her watch again as she entered the lodge. The school bus would be arriving soon, and she quickened her step through the soaring great room, then the breakfast room and finally into the kitchen. Their chef, Bartholomew Lavigne—or Chef Bart, since he'd decided a long time ago that the moniker was more fitting for a Western guest ranch—was sitting on a stool at the stainless steel counter with a big calendar in front of him. She knew from experience that he was working out the menus for November. Typically, that would include a special Thanksgiving week, but she wasn't even sure yet how many guests they'd have by the holiday week.

She'd even been considering closing the property—unheard-of in Angel River's history—for that week until her father had told her about Gage Stanton suddenly extending his stay.

"The Brown cabin party arrived," she told Bart.

"Another guy bringing a woman who's not his wife?"

His dry humor brightened her spirits. "I don't know where you get such a suspicious mind. Two brothers," she said. "Gage and Noah. Do you mind putting together some lunch for them?"

Bart gave her a look above the rims of his black-framed glasses. "And if I do?"

She smiled. "You'll do it anyway, because you always do what's necessary. That's why I love you."

"That's what all the pretty girls say."

There was that word again.

But she'd been hearing it from Bart, who was a very spry sixty-five, since she'd been a child.

"I'm going down to meet the bus, but when I get back we can go over your calendar."

"You've decided what to do about Thanksgiving week, then?"

"The week is going to occur whether we have more bookings or not," she said with more spirit than she felt. "It certainly won't be as busy as the week before, what with the Pith wedding." That had been a huge booking, made just that summer and worth almost as much as the "consulting" fee that Stanton had paid them. "Just plan for everything like usual for now."

Bart's gaze was steady over his horn-rims. "You're sure?"

Despite her misgivings, she nodded. "I don't think holding off another week will make a difference," she admitted. "At least if we finalize everything now, I'll have plenty of time to print up the menus and schedules well before we get busy with the wedding group." She'd taken over that particular task since they'd lost their office assistant the year before. It wasn't everyone's cup of tea to live and work on a remote guest ranch, and so far, finding someone to replace Kaisley had been a bust. The only bright spot had been saving the expense of her salary.

"Speaking of." He riffled through a folder and pulled out a stapled sheaf of order forms. "You owe me ten bucks." He waved the papers. "They chose a tiered cake over cupcakes. Four tiers."

"Four!" She made a face as she pulled a ten-dollar bill from her pocket and handed it over. "That's a lot of cake for thirty-six people."

"Small tiers," he allowed. "But I'm looking forward to something different. Been a while since we've had a traditional cake. Everybody's been having cupcakes or pie buffets and such."

"I'm happy for you," she said dryly as she headed for the rear entrance via the oversize storeroom. "I wish the other details of the wedding day were decided. Mrs. Pith keeps waffling over which location to use for the ceremony itself."

"I hid away a couple of muffins for Killy." Bart's voice followed her. "Send him in here when you get back."

"Will do!"

She took one of the UTVs parked in back of the lodge and was soon bumping her way along the gravel road. It was a mile and a half to the junction where the bus would stop. Plenty of time for the worries on her mind to whip back up again.

She could afford not to replace Kaisley just yet. But she couldn't afford not to replace the spa manager who'd quit three months ago, leaving only Donna, the part-timer, to bear that load. Unfortunately, Rory had been no more successful in finding a new manager than she'd been in finding a replacement for Kaisley. She also needed to either promote Frannie to head of housekeeping and give her the raise she'd been asking for or chance the longtime employee quitting if Rory hired someone else for the job.

She didn't want Frannie to leave. But she also didn't think she was entirely qualified for more responsibility. Things tended to fall through the cracks where Frannie was concerned, which meant the rest of the crew was often left picking up the slack.

Why couldn't Gage Stanton have come to learn the secrets of their success when Rory's father had been at the helm? At least then there wouldn't have been anything *but* success for him to learn.

And she wouldn't be worried that her dad was making secret deals with a developer known to take over struggling properties.

She reached the bus stop to find two other vehicles already there waiting. She waved to them as she parked in her usual spot. The dusty pickup truck belonged to Seth Riggs—there to pick up his daughter, Toonie. Seth ran the cattle operation. The herd wasn't merely for the purpose of lending the ranch authenticity. For as long as Rory could remember, it had been a minor moneymaker for Angel River.

Unless their season improved, that was not going to be the case this year.

Frannie's daughter, Astrid, was sitting behind the wheel of a UTV similar to Rory's, her head bouncing in time to the music only she could hear through her headphones. She was there to pick up her little brother, Damon, who was a year older than Killy and his best friend in the world.

To some, it might seem more logical for all of the schoolkids to be picked up by just one person from Angel River and delivered accordingly to their appropriate locations. But Seth lived nearly five miles away to the west, Frannie and her kids lived nearly three to the east, and Rory and Killian lived in a cabin two miles due north.

She heard the engine, chugging and wheezing, long minutes before the yellow nose of the bus appeared. Sound carried here in the valley. Sometimes when the wind was right, they could even hear semis from the highway.

She had to fight the urge to go over and meet Killy the second he got off the bus. That had been okay *last* year, when he'd been a "baby kindygarder"— his words. Now, though, he was in first grade. He didn't need his mommy waiting for him the moment he bounded out of the bus.

The day she'd learned *that*, she'd wanted to howl with tears.

The three kids from Angel River weren't the only ones still on the bus. It would continue on after this stop for another ten miles, where it would let off the remaining children. Then it would travel all the way back to Wymon. And in the early morning, it would repeat the route.

She couldn't remember how old she'd been when she'd started yearning for something more interesting than this corner of the world. When she'd wanted something more than Angel River. More than the same people day in and day out.

She'd learned the error of her ways, but she dreaded the day when Killy would begin to feel the same way. He'd want to go out and explore the world and she was going to be brokenhearted when he did.

Damon came off the bus first, followed by Killy soon after. Her heart squeezed at the sight of him. He was growing so much. Her baby boy was becoming a little man.

She waved at him. Unnecessarily, of course. None of the kids could fail to miss the presence of their rides.

He and Damon were tossing a football back and forth, and Rory bit the inside of her cheek to keep from smiling too broadly at the way her little boy struggled mightily to keep the football from falling through his arms.

Astrid yelled for Damon, and even from a distance, she could see the boys make faces at each other.

Killy threw the football in a wobbling arc back to Damon, nearly hitting Toonie as she hunched her way over to her dad's pickup. The young teenager had her nose buried in the book she carried. As usual.

Then Killy ran to the UTV and heaved his backpack in before clambering onto the seat next to her. "Damon got detention," he greeted breathlessly. "'Cause old man Frisk thought he threw a spitball at him."

"*Mr.* Frisk," Rory corrected as she started up the utility vehicle, even though Horace Frisk had been old when *she'd* had him in school. She sketched a wave toward Astrid and Seth as they all pulled out and drove away from the bus stop. Only once they'd left would the bus have room to turn around on the narrow road and head along its way. "And did Damon throw a spitball at him?"

"Nah." Killy shook his head, and his messy brown hair fell over his eyes. "It was Amy Carpenter, but Damon says he's gonna marry Amy so he hadda take the fall for her. 'Cause it's shovelruss."

She was used to deciphering, but that one took her a moment. "Chivalrous?"

"Uh-huh." He was leaning over to rummage inside his backpack. He pulled out a crumpled piece of paper. "Can we go to the Halloween carnival?"

He thrust the flyer practically in her face, and she caught it from him.

"I've told you before. We'll see."

His shoulders slumped. "That means no."

She tucked the sheet of paper under her thigh where it wouldn't blow away. "No, it doesn't." She turned onto the Angel River Loop that would carry them back toward the lodge and slowed almost to a crawl. "Give me a kiss."

Out of sight of his buddy, her little boy gave her a quick peck that was followed with a gratifyingly tight hug.

She squeezed him back, hanging on for a second longer just because he allowed it before he started squirming again and she had to let him go. "So what kind of day did *you* have at school?"

"I got a hundred on my spelling test."

"Good job!" She held up her palm, and he slapped his against it. "I told you that you could do it." When it came to math, her boy was off the charts. But spelling and English were another matter.

"Then can we go to the Halloween carnival?"

She gave him a sideways look. "When did you start thinking that earning good grades was a bargaining chip?"

He wrinkled his freckled nose at her. "What?"

She ruffled his hair. She really needed to get him in for a haircut. Usually they could do that sort of thing at the Angel Spa, but Donna was too busy on her own with the guests they *did* have. Maybe Rory could get him in somewhere in town after the carnival. Because there was very little likelihood that she wouldn't take him.

But she didn't want to be a pushover, either. "We can go to the Halloween carnival on Saturday *if* you do all of your chores for the rest of the week without fussing about them."

His dark blue eyes turned very serious as he thought about that. But then he shrugged, evidently deciding the carnival was worth that particular trouble for the next two days. "Okay. I'm hungry."

She smiled, her heart feeling full. Who needed anything else in the world as long as her little boy was around? She sped up again, stirring a cloud of dust behind them. "Fortunately, Chef Bart has you taken care of as usual. He has a muffin or two with your name on them."

"I like Chef Bart's muffins. They're way better'n yours," he said artlessly.

She laughed. "That's true, but it's not very polite telling me so." She could never hope to compete with Bart's kitchen skills. "What if you hurt my feelings?"

He gave her an alarmed look. "I didn't, though, did I?"

She gave him a wink. "Nope. But remember there are things you can say to me, 'cause I'm your mom and you can always tell me anything, and there are things you shouldn't say to people who aren't your mom."

"Like the lady who's with Mr. Pantano this time? She's not as pretty as the one he brought last time. I told Grandpa."

"Yes, like her," she said wryly. And wished that her son wasn't quite so observant about the guests. Generally, he didn't have a lot of interaction with them. He had school and homework during the week, and on Saturdays, he and Damon were usually involved in the sport of the month.

She decided to change the subject.

"So, *if* you do all your chores for the rest of the week without complaint and get to go to the carnival, what costume do you want to wear?" The days of kids wearing costumes to school had gone by the wayside, but she was glad to know that it was still encouraged for the carnival.

"Cap'n 'Merica," he said immediately. "Damon is, too, but we decided we could both be the same."

"That works out well, then." She followed the loop around to the east, heading back to the lodge. It also worked out well since Killy already had the basic elements of the costume. She could just spiff up the cardboard shield she'd already made for him last year. "Do you have any homework?"

He made a glum face. "Three whole worksheets."

"Maybe your grandpa can help you with them." Her dad had helped him achieve that perfect score on his spelling test after all. She pulled up behind the lodge and parked the UTV. "Go on in and see

Chef Bart for your snack," she told Killy. "I'll take care of your backpack."

He needed no further encouragement as he vaulted from the seat almost before the wheels had stopped. She heard the slam of the door cutting off his yelled "Hey, Chef Bart, I got an A-plus on my spelling—" before she'd even hefted his backpack over her shoulder.

Smiling to herself, she followed after him more slowly, reading the carnival flyer as she went. They weren't charging for the games like they had in the past but instead were asking for contributions of school supplies as the cost of admission. They provided a helpful list of items and the quantities needed.

She went through the storeroom, wondering how difficult it was going to be getting her hands on a half dozen wide-ruled notebooks or classroom-size bottles of hand sanitizer. It wasn't as if they had a Shop-World around the corner. With more notice, she could have ordered something online, but at this point there was no way anything would arrive before the weekend.

She entered the kitchen, shaking her head as she looked at the list. "Don't they realize it would be easier to charge admission and just have the schools buy what they need?" She waved the list in her hand and looked up, expecting to see Bart and Killy sitting at the counter in the kitchen.

They were nowhere in sight, however.

Instead, Gage Stanton was sitting at the stainless steel counter, once again with his phone in his hand. He had a plate next to his elbow. He'd eaten part of his hamburger and some of the sweet potato fries.

He raised a brow when she practically skidded to a halt. "I'll take a guess that you didn't mean that question for me."

She made a point of folding the flyer. "Elementary school stuff," she said and tucked the flyer in her back pocket. She told herself it was her imagination that his gaze seemed to follow her hand.

She pulled open the oversize refrigerator and extracted a small bottle of cranberry juice, then nudged the door closed with her hip. She pretended to focus on opening the bottle. "Did you see a small boy run through here?"

"About this tall?" He held out his palm. "Blue eyes like yours, plus freckles?"

Just because he noticed the color of her eyes was no reason to get sidetracked. "That'd be him."

Gage jerked his head toward the doorway. "Went that way with your chef."

"Thanks." She started to leave the room, but her conscience as a host made her hesitate. His water glass was nearly empty, and she picked up the pitcher nearby. "How is everything with your lunch? Is there anything you need?" She refilled his glass and grabbed the basket of cookies and chunky brownies that was usually kept in the breakfast room for guests to help themselves throughout the day.

She was surprised he hadn't chosen to sit there. The breakfast room had a beautiful view of the river.

She set the basket closer to him. "Something sweet? Chef Bart's triple-chocolate brownies are my personal downfall."

He didn't even glance at the basket, but the corner of his lips lifted slightly. "I'll have to remember that."

Warmth suffused her, and she set the pitcher down with what felt like glaring clumsiness. Considering it had been his brother who'd indicated interest in a meal earlier, she wondered why Gage was solo. "And your brother? Noah, he's—"

His dark, intense gaze finally released her when he looked at his phone once more. "He's fine."

She didn't like feeling dismissed.

But she also didn't want to hang around there any longer than necessary.

If he were any other guest—a regular guest—she would take the cue and leave him to his privacy. But he was not their typical guest. He was paying them an astronomical amount of money to learn how they operated. And even though it was her father with whom that bargain had been struck, it fell to Rory to see it through. "When would you like to, ah, to start—" She had trouble finding the adequate words.

He wasn't similarly afflicted. "Learning the ropes?"

She nodded, her lips pressed together in a smile that she hoped wasn't as stiff as it felt. "Once I get

Killy settled, I'll have some free time before the other guests begin returning from their afternoon activities, or…or maybe you'd like to just be a guest for a week?" She couldn't help feeling hopeful at the idea. "See things from that perspective first?"

He quickly dashed her hopes. "Your guest reviews are remarkably positive. So I think we can skip just being a guest. How about we start tomorrow morning?" His tone was smooth. "Let me know what your schedule is, and I'll just—" his gaze slid over her very briefly "—shadow you."

The skin over her spine tingled. She resolutely ignored it and trained her gaze squarely on his earlobe. "I'll put a schedule together for you by dinner."

"Perfect." He looked back at his phone. "Your chef got me onto your Wi-Fi. It's slow as hell."

"Yes, it is," she agreed matter-of-factly and left.

She tracked down her son and their chef in the office. Killy was covered in muffin crumbs while he regaled his grandfather with the day's spitball excitement.

She dropped Killy's backpack on the couch next to where he was sprawled. "Don't get too comfortable there, mister. You have worksheets to do, remember?"

He started rummaging in the depths of the backpack, coming out with the usual six-year-old boy detritus—some rocks, an unwrapped hard candy covered in lint, two plastic dinosaurs—before he pulled out a bundle of crumpled pages stapled together in one corner. "I got this, too." He handed it to her before diving back into the pack.

She took the packet, half-afraid to see what it was about. The last time he'd come home with a packet, it had been a recommendation for placing him in the gifted program because of his math skills.

But that would mean going to a school even farther away. Despite her reservations, she'd talked at length with his teacher and decided to put it off another year. This time, though, it was just registration information for the following school year. Nearly ten months away.

She decided the packet could wait and tossed it aside on her desk. Her father was already reviewing Killy's worksheets with him, and she glanced at the chef. "Do you want to go over your calendar now?"

Bart pushed himself up from his chair and, with a wrinkle of his nose, made his glasses that were propped against his forehead drop neatly down into place where they belonged. "I'll have biscotti for you after school tomorrow, buddy."

Killy grinned up at him. "I like biscotti."

The chef laughed. "You like everything, Killy. That's why you're growing like a weed."

Her little boy suddenly stood on the couch and shot his hand up in the air as high as it could reach. "I'm gonna be *this* tall. Like my dad."

Rory's gaze caught on her father's. Killy had mentioned his dad more than once lately. "Don't stand on the couch," she reminded him and headed out of the office along with Bart.

"How does he know—"

"He doesn't," Rory said before Bart could finish his question. Killian had never even met his father. Rory didn't have any pictures left of Jon, who had, indeed, been very tall. When he'd decided she and their future child weren't worth sticking around for, she'd decided photographs of him had to go, too. One of these days, she knew she was going to have to explain his absence to Killy, but for now she preferred to act as if the man had never existed.

A few of the other guests had returned to the lodge when Rory and Bart walked back through the great room, and she stopped off long enough to greet them.

Tig Pantano was a big bear of a man, handsome enough in his middle-aged way. He owned some sort of business in Colorado and was a regular guest at the ranch—usually staying a month at a time. The flavor of the month on his arm was a giggly, overly made-up blonde named Willow with the voice of a chipmunk who seemed to feel the need to gush over every blade of grass as if she'd never seen one before.

Maybe that's what she thought would impress Tig, and for all Rory knew, maybe it did. So far, she hadn't seen any similarities among Tig's companions except that they were female and none of them were actually his wife, Monica.

Rory had met her only once, several years earlier, when she and Tig had first visited the ranch. Since then, Rory spoke on the phone with Monica at least six times a year—every time she made a fresh reservation for her husband and his latest paramour. Monica even provided their names on the reservations.

It really did take all kinds.

Noah suddenly walked into the great room, and Willow abruptly broke off her latest bubbling rave over her afternoon boating trip. Her eyes followed the young man almost hungrily, and Rory felt an unexpected spurt of sympathy for Tig.

Fortunately, four more guests came in on Noah's heels, and the room livened up. Tig told Willow to put on some music while he headed behind the mahogany bar.

Noah was hovering around looking alone, and Rory went over to him. "Looking for your brother?"

"Surprised he's not looking for me," he muttered. "Since he's my new warden. And he's only my half brother."

He made it sound as if that mattered. Half or whole, it all counted in her book. But she wasn't sure what response was appropriate after the "warden" comment, so she gestured at the small crowd making themselves comfortable in the expansive great room. "Have you had a chance to look around yet? Meet any of the other guests?"

He shook his head.

There was still plenty of time to look over Bart's calendar. Particularly when her only part in the affair was to sign off on the supply order. "Well, then, how about I introduce you to everyone?" She became aware of Gage entering the room. Not only because of the fine prickling on the nape of her neck, but because of the tight expression on Noah's face.

For once, Gage's ever-present cell phone wasn't in his hand, and he'd obviously overheard her words. "You can introduce all of us," he said as he stopped next to her.

She felt that damnable shiver again.

Then she smiled weakly and began making introductions.

Chapter Three

There was a sharp nip in the air the next morning when Rory drove her UTV back to the ranch after seeing Killy onto the school bus.

It was early yet, and even though she could have driven back up to the house to spend another hour in the haven of her warm and comfy bed, she went to the lodge.

If Gage Stanton was going to begin shadowing her that morning, she wanted to be ready.

However, as she walked along the quiet corridor, she could hear the murmur of male voices even before she reached the office door.

"—and Rory was just a toddler when her mother and I bought this place," her father was saying. "Never thought it would become as successful as it did. Figure it was her mom that was the reason. Eleanor had a way of making everyone feel welcome."

Rory hesitated in the hallway, resting her hand on the doorjamb. Her mother had died eight years ago, and there wasn't a day since that she didn't miss her. The ache might not be as acute, but it was still there.

She'd accepted that it always would be. Losing one parent was tragic enough. She was only now beginning to breathe easier where her father was concerned, and it had been two years since he'd received a clean bill of health.

"Did you ever think of selling?"

She winced, easily recognizing Gage's voice, and quickly entered the office. "G'morning," she greeted brightly, not even giving her father a chance to answer the developer's question. "You're up and at 'em early today."

She strode past Gage and dropped a kiss on her father's head, then stood there next to his chair, her hand on his shoulder. She met Gage's eyes, though it took considerable effort.

She didn't know how old he was, but she was guessing somewhere near forty. His dark hair was slicked back from his handsome face, revealing strands of silver near his temples. He'd been clean-shaven the day before, but now his jaw was blurred with faint stubble. Instead of lessening his appeal, it conjured an image of what he probably looked like waking up in bed every morning.

Which was *definitely* not an image she needed

in her head. "I didn't expect you to beat me here to the office. After I left you all after dinner last night, I'm surprised."

"Your other guests are an interesting lot, but a good bottle of whiskey's never been enough to distract me from business the next day, no matter how early."

She hoped that business didn't include trying to acquire Angel River. "They *are* interesting people," she agreed. "Guests come and go here, but each one of them is memorable."

"Exactly what your mama always said." Her dad gave her an approving look as he stood. "And if you'll excuse me, I'll head over to see Chef Bart for my daily oatmeal and leave the two of you to get on with it." On his way out, he straightened one of the framed travel awards hanging on the wall.

She went over to the door and pushed it closed. Now it immediately felt too close inside the room packed with the sofa and chairs along with her dad's oversize desk from two floors up.

She walked back to the armchair her dad had occupied but didn't sit. "My father will never sell Angel River to you." Her words were bold, hiding her shakiness inside, but she kept her voice low and controlled. At least *she* wouldn't be overheard by anyone walking down the hallway.

Gage's brows rose slightly. "I don't recall making an offer to buy Angel River," he said mildly.

Her fingers curled into the worn blue-and-green-plaid upholstery. "But that's what you do," she said. She'd read enough about him to know that. "Buy up struggling properties and turn them into the next jewel in the crown of Stanton Development."

His expression didn't change. "Is Angel River struggling?"

She sank her teeth into her tongue, debating how to answer then cursed herself for not just denying it and being done with it.

Then it didn't matter anyway, because he waved his hand dismissively. "You don't have to answer that." He stood. "I'm not in the market to buy another guest ranch." He smiled. "I'm not sure what to do with the ranch I already *have* bought."

And she wasn't buying his self-deprecation, either.

She changed tacks. "How is your brother this morning?"

His gaze remained steady. "Still pissed at me, I imagine. Or he will be whenever he unearths himself for the day. Is that what you want to know?"

She felt a little ashamed. There'd been obvious tension between him and his brother when she'd left the lodge for the evening. But thanks to the grapevine— i.e., Marni and Megan—Rory had already heard all about the argument between Noah and Gage because of the beer he'd pulled right out of his brother's hand. Marni—on official bartender duty—had carded Noah before serving him. The young man was twenty-two, and to hear the story, he'd been furious and stormed out.

"I heard there was a bit of a disagreement." Understatement of the year. "If there's a legal reason why Noah shouldn't drink, then let me know so we can deal with it without causing a scene next time. Is his ID real?"

"Yes. But he's not long out of rehab, and I'd like him to stay out."

"Is that why he called you his warden?" She hadn't forgotten Gage's curt manner with Noah when they'd arrived.

"I might as well be. He doesn't want to be here. I'm sure you've noticed that already."

"Maybe Noah's feelings about being here will change before too long," she said quietly. Maybe Gage's would, too, but she kept that thought to herself. "Angel River tends to have that effect on people."

"To hear your father, it's not the ranch but the people on it that are the draw."

"Maybe a bit of both." She cleared her throat and brushed her hands together. "So, you're here early this morning, but we might as well get on with things." She glanced at him. "You *did* look at the schedule I gave you last night, didn't you?"

"Yes. Why?"

She shrugged, suddenly wanting to laugh. She was wearing her oldest jeans, held together more by iron-on patches than by thread, a hooded sweat-

shirt and her oldest pair of boots. He was wearing
jeans, it was true. But there was nothing old or worn
about them, or anything else he had on. He looked
like he'd stepped off the cover of a magazine. She
hoped his hand-tooled leather boots survived the
morning or he'd brought a spare pair, because there
wasn't a shoe store anywhere in the vicinity—not
unless you counted the mukluks they sold in the
Angel River gift shop.

"No reason," she said blithely and led the way out
of the office. "Do we need to stop for some oatmeal
for you, too, first?"

He gave a visible shudder. "My mother used to
feed me oatmeal every morning when I was growing up. Hate the stuff."

So did she, but she didn't feel a need to tell him
that.

"Besides, you stocked the kitchen in the cabin
very well. Including coffee. Lots of coffee." A sudden smile hit his eyes, and she nearly tripped over
her own feet. He caught her arm. "All right?"

She focused on the carpet as if blaming it. "Just
fine."

They went out through the front door, and Rory
flipped up her hood against the chill. It wasn't freezing yet, but the way temperatures had dropped
lately, it wasn't going to be long.

He didn't seem to be bothered by it, though. "You
did bring a coat, didn't you?" She blamed the question on the mom in her. Yes, the cashmere hugging

his torso looked great on him but it wouldn't be a match for their weather. "You're going to need more than a sweater if this weather keeps up." The gift shop sold sweatshirts, too, but she had a hard time envisioning him in one. They all bore the Angel River logo—stylized wings and all—across the front.

"Your father told me to come prepared for snow, just in case."

"Smart. I hope we don't get any, though. Not before Thanksgiving, at least."

"Why? Snow means skiing."

"You'd think. But it's not good for business at Thanksgiving when there is snow." She stopped next to the UTV she'd used to take Killy to the bus stop. "I don't know why. Chef's turkey dinner tastes delicious whether snow's on the ground or not. It's just something about the season, I guess." She waited until he'd climbed onto the seat beside her and started the engine. "After Thanksgiving, though? Guests cannot wait for the snow to hit."

"Do you *have* good skiing?"

"If you're into cross-country, it's excellent. But we can't really compete when it comes to downhill." Fortunately, there were plenty of cross-country enthusiasts who sought them out year after year. She hoped this year wouldn't be an exception.

She gunned the engine as they buzzed past the lodge, tires bouncing over the ruts. His shoulder brushed against hers and she drove even faster, wanting a quick end to the ride.

They flew past the big firepit next to the lodge and the rest of the cabins of the main camp. The road evened out slightly when she turned toward the hay barn, but even though that meant they weren't bumping against each other, the damage was done. When she finally parked near the barn door, she quickly hopped out, not waiting to see how quickly Gage followed. She started to rub her shoulder where his shoulder had brushed hers, then realized what she was doing and forced her hand to drop.

She grabbed the cold barn-door handle and pulled. The well-oiled door smoothly slid open, and immediately the three cats sleeping on the floor inside raised their heads.

"Huey, Stewie and Louie," she told Gage, pointing at each one in turn. "They're not very friendly," she warned as they arched their backs and stalked off with tails bushed. "But they keep the mice under control." She headed toward the tractor parked inside with the spreader already loaded up with bales of hay and straw attached to it. "You can climb up and ride on the bales or take the UTV over to the horse barn," she told him. "Your choice." There wasn't room for them both inside the tractor cab.

She was more than a little surprised when he climbed up over the side of the spreader. And that he did it with such ease.

"You don't store the bales in the barn with the horses?"

"We used to. In fact the horses were originally kept in this barn, too. But my father considered it a fire hazard, so he built the horse barn ages ago. It's heated. No need for the insulating factor that the bales offer. Plus it has a sprinkler system. Makes the insurance company happy."

She waited in case he had more questions, but he just sat down on the bales stacked in the spreader, so she climbed in the cab and started the tractor. They rumbled out of the hay barn and slowly circled around the equestrian ring. The tiers of metal bleachers hugging the far curve could accommodate more than a hundred people. Their current guests and staff would only be enough to occupy a third of them.

He raised his voice above the tractor noise. "What do you use the arena for?"

She glanced at him through the cab's back window. "Rodeos," she said loudly. Just not these days. Not since her dad had gotten sick. Now the ring sat empty except as a gathering place for guests heading out on trail and hayrides.

Once they passed the ring, they reached the horse barn. The wide doors on either end of the long structure were already open, and she could see straight through to the pastures on the other side.

Rory drove the tractor right inside and stopped in the wide aisle separating the two rows of horse stalls. She loved the place with its gleaming wood-paneled stalls topped by black pipe. Megan made certain it was meticulously maintained; no one would ever suspect the barn had been built twenty years earlier.

Rory didn't want to think about how long it had been since her father had actually come to the horse barn. How long it had been since he'd been out for a ride.

Gage stood up, pulling her thoughts front and center to focus squarely on him.

The way he was standing on top of the spreader, his head nearly reached the light fixture hanging from the rafters of the steeply pitched roof. "What do you need me to do?"

Stop giving me shivers?

She swiped off her hood, annoyed with herself. What she'd *like* him to do was stay out of her way.

"Start tossing down bales," she told him. "And don't throw out your back while you're doing it." Not that he looked in danger of that, but she'd learned the hard way with overenthusiastic guests who'd helped with the chore in the past.

Naturally, he of the cashmere sweater and all manner of gorgeousness accomplished the task with perfect ease.

There wasn't a great deal of room in the aisle with the spreader blocking it—just enough to walk alongside it and maneuver the bales. After he'd off-loaded half of them, she pulled the tractor forward and they distributed the rest. Then, once the bales were stacked alongside the stalls, he hopped down and she opened the door to the feed room, where the tools were kept, stored neatly on pegs.

She grabbed a pitchfork, shovel, rake and broom. "Ever muck out a stall?"

"No. But I get the general idea."

There was that wry smile again. "You'd be surprised how many people don't." She went back out into the aisle and closed the feed room door with her hip. "The end goal is to save the straw that's not soiled or soaked. The stuff that is gets shoveled up and dumped in the spreader. Do the stalls next to the spreader. Finish them and move the spreader to the next stall, and so on and so forth. Once the stall is clean, we'll spread fresh straw for bedding and fresh hay for feed." She handed him the pitchfork and rake. "Any experience with horses? Livestock in general?"

"I've ridden a time or two."

Which could mean anything. People either overestimated their abilities or underestimated them. It was fairly rare for a guest to be perfectly honest and accurate. And she didn't want to make assumptions just because he could toss a hay bale as though he'd been doing it all his life. "Well, first off, Megan— she's our wrangler—has already done some of our work for us when she checked the horses earlier—" She broke off at his fleeting expression. "What?"

"It's really early now."

She almost laughed. And it was probably a little cruel of her to gleefully anticipate the day when he shadowed her as she helped Bart in the kitchen.

That was early.

Maybe by then Gage would decide he wasn't so interested in how a guest ranch operated. Maybe he'd decide he and his brother didn't need to stay there for the next six weeks.

The thought was appealing until she thought about having to refund all that money he'd already paid.

To say it'd leave a dent in the bank account was putting it mildly.

On one hand, she might sleep better with him gone, but her personal convenience was a high price for Angel River to pay.

"This is nothing. At least it's already light," she told him. "By the middle of next month, it'll be dark at this time of the morning. Anyway, as I was saying, Megan already moved the horses out to pasture." She entered the first stall and walked to the far side to glance in the water buckets hanging on the wall. "And she's already filled the water, so that's one less thing we have to do." Even though she knew she didn't need to, she looked in the feed bucket on the other wall. It, too, had been cleaned.

He glanced down the aisle. "Twenty-four stalls?"

"Twenty-two. All in use."

"You have more horses than staff."

"At this time of year, yes." She didn't elaborate that they were down several people.

"How much waste does a horse produce?"

She was glad for the turn back to matters other than Angel River staffing levels. "Can be as much as fifty pounds a day. Add in the soiled bedding…" She could see his mind working out the math. "That's why we do this daily. A healthy horse needs a good environment. And a guest ranch without healthy horses isn't much of a guest ranch. They work for us six days a week, so we take care of them."

"I saw in the brochure that you give them Sundays off?"

"Yes."

"And you do this chore every day?" He gestured at the stalls.

"Well, *I* don't do it every single day of the week," she allowed. "Megan and Marni take days, too, including Sundays. And during the summer we have a seasonal crew, which helps give everyone a break."

She waited in case he had more questions or comments, but none came, so she pushed up the sleeves of her sweatshirt and took the pitchfork in hand.

"Easiest way to do this is to work from one corner to the other." She jabbed the tines into the straw, lifting and shaking and turning the pitchfork as she tossed it toward the rear wall. "Don't want to leave anything that's wet." She reached a clump of soiled straw, which she flipped straight into the now-emptied spreader. "Manure management is about a lot more than just shoveling horse crap." She tossed another pile into the spreader and rotated the rake to drag it across the hard-packed earth beneath the straw. "Have to collect it then utilize it when you can or institute a disposal system." She glanced at him as she raked, being careful not to look at him too closely, because every time she did, it was embarrassingly difficult to keep a coherent thought in her head. "Sometimes it has to be stored before that happens. In our case, we're able to use most of it year-round. We have a large compost a ways out beyond the Uptown—"

"That's your corporate area?"

She paused only for a moment to answer. "Primarily. It's good for any sizable group wanting to be housed close together without interference from other guests. My father tell you about it?"

"I studied the máp Marni gave us when we arrived."

It was a small matter, but for some reason she was oddly pleased.

She stopped to point at the grilled gate on the exterior wall. Each stall possessed the same emergency gate. The horses could see through it to what went on in the world beyond the barn. It provided them some comfort, because the only times they were ever really happy to be penned up inside was when it was mealtime or there was a blizzard.

"So then you know Uptown is a few miles northwest of the main camp." She was still pointing through the opening. "Can't see from here, but Uptown's just over that ridge." She started scraping and tossing again. "As the crow flies, the compost windrows are between Uptown and Angel camp."

"And Angel camp is where most of the staff lives."

She nodded. Her cabin was in Angel camp. So were her father's, Megan's and Bart's. There were more, but they weren't in use.

"I'd like to see it."

"Angel camp or the compost?"

His gaze slid her way. "Compost."

She was chagrined by the level of her relief. "Then we'll have to fit in a compost tour. A-anyway, like I was saying, we use a lot of what our horses produce. It's either composted—what we can't use for our own gardens gets sold—"

"Good market for it?"

"There's always a market for quality, organic compost." Thank goodness.

"And the rest that isn't composted?"

"Weather permitting, we spread it directly on the fields. That's Seth's call. He runs the cattle operation. If you want to see the typical 'dude' ranch stuff, too, while you're here—"

"Isn't that part of this whole deal?" He looked a little pained. "Playing cowboy?"

"For some," she agreed. "But guest ranching has come a long way since the days of sleeping on a bedroll and going on a roundup. Now, guests come here wanting Bart's farm-to-table food and resort-quality amenities."

"But not high-speed internet," he inserted dryly.

"The ones who really need it to get through their day don't usually bother staying."

His lips twitched slightly. "Touché. So back to the manure. Seth decides whether it gets used now or composted."

She moistened her lips. "Yeah. After we finish the stalls, he'll send someone over for the tractor, dump or spread the stuff, then return the tractor to the hay barn for the next morning."

"Efficient."

"We try. I don't know what sort of setup you'll have on Rambling Mountain—" She hesitated yet again when he gave her a sharp look. "Am I not supposed to know about it?"

"No, I'm just surprised that you do."

She couldn't stop her short laugh any more than she could infuse it with actual humor. She switched the rake out for the shovel, scooping up the pile of debris she'd collected.

She moved past him again and pitched it into the spreader. "Everyone in Wyoming is taking notice. Waiting to see what happens. That ranch you're planning to develop is right on the edge of thousands and thousands of acres of completely undeveloped wilderness. I don't have to tell you how valuable that is. It has everyone worry—*wonder*ing how it'll affect their business." Including them.

"That's a lot of pressure for a little ranch sitting on the side of a mountain."

She held out the pitchfork and nodded toward the stall next door. "You strike me as a man who thrives on pressure."

His fingers brushed hers when he took the handle. "I thrive on lots of things."

Shivers.

She let go of the pitchfork as if it had turned hot. "I hope you thrive on horse manure," she replied, because *surely* there was nothing more effective at killing unwanted shivers than talking about horse poop. "This morning *and* when your Rambling Mountain ranch is up and running. Even a Stanton guest ranch would have to have horses." Then she turned on her heel. "I'm going to get another pitchfork."

Only after she was in the feed room was she able to draw a decent breath. She pressed her palm to her chest, feeling the uneven beat of her foolish heart.

A sound outside the room made her quickly snatch more tools from the pegs and go back out. Megan was there, leaning against the tractor, her arms folded as she openly studied Gage at work inside the stall.

Megan wasn't only Angel River's wrangler. She was Rory's best friend. And there was a glint in her friend's eyes that Rory recognized only too well. Despite Megan's grudge against most of the world's male population, she routinely nagged Rory about her lack of male companionship. As in Rory's total sex-life drought.

She jumped in before Megan could say something. "Are you set to take the trail ride this morning?"

Megan's expression was full of mischief. "I thought maybe you should." Her eyes bounced from Rory's face to the man working inside the stall. She didn't even flinch when Gage pitched a heavy wad of soiled straw in her direction to land unerringly into the bed of the spreader, missing her by inches.

"If I go on the trail ride, I can't help Frannie with housekeeping over at Homestead," Rory told her as if it were breaking news when it was anything but. Homestead was located in the center of Uptown and had higher occupancy than anywhere else on the ranch. It was a lodge in and of itself, though she considered it to have less character than the main lodge. "Are you saying *you* want to change sheets and dust shelves?" She knew Megan would sooner have her fingernails peeled off. She hated cleaning even her own cabin. And she particularly disliked working alongside Frannie.

But Megan evidently wasn't going to give in quickly, because she gave an expressive eye roll toward Gage. "But maybe our newest guest would enjoy the ride." She wasn't going to win awards for subtlety any faster than she'd win one for housekeeping.

"I should introduce you." Rory reentered the stall

she'd been cleaning and looked through the vertical pipes on the upper portion of the partition wall to see that Gage had already cleared two-thirds of the next stall. At the rate he was going, he'd have his stall finished before hers. "Gage Stanton, this is our wrangler I mentioned earlier. Megan Forrester, Gage Stanton."

"*Head* wrangler," Megan corrected with a faint smile.

"She's in charge of the seasonal crew," Rory clarified. "She keeps all the other activities on track, too, not just ones involving the horses."

Gage pitched another load into the spreader. "Sounds like you all wear more than one hat."

"More so in the past year," Megan said bluntly before Rory could telepathically stop her. "The spa director. The office administrator. Head of housekeeping. Everyone's stretched too thin."

It wasn't that Rory intended to hide anything from Gage, exactly. For all she knew, her father had already told him all of this. "It's a temporary bump." She tried to send Megan a mental nudge to hush.

But since Rory was not in the least telepathic, she knew the effort would be useless.

"Maybe Gage's brother would like to join the trail ride," she suggested brightly, hoping to change the subject. She glanced through the bars again toward Gage. "Does Noah enjoy horses? Does he ride?"

"I doubt it." He gave her a quick glance, looking like he regretted the terse comment. He stood the fork on its tines and crossed his arms atop the handle. "I should know whether he likes horses or not, but I don't." He looked toward Megan. "Do you have a big group going out this morning?"

"Only six, so there's plenty of room. And it doesn't matter a lick whether he's ever been around a horse in his life." She pushed away from the side of the tractor as if she'd suddenly tuned in to the mental messages Rory was sending. "I'll just go on over and ask him and leave the two of you to your... work." She gave Rory a wicked look as she turned to leave. "Nice meeting you, Gage."

As much as Rory had wanted Megan to move along, once she had, the barn suddenly felt secluded and too intimate. She avoided Gage's gaze like the coward she was, ducking her head over her pitchfork as she scraped the last bits of muck into a small pile. "You'll want to go on a trail ride yourself at some point. In fact, you could go this morning like Megan said." She hated that she sounded overly cheerful. "Experience isn't necessary, and seeing the place from horseback is one of the best ways to experience it." Their ATV tours were wildly popular, but Rory personally preferred horseback.

"Do you ever go out on the rides yourself?"

"If we have a particularly large group, I help out." She exchanged the pitchfork for the shovel and scooped up the pile, carrying it out to the spreader. "I've been on horses most of my life, but Megan is the one with the real touch with our guests."

She saw that his stall was spotless, with all of the clean straw loosely piled in one corner. "Nice job."

"Cleaning up crap. Been doing it most of my life."

She couldn't help smiling. It was suddenly much too easy to like him, and since she wasn't ready to trust him, that wasn't necessarily a good thing. "Well, now you spread the straw back around, toss in more from the fresh bale—some stalls'll take a whole bale, some'll take less—until there is a nice, good, fluffy bed."

He began deftly pitching the straw about. "What about the hay?"

"We'll put it on the wall next to the water buckets. That's one of the reasons for the concrete apron around the perimeter of each stall," she said.

"You don't stick it in a rack or bag?"

She shook her head. "Leaving it on the ground gives them a natural position to eat. It's also a good reason for checking the stalls as often as we do. Same reason we use water buckets instead of automated systems. Gives us more opportunity to personally attend to the horse. See how his digestion is going, if you know what I mean."

"This guy's digestion seemed just fine to me," he said with half a smile.

"That's a good thing." She took two flakes from the straw bale and went back into the stall with him, handing one to him. "This is Moonbeam's stall." She quickly pulled apart her flake, tossing the fresh, fragrant straw around as she automatically backed her way to the stall door. "He's a big boy, makes a big mess and likes a thick bed. It'll take a fair—" She broke off when her hand collided with Gage's. "Sorry," she mumbled, feeling about as mature as a third grader discovering the boy sitting next to her was cute.

He glanced at her. "Occupational hazard."

She dammed off the flush threatening to flow through her veins and managed a brief laugh. She cast the rest of the straw and backed out entirely, then crouched to pull several more sections from the bale where it naturally separated. She tossed the flakes toward Gage. "Like I was saying, it'll take a fair amount of straw. So grab whatever you need." She glanced up at him as she rose.

His brown gaze seemed to engulf her, and his eyebrow peaked slightly. "Thanks for the offer."

And her flush spilled right around the dam.

Chapter Four

"What happens if it rains on the carnival?"

Rory looked over to Killy where he stood in the open doorway of their cabin. He was looking up at the bleak sky. "Then it rains." She set his dinner plate on the table. "Close the door and come and eat."

Shoulders slumping slightly, he closed the door, immediately cutting off the bite of cold breeze that had been blowing inside. "The costume parade is outside," he said.

"They'll move it inside if they need to." She filled his glass with milk and set it beside his plate. "Don't worry so much. Halloween carnivals sometimes get rained on. Particularly around here. They'll have a plan."

He sat down in the spot opposite hers and propped his elbow on the table, his cheek on his palm. "But—"

"Killy," she cut him off gently, but firmly. She picked up her own fork. "*Eat.* The carnival is the day after tomorrow. Who knows what the weather will be by then."

"But—"

"Killian." She tapped his plate with the fork. He needed to eat dinner then finish his worksheets from school, have a bath and go to bed. Mornings started early around here.

He sighed mightily, then picked up his fork and jabbed it into the mac and cheese that he usually loved, even when she was the one who prepared it. Fortunately, after the first bite, he sat up and looked slightly more interested in eating than worrying about the carnival. Satisfied, she stabbed her fork into her salad.

"Are we gonna live here forever and ever?"

A slice of cucumber fell off her fork as she looked over at him. "Where did that come from?"

He squirmed on his chair and shoveled more noodles into his mouth. "Damon says Astrid says we're all gonna have to leave," he said around his food.

"Don't talk while you're chewing," she said automatically. "And why does Astrid think we're all gonna have to leave?"

"'Cause Frannie says so."

Rory stifled her annoyance. "And why does Frannie say so?"

"'Cause we don't got good business now."

"Don't *have*," she corrected. "And we're fine as far as our business goes." It wasn't strictly true, but she was more worried about her father's state of mind than the state of the business. Which wasn't something her child needed to know.

"But—"

"But nothing, Killy. You and me and Grandpa? This is our home."

"Forever and ever?"

She wanted to tell him yes. When she'd been his age, forever and ever had seemed such a certainty. But life had shown her otherwise.

Still, he was only six. Santa, the Easter Bunny and the Tooth Fairy were still fixtures in his world, and she hoped that they would be for some time to come. "Forever and ever," she assured him, then pointed her fork at his plate again. "Now finish your food."

His worry evidently assuaged for now, he did just that, shoveling in forkfuls with his usual voracious speed, finishing two helpings plus his salad before Rory had made it through her own salad. He clattered his dishes into the sink then spread his worksheets on the table across from her while she finished eating. Then it was bath; then it was bed.

And then, finally, all was quiet.

She went back downstairs and fixed herself a cup of hot chocolate, wrapped a heavy shawl around her shoulders and went out to sit on the porch that ran

the full length of the cabin. In layout, it was similar
to the Brown cabin where she'd put Gage and Noah,
though hers and Killy's was a lot more cluttered.

Such was life with her child, and she wouldn't
change it for the world.

She plumped the plaid pillow on the sturdy rocking chair on her porch and sat down, exhaling deeply.

She didn't bother with turning on the light. She
knew every inch of the cabin and its immediate surroundings with her eyes closed tight. And despite the
distance to the main camp, she could see a glow in
the sky from the bonfire burning down at the beach-
like clearing next to the river.

She stretched out her feet and propped her woolly
slippers on the porch rail. She wondered if Gage
had joined the rest of the guests for the fire. Or had
he stayed closer to his own cabin, where she knew
there'd be a much smaller fire burning in the firepit
near the lodge?

That morning, they'd spent two hours mucking
the stalls, which was actually less time than it usually took. Neither one of them had said much as
they'd worked. She'd expected him to pepper her
with questions, but he hadn't.

If anything, he'd seemed preoccupied as he'd methodically worked his way through the stalls at a
faster clip than even she could manage.

After that task, though, instead of accompanying
her to Uptown, he'd excused himself on the pretext
that he had to take care of some business.

Privately, she figured he'd had enough cleaning chores for one day. He was a good enough sport when it came to shoveling horse manure, but dusting shelves was probably not in his nature any more than it was in Megan's.

Rory hadn't seen him again that day until lunch, which had been served at the cookhouse. Like her, he'd changed his clothes after the mucking chore, and Rory could only hope that she hadn't been as obvious with her ogling as Willow had been. What the man did for a pair of black jeans and a plain white shirt ought to be illegal.

There'd been no sign of Noah at lunch, and she knew Megan hadn't been able to get him out on the morning trail ride. She wondered if he'd surfaced for dinner and the bonfire.

Rory had spent the afternoon with Gage in the office while she put in Bart's supply order. Then she'd given him a general overview of their organizational structure while she worked on the following day's payroll.

She felt certain that all of the Stanton properties would have state-of-the-art technology, but to his credit, he hadn't acted condescendingly when it came to what she knew was an antiquated system.

Nevertheless, she'd been grateful as all get-out when she'd had to leave to pick up Killy from the bus stop.

There was a gust of wind, and she tightened her shawl, cradling the hot mug in her other hand. She wished she felt more content. As content as she had when she'd first returned to the ranch after her divorce. Before Killy was born. Before her dad's cancer. Before she'd needed to take over as Angel River's manager.

When she heard the crunch of footsteps on gravel, she peered into the inky darkness in front of her. It was probably Megan, coming by with her own nightly cup of hot chocolate, though hers would be the boozy variety.

"Thought you'd still be down at the bonfire," Rory told her.

"Gave up bonfires back in my college days," a voice—most assuredly *not* Megan's—replied.

Rory yanked her slippered feet down from the rail and nearly spilled hot chocolate all over herself as a result. She still couldn't see the speaker, but she'd know his voice anywhere now.

She watched Gage's shadowy form solidify as he came closer. "This is a surprise."

"Hope it's not an unwelcome one."

"Of course not," she lied.

"Spoken like the best of resort managers, determined to never offend a guest."

"Careful where you walk, though. There's a tree stump I wouldn't want you knocking into."

He stopped on the other side of the rail, his face a pale blur in the night. "Mind if I join you?"

"Of course not," she repeated, lying yet again. "Have a seat." She gestured at the twin rocker next to hers and ignored her edgy shivering when he stepped up onto the deck and lowered himself into the chair.

She could tell he was finally wearing a jacket, but otherwise it was too dark to see much detail. She held up her mug. "Can I get you something hot to drink?"

"That's probably another offer just to be polite, but yeah. I'll take anything. It was colder walking up here than I expected."

His rueful honesty was annoyingly charming.

She gathered her shawl around her and stood. "If you want to come inside where it's warm—"

"Nah." He stretched out his long legs, sighing a little, as though in relief. "It's a nice night."

Another gust of wind blew past, sending the long, tangling fringe of her shawl slapping across him.

She laughed a little, despite herself. "I noticed." She gathered up the end of the shawl. "I'll just be a minute or two. You prefer coffee or hot chocolate?"

"Right now, plain hot water would work."

She laughed again and quickly went inside. If she had to lean back weakly against the door for a moment, nobody needed to know but her. When the door suddenly rattled under a gust of wind, though, she jumped away from it like she'd been bitten and hurried into the kitchen.

She poured more milk into the saucepan she'd used earlier and set it back on the stove to heat, then nipped into the bathroom. The shawl was ancient.

Her woolly slippers were even older. The fact that she stopped to swipe some clear gloss over her lips embarrassed her so much that she grabbed some tissue and wiped it right back off again.

He's a guest, she reminded herself sternly. A guest's stay always, always ended.

She returned to the kitchen and hurried the hot milk along by turning up the flame. She scooped some of the melted chocolate mixture she'd made earlier into a clean mug, and as soon as the milk was steaming, she stirred it in.

Then, mindful of Megan's preferred recipe, she pulled out a bottle of Irish cream and a clean teaspoon. She topped off her own mug with more hot milk, then—since she didn't have a tray handy—just set everything on a wood cutting board and carried it out the door, hitting the light switch with her elbow along the way.

Gage hadn't changed positions. He was squinting slightly in the sudden light from the fixture next to the door.

She set the board on the narrow table between the two chairs and handed him his mug before sitting back down. "Wasn't sure if you want some more comfort or not," she explained when he eyed the bottle of liqueur. Then she felt a quick stab. His brother had a drinking problem and she, of all people, should know better. Her ex-husband had been a recovering alcoholic. "Sorry if that was insensitive."

In answer, he spun the cap off the bottle and

dumped a shot into his mug. Then he looked inquiringly at her, and she had an oh-well sort of moment and held out her mug. He poured again, then recapped the bottle. He stirred his hot chocolate with the spoon, which he handed to her when he was done.

Her fingers brushed his when she took the spoon, and it clattered a little as she stirred. She quickly tapped it against the edge of the cup and dropped it onto the cutting board.

Then she dragged her shawl back up over her shoulders and stared blindly at the glow of the distant bonfire. "I hope you enjoyed Chef's dinner this evening."

"I don't usually care for fish that much, but it was excellent. If I could figure out a way to steal Chef Bart from you, I would."

She startled only to realize he was smiling slightly.

Expecting a reaction.

"Go ahead and try." She subsided in her chair again. "He's pretty loyal to my father, so it'll cost you a good bit."

Gage's smile widened before it was hidden by the mug he lifted to his mouth. When he was done, he propped his drink on the flat arm of the rocker. "I don't remember the last time I drank hot chocolate. Spiked or otherwise." His boot shifted slightly and the chair gave a soft, comfortable creak as it rocked

gently. "Much less sat in a rocking chair." He made
a sound. "Almost as good as a hammock."

"For relaxation, you mean?" She'd set her own
chair into faint motion without even thinking about
it. "I prefer a rocking chair," she admitted. "Last time
I tried a hammock, I ended up flipping right out of
it. Earned a mouthful of dirt." She looked back at
him. "*Not* relaxing at all," she said dryly.

The corners of his lips lifted. Despite the porch
light, his dark eyes were still too shadowed to see
his expression. "Last time I was actually in a hammock was on my honeymoon."

The hot chocolate suddenly tasted bitter, and she
automatically looked at his hand even though she
knew better than to expect every married man in the
world to wear a wedding ring. Jon certainly hadn't.
At the time, his reasoning had been safety at work.
As a metal artist, he'd done a lot of welding.

As an artist, he'd done a lot of things—mostly
other women.

The fingers Gage had curled around the thick
mug were devoid of rings. So were those on his
right hand.

"If you're married, you could have brought your
wife," she said stiffly. "We have a larger cabin
avail—"

"Think her present husband would've had an ob-
jection or two to that."

Her relief was nearly comical.

But why should she care whether he was married or not? It was none of her business.

Trying to ignore the war between her mind and her emotions, she took another healthy sip of hot chocolate, forgetting all about the added liqueur. She managed not to cough as the heat barraged her throat.

"We divorced a long time ago," he said. "Janie's a good kid, but we never should've gotten married in the first place." He picked up the Irish cream and uncapped it again, adding another measure to his mug.

Rory shook her head when he glanced at her. "I'm fine," she managed hoarsely. "Did you—" she had to clear her still-burning throat "—have kids?"

"Thank God, no."

She thought of Killy sleeping in his room upstairs. "My son was the one good thing that came of my marriage." She couldn't believe the words actually came out of her mouth.

"What happened?"

She wound her fingers in the fringe on her shawl.

"Too personal of a question?"

She opened her mouth, not sure what to say even though she'd been the one to bring up this particular subject.

"Don't worry," he continued. "My staff routinely reminds me that I ask them."

She latched on to her chance to change the topic. "How many people do you have working for you?"

"In my Denver office or altogether?"

"Either." She waved her hand. "Both."

"Thirty-two in the office. Overall, depending on the season, the number varies between two and three thousand. Give or take a couple hundred."

"I didn't realize Stanton Development was that large," she managed faintly. She hadn't researched him anywhere *near* well enough.

He shrugged. "No reason why you would. I'm a developer at heart. Once my projects are up and running, I turn them over to management companies. I just happen to own most of them, too. I have very competent people who take care of the day-to-day operations."

"Yet you came here to learn what we have to say?" She shook her head, feeling both bewildered and alarmed. "You could hire anyone you wanted to deal with your Rambling Mountain project."

"I like personally knowing what I'm getting into before I put it in the hands of someone else." He took another sip and flipped up the collar of his leather jacket against another gust of wind. "If I am going to ask someone to shovel horse crap, I want to at least be able to say I know what it feels like."

She eyed him even more closely. "Have you dug a ditch, too? Walked a high-rise girder?" It seemed inconceivable. "Plunged a stopped-up toilet? Delivered room service? Mopped a floor and changed sheets?"

"If I've been able to find a way, I've tried it."

"Then how do you have time to even be the

boss?" She spread her arms wide. "There are only twenty-four hours in a day."

He looked amused. "Now you understand why marriage—hell, relationships in general—don't work for me. Because all I *am* is work. It's the one thing I'm ideally suited for."

She supposed that was how he had to be to achieve his level of success.

She sipped from her mug, vaguely aware that her rocking was more agitated, and decided to change the subject. "Did your brother get out and do one of the afternoon activities?"

Gage patted his chest in an absent sort of way, as if he were looking for something. "My brother didn't get out of bed until just before dinner." His hand dropped again. "As a warden, I'm not doing that good of a job."

"You're not really his warden, though."

"He had a choice of me or jail after his latest DUI. What's the difference?" He sounded very, very weary.

She pressed her lips together. Regardless of whether or not he harbored intentions where Angel River was concerned, she couldn't help feeling for him. "Is there something I can do to help?"

"Take the trail ride tomorrow," he suggested. "He'll go if you do."

She wasn't sure why that would make a difference. But since she'd gone and offered assistance, she couldn't very well refuse now. "I'll need to switch a schedule or two, but I can do that."

"Great." He suddenly drained his mug and stood, as if he'd achieved whatever it was that he'd walked all the way up there to accomplish. "Thanks for the drink." He stepped off the porch. "Was as good as my mother used to make."

She managed a bemused "thank you," but he was already walking away.

"You said she was going to be here," Noah said under his breath. "Was that a lie just to get me to come?"

Gage inhaled the crisp morning air, reminding himself that biting off Noah's head wouldn't accomplish anything. "No. And I expect Rory will be here. There are two more horses already saddled over there." The saddle creaked beneath him when he shifted, nodding toward the horses still waiting near the fence of the riding ring where they'd all been led by Megan after they'd saddled up.

The tall wrangler was giving a thumbnail course in basic horsemanship before they headed out, and Gage could tell she was gauging for herself how comfortable he and Noah—as the newcomers—were on their mounts. It'd been a while since Gage had been on horseback, but aside from the fact that he was a helluva lot older than the last time, it was sort of like riding a bike.

Noah's ease on his horse, though, was a complete

surprise. Of course, when he'd asked his brother about it, Noah had just given him one of his typical smart-ass responses.

The two of them had a long stay at Angel River ahead of them. If Gage had to put up with Noah's present attitude for much longer, he was afraid he'd haul Noah back to jail himself.

He was already second-guessing his decision not to drag Noah out of bed the previous day. His brother was supposed to be working during his "sentence" with Gage.

But after their set-to the night they'd arrived, Gage hadn't had the stomach to ruin his morning with Rory.

Then he saw Noah's attention perk and followed his brother's gaze.

Rory was striding toward them.

The breeze had her long hair blowing around her shoulders in a tangle of brown and gold. She was wearing a worn-looking coat in a muddy red shade. Its only real attraction was the fact that it ended at her hips, where equally worn-looking blue jeans clung to her lithe figure. Her cheeks were ruddy from the cold air, and her eyes were as blue as the sky—at least what could be glimpsed of the sky among the gray clouds scudding across it.

He'd dated women who were far more beautiful. More polished. But as he watched Rory approach, he couldn't recall a single one of their names.

He might not know where Noah had acquired his familiarity with horses, but one sideways glance at him watching Rory, and Gage knew that Noah was feeling the same way as he did.

Not an issue, he reminded himself.

He didn't do relationships and he wasn't there to strike up a fling. He'd learned a long time ago to use the tools at hand. And if Rory's mere presence was enough of an enticement to get his brother out of bed without a battle, Gage would take advantage of that fact.

Megan barely paused in giving her horsemanship spiel when Rory reached the ring and ducked down to slip between the top and middle fence rungs. When she straightened, she gave a quick wave in acknowledgment as she headed toward the taller of the two remaining horses.

The wrangler's words were nothing more than a buzz while Rory checked her saddle. The horse was striking. Chestnut colored with a flaxen mane and tail, she butted her nose against Rory's shoulder until she turned with a smile and pulled something from her pocket. The horse greedily nuzzled her palm, taking up whatever the treat was, and then Rory nimbly swung up into the saddle.

It seemed that she'd hardly taken any notice of the rest of them gathered in the center of the ring, but the second she took the reins and turned the horse slightly, those blue eyes of hers seemed to slam into Gage.

There was just enough time for him to catch her pupils dilating before Noah and his horse cut across his line of sight, heading toward her.

Gage shook off his quick jab of irritation and looked back toward the wrangler, who'd evidently concluded her talk, because she was swinging up into her own saddle.

"All right," Megan said over her shoulder as her horse plodded out of the ring, "next stop will be Angel's Lookout. Your horses know the way, so just remember to keep your heels down and your attention up!"

As if on cue, Gage's mount—Moonbeam of the well-used straw from the day before—lurched forward with no direction from Gage at all. Everyone else's horses seemed to be doing the same.

They knew the way, and they obviously knew how to follow.

Including Megan and Rory, there were only seven riders in their group: Gage, Noah, the chatty Willow and another couple who must have arrived after dinner the night before. He'd only caught their last name. The Coopers were older and seemed excited with everything around them, as if they were on the trip of their lifetime.

Maybe they were.

Moonbeam fell into line behind the couple as they all settled roughly into a single line. Willow was after him, then Noah.

Rory brought up the rear.

Gage couldn't see her without turning around in his saddle. But he was nevertheless aware of her.

Aware in a way he hadn't been in quite a while.

Behind him, he heard Willow's high-pitched chatter as she talked to Noah. Heard the deeper, less enthusiastic responses from his brother.

The distance between each horse grew the farther they got from the main camp. Eventually, the trail began to curve, heading in a different direction than he'd taken the evening before when he'd found his way to Rory's cabin.

He could hear less of Willow now and more of the breeze in the trees. It sounded like water.

Leather creaked. Horseshoes scuffed on rock.

It was lulling in a way he didn't expect.

Eventually, they headed up a steep hillside and the trail curved like a hairpin. Without needing to turn around at all, Gage could see Rory below. She was nearly abreast with Noah, and even as Gage watched, she threw her head back and her laughter floated up to him. Musical. Infectious.

And then he heard something else he hadn't heard in a very, very long time.

Noah laughed, too.

Gage exhaled and looked up at the horse ahead of him.

Not an issue, he reminded himself yet again.

Not an issue at all.

Chapter Five

"It's a beautiful view, isn't it?"

Gage turned away from the precipice overlooking a group of cabins by the river toward Megan.

After reaching Angel's Lookout, they'd all dismounted so everyone could walk farther out beyond the natural outcropping onto the cantilevered deck that had been built into the side of the steep, rocky incline. It was a beautiful view.

No more so, though, than the mountainside view from the ranch he'd purchased on Rambling Mountain.

"It's a good view," he agreed. "The deck's a nice touch. Looks recent."

Megan rested her hands on the top of the deck rail surrounding the hexagonal structure. She was taller than Rory. With fewer curves and, he suspected, more hard-edged nerve.

"It's almost five years old now," she told him. "It was Rory's idea to have it built. The most recent thing that's been added around here." She glanced over to where Rory was talking with Noah. She was pointing out something in the distance, and his brother's head was angled slightly toward her. The Coopers were busy taking selfies with their cell phones, and Willow was hovering well back from the deck, her fear of heights evidently superseding her interest in anything else.

Gage's gaze slid toward Rory again.

"Does that bother you?"

Gage gave Megan a questioning glance.

She jerked her chin toward Noah. "Your brother's obviously got an eye for her."

"Why would it bother me?"

Her smile had a biting sort of edge to it. Not exactly unkind. But definitely not without cynicism.

His smile was probably not much different.

He looked out at the spectacular view again then turned his attention to the deck. He didn't remember it being on the map Marni had given him when he and Noah arrived at the ranch. The brochure must not have been updated in a long time. "What's the space used for?"

Megan shrugged, apparently content to let the matter of Rory and Noah drop. "We've had wedding ceremonies up here. It'll seat about fifty people, but it's a pain in the butt hauling the chairs up here. We do it if it's requested, of course, but it's a helluva lot easier when people coming here to get hitched just use the wedding barn and gardens."

"Get a lot of weddings?"

"A fair amount. Have one coming in a few weeks. Who knows where they'll end up wanting the ceremony. Their party booked all of Uptown. Ten full days of pre- *and* post-wedding festivities planned." She rubbed her thumb and index finger together. "Lot of money in weddings." She made a face. "Lot of work in weddings, too."

"Not to mention the marriage that follows."

She laughed. "Amen to that."

"Anything besides weddings?"

"Oh, yeah." She spread her arms. "We've done yoga sessions during the summer season. Painting classes. There was even a writers' group who rented out Uptown last spring. They held brainstorming sessions out here."

"Only thing that limits the uses here is imagination," he concluded.

"Basically."

"Anyone in the cabins down there?" He pointed toward the roofs far below.

"The Overlook cabins?" She shook her head. "These days they mostly just get used in summer. They're not as well equipped as the cabins in the main camp or Uptown. Little more rustic, you know? But I can remember years when even those places would be booked all year round. And see where the river bends east of the cabins?" She waited until he nodded. "The rapids are just beyond that. So people who are into white-water rafting love the location of the cabins. But the only time it's safe is in the dead of summer, otherwise the water gets pretty wild. That's why we don't let anyone on the river anymore beyond the bridge to the wedding barn unless it's summertime."

"Have you rafted, too?" Rory asked after appearing at their side, miraculously without Noah. She was looking up at Gage, and a tangle of goldish-brown hair kept drifting into her eyes.

He shoved his hand in his pocket, curbing the desire to tuck the silky-looking strands behind her ear. "Yeah." He'd done quite a lot of it back in the day. But that was before his business began demanding all of his time. "Been a long time, though."

"You should come back in the summer," Megan said, and he couldn't miss the quick look that passed between the two women. She didn't seem bothered by it. "We take groups out on the rapids every day," she finished.

"But not at this time of year." He was watching Rory.

She shook her head, her eyes suddenly looking distant. "Not at this time of year," she confirmed. She shot the cuff of her dull-red coat and glanced at her watch. "It's getting on toward lunchtime, Meg."

"Right." Megan clapped her hands once and

quickly moved away from the rail. With a single whistle, the horses who'd been left to roam began circling around her.

Despite her words, Rory didn't head to her own horse, though. Instead she hung back with Gage. "What do you think of our little overlook?"

"Great view." He told her the same thing he'd told Megan. "The deck's a nice touch."

"Thanks." She looked out at the cabins and river below. "This was my mother's favorite place on the ranch. But she wouldn't let my dad build their cabin here because she thought it needed to be shared with everyone who visited."

Her gaze seemed to linger on the vista for a moment before she turned away.

"Her favorite place, but you're sad," he said quietly.

Her brow knitted for a fraction of a second before she gave a quick little shake of her head. "Not at all," she denied. Then she held out one hand in invitation toward the waiting horses and touched his elbow with her other hand, but just as quickly drew back. "Chef has his famous ribs on the menu out at the chuck wagon." Her voice sounded deliberately bright. "And they are *not* to be missed." As if to urge him on, she headed off toward the horses.

He followed more slowly, watching the way Noah materialized at her side, offering her a leg up even though she was more than capable of mounting her horse without assistance.

Gage passed Willow on his way to Moonbeam. "Not one for heights?"

"Hate them," she admitted with a wrinkled nose. Beneath her heavy-handed makeup, she was a pretty girl. "Tig thinks it's silly."

Gage thought it was silly of her to worry about what Tig did or didn't think. "He didn't come riding with you."

She shrugged one shoulder, trying and failing to look unconcerned. "He had business to take care of."

It didn't matter that the girl was at the ranch with a married man who was old enough to be her father. There was still something sadly sympathetic about her. "Need help up?"

Her expression brightened. "Yes, please."

He walked over and linked his hands together just as Noah had done for Rory. Willow placed her expensive cowboy boot in his palms. She was excruciatingly thin. It took no effort at all to boost her up.

She gave him a beaming smile that seemed to stay there for the duration of the ride back down to the main camp. There, they left the horses in Megan's hands and walked over to the chuck wagon for ribs.

Gage followed along with the rest, returning Bruce Cooper's rueful smile as the other man stretched his legs with feeling. "Don't remember if this place has a whirlpool or not."

Rory overheard him. "We do." Her smile skated

over both Gage and Bruce. "Two, actually. One at the lodge and one at the Uptown camp."

"Thank goodness." Missy Cooper caught up to her husband. She was rubbing her backside. "I used to ride horses when I was a little girl. Why is it that even though I have so much more padding than I did then, it hurts more now?"

"The universe's practical joke on us." Bruce gave her a wink as he dropped his arm around her shoulders.

"How about you?" Rory asked Noah. "Feeling saddle sore yet?"

Noah shook his head. "From a little ride like that? Nah."

"Great," Rory said cheerfully. "Then you'll be all set for our daylong ride next weekend. I'm going to put your name down on the list as soon as I get back to my office."

Gage tucked his tongue in his cheek, looking away from his little brother to keep from laughing at the chagrin Noah couldn't hide.

He joined the line in front of the covered wagon with its long table loaded with food protruding from the back. Beyond the wagon was a cooking pit with two enormous blackened pots hanging from an iron rack. The rack had the same forged wings as the ones on the ranch entrance sign. It reminded him that he wanted to talk to April and Jed about a new name for the Rad.

April had been his go-to when she'd worked for

him. But he'd ended up losing her to Jed Dalloway, who'd been running the ranch for Otis Lambert before he died. Now she and Jed were living in the ramshackle ranch house wallowing in wedded bliss, and they were his partners in turning the Rad into something profitable.

"Who did the ironwork?" he asked the chef when it was his turn in line.

Bart followed his gaze then served him several glistening ribs. "Better ask Rory that," he said. "Corn bread and beans?"

Gage nodded absently. Once his plate was full, he turned toward the weathered picnic tables arranged under several trees. He sat down next to the Coopers, wincing a little as he sat.

It turned out that Bruce Cooper wasn't the only one who could use a hot soak.

Rory eyed the guests as they settled themselves around the picnic tables. The Coopers and Gage sat together at one. Willow and Tig, who'd been at the chuck wagon when they'd arrived, joined Marni and Chef Bart at another.

Even though there was plenty of room at either table, Noah had chosen to sit at the third table, alone. He had a plate of food in front of him that he seemed to have no interest in eating. Instead, he just watched his brother with a vaguely sulky look on his young, handsome face.

She picked up a jug and a couple of glasses and

headed toward him. "You don't have anything to drink, Noah." She set the glasses on the table and held up the jug. "How about some cider?"

"Is it hard?"

"Nope," she said cheerfully and filled one of the glasses with the deep, golden juice. "Just good old-fashioned apple. Chef Bart makes it himself every year."

She set the jug in the center of the table and retrieved her own plate of food before sitting across from him.

She thought she saw surprise in his blue eyes—at least enough to replace the sulkiness for a second.

He hadn't filled his glass yet, so she did it for him. "Just one drink," she encouraged the same way she would have with Killy.

Then she picked up one of the ribs on her plate and began eating.

Before long, she heard Noah's grumbled sigh as he took a sip from his glass.

She didn't act as if she even noticed, and eventually, he tried the ribs.

She hid a smile. It really was like dealing with Killy. Before she'd made it halfway through her own plate of food, Noah had finished all of his and gone back for more. When he sat down again, the sulky look seemed to have been retired altogether.

At least for now.

She refilled his glass and looked past his shoulder to see Gage watching them. It seemed to take a mammoth effort just to look away.

Now she felt too warm. She unbuttoned her coat and focused more narrowly on her tablemate. She didn't want to be getting too warm over any man, much less a *guest* who had the capacity to buy them out if he took it into his mind to talk her father into it.

"So, Noah, tell me more about when you played polo." He'd mentioned it during the ride up to the lookout. "Were you in college?"

He nodded. "Played when I was in high school, too."

Noah made it sound as if high school polo teams were commonplace, and she couldn't help but laugh. "Polo most definitely was *not* on the roster of sports at the high school I went to."

"It was a private school." He wiped his fingers on the bright red bandanna-patterned napkin.

"Did your brother go to the same school?" She cursed herself even as the words came out. Not only because it proved how miserable her self-control was when it came to keeping her mind off Gage, but because Noah immediately shut down.

"No."

"Did you play other sports?" she asked quickly. Brightly. Hoping to rectify her mistake. She gave him a coaxing smile. "Or were you chasing girls?"

The look he gave her underscored his resemblance to Gage. Luckily he seemed to relax enough to ask a question of his own. "Where was your high school?"

"In Wymon. It's the closest town to the ranch here."

"Never heard of it."

"Not surprising," she said wryly. "Population is less than eight hundred people. Wymon has an elementary school, which my son attends now, a middle school and a high school that share the same building, five churches and no bars."

He shuddered visibly. "What about college?"

"I went to art school, actually."

He raised his eyebrows. "You *paint*?"

He made it sound as if she'd told him she danced naked on the moon every third Friday. "Ceramics, actually. Pottery. Clay. That sort of thing."

"So what're you doing in *this* place?"

"It's my home," she said mildly.

"Yeah, but—" He leaned forward. "What do you do all day? Don't you get bored?"

"We're too busy to get bored." Not as busy as they ordinarily were, but she brushed aside the nettlesome fact. "What do *you* do all day?" She grinned. "When you're not enjoying all the comforts here at Angel River, that is."

He shrugged again. "Nothing that matters."

She folded her arms on the table in front of her and leaned toward him. "What *does* matter to you?" Out of the corner of her eye, she couldn't help but be aware of Gage rising from his seat.

Noah seemed to have noticed, too, and didn't answer her question. He couldn't stop watching Gage any more than she could.

Gage carried his tin-style plate over to the chuck wagon and dropped it in the container for dirty dishes.

When he started their way, Rory tried to blame her shiver on her coat falling open but knew better.

She hoped that this particular affliction wore off soon. She wasn't a masochist. She didn't relish another six weeks of butterflies and hypersensitive shivers every time he got within ten feet of her.

He stopped next to their table, obviously taking note of Noah's nearly empty plate. "Glad to see you finally ate something."

As if controlled by a light switch, Noah's expression turned pugnacious.

Hoping to stave off an argument between them, Rory quickly stood. "Nobody can resist Chef Bart's ribs," she said loudly. "Isn't that right, everyone?" She glanced around at the rest of the guests, and by some divine intervention, they seemed to grasp her intention.

To a one, they began clapping and cheering for the chef, who blushed at the sudden accolades.

"Only thing to top it off is dessert," Marni added as she rose and went over to the chuck wagon. She pulled out a container and flipped off the lid to reveal a display of enormous cookies individually wrapped in cellophane. She offered Noah first choice. "Plenty of options," she coaxed. "My faves are the oatmeal raisin. Chef Bart dries his own grapes, if you can believe it. Best raisins you'll ever taste."

While Marni continued extolling the glories of Chef's cookie selection, Rory took her plate over to the plastic bin and set it inside. Gage followed her.

She glanced at her watch. "There's still time for a few hours in the office. I'll be working on a couple of inquiries that came in last night." Hopefully she could convert them into actual bookings.

She couldn't help being disappointed when Gage declined, even though she'd expected him to. She doubted that he needed a lesson in processing reservations now that she knew he maintained an interest in the projects he developed. It was probably one of those tasks he prided himself on having tried at least once.

"All right, then." She looked over at Noah. "Be sure to participate in one of the afternoon activities."

"Skeet shooting or rock climbing," Marni interjected. "Can't go wrong with either one."

"Or a session with me in the bakery," Chef Bart reminded. "Soufflés."

"There you go." Rory just couldn't help herself. She looked from Noah to Gage. "Hopefully something whets everyone's interest. And if not, there's nothing wrong with relaxing at the lodge with a book or a game of horseshoes."

"Or a cold beer," Tig said with a hearty chuckle.

Pretending she didn't see Noah's grimace, Rory said her goodbyes and escaped.

As soon as she set off on foot toward the lodge, though, Gage fell into step right alongside her.

She shoved her fists into her coat pockets, watching him from the corner of her eye. "Thought you were giving the office a pass."

"I am." He gave that now-familiar pat at his chest before he dropped his hand. "I need to take care of some business with my lawyer."

"Every time we have a lawyer here as a guest, I have nightmares of being sued for something trivial. Like the baking lesson with Chef Bart is a sham 'cause the lawyer's soufflé fell flat."

Gage laughed.

She was almost getting used to the shivers slipping delectably down her spine every time he did so.

She ducked her head slightly and walked a little faster.

He didn't have to make any effort to keep up. "Thanks, by the way, for coming on the ride this morning."

"Sure. Noah rides very well." Deep inside her pockets, she curled her fingers into her palms. *Just leave it at that, Rory.*

She repeated the admonishment to herself in time with her boots hitting the gravel road. *Leave...it...*

She sneaked a look at Gage from beneath her lashes.

Leave...it...

"He even played polo." So much for leaving it.

If she'd expected him to be surprised she knew that, maybe even a little jealous, she was disappointed.

"Which is the reason he rides well," was all Gage said.

In a neutral voice.

An I-don't-really-give-a-damn voice.

She kicked a pebble out of her path and watched it skitter and bounce until it came to land on the side of the pathway. "It's obvious you've ridden horses more than just a time or two, yourself," she said. "Did you play polo, too?"

"No." He didn't elaborate.

It was like pulling teeth. And she'd never enjoyed dentistry.

As she struggled to come up with something to say, she spotted Megan on one of the UTVs heading away from the lodge. Divine intervention. "There's Megan. I need to go over some stuff with her." It wasn't an outright lie. There was always something she needed to go over with every single person on the Angel River crew. "Good luck with your lawyer."

She barely waited for a response before she waved to get Megan's attention and ran after her.

She was breathless once she reached the UTV. "Hey." She propped her hands on her hips and hauled in a deep breath.

Megan had a definite glint in her eye. "Running from temptation always makes a person out of breath."

"I don't know what you're talking about." Of course, Rory went and ruined that particular pronouncement by sneaking a look back in Gage's direction.

He was too far away to see his expression, but he'd nearly reached his cabin. His stride was long. Ground-eating. All business.

He didn't look her way as he reached the deck surrounding the cabin and disappeared inside.

She felt her breath leak out of her.

"He's been here only a few days," Megan said. "What're you going to be like after he's been here two months?"

"He's not staying two months."

"Okay. A month and a half," Megan allowed. Her voice was tart. "Huge difference. Astronomical."

"Oh, be quiet."

Megan looked at the imaginary watch on her wrist. "Let's see. October's kaput."

"Don't let Killy hear you say that. He's been talking about nothing but the Halloween carnival in town."

Her attempted change of subject was lost on Megan. "Gorgeous Gage will be here until after gobble-gobble day. I give you—" She squinted as if in great thought. "Three weeks. Less if you dress up as something sexy for the bonfire on Saturday."

Rory climbed into the UTV beside Megan. "For

what?" she asked even though she knew better than to encourage her friend.

"Before you're knocking boots."

Rory rolled her eyes, trying to squash the images that suddenly filled her head. "I don't get involved with our guests," she said severely. "You know that."

"Yeah, not since Jon." Megan ignored the stony look Rory gave her. "You told me yourself. Gage isn't the typical garden-variety guest."

Rory pressed her fingertips to her temples to stop the pain suddenly throbbing behind her eyes. "Can you just drive or something? At least *look* like we have important things to take care of?"

The UTV lurched into motion, but instead of continuing to drive away from the lodge and the adjacent cabins, Megan made a wide, loopy U-turn. "I think it's fairly important for you to venture out of your self-imposed sex desert."

Rory dropped her hand. "Megan!"

The other woman just shrugged, unrepentant.

"I could say the same about you," Rory grumbled. "And if you expect *me* to put on a costume for the bonfire Saturday night, then you'd better do so as well. And that does *not* include showing up like Annie Oakley, because that's your usual look. And *where* are we going right now?"

"Forgot I need to drop off the firewood." Megan jerked her head to indicate the split logs in the cargo box. "And I'm *not* the same as you, because *this*

Annie Oakley freely admits that the only thing she thinks men are good for is a good scr—"

Rory lifted her hand, cutting her off. "Yes, you've told me that numerous times." She was already stepping out of the vehicle next to the firepit before they came to a full stop. She grabbed the logs and deftly stacked them near the pit, then swung right back into the utility vehicle.

Megan hit the gas even before Rory's rear hit the seat. She zipped toward the road between the lodge and the cabins. "Whereas you, missy, still believe in all that happily-ever-after stuff. In fact, I think you should dress up like a bride Saturday night."

Rory tossed up her hands. "A minute ago, I was merely sex-starved!"

As Megan snorted with laughter, Rory spotted Gage standing in the doorway of his cabin.

Close enough to have heard every darn word.

Chapter Six

"Cap'n 'Merica saves the day!" As Rory turned off the engine, Killy hopped out of the truck, the buckle on his safety belt clanking hard against the door frame.

He didn't notice.

He was too busy running around, brandishing his cardboard shield and enjoying the swish of the superhero cape that he'd won in the costume parade at the Halloween carnival. He climbed atop a tree stump that was almost as tall as he was, hopped onto the corner of the patio deck, then back down again.

She was still gathering their belongings from the back seat of the truck—including his stuff that she'd told him to carry in himself—when he disappeared around the corner of the cabin, though she could still hear his enthusiastic whoops.

"That's a lot of energy."

She dropped the armload of gear she'd gathered as she whirled to see Gage standing a few feet away. He'd obviously walked over again. There was no sign of his vehicle or one of the UTVs. "I let him have more Halloween candy than was probably wise," she said, sounding breathless to her own ears.

To hide her reaction, she stuck her head back inside the truck, gathering up her canvas shopping bag, the jacket Killy had abandoned hours ago, the enormous plastic pumpkin filled with his sugary loot from the carnival and the plastic bag containing the goldfish also won in a water pistol game.

"Can I help you with something there?"

"I've got it," she answered brightly and shoved the truck door closed with her hip. She could sense him looking at her and felt her cheeks turning hot. It was pretty annoying. "Have a delicate balance going here." She slipped between him and the truck, heading toward the cabin. "Lose one item and the whole wagon's in danger." From the corner of her eye, she could see Killy now squatting in the road, undoubtedly gathering another fascinating piece of gravel to add to the jumble of rocks he kept in his room. She headed up the steps to the front door, but before she could maneuver enough finger strength to turn the knob, Gage beat her to it.

She felt the brush of his shoulder and hurried

even more quickly inside—so quickly, in fact, that she managed to catch the heel of her boot on the threshold. She didn't even have a chance to gasp or groan or curse her own clumsiness as she pitched forward.

Gage caught her just as the plastic pumpkin bounced against the hardwood floor, shooting out a shower of penny-candy shrapnel. She barely managed to keep from dropping the poor goldfish, and her breath left her in a whoosh when she came up hard against Gage's side. Her canvas bag of groceries was caught between them, and no amount of self-consciousness was enough to keep her gaze from flying up to his.

He may have kept her from falling flat on her face, but she still had the sensation of falling headlong into his intense brown eyes.

"You okay?"

She managed some sort of a croaky sound.

"Squashed, I'm afraid." He reached between them and heat rushed through her veins as his knuckles brushed briefly against her breast. She stared stupidly at the loaf of bread he'd extracted from the bag.

"Mommy!" Killy shoved her from behind and dived to the floor, intent on rescuing his carnival treats. "You spilled my candy!"

Pushed together once more, she and Gage both winced at the sharp edges of the cans inside the grocery bag pressed between them. She tried to step back, but her foot landed on Killy's superhero cape, pinning him to the spot and earning her a second, even more outraged yelp from him.

She heard Gage's faint oath, then squealed like a stuck pig when he suddenly wrapped his arm around her waist and lifted her out of the tangle of her son's legs—he surely had sprouted a few extra in the last millisecond—and took a long step right over him.

They could all hear the crunch of hard candies beneath his boots before he set her back on her feet beyond the debris field. Killy's "Mo-om!" contained a new level of despair.

"Killy, it's just a few pieces of hard candy!"

The mulish look he gave her encompassed Gage as well. She'd finally managed to extract her arm from the tangled loop of the grocery bag and dumped it on the couch, then set the poor fish on the mantel. At least she hadn't dropped that, too.

She pointed toward the kitchen. "Go and get a big bowl to put your candy in," she told Killy. "The red one we use when I make popcorn."

He was scooping candy into a pile. "But—"

"Now."

He huffed and got to his feet, then stomped out of the living room.

Rory gave Gage a quick glance. "Sorry. He's overtired and needs a nap, but he's six and there's not a chance in the world I'll get him to take one."

"And I crunched his—" he'd crouched down to pick up one of the wrappers "—Spicy Hots. Major crime. Used to eat these things by the pound when I was a kid. Didn't know they still made them."

So had she. "He'll survive. Which is more than I can say for the pumpkin." She scooped up the two pieces of brittle plastic and dropped them on the couch, too. With Gage there, she was very aware of the general untidiness of the room. Killy's discarded school backpack on the floor. Her coffee mug and Killy's unfinished bowl of cereal from that morning still sitting on the table in the dining area.

She could hear her little boy slamming all the cupboard doors in the kitchen even though he knew very well where the large popcorn bowl was. She couldn't fault him too much, though. She'd been known to slam a door or two herself when she was angry.

"Have a seat," she told Gage as she transferred one of Killy's oversize plastic dinosaurs from the cushion of an armchair to the coffee table. "Sorry about the, uh, the—" She broke off at the sound of a loud crash from the kitchen. She'd been about to say "mess," but she sighed. "Insanity," she said instead and hurried into the kitchen.

Killy was sitting on the floor in the midst of several pots and pans, unharmed despite the terrific crash he'd caused.

She crouched beside him. "Where do we keep the popcorn bowl?"

His chin was set, but at her continued silence, he

finally pointed a finger at the cupboard on the other side of the stove. "Over there."

He sounded so disgruntled she had to work hard not to smile. "So why were you looking in here where the pots go?" She picked up a small frying pan and set it back inside the cupboard.

"Dunno."

She rubbed her palm over his sweaty forehead, pushing back his hair and gently directing his focus up to her face again. "If you had carried your candy in like I asked you to in the first place, none of this would've happened," she said calmly. "So you can put the pans back where they belong and get the popcorn bowl or else I'll get the broom and sweep up your candy and whatever I sweep up is going in the trash. So you choose."

He began shoving pans back into the cupboard. It was a disorderly jumble, but she took it as a win and went back into the living room.

Gage was standing near the fireplace, studying the goldfish swimming around in its water bubble.

She watched him for a moment and then flushed all over again when her gaze collided with his in the mirror hanging above the mantel.

Then she caught her own reflection. She'd entirely forgotten her face-painting session at the carnival. Purple-and-green fairy wings radiated from her eyes and met at the center of her forehead in a sunburst of silvery stars.

No wonder he kept staring at her.

"Halloween carnival," she explained, gesturing vaguely at her face. "If I manage not to smear it before tonight, I figure it'll do double duty for the bonfire." She rubbed her hand down her thigh. "You, uh, you plan to go, don't you? Sooner or later you should, and tonight all of the staff'll be celebrating there, too. I have a small group coming in to provide live music."

"Hadn't planned on it. But maybe I need to reconsider." A faint smile was playing around his lips. Lips that were perfectly sculpted. Perfectly shaped. Perfectly—

She cursed her vivid imagination and walked over to the mantel to grab the bag containing the fish. "You should. And your brother, too." She held up the bag, wishing she hadn't mentioned the bonfire at all. "I'd better get this guy in a real fishbowl."

"Do you have one?"

"Somewhere." She pulled open the lowest drawer in the built-in shelves by the fireplace and began poking through it. "From the last time we attempted to keep a fish. Also won from a kids' carnival last spring." The more she talked, the less she had to think about the silly fairy wings painted on her face. "But at the time I figured better a goldfish than a bunny or a chick, which were also prizes."

"Attempted?"

"Voilà." She extracted the bowl and plucked out the can of fish food that had been stored inside it.

"Yeah. He lasted about three weeks. Think we over-fed the poor thing."

"Or maybe it was from trying to keep a goldfish in a bowl like that." Gage's fingers brushed hers as he took the glass sphere from her. "Even goldfish need the proper temperature. Proper water filtration."

"Well." She shook the fish food. "This is all we've got. Has to be better than a zip-top bag." She rounded the couch, avoiding the scattered mess of candy, and went into the kitchen, where Killy was just finishing putting away the pots and pans.

Gage followed and set the fishbowl on the counter. She rinsed it out and then poured the contents of the baggie inside the bowl. The fish darted around its expansive new digs. She bent over, looking closely at it. "All right, Nelson. Hang in there the best you can, right?"

"Nelson?"

She glanced over her shoulder at Gage. "Yeah. Nelson. Something wrong with that?"

His lips were tilted in a faint smile. "Nope. Did you name him, Killy?"

Her son was holding the popcorn bowl. His expression when he looked at Gage was still accusatory. "No." He carried the bowl with him out of the kitchen. "Mommy won him," he said as he went.

Gage looked at her, and she felt the blush creeping up again.

"Water pistol race," she explained. "You know.

Who can fill the balloon the fastest with the water you shoot into the target?"

His smile widened, and she felt more self-conscious than ever. "What, uh, what brought you here this afternoon, anyway? Everything going all right with your visit so far?"

"Had breakfast with your father again."

She hoped her fairy paint hid her worry. "Has he brought you over to the dark side of oatmeal yet? Or did Chef Bart come to your rescue?"

"Actually, Chef Bart let me loose in his kitchen."

"You don't say." She was surprised. "What did you make?"

"Breakfast burritos." He shrugged dismissively. "Throw everything in with some scrambled eggs and cheese and wrap it in a tortilla."

"Breakfast of the gods." She leaned around him to look out at Killy. His legs protruded from beneath the sofa. She wondered what all he would find beneath it besides a piece or two of his precious candy.

She leaned back again, pressing her hands against the countertop behind her. Gage had had breakfast with her father the previous day, too. Before the trail ride. She'd only learned about it when she and Killy had dinner with her dad the night before. "Discuss anything interesting?"

"Nothing in particular. He didn't stay long after his oatmeal. Thought he looked tired."

That answer wasn't exactly a comfort.

"I might be able to help you when it comes to finding someone for your spa," he said out of the blue.

She didn't want to admit they needed help with anything. "Oh?"

"Someone I've known for a long time. She owns a string of day spas in Colorado. Successful ones."

Rory began shaking her head before he even finished speaking. "If she owns spas, she wouldn't be interested in working for Angel River as an employee."

"You could contract out the space. Remove that burden from your payroll but still offer spa services. She owns and operates the spa in one of the residential towers I own."

"That's not the way we've done things here."

"Change isn't always a bad thing, you know."

How many times had she said that to her father? And then he'd been diagnosed with cancer and everything had changed. "We're like a family here. The reason why Angel River is as special as it is, is because our particular way of doing things runs through every inch of our operation."

"From horses to hot tubs?"

She couldn't tell if he was mocking or not. "As a matter of fact, yes."

"She still might be of help," he said. "Sybil cut her teeth in a five-star resort in Switzerland."

"This is Wyoming," Rory reminded. "We're a long way from Switzerland."

"With the prices you charge, not so much."

Her chin went up. "You think we're overpriced?"

"I didn't say that." His voice was mild, but that didn't stop her from being defensive. "What I am saying," he continued, "is that you have some key positions that have needed filling for too long. Particularly when you're trying to maintain a certain level of service. Sybil might be able to help you with one of them." He pulled a small leather case from his back pocket. He flipped it open and removed a business card that he set on her counter next to her clenched fingers. "That's her number." He returned the case to his pocket.

Rory wished she didn't notice the way his movements stretched his expensively casual gray sweater across his chest. "Is that why you walked up here? Just to give me Sybil's contact information?"

He frowned slightly. "Actually, I came up here because it's a nice walk and if I'd spent another minute with my brother, somebody would've been fishing him out of the river where I wanted to throw him."

Her jaw dropped.

"And I wish I were exaggerating," he said grimly.

Then he turned on his heel and left the kitchen. "I'm sorry I stepped on your candy, Killy," she heard him say a moment before she heard the front door open and close.

Rory's shoulders slumped.

She pressed her hand to the fluttering in her

chest, then dashed through the living room and followed him out the door.

Gage's stride was something to behold. She had to jog to catch up to him. When she did, she stared at the unlit cigarette he'd tucked in the corner of his mouth. "I didn't know you smoked."

He gave her an irritated look and palmed the cigarette, returning it to the battered pack he pulled from his jacket. "I don't."

She raised her eyebrows. "Looks are deceiving, I guess."

He exhaled and gazed behind her at the cluster of staff cabins that comprised Angel Camp, probably wishing she'd return to hers. "I quit smoking years ago. I carry the pack because—" He exhaled softly and shook his head, pocketing the pack again. "I don't know why," he muttered.

"My ex-husband was a recovering alcoholic," she admitted. "He kept a full bottle of whiskey on the shelf. Like a reminder. But if he was feeling stressed about something, he'd take it off the shelf. Set it on the table and just stare at it."

"Is that why you split up? Because he drank?"

"We split up because he was a liar and a cheat," she said evenly. "But actually, to be fair, Jon never did fall off the wagon. Not while we were together, at least, no matter how many times he took that bottle down. So maybe in his case, the method worked."

"Maybe he stayed sober for you and his son."

She couldn't help the derisive snort. "Jon's never even met Killy."

"Never?" Gage's expression made her wish she'd controlled her wayward tongue.

She scuffed her boot sole against the gravel and shook her head. "Why were you frustrated with Noah today?"

"Because I'm always frustrated with him," Gage muttered. He slowly turned his head as if his neck were paining him. "He's lazy. Moody and spoiled. Kid has never appreciated everything he has going for him."

"Sounds like a teenager."

"Which he isn't."

"Obviously you know him best, but he certainly admires you."

It was Gage's turn to snort. "He can't stand the air I breathe." He started to reach into his pocket again but checked the motion. "Which he told me in no uncertain terms earlier today."

"Why?"

He spread his hands. "Imagine any reason under the sun," he said. "There's a good chance he's thought of it and blames me for it."

"Like bringing him here in the first place?" Gage had told her Noah's choice had been Gage or jail, but she found that a little hard to believe. "Is he feeling too cooped up here at the ranch?"

"It's what I expected, but—" He shook his head. "He's very taken with you," he said abruptly.

She gave a half laugh. "Please. Marni's a much more likely object of his attention. She's the one who has a crush on him. I'm just a...a big sister figure or someth—"

Gage touched her lips with his finger, shocking her into silence. "There are a lot of things I don't know about my brother." His voice was low. "But this isn't one of them."

His hand dropped away immediately, but the damage was done. She could hardly think past the tingling in her lips. She took a step away, clearing her throat. "You don't have to worry," she finally managed in an only slightly garbled tone. "We discourage our crew from having personal relationships with guests."

He looked skeptical. "And the rule applies to you?"

The memory of him overhearing her conversation with Megan was much too fresh. "Yes." Her tone grew firmer. "Even me." *Especially me.*

"Is it worth someone's job if they violate the policy?"

"You mean would we fire someone over it?"

"You're a family here," he reminded her. "You going to fire one of your 'family' for getting too cozy with a guest?"

Now she was certain he was mocking her. The way he'd air-quoted the word *family* clinched it, and it set her teeth on edge.

"If I had to," she said flatly. "Maybe you can't

prevent those lines from being crossed in a company as large as yours, but here?" She crossed her arms over her chest. "You needn't worry about your brother where I'm concerned. Or Marni or Megan or anyone else, for that matter. I can promise you that your little brother is perfectly safe from all of us."

"I'm more worried that all of you aren't perfectly safe from him."

That took the wind out of her sails for a moment. "Marni can handle herself."

"Oh, for Go—" He broke off, swallowing his obvious impatience. "Not Marni. *You.*"

She tossed out her arms, exasperated as well. "What on earth for? I just told you I don't get involved with guests!"

He closed the distance she'd put between them. "Noah has a way of getting under people's skin."

"Well, not mine," she quickly assured him. The only one getting under her skin was Gage, and she had no intention of admitting it.

The only question was how long she'd be able to hide it.

Chapter Seven

Despite Rory's anxiety, the following days slid into a fairly easy routine.

Gage mucked stalls several times—with and without her. She showed him the compost setup and drove him over to Seth's place to introduce them. She'd been surprised by the knowledge Gage had when it came to the vagaries of cattle ranching. But by then, she ought to have known better where he was concerned. The man really did seem to know something about most everything. By the end of the week, he'd spent as much time with Seth as he had with her.

She knew Gage had seen plenty of her father, too, because half the time when she returned with Killy from the bus stop, she found them together in the office. The day before, in fact, they'd been playing chess.

She hadn't seen her dad play since before her mother died.

She'd crept back out of the office, leaving them to it, and spent a few extra hours with her son, which was never a bad thing.

She rarely saw Noah, though. Even though she'd joked about putting him down for the daylong ride that weekend, she hadn't. Nor had he added his name to the list, which settled Gage's claim that Noah was "taken with" her as far as she was concerned. According to Marni, Noah emerged daily when Frannie got there to clean the cabin, usually walking down to the river.

Always alone.

Rory considered asking Gage if Noah would be better off with his own cabin—they had plenty available, and maybe it would be less stressful for the brothers if they had more space between them. But she decided against sticking her nose where it didn't belong. If Gage had thought that arrangement would be better, it would already be a done deal.

In fact, after their last conversation about Noah, Gage had barely mentioned his name to her again. She hoped that meant they had reached some sort of détente, but she had her doubts.

Gage didn't offer any more staffing suggestions, either, and she was glad. She posted the spa manager position again on a few more websites and even scheduled a phone interview with a possible office assistant.

But when the candidate didn't bother to answer the phone at their agreed-upon time—or even bother to return the message Rory had left—she'd tossed the girl's application in the trash. It briefly made her wonder if she should have accepted Gage's help. But only briefly.

Regrettably, Gage still gave her that shiver down her spine whenever he was around. But at least by the end of the week she'd more or less regained her ability to keep her train of thought whenever their gazes happened to meet.

Though she'd succeeded on that score, her dreams at night were still rife with him. She'd gotten so she was afraid to go to sleep for fear that she'd be blushing the next day when she had to face him again.

Of course, Megan thought the entire situation was hilarious when Rory admitted the problem and tried to get out of the long trail ride she'd committed to before Gage and his brother had even arrived at the ranch.

"No way, girlfriend." Megan was using a curry brush on Moonbeam and didn't miss a stroke as she gave Rory a look. "Willow is signed up and if I have to listen to her exclaim over every little thing for hours on end, so do you. This was your idea, if you recall. So you're going. You're just getting the heebie-jeebies because Gorgeous Gage will be there. Besides. You want to disappoint Killy? This is the first time you're letting him go out with us."

Knowing that Megan was right didn't help. Feeling entirely out of sorts, Rory returned to the lodge. The sight of Gage pacing back and forth on the deck outside the great room while he talked on the phone was now commonplace.

She supposed a man like him couldn't get away from his business demands for long. Even Tig—who rarely spent less than a month at a time at Angel River—had to check in occasionally, and it was his wife who actually ran their business.

Two new bookings had arrived that week—the Murphys and the Delgados—and she stopped long enough to check in on them where they were sitting near the fireplace before heading back to her office.

She paid some bills and made some calls, including one confirming the officiant she'd arranged for the upcoming wedding. She was doodling on her desk pad while she listened to yet another voice mail from Bitsy Pith—the mother of the bride—when Gage entered the office. His gaze skated over her face and she pretended to give the voice mail more attention than it actually warranted. Before long his cell phone rang and he left again.

She hung up while Bitsy's message was still playing. So far, in the half dozen that the woman left, she'd changed her mind over the welcome reception menu every single time. Now she was back to the one she'd originally chosen four months ago.

Rory made yet another note for Chef Bart to add to his increasingly thick pile and left the office to pick up Killy. She was just pulling away from the lodge in the utility vehicle when she noticed Noah sitting on the front porch of his cabin.

She didn't have a lot of patience with someone who was guilty of driving under the influence, but there was still something about the young man that tugged at her. No matter what Gage said about his brother, she recognized unhappiness when she saw it and felt sympathy.

She pulled the UTV around to stop in front of his cabin and sent him a smile. "Hey there, stranger. Want to go for a spin?"

His hair was in a messy twist on his head, and he needed a shave. With the slouchy athletic pants and shapeless sweatshirt that hung on his thin frame, he definitely looked the part of the lazy brother. But he pushed off his chair and climbed in. "Where to?"

"Nowhere exciting. The bus stop. I need to pick up my son after school." When he didn't make any attempt to climb back out, she started off again. "Frannie cleaning?"

He nodded.

"Hear you've been exploring down by the river. You know that's the route we'll be taking on the ride tomorrow. We'll follow it all the way around to Overlook Camp. Those are the cabins I pointed out the day we rode up to the lookout. The leaves are about at their peak. It should be a beautiful ride."

She gave him a coaxing smile. "You really should come along. It'll be fun. Chef Bart sends us off with boxed lunches."

He gave a half laugh. "Is that supposed to be a real perk?"

"Some people think so." She grinned. "My son does, at any rate."

"Killy, right?"

"Yep. He's six. Nearly everything is an adventure where he's concerned. It'll be his first time going on a long ride with us. Usually he spends the day with my father or his friend Damon. Frannie's boy." She slowed to take the fork in the loop road. "This time they're both coming."

"Who else?"

She wondered if that was his way of finding out if his brother was going. "Most everyone here. We don't have any new guests arriving for a while." Not until the wedding group was due the following weekend.

"You don't have a lot of business, do you?"

"Ouch." She gave him a pointed look. "I'm surprised you noticed, considering you barely stick your nose out of the cabin."

His lips twitched. "Ouch," he returned.

The first day they'd arrived, she hadn't thought there was much resemblance between him and Gage, but times like this had her rethinking. "We don't have as much business as we usually do this time of year," she admitted. "But I'm working on it."

"Is that what Gage is doing with you?"

She gave him another look, longer this time. "Do the two of you *ever* talk?"

"Not if we can help it."

That was inconceivable to her. "He's learning how we do what we do."

"Why?"

There didn't seem to be any point in hiding it. "So he can turn around and do it better with his own guest ranch." They were jostled as they drove over bumps in the road.

"That's Gage. Always has to be better than everyone else."

She didn't see it. Not after the past week. Yes, he collected information and knowledge like some people collected coins, but when it came down to it, he was a lot less arrogant than she'd expected.

It still didn't mean she trusted him.

They arrived at the stop just as the big yellow bus was pulling up. Toonie came off first, not looking up from her paperback as she headed to her dad's pickup. The boys were next, throwing the usual football. But this time, when it went sailing over Killy's head, Noah leaped out of the utility vehicle and caught it neatly.

It was the fastest she'd seen him move, so she probably had the same look of astonishment on her face as her son did. Noah flipped the ball expertly to her son, and this time Killy did catch it. Astrid was yelling for Damon to hurry up, so the boys waved at each other and Killy jogged over to the UTV.

He peered up at Noah. "Are you my mom's boy-friend?"

Rory gaped. "Killy! Of course he isn't."

Noah just laughed.

"Noah's staying in one of the guest cabins." She gestured for Killy to climb into the narrow wedge of a rear seat. "Use the seat belt."

He did as told, but hung forward as she turned the vehicle around to leave. "Are you a football player?"

Noah laughed again. Which had to be a record for number of times that happened in a day. "No. Are you?"

Killy grinned broadly. His skinny chest puffed out beneath his jacket. "I will be."

"It's good to have goals," Noah told him.

"Yes, it is." Rory caught his eye. "So. About the ride tomorrow?"

He looked from Killy back to her again. "Yeah, fine. I mean, who can resist a boxed lunch?"

Turned out, no one got a boxed lunch after all.

Because the next morning, they woke to a torren-tial downpour that lasted the entire day.

"If I didn't know better, I'd think you did some fancy rain dance to conjure this up," Megan said as she and Rory stood together in the lodge staring out the window over the deck. "But as much as I know you wanted to avoid another full-on day with the

Gorgeous G, not even you have the skill for this."
Outside, the rain was coming down in sheets.

Behind them, the guests were all sprawled out
waiting for Bart to ring the dinner bell. The rainy
day had turned them into happy couch potatoes.
Even Willow was quiet for once, her legs over Tig's
lap while he read a book.

The only ones missing were Noah and Gage.
She'd seen Gage for a while earlier; he'd been talking to Willow and the Delgados. But then he'd disappeared.

She doubted that he was happily couch potato-
ing along with his brother in the Brown cabin. More
likely, he was off somewhere talking on his phone.

Killy and Damon, on the other hand, were practically bouncing off the walls after being cooped
inside all day long. Right now, they were running
up and down the hallway near the office. "I need to
get these guys out of here," she told Megan. "You
and Marni okay holding down the fort with Bart?"

"Have we ever *not* been okay?" Megan's brows
rose meaningfully. "I'm gonna set up the white
screen in here while they're having dinner, and we'll
watch Humphrey and Ingrid stare longingly at each
other while we make s'mores in the fireplace. It'll
be one of those unexpected nights that guests go
home raving about."

So Rory corralled the boys and tucked them into
her pickup to drive them back up to Angel Camp.
She stopped off in front of her dad's cabin to see if

he wanted to come up to their place to share the pan of lasagna she'd stolen from Bart. Leaving the boys in the truck, she darted through his front door. "I've got food—" She broke off.

Her dad was sitting at his table eating pizza with Gage, and both of them gave her a surprised look. "Everything all right, honey?" her dad asked.

She knew her jaw was flapping in the breeze. She nodded. "Just, uh, just checking that you—" she bumped into the door as she backed her way out "—you got dinner okay. Gottheboys. Gottarun." She slammed the door on her way out and ran back to the truck.

Rain was dripping from her hair into her eyes when she slid behind the wheel again.

"Thought we was getting Grandpa," Killy said.

"We *were*," she corrected absently as she drove the rest of the way to their cabin.

Chess. Pizza.

What else was going on that she didn't know about?

She got the boys inside, fed and eventually settled for the night in sleeping bags on the floor in Killy's room. She could still hear them giggling and whispering an hour later, but she didn't have the heart to come down on them. It meant that getting them going would be harder than ever the next morning, but since it wasn't the week she helped Bart make bread, it didn't matter.

She decided to draw herself a rare bath, then

poured a glass of wine and sank up to her neck in bubbles.

It was a small amount of bliss.

Which naturally meant it didn't have a chance in Hades of lasting.

She hadn't even gotten to the bottom of the wineglass when she heard knocking on the door.

Somehow she knew it wasn't just anyone. Because everyone else would have just picked up the phone and called her. Gage was the only one to show up unexpectedly at her cabin time and time again.

She stood and sluiced away the bubbles before stepping out of the tub and pulling on her ancient bathrobe.

She tugged Killy's door the rest of the way closed as she passed his room and hurried downstairs. But by the time she reached the door, the knocking had stopped.

She opened it and stuck her head out. "Gage?"

He was just stepping down the porch steps and he turned. Not even he could act oblivious to the rain pouring down over the umbrella bearing the small Angel River logo. He had to have gotten the umbrella from her dad. The gift shop had run out of them months ago, and she hadn't yet reordered more.

She held her robe close to her throat. "Did you need something?" Even though most of her was tucked behind the doorway, he couldn't fail to notice she wasn't dressed for visitors.

"Sorry." He sounded oddly gruff. "Didn't mean

to interrupt your—" He broke off, gesturing. It seemed unlikely that he was as thrown by the sight of her as she'd been to find him eating pizza with her father, but for a gratifying moment, it felt that way.

"But you *are* here," she prompted. "And I can't help wondering why."

He took one of the porch steps. "Sean was telling me about the holiday season here."

Great. "What about it?"

"That it should be one of your busiest times, but this year it's not," he said bluntly. "Ever thought about offering a flash deal?"

She pushed her hair behind her ear, this time legitimately shivering from the cold and not his presence. "Done it, and we didn't even get a bump."

He moved up another step. "But did you do it for a holiday getaway? You know, most of your guests are coming here and staying a week or better. Tig—"

"Tig doesn't represent the majority of our guests."

"Fine. But my point is they're here for more than a couple nights. The Delgados? They're using all of their two weeks of vacation here."

"You think it's not a good thing for someone to *want* to spend an entire vacation here?"

"No, I'm saying it's expensive as hell." He raised a quick hand. "And I know Stanton resorts are expensive, too. But not a one of them is all-inclusive. It's a different animal entirely."

She wasn't convinced of that, but she grabbed her coat from its hook and swung it around her shoulders before opening the door a few inches more. "Okay. So?"

"So I'm saying there's also a whole market of people who don't have time to invest in a full-blown vacation. They just want a quick getaway. Two nights. Three nights. Christmas is on a Friday this year. People come in Christmas Eve. Stay until the day after Christmas. Or even two days after. Still have time to get back to work on Monday before they start celebrating New Year's."

She tilted her head. "You make your people come into the office between Christmas and New Year's, don't you."

He just gave her a look. He'd reached the top of the steps, and he lowered the umbrella to one side.

She sighed and pulled the door wide. "I'm freezing. You might as well come in." Still wearing the coat over her robe, she went over to the couch and curled in the corner, dragging an afghan over herself for good measure.

He left the umbrella outside and closed the door. He didn't really look away from her, but she was certain that he was taking in every detail of the cabin. At least it was a little more orderly than the last time he'd been there.

"How's Nelson?"

She glanced at the fishbowl on the dining room table. "Still swimming. Don't you think it's a little late to start promoting a deal for *this* Christmas?"

"In a perfect world. But nothing's perfect. Come

up with a new angle. Offer a flash deal—a little taste of Angel River at a price they can't resist in a short-stay package. And promote the hell out of it in places you don't ordinarily think about."

He wasn't bubbling over with Willow-level enthusiasm, but still it was enough to intrigue her. "Say we did it," she said cautiously. "What happens if we actually get a good response? I don't have the staff to—"

"Keep your staff focused on a few key areas. You're not getting people in the door for the full Angel River experience." He wasn't quite pacing, but he was moving around the room as he talked. Same way she'd seen him do so often when talking on his phone. "You don't have to offer eight different activities every day to keep them entertained. You're giving them a taste, remember?" He held up his hand. "Food, booze, ambience." He ticked them off. "You've got that covered without anyone having to step foot outside the lodge. Play up the season. All the feel-good stuff people fantasize about for the holidays." He stopped moving and closed his hands over the back of the couch beside her.

She looked away from those long, blunt-edged fingers. "You think that feel-good stuff is just a fantasy?" It was hard to even voice that particular word in his presence without feeling hot inside.

"I think people get caught up in the season and then reality hits."

"Well, hello, Mr. Scrooge," she murmured. "Is

this 'taste of'—" she air-quoted the words "—the sort of thing you have in mind for your ranch on Rambling Mountain?"

"Right now the only thing I have in mind for the Rad is a new name." He suddenly leaned forward on his arms, which brought his head almost down to her level. She couldn't help sucking in a silent breath and shrinking back against the cushions.

Fortunately, he didn't seem to notice. "Speaking of the name, I keep seeing the Angel River logo forged onto metal signs and things. Custom work, obviously. What company did you use?"

She managed to slide off the couch with something approaching casualness. "Nobody you want to work with."

"Why? Difficult to deal with?"

"Something like that." She clasped her arms in front of her. "My ex-husband did it for us."

Gage's eyes glinted with surprise. "When you said he'd never met Killy, for some reason I assumed he'd also never been here at all."

"It was before Killy," she said. "Jon was a guest here."

He straightened slowly. "Is that how you met?"

She wished she'd left off that detail. "I designed the logo, but he did the work." She'd been falling for him from that moment on.

"*You* designed the logo?"

"Don't look so shocked. I do have some skills besides mucking out horse stalls!"

His gaze seemed to look straight down inside her. "Never doubted it."

She was afraid that the shivers resulting from his innuendo would plague her for days.

Chapter Eight

She was right on that score.

In fact, even a week later, she was afraid they'd actually worsened. She felt like she was living on pins and needles where the man was concerned, and by the following Saturday, without Killy there to distract her because he was at Damon's, she resorted to desperate measures.

She got out a chain saw.

If shoveling horse manure couldn't relieve her tension, maybe cutting down the stump in her front yard would.

The torrential rain that postponed their trail ride had moved on after only a day, leaving in its wake a glorious week, weatherwise. The only downside was that the downpour had knocked all the fall leaves from the trees. Every time she looked down at the river, the bare, knobby branches reminded her of skeleton fingers. With everything looking so barren, she wanted the snow to come and soften the landscape whether it was good for Thanksgiving business or not.

She'd also had to spend a day polishing windows at the Uptown camp all over again after the storm. The wedding party was coming in the next day, and she wanted everything to be perfect.

The stump was a good four feet tall and half again as wide. Reducing it to smithereens would take time, even with the chain saw. She was counting on the task to do the trick of reducing her Gage nerves.

She circled the stump, feeling the bright sun on her bare head as she throttled the engine.

But as she eyed the thing, she suddenly saw potential in the dead wood.

She dropped her safety glasses down onto her nose and revved the engine on her chain saw again. The first dip she made against the stump sent a jolt right up through her shoulders.

After that, everything else fell away as she worked. First she made broad, rough swipes that cut away the excess wood from around the shape she saw within. Then she got a little more detailed. A little finer.

Gage heard the chain saw long before he realized that Rory was at the center of the sawdust arching out around her.

And then he couldn't do anything *but* watch, half his heart in his throat and his blood pooling hotly because of the way she swung the dangerous saw around.

It was like watching a dancer. She was so intent on what she was doing, she never even noticed him standing out of range of the spray of disintegrating wood. The saw whined as she angled an incision here, coaxed a curve there.

And then, suddenly, she was done.

She killed the engine and let the tip of the guide bar down at her side. She was breathing hard, her shoulders rising and falling from the exertion. And the expression on her face...

Euphoric.

He ran his hand around his neck, reminding himself that following the instinct to toss her over his shoulder and haul her back to his cave would be universally frowned upon.

She was circling the stump again. But it was no longer a stump at all, and her fingertips danced over the delicate-looking tip of the single unfurled wing that had taken its place. The graceful arc of wood could have been modeled after a peregrine, it was so vividly perfect. "When you talked about skills, you weren't joking."

She jerked around, obviously startled, and pulled off her safety glasses. "I didn't realize I'd gained an audience."

Her cheeks were flushed. Her eyes brilliant.

Everything about her radiated joy. "How could you, when you were playing with that toy?" He gestured toward the wicked-looking chain saw. "Remind me never to get you angry."

Expression sparkling, she set the saw on her patio along with the glasses and began swiping at the slivers of wood clinging to her sweater. It looked like a fairly hopeless endeavor to him, but his fingers still itched to lend aid.

"Are you here for a reason or just to make fun?"

"Not making fun," he assured her as he walked around the creation. "Have you always had a thing for wings?"

"Well, this *is* Angel River." Her smile was sexy as all hell.

"Where'd the name come from, though?"

She laughed outright. "The river, obviously. That's the name of it. Was the name of it before my dad bought this place and will be the name of it long after we're all gone." She leaned over to rake her fingers vigorously through her hair, releasing another cloud of sawdust before straightening and flipping it back.

He nearly swallowed his tongue.

"Now, back to the reason you're—" She broke off at the sight of Megan racing up the road in a UTV, waving her hand wildly.

The exuberance in Rory's expression drained away along with every speck of color in her face. "It always happens," she whispered. "Every time."

"Every time, what?" He slid his arm around her shoulder, because as strong and vibrant as she'd looked carving a falcon's wing out of an ugly tree stump, now she looked brittle enough to shatter to pieces.

But she didn't answer. She just waited until Megan's vehicle skidded to a stop a few feet away.

He saw the quick concern in the woman's eyes as she took in Rory's obvious alarm. "The Uptown group arrived."

Gage felt Rory sag before she suddenly spun away from him, racing inside her house and slamming the door shut after her.

"What the hell?" He glanced at Megan. "One minute she's—" he waved at the stunning bird wing "—and the next it's like she's seen a ghost."

Megan looked from the cabin to the sculpture, seeming to realize something. "Rory created that?"

"With a freaking chain saw. I've never seen—" He broke off. "I'm checking on her," he muttered.

"Be gentle," Megan called after him, entirely unlike her usual self. "Remember what I told you about Sean?"

It took him a minute to make the connection. Earlier that week, when the two of them had been cleaning the horse barn, she'd been recounting the days when Sean had run the place. She'd told him about the day he collapsed, seemingly out of the blue, leading to his cancer diagnosis. "What about it?"

"I was the one who found him."

"Yeah, you told me."

"And I was the one who came up here to tell Rory. She was in her studio working." She looked pointedly at the carving. "Something she hasn't done until now."

Every time. That's what Rory had whispered.

He realized it would have made a lot more sense for Rory's best friend to go in and check on her now, but he went inside the cabin instead. He found Rory in the downstairs bathroom, retching.

He swallowed an oath and slid in beside her— not sure what he could do, but only knowing he needed to do something. She swatted a hand at him, obviously thinking otherwise, and yanked down a towel that she pressed to her face as she flushed the toilet and sat back against the wall. "Go away." Her voice was muffled by the towel.

He wished he could. His life was complicated enough without this. The simple solution would have been to let Megan deal with this.

But he hadn't. And he knew he wouldn't.

So he ran another small towel under the faucet and nudged it into Rory's lax fingers.

Her shoulders moved with a heavy sigh and she exchanged the bath towel for the smaller one, pressing it to her face.

She seemed out of danger of needing the commode, and he lowered the lid to sit. "You're an artist."

Resignation filled her eyes above the edge of the wet towel.

"So why are you running Angel River?"

She swore suddenly and pushed to her feet, using his thighs as leverage in the small space. She stuck her mouth right beneath the sink tap, rinsed and spat, and hurried out of the bathroom.

He followed her back outside to where Megan was still sitting in the UTV.

"The wedding party's not due until tomorrow afternoon," Rory said as if she hadn't just taken a momentary detour.

Megan spread her hands. "Nevertheless, they *are* here. Seth heard they'd landed at the airstrip, and he and Marni shuttled them all to the lodge. Marni said she called you but you didn't answer." Her gaze slid briefly to the wing. "They just arrived." She took a bracing breath. "All fifty-four of them."

"Fifty-four!" Rory's voice rose with disbelief. Her color had returned, and she propped her hands on her hips. Wood splinters still littered the shoulders of her sweater. "Last week they confirmed thirty-six!"

"Gonna be a fun ten days," Megan predicted.

"Why?" Rory tilted back her head. "Hardly any business and now too much?" She had a newly determined look about her. "Uptown has the space, but we're talking eighteen extra people. Do we know if it's just a few extra families?"

"Marni was trying to work that out when I left. I saw some kids in the group, but as for the adults… I recognize a bunch of bar patrons when I see them."

She nodded sagely. "Mark my words, we're going to burn through some booze with this group."

"I'm not worried about the liquor supply. I'm worried about the workload." Rory rubbed her cheek, swiping at the fine sawdust clinging to her skin. "The bride's mom has told me more than once they'll want a babysitter. Call Astrid. Make sure she'll be available. Marni won't be able to do it now. We'll need her to run activities. Chef knows we've got extra heads?"

Megan nodded.

"All right, then." Rory looked like she was about to climb into the UTV. Then she flushed, dusting her hands off on her jeans. "I'll clean up first before heading down there." She raked her hair back from her face. "Can you help Marni in the lodge until I get there?"

Megan shook her head. "I have the afternoon ride in less than an hour. I don't even have the horses ready yet."

"I'll help at the lodge," Gage offered, and both women looked at him almost as if they'd forgotten he was there.

It was curiously refreshing. And surprisingly deflating. "I *can* mix a drink, at least."

"But—" Rory broke off whatever protest she was about to make. Obviously, she'd decided desperate times meant even his help was better than nothing. She tugged down the hem of her splinter-ridden sweater, her eyes skipping away from his. "I appreciate it."

Then she gestured at the utility vehicle. "Megan can take you down to the lodge before she gets going on the ride." She didn't wait for his agreement but headed straight back to her cabin, scooping up the chain saw along the way.

Gage sat down beside Megan in the UTV, his attention still on Rory's departing form. "How much time did she spend in her studio before Sean got sick?"

Megan hit the gas and pulled out of the drive, aiming down the hill toward the main camp. "All of it. I know that was just a knee-jerk reaction back there, but after this long, you'd think—" She broke off and shook her head. "Losing her mom was bad enough. I was the one who called her about that, too."

"What happened?"

Megan glanced at him. "She died on the rapids."

Rory's sad eyes the day they'd been up on the lookout finally made sense to him.

"Rory and Jon hadn't even been married a year when it happened. They'd just moved to Seattle."

He had a hard time envisioning Rory anywhere other than Angel River. "She told me he's the one who did the ironwork with the logo."

Megan's eyebrows rose. "She usually acts like he never existed."

"And that he was a liar and a cheat."

That earned him another surprised look. "He

was. And he walked out on her right after she discovered she was pregnant with Killy. Miserable worm," she added under her breath.

It didn't take a math whiz to realize her marriage had lasted about as long as his. Or that it had ended shortly after her mother died. "She came back here after that."

"Yeah. Her folks built the studio before she went to art school. She used to make a ton of stuff that got sold in the gift shop. When she came back after Jon, she didn't go in the studio much. After Killy was born, she got back to it. Like she'd found the joy again because of him. But once Sean got sick, she closed the door and stepped in as manager."

He knew that much from Sean. Knew too that the awards from travel magazines had come less often. That the occupancy rates had been on a slow decline. It wasn't that Rory wasn't good at running the guest ranch.

But the problem was plain as day to him now that he'd seen her artistry. Rory might love the guest ranch. But her heart wasn't in it the way it was in her art.

As if she'd been reading his mind, Megan shook her head. "I still can't believe she carved that wing." She whipped around the fork, aiming for the main camp.

He could hardly believe it, either, and he'd watched the live performance. "Drop me at the Brown cabin. I'll walk across to the lodge."

She spun the wheel again, and gravel spit from the tires as they slid to a stop in front of his cabin. He stepped out and had barely cleared the front bumper when the wrangler took off again.

He noted the two shuttle buses parked in front the lodge as he quickly went inside. Noah was still sprawled on the couch in the exact position he'd been occupying earlier.

"Get up," Gage ordered, shoving his brother's bare feet off the coffee table. "Put on clean clothes. Time you started earning your keep."

Looking bored, Noah lifted his middle finger.

Gage ignored it. "Rory needs help."

"So?" Despite Noah's insolent tone, his hand dropped.

Gage pulled off his jacket and started up the stairs. He wanted a clean shirt. "That wedding group she's been expecting came a day early and with a lot of unexpected plus-ones." He pulled off his sweater and looked over his shoulder.

Noah was sitting straighter on the couch, though he still hadn't made any effort to stand.

Gage continued up the stairs. "You and I," he said over the banister, "are going to do whatever we need to do to help her out."

"Like what?"

Gage entered his bedroom and pulled a clean white shirt from the closet. As he buttoned it up, he grimaced at his reflection in the mirror on the back of the door. Noah wasn't the only one who needed a shave.

He headed back downstairs, shoving his shirttails into his jeans. "Bartending, for one thing," he told Noah, picking up where he'd left off. He knew it would get his brother's attention even more than mentioning Rory had.

Noah's head lifted. In the weeks they'd been there, his blue eyes had finally lost their bloodshot tinge. They were clearer than Gage could remember them being in a long, long while. Even after the last stint in rehab.

"That doesn't mean you get to imbibe. And if I see you try, I'll kick your butt from here to Denver," he warned. "And I'm assuming you know how to actually mix a cocktail without having someone do it for you."

Noah sneered as he unfurled himself from the couch. "Better mixologist than you'll ever be." He bounded up the stairs with more energy than he'd shown in years.

This huge inconvenience for Rory and Angel River was so far proving to be the best thing that had happened to Gage in dealing with the Noah problem.

He scrubbed his hand down his jaw, thinking about shaving again, but his cell phone interrupted the thought. Seeing the name on the display, he briefly considered ignoring it. He spoke with Archer routinely, hoping for a resolution about Rambling

Mountain, and they were still in limbo. He swiped the screen. "Tell me something good, Archer."

"Nell's having a boy."

Gage forgot about business and smiled broadly. "No kidding? Congratulations!" He pulled on his jacket again and went out onto the porch. Over at the lodge, a trio of women was dancing on the deck outside the great room. Their laughter carried easily. "When're you going to get her down the aisle?" The two had been engaged for a few months now.

"Before the year is over," Archer said. "I told Nell I wasn't waiting any longer. She should be getting past the morning sickness sometime soon. It's not as though we're planning some huge, formal wedding. We just want our family and friends there. That includes you, in case you're entertaining some notion of hiding out at Angel River to get out of being my best man."

Family and friends.

Gage rubbed his forehead, feeling a sudden headache coming on. He should never have agreed to be Archer's best man. It was getting too complicated.

"My grandmother's already offered up her mansion for the I dos," Archer continued. "Since Nell started working for Vivian this summer, they've gotten pretty close. We'll probably take her up on it."

Which meant Gage definitely needed to get out of being best man. He'd avoided meeting Vivian Templeton in person for several years now.

He looked over his shoulder into the cabin, holding his phone away from his mouth. "Noah," he yelled. "Get the lead out." The noise from the lodge was growing louder. At the rate Noah was going, Rory would beat them there.

Gage put the phone back to his ear. "Sorry about that."

"How's everyone's favorite little brother doing?"

"If he's not ignoring me, he's telling me to go to hell." Or worse. "But he's sober. Been that way since we got here."

"And you're what? Halfway through the stay?"

"Nearly." It felt like a small eternity even to him, and he wasn't plagued by the same demons that his brother was.

"Learning anything important about running a guest ranch?"

"Yeah." Gage eyed the group at the lodge. Despite the temperature hovering somewhere in the mid-forties, one of the girls was dancing around in a bikini, and someone was tossing confetti over the side of the deck. "You gotta know how to manage manure."

Rory felt the pulse of music from the lodge even before she entered through the storeroom.

Bart was working in the kitchen, prepping a mountain of vegetables. He wore a pair of noise-canceling headphones and gave her a benign smile as she passed through. She was pretty sure nothing ever knocked him off his even keel. Not even eighteen extra mouths to feed.

In the great room, the music was almost deafening. She glanced at all the unfamiliar faces and was glad that the guests they'd welcomed that week—the Jorgensons, Lilys and Mattas had replaced the Delgados and Murphys—were out on the afternoon ride with Megan. Tig and Willow were gone, too, spending the afternoon at the spa with Donna.

Megan had said the arrivals totaled fifty-four, but as Rory sidled through the crowd, it felt like twice that many. Which just reminded her how long it had been since they'd had such a full house at Angel River.

She spotted Marni's pink hair and angled toward her.

The young woman was gamely trying to deal with an angry, red-faced man. "Missy, I've paid good money to—"

Rory stopped next to him, her hand extended. "Good afternoon," she said loud enough to be heard above the music. "I'm Rory McAdams, manager here at Angel River. You must be Mr. Pith." Before he had a chance to transfer his baleful look to her, she took his clammy hand and pumped it enthusiastically. "How was your flight from Florida?"

"Bumpy," he complained.

"Landing at the airstrip often is," she said with a nod. "Has something to do with the mountains. Is Mrs. Pith here?"

"She's off with Sabrina somewhere," he said dismissively. Sabrina was the bride. "She's not real pleased the welcome spread we expected is nowhere to be found."

Rory kept her smile in place. The "welcome spread" would have been quite in place if his party had arrived on the right day. "Perhaps we could go to the office for a few minutes," she suggested. "Finalize some details."

"Bitsy said everything was all set." He looked irritated, the lines on his bulbous nose turning even bluer. "What's there to finalize?"

She leaned closer so she didn't have to yell to be heard. "She confirmed your group for a few less people than you actually have, so we need to review the rooms and cabins you'll need." She wasn't mentioning their early arrival until she knew that *she* hadn't made the error. "My office is just this way." She extended her arm and, since she was still clasping his hand, managed to get him to take a few steps in the right direction.

Fortunately, once he'd started moving, it was easy enough to keep him moving.

They were nearly out of the great room when she spotted Gage and Noah standing behind the mahogany bar. They were both wearing white shirts rolled up at the elbows and tucked into their jeans. Noah's long hair was tied up in a man bun. Gage's shorter hair was tumbling over his forehead.

They both had cocktail shakers in their hands, and a row of young women—she'd bet her goldfish that they were bridesmaids—was lined up in front of them.

More striking than anything, though, were both men's huge smiles.

It was enough to make *her* want to line up in front of them, too.

"Are we going to your office or not?"

She hadn't realized she'd slowed. She quickly looked away from Gage.

He's a guest. Only that particular line was getting blurry right now.

"Yes, Mr. Pith." She let go of the man's beefy hand and briskly led the way. When they reached the office, she invited him to sit in the living area. "Can I get you something to drink?"

"Coffee," he muttered.

She was relieved it wasn't a cocktail.

She flipped on the coffee maker behind the desk and stuck in a pod, leaving it to heat while she pulled out the reservation book and the Pith file. She distinctly remembered that Bitsy Pith had sent a fax with the original dates of the registration, and Rory flipped through the file until she found it.

She relaxed slightly when she had confirmation that the arrival date error was on the Piths' side. She found it much easier to be accommodating when she knew she wasn't in the wrong.

When the coffee was done brewing, she carried the cup and the reservation book into the living area. "Do you take sugar or cream?"

He shook his head. "Whiskey."

Probably explained the state of his nose. She set the coffee in front of him and pulled a bottle of whiskey she kept for just such occasions from the desk drawer.

She added a measure to his cup and then sat beside him, opening up the book. "These are the room configurations at Uptown Camp," she told him as she unfolded an oversize diagram.

"We're not in the lodge here?"

She couldn't help but wonder how much conversation went on between Bitsy and Bobby Pith. "The Uptown Camp is a private setting for you and your guests," she explained, pulling out the brochure containing the map of the entire Angel River valley. She pointed out the collection of cabins with her pencil. "It's an easy ride from here to there." She pretended not to see the face he made and returned her attention to the Uptown reservation chart that contained head counts for each cabin.

She also used the chart to keep track of everyone's individual welcome totes, which she hadn't put together yet because they'd arrived a day early. "If you can let me know the additional number of rooms or cabins that you need, I can—"

"We don't need any additional anything. We're already paying you a living fortune for this wedding business."

Her fingers tightened on her pencil. The inclusive wedding package the Piths had chosen had a built-in discount, which even at the original count amounted to a considerable sum. She was willing to negotiate the extra cost of the unexpected guests to smooth over the situation, but she wasn't going to accommodate them for free. "Mr. Pith, just the other day, your wife confirmed your final number of guests at thirty-six."

"So?"

"You arrived with more than fifty," she said, making an effort to keep her tone gentle.

"It's all the kids," he said with a dismissive flick of his fingers.

"And we're happy to have them," she assured him, swallowing another spurt of annoyance. "We pride ourselves on being family-friendly. We can configure all of our cabins to accommodate more children per room. The Homestead lodge in particular has a wing that can even be fashioned into a bunkhouse if all of the kids would like to sleep together, for instance." She smiled. "I have a six-year-old myself."

He gulped his hot, spiked coffee, seemingly undeterred by the steam coming off it. "You need to work this out with Bitsy."

She wanted to gnash her teeth. Instead, she rose immediately, tucking the book under her arm. "Certainly." Considering the state of things already, she'd be reviewing every single detail the woman *had* confirmed for the coming ten days, including the reception menu that Bart was working on.

Rory didn't want the entire ranch thrown into chaos for one minute longer than necessary.

"Let's go find her and get things sorted, and we can begin transporting luggage while you and your guests continue enjoying the lodge here. There's a bonfire near the river after dinner. It's always a lot of fun."

With a harrumph, Mr. Pith stood, too, and followed her out of the office.

He took the whiskey bottle with him.

Some guests were a positive joy. She was already certain that was not going to be the case where the Piths were concerned.

When they reentered the great room, it was slightly less crowded than it had been before. Her attention swerved to the bar.

Gage and his brother were both still working behind it, smiles on their faces.

With the bevy of bridesmaids still watching them raptly.

Maybe the Pith party hadn't stepped off on the most ideal footing. But if it kept a smile on the faces of Gage Stanton and his brother while they actually *worked* together, she had to admit that maybe, just maybe, it might all be worth it.

Chapter Nine

The lodge was finally empty when Rory reentered her office later that evening and closed the door.

At the sight of the white stationer boxes sitting on her desk, she let out a deep sigh. They contained the monogrammed paper that Bitsy expected to be used for anything relating to her daughter's wedding. Using special paper wouldn't be so bad. But there were ribbons to be added. Elaborately printed folders to be folded and filled with every manner of information for their guests.

And Bitsy expected Angel River to take care of it all.

At least Bart had told her that the dinner hour went well. While Rory had been here in the office trying to rearrange several months of effort in a single afternoon, the chef—not surprisingly—had more than risen to the occasion of feeding everyone.

Now, all the guests were down at the river for the bonfire, which left her time to finish the welcome totes and get them delivered to Uptown before they turned in for the night. Megan was coming by later to help.

She wearily pushed away from the door, popped a fresh pod in the coffee maker and rearranged the boxes that she'd stacked there earlier.

Then she pulled out the chart she'd redone and set to work. She was on her third cup of coffee and coaxing a piece of the fussy, deckled paper through her reluctant printer when the office door opened a few hours later.

"I hate this printer. And this paper—" she snatched up one of the ruined sheets from the floor and spun around in her desk chair "—is not help—" She broke off at the sight of Gage. Her grip tightened, wrinkling the paper even more. "I thought you were Megan."

He spread his hands slightly. "Not quite."

Her stomach suddenly felt jittery. She realized she was still clutching the paper and pitched it into the overflowing trash can beside the desk.

Behind her, the printer on the credenza clicked ominously, followed by the sound of paper crumpling. Again.

She sighed and grabbed her coffee mug, looking at Gage over the top of it. "Thought you were down at the bonfire." She'd seen him heading that way along with Tig and Willow.

"I was." He unzipped his leather jacket as he approached the desk. His gaze took in the mess of papers. "What's all that?"

She plucked one of her successes from the woefully small pile of them. "Next week's activity schedule."

"And those?" He nodded to the second stack of folded items sitting on the corner of her desk.

"Next week's activity schedule for anyone *not* involved with the Pith wedding." She sipped her coffee again. It was already lukewarm. "Thank you for your help before. Tell Noah how much I appreciate it. The extra hands really helped." She dragged her eyes away from the perfect fit of Gage's shirt against his chest. "You and Noah seemed to be quite the popular duo with the ladies."

He shrugged off her words and picked up one of the schedules. "What's the difference between the two? Their options are the same as everyone else staying here."

She set aside her mug. "Yes, but Bitsy Pith—" just saying the name annoyed her "—insists that for *her* guests, everything must match the wedding decor. Even our ordinary old activity schedule." She pointed her finger at him. "And get that expression off your face," she warned. "When it comes to weddings, you can expect all *sorts* of demands like this." She flicked one of the white boxes with her fingertip. "Wedding programs. Reception programs. Brunch programs. You name it and I'll bet you that Bitsy Pith has planned for it."

"Just because a demand is made doesn't mean it has to be met."

"It does when we're talking this much money," she muttered and spun around in her chair again to face the printer. She began freeing the jammed paper. "Is Noah at the bonfire?"

"He was when I left. First time he's actually gone down for one."

"When the two of you were serving drinks, he looked like he was enjoying himself. You both did." She glanced over her shoulder. He'd tossed his jacket on the couch, as if he planned to stay. She moistened her lips and quickly turned back to her printer. "It was a nice sight." She pulled harder on the paper and swallowed an oath when it began to tear.

"Did you even break for dinner?"

"No time." She flipped open a panel on the printer and pulled out the cartridge to work on the jammed paper from the inside. "I want to get the welcome totes over to Uptown before the bonfire breaks up." Which, considering her luck right now, could be any time. "The fire *is* still going strong, isn't it?"

He nodded. "Their group wasn't supposed to be here until tomorrow. Can't the totes wait until then?"

"Mrs. Pith—" she nearly spit the name "—doesn't understand that her group arrived a day early."

"Then she's a twit."

Rory couldn't help feeling a rush of gratitude at his words. "That's entirely possible. She didn't even have the actual ceremony date right in her paperwork. It's on Saturday instead of Sunday. Makes a person wonder what the wedding invitations were like, doesn't it?" Getting the date corrected wasn't as simple as just fixing the ranch calendar. It also meant Rory rearranging the officiant from Wymon. The flowers. The musicians. The bartenders and waitstaff she'd hired from town. Everything had needed to be moved forward a day.

"What about her husband?"

"Mr. Pith believes Mrs. Pith has everything organized like a top. And even though she most certainly does not, they're the clients, and our clients are never wrong."

"Even when they are."

"And particularly when they've written a big fat check," Megan said, walking into the office. She'd obviously overheard. When she spotted Rory's mess, her eyebrows rose. "Having fun?"

Rory ought to be grateful for Megan's arrival. "A blast. Exactly how I like spending my Saturday nights."

Gage had wandered closer and was watching the printer. "What do you usually do on Saturday nights?"

Megan laughed. "Rory? She hits the hay early, because she's in the kitchen with Bart making bread at the butt crack of dawn on Sunday mornings."

"Dawn would be too late," Rory murmured. She'd finally succeeded in working the ragged strip of paper free, and she replaced the cartridge and closed the panel. "And it's not every Sunday."

The printer whirred and clicked, warming up again. It was hard ignoring Gage standing so near, and she was grateful that her hand didn't shake when she reached for a fresh piece of paper. "Did you get the luggage over to Uptown?"

"Left it all in Homestead just where you told me," Megan said. "I'm surprised you didn't want it delivered to everyone's individual rooms like usual."

"If they hadn't come in a day early, I would have," Rory muttered. Maybe it was petty of her not to provide that particular convenience, but she chose to think of it as expedient.

"Pretty hoity-toity." Megan plucked a piece of marbled blue paper from an open box and ran her fingertip along the thin, rough edge. "This the part causing the problem?"

"I don't know if it's the deckled edge or the raised monogram." Rory held the paper lightly until the feeder finally gained traction, then didn't dare breathe while the sheet disappeared inside. A moment later, it emerged and settled lightly on the exit tray. "Hallelujah." She pulled it off the tray and folded it carefully.

She was painfully aware of Gage watching the whole process. She wasn't sure she'd ever felt quite so inept, and she really, *really* wished he'd stayed at the bonfire. So far, it'd been a banner day. First he saw her lose her lunch, and now this?

"These the directories?" Megan had transferred her attention to another stack of brochures with a map of Uptown and guest locations on one side and a map of the entire facility on the other.

Rory barely glanced her way as she turned to feed another sheet into the printer. "Yes."

It had taken her all afternoon to get the reservation mess straightened out and room keys distributed to the proper parties. The fact that Bitsy Pith was tipsy—and probably had been since before their private charter touched down in Wymon—hadn't helped, either. Keeping Bitsy focused on the matter at hand hadn't been easy.

Her husband's offhand dismissal of the additional guests as just being "kids" hadn't been remotely accurate, either.

Oh, yes, there were kids. Seven in all, but only two weren't in the original confirmation. The remaining additions to the party were adults.

"No wonder you said to just pile up all the luggage for them to sort out themselves."

"Yup." She held her breath again as the printer whirred softly. Rearranging the rooms and cabins had been easier than swallowing Bitsy's blame for the mix-up on the dates. Rory had proof that Bitsy was wrong, but she didn't argue. It had been more important that the woman had at least acknowledged they'd arrived with "a few" more people than they'd intended and was willing to negotiate the additional cost.

Rory wasn't willing to chance the ill will from the people paying for an extravagant wedding over an incorrect date. Angel River needed good word of mouth. Good reviews.

"What's all this other stuff?" Megan didn't wait for an answer as she lifted one of the box lids.

"The rest of their custom printing. She expects us to assemble everything for them."

"Good grief." Megan pulled out a slim, engraved card and started reading. "'Sabrina Larissa Pith and Dante Cruz Castellano met on a cool spring evening—' oh, gag." She tossed the program back into the box. "I thought putting this stuff together was what bridesmaids were good for."

"Evidently, not in this case." The printer had managed to emit another page unscathed. Rory folded it and dropped it on the stack. But before she could add another sheet, Gage stepped in the way.

"Let me take a look at it."

"Printer maintenance another one of those things you've tried yourself?"

He gave her a sidelong glance, amusement in his eyes. "You'd be surprised at the things I'm capable of doing."

A flame flickered low inside her. At this point, she was pretty sure she *wouldn't* be surprised.

"How many more do you need to print?"

"Twenty." She didn't bother pointing out that

she'd already ruined more sheets than that. He could see her failures in the trash.

He suddenly crouched down in the narrow space between her and the credenza, and she couldn't help catching her breath.

He noticed. "Afraid I'll make things worse?"

Better for him to think she was worried about the stupid printer than to think it was his proximity making her nervous. "Maybe." She looked away, only to find Megan watching her with a knowing expression.

She turned back to Gage. He'd pulled open the panel, removed the cartridge and was feeling inside. "Have a small screwdriver? A piece is still jammed beneath that plate there. Here." He grabbed her hand and directed it into the printer cavity. "Feel."

Her pulse was suddenly pounding inside her head, and the only thing she felt was his fingers on hers. It was ridiculous. There was nothing intimate whatsoever about sticking one's hand inside an overworked desktop printer. Until Gage Stanton was involved.

"I feel it," she said quickly. A bald-faced lie that made even more heat rise to her cheeks. She tugged her hand free and bolted out of her chair. "I'll go find a screwdriver." She hurried out of the office, aware of the unholy glee in Megan's eyes as she followed.

"What'd I give you?" Megan asked in a loud whisper. "Three weeks?"

Rory slashed her hand in the air. "Shh!"

Megan's laugh wasn't even remotely muffled as they reached the empty great room. "You should have seen your face when he grabbed your hand. I thought your eyes were going to bug out of your head."

Rory glared at her. "Isn't there something more productive for you to do right now? I can find a screwdriver on my own."

It shouldn't have been possible, but Megan looked even more gleeful.

"Grow up," Rory muttered as they turned into the kitchen.

That room was empty, too. The counters were spotless and gleamed under the overhead lights.

"You're the one acting like a sixteen-year-old virgin around him." Megan followed her into the storage room.

Rory slammed shut the drawer she'd just opened. "Remind me why we're friends?"

"Because nobody watches your back like I do," Megan said tartly.

Rory's shoulders slumped. She looked at Megan, contrite. "I know." She pressed her hands on top of the counter and inhaled deeply.

"You are making too big a deal about this." Megan pulled open a drawer and poked through it. "If you've got the itch, scratch it. What's the harm?"

"He's a guest and he could buy us out," she said in a fierce whisper.

"So what? He's a man who has your stirrups all twisted up." Megan lifted an ice pick, giving it a considering look. "When's the last time that happened? The last time you were a mass of *quivering loins*." She drew out the words with dramatic flair.

Rory nearly choked. "There's no quivering going on."

"My foot." Megan tossed aside the ice pick and opened another drawer. "Why are we looking for a screwdriver in here? It's all kitchen stuff. Admit it. You just needed to put some space between you and the delectable developer."

"If you think he's so delectable, *you* do something about it."

"Noah's more my speed." Megan winked. "Young. Lots of energy."

"I need to disinfect my ears now." If she could just remember where she'd seen that screwdriver. "Guest. Remember? Hands off. Besides, Noah's a boy."

"Gage, on the other hand, is all man," Megan countered as if Rory had played right into her hands. "And screw the rules. The world isn't going to stop rotating if you just happen to break your sexual fast with a guest! He's not Jon, for Pete's sake! You don't have to be looking for Mr. Right. Gage strikes me as a great Mr. Right Now."

Rory pressed her palms to her hot cheeks. "It's bad for business."

"Yeah, well, the business hasn't been so good lately!"

One more thing she already knew. "Right now, all I care about is keeping Bitsy and Bobby Pith happy. You know how it works. One good wedding begets another. That's as much as I can concentrate on right now." She snapped her fingers. "I remember now. It was behind the bar." She strode back through the kitchen, flipping off the lights as they went.

The sight of people on the deck outside the soaring windows had her stopping short. "Well, that's just perfect." She gestured. "They're coming back already. Do what you can to stall them for a while yet."

"How am I supposed to do that?"

"From what I've seen of this crowd so far? Just tell them the bar is open." Then she jogged out of the room and back to the office.

Gage had moved to her chair, and he looked up at her when she entered.

It was jarring to see him sitting at the desk, and her footsteps faltered. The only person to sit behind her father's desk in years had been her. "I didn't get the screwdriver. But they're starting to come back, so I'm going to have to settle for what's already done." She retrieved a crate containing custom tote bags from the closet and set it on the couch. After counting the bags, she went back for another dozen.

Gage had left the desk, and his hands brushed

hers as he took the new totes from her when she emerged.

She stopped in surprise as she turned toward the desk to get what she'd prepared so far.

"I finished printing the schedules," he said.

"I see that." She picked up the tidy stack—more than double the size that she'd left. "How did you do it?"

"Made an adjustment to the printer configuration. Overrides everything." He looked at the bags on the couch. "One for each bag?"

"Yes."

As if it were a perfectly ordinary thing for him to do, he began doling out the schedules among the bags. She grabbed the stack of directories, following along behind him.

They could hear voices from the great room now. Laughter. Music when someone turned on the sound system.

She darted back into the closet for the child activity sets and added them on top of the crate. They were color-coded by age range and filled with appropriate games and crafts. She'd learned a long time ago that the easiest way to keep kids happy was to keep them occupied. She pulled on her coat, Gage grabbed the crates and she led the way to the rear of the building where the laundry was located. At the sight of the rolling bins still filled with sheets and towels, her lips tightened.

Before she could hide her reaction, Gage noticed.

His gaze followed hers. "Frannie's supposed to be in charge of all that."

There was no point denying what was perfectly obvious. She pushed through the door leading outside, and it closed heavily behind them.

They stored the stuff in the cargo box of the one UTV parked there and set off. She flipped on the heater even though it wouldn't do a lot to combat the chilly night air, not without one of the cold weather enclosure kits they installed every year. The weather had been so up-and-down lately that she wasn't sure when the time would be right for them.

"What happens when we get to the Uptown Camp?"

"We'll put totes in each room."

"One per?"

"One per adult." She veered around the cabins and sped up. "Each child gets a box. The directory that I printed will tell us who gets what and where it belongs."

Their shoulders collided when she hit a bump and he grabbed the roll bar. But his shoulder stayed pressed against hers.

He was warm. Warmer than the feeble puffs from the heater vents. As distracting as he was, his presence also felt strangely comforting. The same way it had been comforting when he handed her the damp towel to wipe her face that afternoon.

It seemed like days ago by this point.

"How often does this happen?"

Since she'd felt companionable comfort from a man besides her father and Bart? Never.

She shook herself and focused on the present. "Sorry?"

"Parties arriving early. Confirmations for the wrong number of guests."

She fought back her instinctive burst of defensiveness. "You own resorts all over the country. You know how it goes. Some people operate on the spur of the moment. They don't plan ahead. They don't make advance reservations."

"And during high season, those people would be out of luck. If there are no vacancies, there are no vacancies."

"Well, this isn't our high season."

"When is Angel River's high season?"

At least he hadn't asked if they even had one. "End of May to the middle of September. And then again from late December through February if the snow is good. I've been thinking about your idea for a flash promotion. And I, uh, I think we should do it." She glanced at him. "But to answer your question, generally people don't show up on the wrong day, and particularly not for something as important as a destination wedding."

"Or with additional walk-ins in the party."

"Not to this extent." They'd reached the fork in the camp loop. "A few times a year, we'll have someone show up just because they've been out exploring and they've stumbled on us. It's rare when we actually have to turn someone away." He and his brother were perfect examples. "The Pith party isn't a disaster." She wanted to convince herself of that as much as him. "I just don't like being caught unprepared like this. We'll spend their entire visit making up for what they consider to be our error, even though it wasn't. It's not a position I like being in."

"Think they did it deliberately?"

Her foot unconsciously eased on the gas as she gaped at him. "Who would do such a thing?"

"You're comping all of them an extra day and cutting a deal for the extra eighteen guests for more than a week. You think the Piths don't know how much they're saving?"

She hadn't told him about that decision, so she could only assume that Megan had. "You think I should charge them full board?"

"Does it matter what I think?"

She focused on the road for a while. "No," she said finally. Truthfully. "I don't think it does matter." Her voice grew firmer. "I did what needed to be done, and I'm not going to worry about it anymore."

It was too dark to see his expression, but for some reason, she thought she'd pleased him.

At least until he spoke again. "How often does Frannie let you down?"

"She doesn't let me down. Exactly."

"You didn't expect to see those sheets and towels in the laundry."

She flexed her cold fingers around the steering wheel. She should have worn gloves. "We're shorthanded. Everybody is pushed to the limit." She wished she'd taken the time to dump the sheets and towels in the wash before they'd left the lodge. They'd still need to be dealt with when she got back.

"You need help."

She hit the brakes, bringing the utility vehicle to a juddering stop in front of the Homestead lodge. She supposed she should be glad he hadn't started in again on why she was even running the place. "Finding the right people to live and work out here isn't exactly easy. Wymon is *way* smaller than Weaver. That's the closest town to the ranch you bought, right?" Afraid he might bring up his friend the spa owner, she quickly hopped out of the vehicle. "I'm sure you'll have an easier time finding and keeping staff."

"Have you ever been to Weaver?"

"Sure. Wymon High plays football against the schools in Weaver and Braden. That's not too far from Weaver—"

"I know where Braden is. My attorney's from there. I'm pretty sure you didn't play high school football." His voice turned dry. "Cheerleader?"

She laughed shortly as she poked through a bag in search of a directory. "Hardly. Marching band. There were a whopping twenty of us."

"What did you play?"

"Trombone." She gave him a sharp look. "What?"

"Nothing." He lifted his hands peaceably. "Just that you are one surprise after another."

Directory in hand, she pulled out her master key. The main entrance wasn't locked, but all of the interior rooms would be. "Grab a handful of bags." As he gathered as many totes as he could, she did the same, stacking the loops like bracelets that went all the way past her elbow, and they went inside.

Soft lights came on automatically as they walked through the central common area, where the focal point was an enormous stone fireplace. It was surrounded by overstuffed chairs arranged in cozy groupings.

"That," Gage said, "is a lot of luggage."

The pile that Megan had left was far more orderly than she'd implied. But it did take up a considerable amount of floor space, entirely obscuring the long reception counter behind it.

"Fifty-plus people," she reminded him. "Ten days. Not to mention a wedding. Weddings always mean a lot more luggage." She gestured to the wing branching off to the left of the fireplace. "We can start over there."

They quickly settled into a rhythm—Gage unlocking the door and Rory leaving the welcome packages inside. It also gave her one last chance to smooth a wrinkled quilt here. To straighten a stray pillow there.

They finished the first floor and went up the stairs to the second, working their way back to the wing right of the fireplace, then back down to the first floor again. Gage only had to return to the utility vehicle once for more totes.

When they were done in the main building, Rory turned on the big gas logs in the fireplace, made sure the protective glass was in place and they moved on to the individual cabins, situated in a wide circle around the swimming pool. He took over driving, which let her nip in and out as she delivered the rest of the totes and craft boxes.

She'd just finished the very last one when she saw the distinctive pinpoint of headlights off in the distance. There was a whole string of them.

Gage noticed, too. "They're on the way."

Adrenaline surging, she hopped in beside him. "Drive over to that shed." She gestured at the shadowy structure. "On the other side of the horseshoe pits."

He didn't question why. He just hit the gas and drove around to the shed. She got out again and nearly dropped her passkey in her hurry to get the door open. Inside, she flipped a switch, and the hanging bulbs spanning the expanse of the pool area came on, bathing the water and everything else in a gentle dance of golden light. She hit another switch, and the automatic cover on the big hot tub rumbled softly as it rolled open. Steam billowed as warm water met cold air. A third master switch started the water churning softly. If the controls next to the tub weren't used, the master would automatically shut off in a few hours.

She relocked the shed and jogged back to him. "Let's get out of here," she said breathlessly. "If you drive up behind the cabins, there's a hiking path that's wide enough to drive on. It's the long way around, but at least nobody'll see us."

Soon he was guiding the vehicle up the narrow ridge well beyond the cabins, stopping and turning off the headlights when she told him.

The panorama of Angel River Ranch was spread out below. The soft glow of the main lodge off in the distance contrasted with the brighter one from the nearby Uptown Camp. "We're up behind Angel Camp." He sounded surprised as he pointed. "That's your cabin, isn't it?"

"Yes." They watched the string of headlights from the wedding party work their way nearer. Above them, stars glittered in the inky sky.

"My mom's favorite spot might have been the lookout," she admitted softly, "but this spot is mine. My studio is only a few yards away from here."

She felt his look. But he didn't comment. "Why didn't you want any of them to see us?" he asked instead.

She pushed her cold hands into her coat pockets, hunching toward the heater vents again. "My mother made all these little touches seem effortless," she finally answered. "*She* was never once caught unprepared. Not where guests were concerned."

"Is that why you were so determined to get this all done tonight? Trying to live up to the bar she set?"

She looked at him. As bright as the sky was with stars, his eyes were still dark, unreadable in the shadows. "You said it yourself. Why am I managing Angel River? I'm an artist." She looked away. "Or I was. For a while." She shrugged, pushing her hair out of her eyes as she watched the procession of UTV headlights. "No matter how bad I am at this, Angel River is a special place. It doesn't matter what kind of problems we had today—I still want everyone to leave here feeling that, too. I guess I just don't want someone seeing behind the curtain," she admitted.

"You want them to only see the magic," he said quietly.

"Yes." She looked at him again. "That's it exactly."

"You're safe, then." His voice was low. Deep.

Even as impossible as it was to see his expression, her heart still lurched. She could make out the shape of his lips and couldn't make herself look away. "Why?"

He lifted his hand, and she couldn't help starting when he brushed her hair away from her cheek. "Because magic is all I see."

Then he leaned closer and lightly brushed those perfect, perfect lips once, twice, across hers.

"And for the record—" his voice dropped another notch "—you're not bad at anything."

And he kissed her a third time.

Chapter Ten

"Stupid," Gage muttered for the tenth time as he walked to his cabin from the main lodge. "Stupid, stupid, freaking stupid."

What had possessed him to kiss her?

One minute she was sitting there, looking vulnerable and talking about her mom, and the next he was kissing her.

"Stupid," he said again through his teeth as he stomped up the cabin's wooden steps.

"Pathetic, too." Noah's voice cut through the dark, and Gage realized his brother was sitting in one of the wooden rockers on the porch. "I've heard of old dudes like you talking to themselves, but now I see it's true."

Noah hadn't turned on any lights, but the stars

were just as bright here as they were up on that ridge beyond the Uptown Camp. Gage could see the slender bottle in his brother's hand just fine.

Same as he'd been able to see the shock in Rory's eyes when she'd jerked back after he'd kissed her.

Stupid. He managed not to voice it, but the word still circled around inside his head.

So maybe his voice came out colder than it should have. "Better not be anything stronger than root beer in that bottle."

"And if it is?"

Gage's fists curled. He didn't want to fight with Noah. But it was easier to justify falling into that familiar routine than his behavior with Rory. "Then we can call it quits right now and you can spend the holidays in a jail cell."

Noah didn't reply. He just lifted the bottle and took a long, long pull on it.

Gage wanted to yank it out of Noah's hands. Instead, he wrapped his hands around the top rail surrounding the porch. "Rory said to tell you thanks for helping out today."

Noah lowered the bottle. It was pretty much predictable at this point that Noah reacted more positively to the slightest mention of Rory than he did to anything else.

"That where you've been?" Noah's voice went tight. "With her?"

"I helped her get some things done for the group that came in."

And you kissed her.

He thumped his palm on the wooden rail, trying to beat back the voice inside his head. "She needs more help than just mixing drinks."

"What's your point?"

His jaw ached from the way he'd been clenching it so much lately. "What else do you know how to do? Anything besides the cocktails and the horses?"

Noah didn't answer. He lifted his bottle again.

Gage looked across to the lodge. There were lights on in several of the rooms. One of them would be the laundry, where Rory had headed when they'd gotten back to the lodge.

After he'd shocked her into silence by his damn stupidity.

She hadn't said a single word. Not after he'd kissed her. Not on the drive back down to the lodge. And not when she'd used her key to get into the laundry room and disappeared inside like the devil was on her heels.

He'd put her in a hell of a position with that kiss. Worse than anything the Piths had done, that was for damn sure. Particularly after he'd witnessed how hard she'd worked to salvage that situation. All to keep the clients happy.

Add thoughtless to stupid.

She was never going to relax around him again. The last thing he wanted was for her to think he believed he had some sort of right to touch her, just because he'd paid a fortune for her time and for the lodging.

Stupid. Stupid, freaking stupid.

He should have cleared it up immediately. Promised her it would never happen again.

He realized Noah was silently watching him. Probably wondering what the hell had gotten into him.

Fine. Whatever. Noah was Noah. He always would be.

Gage shoved open the cabin door.

"It's cider," Noah said abruptly.

Gage froze.

"*Plain* apple cider," Noah added darkly. "Chef Bart makes it."

"I know," Gage said slowly. "Rory's father drinks a glass in the mornings along with his oatmeal." He let the door close and shoved his hands into his pockets. He could feel the worn edges of the cigarette pack with his thumb. "Was it hard? Working behind the bar earlier?"

When Noah didn't answer, he squelched another sigh, feeling older than he should. "I'm glad it's cider," he said.

But he didn't go so far as to admit he was proud of Noah. Then his brother would know for certain that Gage had lost his marbles.

He pushed open the door again.

"It wasn't a piece of cake." Noah's voice was low.

Barely audible. "And I don't know how to do any-thing else."

Gage stopped, one foot across the threshold. Noah's words could have sounded self-pitying. But instead, his brother's tone was matter-of-fact. "That's hard to believe."

"Why?" The question was more like Noah. Full of insolence. "Because *you* know how to do every-thing?"

Gage didn't know how to rewind the last hour. How to undo that kiss.

He wearily rubbed the back of his neck and con-trolled the impulse to pull out the cigarettes. "I don't know how to help you," he admitted.

"I don't want your help."

He sighed deeply. "It's not a choice, Noah."

He could see the grimace on his brother's face. "Because you promised my mother you'd take care of me."

"She was my mother, too."

"And it would kill her to see what's become of me," Noah muttered. "That's what you're thinking."

"Althea Stanton was made of sturdier stuff than that," Gage countered. She'd survived his father's premature death. Then Noah's father's death. "It wouldn't have killed her." It had taken a massive stroke that hit out of the blue several years ago to do that. "She'd have just been mighty pissed off with you. And she would've kicked your hind end until you could recognize for yourself what the right path looked like."

"There's nothing I know how to do that is gonna help Rory."

"A pair of willing hands is what she needs the most. That and a person who doesn't sleep past noon."

When Noah didn't respond, Gage turned to go inside. "You're my brother," he said abruptly. "*That's* why it's not a choice."

Leaving Noah to chew on that, he went inside and closed the door.

The fireplace was cold and black, and he thought of the fire that Rory had left burning for the wedding group. About the way she'd bent over backward to accommodate them. He had employees to handle all those sorts of things at his resorts.

He turned the control on the fireplace, and a flame immediately began licking at the realistic-looking logs. He'd always preferred a real wood fire to a gas-fueled one. But he had to admit that it was still a welcoming touch.

He left the fire burning for his brother and went upstairs. But once in his room, he didn't go to bed. He stood at the dark window and stared out at the infinite stars.

Rory could smell the coffee when she entered the lodge kitchen the next morning.

"Sorry I'm late," she greeted Bart, who was

standing behind one of the stainless steel prep tables, folding a perfect rectangle of pale dough into thirds. "I overslept." She crossed to the coffeepot on the stove, filled a clean mug and took an appreciative sip. "Oh, yessss. I still don't know what your secret is."

"Actually brewing it," he said dryly.

She tied an apron around her waist and washed her hands before joining him at the table. He'd been busy while she'd been snoozing her alarm clock into oblivion. Not only did he have his chocolate croissants well underway, but several batches of dough were already waiting in bowls. "What do you need me to do?"

"Knead," he joked. "Same thing as always." He nudged one of the bowls toward her.

Using a clean cup, she scooped flour out of the enormous canister and moved farther down the long table. She sprinkled the surface with flour, dumped the sticky dough out of the bowl and lightly sprinkled more flour on top of it.

It would be a lot easier to just add baked goods to the supply order, but there simply was nothing better than what Bart made by hand.

He didn't even use a bread machine. By hand literally meant by hand, and she'd been rolling and kneading bread dough in this kitchen with him since her mother was alive. She was no great shakes as a cook, but after years of practice under his watchful eye, at least she could do this part.

But Rory did feel bad for being nearly an hour late. She didn't have to ask how much extra they were making because of the Pith group. She could see for herself there were three times more rattan cane proofing baskets stacked to one side than usual.

Bart didn't just make beautiful loaves of sourdough bread, though that was his primary staple. He made marbled rye bread. Seven grain. Italian olive. He made dinner rolls. Sandwich rolls. Pretzels. Bagels. The occasional quick bread, though he usually made those later in the week. But always, always the most delicious chocolate-filled croissants on the planet.

Spending these early hours with the chef— pressing, folding, turning the dough—while the kitchen smelled of yeast and coffee was as close to healing meditation as Rory had ever gotten outside of sitting at her potter's wheel.

But that morning, all she could think about was the night before. About Gage.

She couldn't believe the way she'd acted. As if she'd never been kissed. It hadn't even been that much of a kiss.

Actually, it was three kisses.

Her lips tingled in remembrance.

The kiss—okay, the three kisses—had nearly been chaste.

She'd overreacted. So much so that she wasn't sure how she'd ever recover from the embarrassment.

It wasn't as if she could avoid Gage until he left

Angel River. The man was going to be there for weeks yet.

"So why'd you oversleep?" Bart's voice cut into her self-flagellation.

She realized her dough that had started out wet and sticky had already turned smooth and elastic under her palms. Overkneading was a bad, bad sin. She walked over to the stack of baskets. "A person oversleeps now and then."

"Not you."

"Maybe it's the rain." It had started falling again when she'd finally left the lodge after she'd finished laundering the sheets the night before. The rain hadn't stopped since. Even now, she could hear its soft drum against the kitchen windows. But at least it wasn't like the downpour they'd had the previous week.

She snatched a basket from the stack and carried it back to her working area. She sprinkled the basket with more flour, rubbing it into the crevices between the circular rattan coils so the dough, once raised, wouldn't stick when it was turned out. "It was a busy night last night. You know. With the wedding party arriving the way they did." She winced, knowing how defensive she sounded.

"Everything's going to be just fine with that group," Bart said calmly. "We've juggled twice as many people many, many times. Remember—oh, it has to be nearly five years now, because the lookout deck was brand-new—when we had three weddings going on during the same weekend?"

She gently placed the round of dough inside the basket, smiling despite herself. She'd been so horrified when her dad had accepted the concurrent wedding reservations.

They'd had a full contingent of staff, full-time and seasonal. And even *she* had been pressed into service. "I remember. Killy was just a baby, and I was trying to nurse him between racing around between the three events." She smiled. "Remember the Torres reception at the Overlook Camp?"

"It was so hot, the icing on the wedding cake melted and the tiers started sliding and—"

"The best man fell into the river trying to catch it," she finished. "Hard to believe we can laugh about that now."

"Let enough time go by, and a person can laugh about all sorts of things." Bart shook his head, chuckling. "Try as I might, I could not convince that sweet little bride that whipped icing was a bad idea on a hot June day." He pointed the end of his rolling pin at her. "Mark my words." The pin punctuated each word. "Won't be long and you'll be laughing about *this* wedding, too." Then his gaze went past Rory. "Wasn't sure you were going to make it."

That was how much notice Rory had.

She felt a fine shiver on the back of her neck and turned to see Gage entering the kitchen. His unshaven jaw was darker than it had been the day before. He was wearing a black mock-neck sweater with a short red zipper that was open halfway down his neck and faded blue jeans.

Just looking at him made something inside her feel weak.

"Wasn't sure I was, either," Gage answered. His dark gaze slid over her before he pulled a mug from the shelf and turned to the stove to fill it with coffee. "I've had more nights that lasted until four in the morning than days that started at four."

With some difficulty, Rory looked away from the black knit sweater hugging his wide shoulders. She felt too warm, and when she scraped her work area clean, her hand shook.

Coffee mug in hand, Gage turned and went over to the table midway between her and Chef Bart. "Quite the production. Smells like a bakery."

"Wait until we start pulling the goods out of the ovens," Bart said. "Takes me back to my *boulangerie* days in Paris." He kissed the tips of his fingers. "Superb."

"Can't wait," Gage murmured. His eyes were as dark as the block of Belgian chocolate that Bart was unwrapping. "When were you in France?"

"My early twenties," Bart said, looking reminiscent. "I studied at Le Cordon Bleu." He gave a broad wink. "And the lovely French girls."

"I've studied a few French girls myself," Gage said, smiling slightly.

Maybe *Sybil* had been in France as well as Switzerland.

Rory flipped the dough in front of her and mashed it beneath the heel of her palm.

"How'd you get from Paris to Angel River?"

"A woman, of course," Bart answered him.

"That'll happen," Gage said. "Or so I've heard."

Rory flipped the dough again, accidentally knocking over her cup of flour. A cloud of white puffed up around her. "Can I talk to you for a minute?"

Gage looked at her over the rim of his mug, and she jerked her head in the direction of the storage room. She didn't wait for him to answer; she just walked through the doorway.

She pushed the door closed when he joined her, even though she knew she'd have to deal with Bart's unrelenting curiosity as a result.

Her stomach was in knots, and her entire body felt flushed. She would rather have been anywhere other than there. Maybe. Because closed in the storage room with him, she noticed just how good he smelled. "Look," she said raggedly, "about last night."

His lips thinned. "Yeah. About that."

"I shouldn't have—"

"I shouldn't have—"

Her gaze collided with his as they both broke off. Feeling even more awkward, she rocked on her tennis shoes and tucked her dusty fingertips in the back pockets of her jeans.

He gestured with his mug. "You go."

Go? She'd like to go out the back door and keep right on going. But that wouldn't solve anything. She drew in a breath. Held it for a moment. Then went for broke. "I shouldn't have reacted the way I did," she said as she exhaled. "I just, uh, well, you just, uh—"

"Surprised you."

He had. With the way he'd read her mind. About the Angel River magic. And about the kiss. She'd wanted him to kiss her. As illogical as it was, she'd still wanted it. "Yes. I...panicked. I'm sorry."

If anything, his expression turned even grimmer. "I noticed. You don't have to worry, though. It won't happen again. You have my word on that."

She tried to smile. Considering she felt worse than ever, she had doubts she succeeded.

Of course it would never happen again. Why would a man like him want a repeat of that abysmal moment? Especially after all her claims about not getting involved with guests. She gave a jerky nod. "Then we'll just...just erase the board as if it never happened."

As if *that* were remotely possible.

She sidled around him to reach for the door to the kitchen. "You don't really need to see how Bart makes his bread. I know I put it on the list when you first got here, but it doesn't have anything to do with running a guest ranch."

"Maybe not. But Bart mentioned it at dinner last

night, and you said extra hands were welcome. And I couldn't sleep. So." He held out one of his hands, wide palm up, long fingers spread. "Extra."

She hadn't been able to sleep, either. Not until it was too late and she was supposed to get up.

We could have been not sleeping together.

She quickly looked away, hoping he wasn't reading her mind, and yanked open the door. "If you're really offering extra hands, how are you at folding towels?"

"The ones from the laundry last night?"

"I finished the sheets last night, but I didn't get the towels into the wash until this morning. They should be ready for the dryer by now."

"I'll take care of it." He set his mug on the counter and strode out of the kitchen. Almost as if he couldn't wait to get away.

She chewed the inside of her cheek. Relieved. Of course she was relieved.

"You want to tell ol' Bart what's going on?"

She jerked guiltily and looked at the chef. He was babysitting his chocolate at the stove. "Sorry?"

"Haven't seen you so distracted by a man since you went to the prom with Donny Thomas."

"Donny Thomas!" She hadn't thought about her high school crush in forever. "I'd have thought you'd have said Jon. I *did* marry him, at least."

"And I'd say he was a total waste of space on this planet, except that he did give you Killy." Bart turned off the flame under his pan and stirred the glossy chocolate, watching it ribbon off his wooden spoon. Then he tapped the spoon gently and held it out to her.

She took it, just as he'd known she would. She sucked some of the chocolate from the tip, then stirred it around inside her coffee mug, watching the rest slowly disappear in a swirl. "He's a guest."

"He's a man who's got your flutters in a twitter."

She smiled reluctantly. "Flutters in a twitter?"

"Jugglies in a quiver? Wannas in a whirl?"

She rolled her eyes, laughing slightly. "Worry about your own love life, Bart."

"So you admit you're thinking *love life*." He gave a satisfied nod and wiped his hands on the towel wrapped around his waist before reaching for his rolling pin again.

"I'm not thinking about anything besides getting through all of this bread dough," she said and plopped the uneven lump she'd abandoned into another proofing basket. Then she scraped her work area clean and started on yet another batch.

Before long, Gage returned. But she had herself under control by then. Or else she was sedated by a suitable amount of chocolate-spiked coffee by then.

She didn't even shiver, flutter or whirl when he cleared a space on the table, washed his hands, then scooped some of her spilled flour to dust his own work area.

Okay, so maybe she did stare a little.

What else could she do when he pushed up the

sleeves of his sweater, tipped out a bowl and began working a batch of sweet roll dough as if he'd done it for years?

Only catching the delighted expression on Bart's face as he watched her got her moving again on her own task.

Soon enough, all of the baskets were full and resting beneath the sackcloth towels spread over them. Once the loaves had risen, Bart would turn them out to bake, but the pretty imprint of the basket coils would remain.

While Rory had portioned dough for rolls and twisted ropes into giant pretzels, Bart had shown Gage how to form the bagels. Those were now resting on sheets stacked in the upper half of a tall rolling rack. The bottom half of the rack contained Rory's efforts. Chef Bart would take care of baking everything throughout the rest of the day.

She was cleaning up the worktable and Gage was sweeping the floor when she heard Killy's voice. A moment later, he and her dad entered. The real surprise, though, was the sight of Gage's brother ambling along after them. His long hair was hanging down around the shoulders of his dull gray hoodie, and he looked as though he'd just woken up.

"Is there coffee?" he asked.

"Sure." Rather than make a big deal about his unexpected presence, Rory handed him a clean mug, indicating the pot on the stove, and then crouched down to grab Killy and give him a quick nuzzle. His hair was sparkling with raindrops. "Good morning, handsome. Did you have a good night with Grandpa?"

"We watched a Christmas show this morning. It was a cartoon about Frosty the Snowman." Killy squirmed out of her hold and ran over to peer at the first batch of croissants that were already cooled and drizzled with chocolate. "Can I write a letter to Santa now?"

From the corner of her eye, she could see the wary looks passing between Gage and his brother. "We need to get through Thanksgiving before we start worrying about letters to Santa."

"Thanksgiving's just turkey. Santa brings presents." He sneaked a finger up to touch one of the croissants but snatched his hand back, looking innocent when Bart reached over his head to move the cooling tray to a safer location. "Can I have pancakes for breakfast?"

"You can have pancakes only if you eat eggs first. Because you need some protein, too." She held out her hand toward him. "Let's go home so I can fix it for you."

The way her son's expression dropped was almost comical. "But Chef Bart—"

"Has a lot to do this morning for the actual *guests*. He's too busy to make you pancakes." They'd already spent hours in the kitchen just preparing baked goods. He still needed to start on his preparations for the actual meals he'd be serving that day.

"But your pancakes are…"

She raised her eyebrows, and Killy's voice trailed off. He wrinkled his nose but took her hand without further protest.

"Frannie called me this morning," her dad said before she could take a step toward the storeroom and the back exit.

"Hope it was to apologize for not getting the sheets and towels done yesterday."

"She said they've all got chicken pox. The kids and her."

"Chicken pox!" Rory cried in dismay. The timing couldn't have been worse. "She's sure?"

"You know it's been going around. Damon probably brought it home from school."

If Damon had, so had Killy. She looked toward Gage and Noah. "Please tell me you've had them already."

Noah shrugged. He was showing as much interest in the croissants as her son had. "I can't remember."

"You were four," Gage said abruptly. He glanced at Rory, seemingly oblivious to the frown that crossed his brother's face. "We've both had 'em."

"Thank goodness *you've* already had them, too." She brushed Killy's hair out of his eyes. So had she when she was a kid.

"You painted me with the pink stuff that stopped me being all scratchy." Killy squirmed out from under her hand. "Damon and me were gonna build a fort today, though."

"Damon and I, and I'm afraid that's not going to happen today, sweetie."

"Not *you* and Damon. *Me* and Damon."

She shot a glance toward Gage at the faint sound he made. But he was focused hard on his coffee. Noah, on the other hand, watched like they were a tennis match, his head bobbing back and forth.

"I was counting on Astrid to help mind the Uptown kids. Bitsy Pith's expecting it." She looked to her father. "Do you think Toonie—"

Rory's father shook his head. "You know how shy she is. She can barely look Bart in the face when she drops off the fresh milk, and she grew up here. Plus she's too young."

"She's fourteen," Rory argued, but in her heart she knew her dad was right.

The day's offering of activities had changed slightly because of the rain. Sunday was always a day off for the horses. But the other outdoor activities—climbing Angel's Lookout, ATV rides and disk golf—were out.

Instead, the default was a friendly poker tournament in the lodge or square dancing and a leatherworking class in the activity barn. If the rain continued for longer, they had more alternatives waiting in the wings.

It was going to be interesting, to say the least, where Bitsy Pith was concerned. But the woman could hardly blame them for the weather.

Rory looked to her father. "Are you up to monitoring the poker games?"

"Of course." He looked vaguely insulted that she'd asked.

She really was batting a thousand.

"Killy will have to come with me while I take care of the housekeeping. Marni's going to have to handle the square dancing. Megan's on the leather craft." She glanced at Bart. "That leaves you without any kitchen help for most of the day."

"No, it doesn't." Gage had lifted his nose from the mug. He raised his palm again, his eyes capturing hers. "Extra."

"He does know how to make a breakfast burrito," Bart said. Of everyone there, he seemed the least concerned about the situation.

Gage was still watching her. "Unless you need me more."

Flitters. Twitters. Juggles galore.

She tore her eyes away, focusing instead on the rain-streaked windows behind him. She knew he meant with the housekeeping but that didn't stop her nerve endings from acting out their own personal Fourth of July fireworks.

Only the knowledge that everyone was watching her helped her keep her wits together. "I can get Uptown cleaned this afternoon while everyone's out for activities."

"That doesn't solve the problem of who's watching the kiddos," her father prompted.

"Right." She went over to the coffeepot, but Noah had emptied it. "Seven kids. All too young to be left to their own devices while their parents go out and play."

Noah suddenly spoke. "Let 'em build forts." He looked vaguely uncomfortable with the attention he'd earned, and he focused on Killy. "That's what you were going to do, wasn't it?"

Killy turned his pleading eyes to Rory. "Can we? I could do it, too, right?"

"Homestead's common room has plenty of space," her dad said. "They can either use the furniture to build the forts or push it all aside and set up the pup tents we've got in storage."

"*Real* tents!" Killy practically bounced on his toes at the prospect.

Rory wasn't sure she liked that suggestion. "But who do I put in charge? Killy? Without Frannie and Astrid, I don't have enough people to—"

"I'll do it," Noah said, and once again, all eyes turned to him. "How hard can it be?"

Beneath that bit of bravado, Rory was certain she saw uncertainty. Uncertainty and the same desire to please that she saw so often in her little boy's eyes. Noah just worked harder to disguise it. "There will be *seven* kids," she felt compelled to caution.

"Eight," Killy piped excitedly.

No matter how much compassion she felt for Noah, she wasn't thrilled at the prospect of her son thinking he'd found his own new personal superhero. Which was exactly how Killy was looking at Noah.

"Eight," she repeated. She reminded herself that Noah had pitched in the day before when the wedding party arrived. Helped to keep them entertained and happy with cocktails in their hands.

But cocktails weren't children. She couldn't chance any mistakes where they were concerned.

She looked toward Gage.

Nothing in his expression helped her feel any more confident, because he was staring at his brother as if he didn't recognize him.

She turned back to Noah again. "Are you sure?"

He might look as though he'd just rolled out of bed, but his eyes were clear. His gaze steady. Remarkably similar to his brother's despite the different coloring. "It matters, doesn't it?"

She felt a little sigh escape. People tended to live up—or down—to expectations. Maybe he just needed someone to have some faith in him.

She could save cleaning Homestead until he was there building forts—or pitching tents—and babysitting. At least she'd be on the premises.

She nodded. "Yes," she said. "It matters."

Chapter Eleven

The rain continued.

And with each passing day, Rory felt the mounting blame that Bitsy and Bobby Pith sent her way. Because it seemed they really *could* blame her for the weather.

Fortunately, the bride- and groom-to-be were much more adaptable. As were the rest of their wedding party and the guests. Once Rory had a chance to actually get to know her, Sabrina Larissa Pith turned out to be the least Bridezilla-ish bride who had ever visited Angel River.

It was the only reason that Rory managed not to lose her mind when Bitsy Pith—the *mom*zilla of all time—rained a fresh batch of demands on their heads.

For the fourth day running.

Bitsy started with a request for all of the meal-times to be changed, because her "delicate" system just was not accustomed to the different time zone.

Evidently, she couldn't digest her mimosas two hours earlier than she was used to back home in Florida.

Rory sat behind her desk, her hands clasped atop her heavily doodled blotter as her mind took a quick little vacation, imagining Bitsy Pith far, far away.

"…and you have to do something about this ridiculous weather," Bitsy was saying when Rory tuned back in for a quick check. The woman wasn't running out of steam at all. "Ludo is arriving tomorrow. How is he supposed to make Sabby look beautiful enough for the cover of *Miam-I-Do* magazine when it's all gray outside? I *knew* this was a bad idea having the wedding here, but my daughter just *had* to insist." She was pacing in front of the desk. "I had everything all arranged for the club *next* year, but no." She slashed her hand through the air. "That wasn't good enough. She had to get married *this* year."

For a moment, Rory watched her pace back and forth, back and forth. Bitsy was wearing a sleeveless pink blouse and white slacks, which might work in Florida at this time of year but was an insane choice for northern Wyoming in the middle of November. There were spatters of mud around the hems of her cropped white slacks, and Rory could easily see the goose bumps on Bitsy's thin arms.

"Would you like something warm to drink?" Only after she'd asked the question did she realize that she'd spoken right over whatever it was that Bitsy was blithering on about. "Coffee? Hot chocolate?" Not that the woman seemed to need any more stimulants. It was also too early in the day for something stronger—though that never seemed to stop her husband.

Or a lot of their guests, actually. They were definitely a group who knew how to have a good time. The rainy days hadn't stopped them in the least.

Bitsy planted her palms on the desk, the sharp points of her vermilion fingernails pressed like daggers against the wood. She leaned over Rory. *"What I want is this effing weather cleared up,"* she screeched.

Startled, Rory rolled her chair back and bumped the credenza behind her. Definitely no more stimulants for Bitsy Pith. "Maybe some herbal tea would be a good—"

"If I'm offered another cup of herbal tea—" Bitsy bared her teeth "—I'm going to scream."

Rory decided it was prudent not to point out that she'd already done so. "Mrs. Pith, I understand your frustration, but—"

"You understand nothing!" Bitsy leaned over the desk even farther. "Do you *care* at all that you are *ruining* my daughter's wedding?"

"Mother!"

Bitsy jumped as though she'd been bitten on her bare, mud-spattered ankles.

Sabrina entered the office, casting Rory an apologetic look. She was as different from her mother as night and day. Bitsy was a tall, bleached rail of nerve. Sabrina was shorter than Rory, comfortably plump and curvy with a smile that could light a room. She was, without question, head over heels in love with her fiancé and he with her.

She also had more sense than her mother when it came to suitable attire, because Sabrina's jeans were tucked into duck boots, and she wore a bright yellow rain slicker over her flannel shirt.

"Don't look at me like that, Sabby," Bitsy said tearfully. She clutched her daughter to her. "This is *the* most important time of your life! It should be absolutely perfect." She looked reproachfully at Rory over Sabrina's head.

"It *is* perfect." Sabrina gave a light laugh, no doubt meant to reassure her mother. "Dante and I don't care about a little rain."

"But everyone is *dying* of boredom." Bitsy's voice rose again.

With visible effort, Sabrina wriggled out of her mother's tight grasp. She looked a little breathless as she tightened her ponytail and sent Rory another look—this one more embarrassed than the last. "No one is bored, Mother," she soothed with what was obvious long practice. "When is the last time you ate?"

Bitsy threw herself dramatically onto the couch. "Who can eat at the outrageous times these *people*—" she said it as if they were pock-ridden aliens from another planet "—see fit to serve meals?" She dropped a goose-pimpled, bony arm over her eyes.

Rory caught a faint eye roll from Sabrina. "Well, it's brunch time at home. So perhaps a little food. Hmm? For me?"

Bitsy shuddered visibly. "I *suppose* I could try to choke down a little something. For you, darling. You're suffering so much this week as it is."

Rory stood. "I'll send a tray right in for you, Mrs. Pith."

"We can go—"

"No, no, Sabrina. Happy to take care of it." Rory was already halfway to the door and escape. She waved a hand at the couch. "You two just relax." She darted out of the office, only to bump squarely into Noah.

She pressed her finger to her lips. "Shh," she mouthed and grabbed his arm to drag him out of sight of the doorway. She kept hold of him until they reached the great room, where a giant fire was crackling in the fireplace. She'd always been glad the gas logs had only been installed in the Homestead lodge and some of the newer cabins, because she loved a wood fire.

The few guests there seemed to like it, too. The MacArthurs were cozied up together in an over-stuffed love seat near the fireplace, working on a puzzle they'd brought with them. The young couple had replaced Tig and Willow, who had departed two days ago.

On the other side of the fireplace, the Jorgensons were playing backgammon with one of the married couples from the Pith group. They barely gave Rory a glance as she let go of Noah, still aiming for the kitchen.

"Sorry," she finally told him. "Pith emergency." She glanced at him. "What's up?"

"Been thinking about what to do with the kids tomorrow," Noah told her as they turned into the breakfast room.

"Okay." She had been nervous about his ability to handle the kid duty, but he'd come through like a champ. And in the days since—while their parents were busy participating in the daily activities—he'd hosted DVD cartoon fests with the kids in the Homestead lodge and straw-bale mazes and pony rides in the barn. He'd even hauled one of the rowboats up from the river to the barn to play pirates. As far as all the children were concerned—including her own son—Noah was the absolute greatest.

Her eyes skated over the basket of muffins on the wood buffet. Only gluten-free would work for Bitsy, even though Sabrina had told Rory in an aside that her mother wasn't allergic or even remotely gluten sensitive.

Fortunately, Bart was used to accommodating

dietary requests—real or imagined—and had taken to preparing a special "Bitsy basket" just for her.

"I'm thinking art projects," Noah went on.

"Art sounds good. We keep a stock of basic supplies. Paper. Paints. That sort of thing. Just let me know what you need."

She didn't see Bitsy's basket, so she continued into the kitchen. When she caught sight of Gage filling the dishwasher, she prided herself on not breaking stride.

Okay, every nerve ending she possessed tingled, but she didn't trip over her own feet, which had to be a tick in the win column.

"I was thinking we need you," Noah said just as Gage glanced their way.

He gave her a fleeting smile as he leaned over to slide the rack into the washer, his black hair falling into his deep brown eyes.

His hair grew so fast, she thought to herself, mesmerized.

He straightened then, and almost as if he'd been reading her mind, shoved his fingers through his hair, pushing it back off his face. She realized the thin leather wrist wrap they'd made during one of Megan's activities this week had replaced his expensive watch.

It also dawned on her then that she couldn't remember the last time she'd seen him with his phone in hand.

She belatedly focused on Noah. "Sorry, what?"

"What I need is you."

Another rack clattered into the dishwasher.

It took all of her willpower not to look over at Gage again. "Need me for what?"

"You said you went to art school. I don't know anything about that stuff."

She started shaking her head before he'd even finished. "You don't need me, Noah. All you have to do is stick a big sheet of paper and a pot of finger paints in front of kids—doesn't matter *how* old they are— and they'll do the rest. Well, probably better cover every surface that can be covered with plastic first. The paints we have are nontoxic and washable, but finger painting makes a huge mess." She gave him an encouraging pat on the shoulder, stepping around him with the intention of escaping the kitchen. "It's great how you're planning ahead. You've really been a huge help this week."

She made it back through the breakfast room to where the basket of muffins sat on the buffet in all their gluteny glory.

Mocking her.

She spun on her heel and went back into the kitchen.

Avoiding looking at both men, she slapped a serving tray down on the prep table without a word, then yanked open the wide fridge. She pulled out a plastic bin of sliced fresh fruit and filled a small bowl with it. When she added a crystal cup full of yogurt that Bart made from the milk produced by the cows

Seth kept for just that purpose, she caught the look passing between Noah and Gage.

Her cheeks warmed, and she ignored the two of them even harder. She went into the storeroom—it was chillier in there because of the poor weather—and grabbed one of the little stoneware honey pots imprinted with the Angel River logo. When she went back into the kitchen, Bart was entering from the other side. He was wearing a rain slicker and carrying a flat basket full of leafy greens he'd obviously just picked.

"I wasn't thinking of paint so much as clay, Rory." Noah picked up the discussion as if she hadn't ended it. "You did that stuff. Right?"

"You bet she did." Bart set his load next to the tray she was preparing. "I remember the days when we could barely peel her out of her studio."

"That was a long time ago."

"Not that long." He slid the honey pot out of her fingers and held it up. "These were your design."

She snatched it back and set it on the tray with a soft thunk. Since she'd carved the wing in front of her cabin, she'd been thinking more and more about her studio. "A long time ago," she reiterated more for her own benefit than anyone else's.

And then, because she couldn't put it off any longer, she reached around Gage to grab the Bitsy basket.

She saw the amusement in his eyes and was certain that he knew she'd forgotten what she'd come into the kitchen for the first time.

She shot a warning finger in the air between them. "Not one word."

He was hardly containing his smile at this point. "I was just going to ask you how Nelson was faring."

"Nelson!" Amusement overrode everything else. "He wasn't belly up when I got up this morning, so I guess he's managing. Why do you keep asking?"

"Doing my part to keep tabs on the goldfish of the world."

She let out a laugh and escaped with the tray.

What with the rain and the chicken pox, Rory had been depending on Gage lending a willing hand just as much as she had everyone else. Despite having his own business to run from a distance, no less, he'd continued mucking stalls and added hauling firewood daily to all the cabins that burned the real thing. He'd brainstormed ideas with her in the office for the holiday flash deal and then helped her find the best places to advertise it. He helped Bart prep mountains of food in the kitchen and had even run interference a time or two between Rory and the Piths.

Familiarity ought to have helped her gain more control over her reactions where he was concerned, but the reality was just the opposite.

She wasn't thinking of him as a guest. She wasn't thinking of him as the competitor. Or the person with the wherewithal to acquire the ranch if he saw fit to convince her father to sell.

She was just thinking of him. Period.

Day and night. The dreams were even more vivid now. The yank-awake kind that left her breathing hard and her body weak.

She wasn't sure if her subconscious was more or less annoying than Bitsy Pith's constant criticism.

The momzilla was still dramatically draped over the couch when Rory reached the office. She set the tray on the coffee table and smiled at Sabrina. "Feel free to stay here until your mother feels better. But I'm afraid I'm going to have to leave you for the moment."

It was going to be more than a moment, though. The morning activities would be starting soon, and that meant it was time for Rory to gather up the cleaning supplies.

And wasn't it quite a statement to know that she preferred cleaning toilets to spending one more minute in the company of Bitsy Pith?

Sabrina followed her into the corridor. "Rory," she said under her breath, "I want to apologize for my mother again."

Rory shook her head. "Not necessary, Sabrina."

"But it is." She kept pace with Rory. "Dante and I just want to be married. All this wedding stuff—" She waved her hand. "None of it really matters to us."

Rory couldn't help thinking of all the fancy papers. The ribbons. The programs that still had to be dealt with.

"We wanted to elope," Sabrina went on. "But my parents were completely opposed." She spread her hands, looking helpless. "Mother wanted us to wait until next May. Get married at their club with three hundred of their nearest and dearest in attendance. I swear, the day after we told her we were engaged, she already had chosen a date for us and booked it! And it would have been a nightmare."

Rory's steps slowed as they reached the great room. She couldn't help herself. "How did you end up here at Angel River?"

"Dante had a friend who got married here a few years ago. To this day, Matteo and Margo talk about how perfect their wedding was."

She jerked slightly. Surprised. "The Torreses?"

"You remember them?"

Rory couldn't help laughing slightly. Happy weddings—even ones where the best man landed in the river—begot happy weddings. "I remember them very well."

Sabrina smiled, too. "If my parents were going to be adamant about an actual wedding, then we were adamant that it was going to be *here* and we weren't going to wait. Mother still gets all her wedding folderol, and I get to marry the man of my dreams in a few days." Her eyes suddenly glistened. "I've already told Dante that we're coming back for our first anniversary. My mother aside, this place is just magical."

Rory could do only one thing. She hugged Sabrina. "I'm glad," she said huskily.

"Everything all right here?"

Sabrina pulled back as she slid her arm through her fiancé's. "Everything's perfect." She lifted her lips for his kiss.

Immeasurably touched by Sabrina's words and maybe a little envious of the pure happiness the couple radiated, Rory looked away, giving her cheek a surreptitious swipe.

Gage, now stacking firewood next to the hearth, was watching.

He smiled slightly, and it wasn't simply shivers that danced down her spine then. Something warm and sweet and far more dangerous than mere attraction was seeping through her veins, too.

And it stayed there for the rest of the afternoon.

Even through scrubbing toilets.

"So," Megan said later that night as she sipped her spiked hot chocolate on Rory's porch. "I heard about you turning down Noah this morning."

Rory adjusted the pillow behind her in the rocking chair. The rain was more of a mist now, not strong enough to get past the covered deck. "About what?"

"The art thing with the kids."

"Oh, that. It was nothing."

"If it was nothing, you'd have agreed to free up a couple hours to play with modeling clay with them."

Rory gave Megan a look that was entirely wasted since she hadn't turned on the porch light. "I can play with modeling clay or I can cover for Frannie. I still have to keep the office going. I'm just a regular superhero. I can't do it all."

"You're a super chicken." Megan lifted her mug in a toast. "I'll give you that."

Rory huffed. But the truth of it was, she really didn't have the energy to back it up with real annoyance.

So the two of them sat there. Both cradling their mugs. Rocking chairs rocking.

"Who do you suppose that is?" Megan asked when the sound of an engine joined the soft squeak of the chair runners. Headlights were visible in the distance.

"As long as it isn't Bitsy Pith, it doesn't matter to me," Rory said. She relayed Sabrina's conversation from that morning. "What do you bet that Bitsy didn't think to check the actual weekday when she made the reservation here? She just switched the date from May of next year at her *club* to November of this year."

"At least it would explain why they arrived a day earlier—" Megan broke off when the headlights swept over the porch and stayed there as the mystery vehicle came to a stop. "I guess we know the answer now," she said under her breath when the door of the low-slung car opened and Gage stepped out.

Her friend—big help that she was—immediately offered a slyly cheerful "time to go" before she ducked her head against the damp and headed off in the dark.

Rory nervously curled her fingers over the wood rail as she watched Gage retrieve something from inside the vehicle before closing the door, switching off the interior light that had illuminated both his tall form and the wooden bird wing in the yard. "Hey," he said as he climbed the steps.

"Hey," she returned faintly. If her heart pounded any harder, it was going to jump out of her chest. She couldn't make out what he was carrying, except that it was large. "Everything all right in the main camp?"

"Far as I know. Got something for you."

"What is it?"

He laughed softly. "Maybe turn on a light and see," he suggested. "Is Killy asleep?"

"He was an hour ago." She tightened her shawl and pushed open the door, turning on both the porch light and a lamp inside. "Come on in."

She couldn't help but remember the last time he'd been there, and she slowly closed the door while he deposited his box on the coffee table.

"What is it?" she asked again.

And again, he laughed slightly. "Open and see."

Smiling a little shakily, a little uncertainly, she

unwound her shawl and dropped it on the back of the armchair before sitting on the couch in front of the plain brown box. It was definitely bigger than a breadbox.

When he sat down beside her, a fine shiver worked through her. Her gaze was skittering all over the place. From the box to his jeans-clad thigh all of six inches away from hers to the braided leather circling his wrist and back to the box again. Her hands felt unsteady as she folded back the cardboard flaps.

Then her lips parted, and her heart just melted.

It was an aquarium kit.

Her nose prickled warningly.

"Nelson deserves at least a fighting chance," he said.

She blinked hard and pressed her lips together as she worked the aquarium free. Inside the glass she could see a water test kit, filter, gravel and several varieties of plastic plants. "Where on earth did you get all this?"

"Ordered it a week ago. Drove into Wymon to pick it up this afternoon. It's just ten gallons, but it's a good starter size. Nelson will have room for a friend or two once you've got the water cycled. That'll take a couple weeks at the very least, so let's hope he sticks it out in the fishbowl long enough."

She'd been so busy that day she hadn't even realized he'd left Angel River at all. "I can't believe you did this."

He swept the cardboard carton aside. "Got these,

too." He pulled a small plastic bag from his pocket and dropped it next to the tank.

The hard candy in the bag was very distinct. "Spicy Hots," she murmured.

"Figured I still owed Killy."

She let out a garbled sound. Half a laugh. Half a sob. "'Scuse me." She launched herself from the couch and raced into the bathroom, slamming the door shut. Her hands shook as she blew her nose. Wiped her eyes. Then she looked at her reflection. Her eyes looked just as red as the tip of her nose. She yanked her ponytail tighter and dashed a quick smear of gloss over her lips.

This time, she didn't scrub it right back off.

"Rory?" Gage's voice was soft on the other side of the door. As soft as the knock he gave. "You all right?"

Her eyes burned again. She sniffed hard, squared her shoulders and opened the door.

His eyebrows were pulled together above his dark eyes. "I didn't mean to upset you."

She shook her head. "You didn't."

"That'd be more convincing, except—" He lifted his hand toward her cheek but halted just shy of it, then curled his fingers and cleared his throat. "Tears," he said abruptly.

"It's been that kind of day," she said on a choked laugh. "I can't remember the last time anyone did something so…unexpected." So sweet. So captivating.

"It's just candy and a fish tank."

She laughed again and swiped her cheek. "Killian will love it. *I* love it." Aware that they were standing in the doorway to the bathroom—reminding her of the scene she didn't want to relive—she took a step out and he shifted to one side, pushing his hands into his jacket pockets.

She ducked her chin slightly, pressing her glossed lips together as she returned to the couch. She sat and began removing the items from inside the tank only to realize that he wasn't going to also sit. And she was suddenly afraid that—now that he'd stolen half her heart so easily—he was going to drop tank and run. "You're going to show me what to do with all this, right?"

If she hadn't been watching closely, she would have missed the quick glint in his eyes. As though he was relieved. He pulled his hands free of his pockets. "Yeah." He pushed his fingers through his hair and nodded. "Sure."

She chewed the inside of her cheek to keep from smiling. Apparently even developers with employees all over the country had tender boys lurking inside.

"What do we start with first? Probably should do this in the kitchen." Thank heavens she had actually taken the time to do the dishes for once.

"Yeah. Everything needs to be rinsed off before it goes in the tank." His hands brushed hers as he took the aquarium kit from her and carried it into the kitchen.

Before long, the tank was set up, gravel, plants, water and all. "Just follow the directions and keep testing the water. Once it's ready, you can introduce Nelson to it," Gage told her as he moved the tank to a shelf that she'd cleared. "You could do it now, but it's pretty hard on fish to dump them into a tank before the nitrogen's cycled. I've done it, but—"

She leaned against the back of the armchair. "You keep fish?"

"Is it going to cement the whole nerdy image?" His smile was swift and entirely, wholly *non*-nerdy. "I think I was ten when I got my first tank. Pretty much just like this. By the time I graduated from high school, I had two fifty-gallon ones. I ended up selling both, though, 'cause Noah was a toddler and he kept wanting to dive in and play with the fishies. I was sixteen when he was born," he added as if he'd read her mind.

Which made Gage thirty-eight. Younger than she'd first thought. "Was that the end of your fish-keeping days?"

The lamplight shined on his dark hair as he looked down at the aquarium again. "I have salt-water tanks now in most of my offices. And people to keep them in perfect condition. Killian's an un-usual name."

She blinked slightly at the abrupt change of sub-ject. "Depends on your point of view. It was my mother's maiden name."

"Megan told me about her. The rapids."

"Seems Megan likes to talk more than I thought."

"Losing your mom is hard." He spoke from obvious experience.

"You, too?"

"Several years ago. Stroke."

"I'm sorry. What about your dad?"

"He died in a skiing accident when I was little."

She frowned. "Any other family?"

His lips twisted slightly. "Yeah, but that's a whole other story." He didn't elaborate.

Which naturally only increased her curiosity. "Noah's father? Were you close to him?"

He snorted softly. "Guess he told you we're half brothers. But no. I was not close to Noah's father. For that matter, neither was Noah. My mom worked for Julian for years, but they never married. Didn't even live together. He left a fortune for Noah, but that's *all* he ever did for him." He glanced at her. "She didn't marry my father, either. She wasn't traditional that way. But she did want me to watch out for Noah. He's never really been happy about that."

"Maybe he's just trying to figure out where his place is in this world. He even said it. He wants to be something that matters to someone."

"He's always mattered," Gage said quietly. Then he lifted his head, and it was as though a light had been switched off. "I don't need to keep you any longer. Stables to muck in the morning." He reached for the door and stepped outside.

She snatched up her shawl and hurried after him. "Gage, wait—"

He hesitated, but her spurt of bravery suddenly failed her. "Thanks again for everything." She moistened her lips. The gloss was long gone. "The tank and the candy." A sharp wind whipped over them, but all she did was clutch the shawl in her hands. "Not to mention everything else you've been doing. I really owe you. I know you came to learn what made us tick, but this last week has been—" She broke off, because she didn't have adequate words to describe it.

He startled her slightly when he tugged the shawl out of her grip. He shook it out and swung it around her shoulders. "I don't want you owing me anything."

Her pulse throbbed inside her head all over again, and she blamed it on the way his hands were holding the shawl together beneath her chin. "Considering everything you've been doing, that's kind of a hard thing to avoid."

The shawl grew more taut around her shoulders, as if he were reeling her in. "That's what makes this worse."

She looked up beyond that perfect mouth until she could see his eyes. "Makes what worse?" But she knew. She could feel it in every cell.

And he knew that she knew. The thumb he brushed whisper light over her chin told her so. "I made a promise." His voice was low. Deep. "That you didn't have to worry about this happening again."

"I'm more worried that it won't," she blurted, then wished the ground would just open up right then and there. Her tongue felt thick, and she looked away. "I don't know why that came out."

"But it did. And now I'm just going to have to take back that promise," he finished, his deep voice seeming to drop another octave.

It took a moment for the words to seep beyond the heartbeat clanging in her head, and when they did, everything just went still.

Her gaze slowly crept up his throat. Over his sharply angled jaw.

They never had a chance to make it to his lips, because his head was lowering toward hers. "All you have to do is say no if you—"

"No." She swallowed hard. "I mean no, I'm not going to say no."

His fingers touched her cheek. They were so, so warm. "Is that your way of saying yes?"

"Yes." It was hardly a whisper. Barely a breath.

"Good."

And then he slid his hand along her neck with just the perfect pressure and his mouth found hers.

And she was *very* glad the ground hadn't swallowed her up after all.

Chapter Twelve

The next morning, the day before Sabrina Larissa Pith and Dante Cruz Castellano would be pronounced husband and wife promptly at sunset, the sky was at last clear.

But it was freezing cold out.

Frost clung to the trees and fence posts. It coated the ground, looking almost like snow, and lent an extra crunch under Rory's boots as she pulled open the door on the hay barn.

The trio of cats inside was sleeping, their bodies pressed up against each other. Only Huey lifted his head and gave her an unwelcoming stare when she walked past them on her way to the spreader. "Good morning to you, too."

Huey blinked twice and snuggled his head back into his curled body.

"They look ambitious this morning."

She whirled around, and though she knew a goofy smile was forming, she didn't really care.

"Good morning." She watched Gage close the door and head toward her. It was the first time that week that he hadn't beaten her to the hay barn.

His eyes crinkled. "G'morning."

She almost giggled from the jittery excitement inside her. Instead, she gestured at the cats. "Really ambitious," she agreed. "Good thing we're not plagued with mice."

"Good thing."

Her gaze might as well be a fishing line reeling him in considering the way she couldn't look away from him. "I wonder where Megan is. It's not like her to be late."

"I don't really care," he said, smiling slightly. He slid an arm behind her back and pulled her close.

His lips were cold. Until they weren't.

And then, it was only a loud "ahem" that finally broke them apart.

Rory couldn't pull away, though, because if she did, Megan just might see the way her flannel shirt had come undone. So Rory rested her head against his chest and gave Megan a slit-eyed look. It was her fault for the barn door being so well oiled they hadn't even heard her entering.

The look was wasted on her friend, who was

grinning broadly. "Looks to me like the drought is finally ending." She gestured with her gloved hands. "Go ahead. Proceed. For once in my life, I think I'll go and see Bart about a chocolate croissant." And she turned on her heel and left the barn, sliding the door closed after her.

Gage's hands rubbed down Rory's arms. "The drought?"

She felt flushed. From his touch. From everything. "Megan's idea of a joke."

He laughed softly, and she was pretty certain he knew exactly what Megan had meant.

"Enticing as it would be to take advantage of the sleeping chaperones there—" he nodded to the cats, who were not giving them the time of day now "—we should probably get on with the work."

She nodded. "Probably." The fact that his maddening thumb was circling her rigid nipple brought into question what exactly he meant by "work." She angled her chin when he kissed her neck right below her ear. "But, uh, that's uh… Oh, you." She dragged his mouth to hers, luxuriating in his soft laugh as they fell back against the stacks of sweet-smelling hay.

And then his hands were delving even farther under her wool jacket, rearranging more than just her flannel shirt and slipping beneath waffle-woven thermals. She was catching her breath, gasping his name when his tongue found her nipple and his fingers found her center and she very nearly dissolved right then and there. "Wait, wait. We can't." So then why were her fingers twined in his belt loops? "I'm not on the pill."

He hesitated, his oath muffled against her breast. "And I'm not exactly packing condoms here." Suddenly, his shoulders shook, and it took her a second to realize he was laughing.

Hard. His fingers retreated from her thermals and she couldn't even protest, not really, because he kept laughing until he was positively roaring. He slid down until he was sitting on the ground, taking her right along with him.

And then she was laughing, too, and it felt so good, so wonderful, really, to just laugh and laugh until they were breathless and exhausted from it.

She leaned against him, sliding her fingers through his. "I haven't laughed like that in a long time," she finally managed. "It's almost as good as—" She broke off when he lifted their hands and kissed her knuckles.

"No," he drawled. "It's not. But that's something easily solved in time."

Her cheeks heated even as need threatened to devour her from the inside out. But she thrilled to the "in time" part.

Then he turned her hand over and kissed her palm. "Right now, we've got a crapload of stalls to clean." He stood up and tugged her to her feet. "And yes, pun intended."

Before she could even roll her eyes, he grasped

her waist and lifted her up and over the side of the spreader. "Fix your shirt," he said when he deposited her. "It's buttoned all wrong." Then he yanked a pair of work gloves from his back pocket and pulled them on.

She quickly refastened her buttons before pulling on her own work gloves. Then he started tossing up hay bales and straw, and she scooted and stacked them. "I could help you do that, you know."

He didn't even slow. "I know."

"When you made your deal with my father to learn all our secrets, was this what you had in mind?"

He grunted, and a moment later, another heavy bale landed near her feet with a fragrant puff. "When I made that deal with Sean, I didn't intend to even *be* the one who was here. Got room for a few more?"

"A few." She used her knees to push the stacks together more closely. "Who did you intend to be here?"

"Anybody else but me."

"Oh. Flattering."

His smile was long and slow. "I've learned my error." He hefted two more bales, then rested his arms on the side of the spreader. "Noah had earned himself another DUI. It should've been his last strike, but I convinced the judge to give him another shot at proving himself. That he could be responsible. That he could actually work and be a productive member of society. So I dragged him along with me, figuring I'd come up with some sort of job for him to do along the way." Gage circled her calf with his fingers almost absently. "Never thought it would be wrangling a handful of little kids for about eight hours a day. He's doing it to impress you, but the bottom line is at least he's doing it."

She shook her head. "You keep saying stuff like that, but I think you're wrong."

"Wrong that he's infatuated with you?" He squeezed her calf and smiled wryly. "Half brother or not, we've got some things in common." Then his hand slid around, and he lightly smacked her knee. "Stay there. I'll drive this thing over to the horse barn."

In seconds, he'd climbed into the cab, and the tractor engine rumbled to life. She swayed on her perch as they jerked into motion. He got out again to open the barn door when they reached it, and they rolled out into the frosty morning.

But she was blind to the wintry beauty. Instead, she was entirely rattled at the idea of Gage being infatuated with her. He hadn't said it expressly, but he might as well have.

Infatuated.

Was that what she was feeling, too? Infatuation was harmless enough, wasn't it?

But as they continued making their way around to the horse barn, all Rory could think about was fish aquariums and Spicy Hots.

* * *

She was still thinking about them thirty-six hours later, when she was sitting in the wedding barn watching Sabrina and Dante circle the dance floor.

"Dance?"

Rory glanced up at Noah and smiled. All was right with the world—except when it came to worrying that she was falling in love with Gage.

The wedding ceremony on Angel's Lookout had gone off without a hitch, the timing of Sabrina and Dante's first kiss as husband and wife perfectly co-ordinated with the golden rays of the lowering sun.

Not even Bitsy Pith could find fault.

Rory had seen enough weddings to know that the photographs would be spectacular. The subject matter was too perfect to fail.

Now, the bride and groom, their attendants, and all of the guests were here in the wedding barn, where Chef Bart's spread was on glorious display. The champagne was flowing, the music was playing and everyone—including mom- and popzilla—was dancing beneath the glittering fairy lights twined among the barn rafters.

Noah was still holding out a hopeful hand.

The last thing she wanted to do was get up on her feet and dance. The grueling week of splitting housekeeping duties with Marni was still fresh, with no end yet in sight. Rory was fairly certain she'd never scoured so many bathrooms and vacuumed so many floors in her life. The Pith group would be departing in a few days, and even though she'd worried about not having any guests for Thanksgiving week, now that they'd gotten several bookings, she longed for a break.

But she ignored her aching back and her tired feet and put her hand in Noah's, because he'd helped haul the chairs up to the lookout. Because he'd woven Bitsy's blue ribbons through the white wood so Rory could affix the floral sprays that had been delivered just in the nick of time.

For once, the children of the Pith group were actually spending time with their families and he wasn't on babysitting duty.

And her duties—until the reception concluded— were pretty much done.

"I would love to dance," she told him.

His smile was somewhere shy of brilliant, and she couldn't help but think that one day there'd come a girl who would look past that silly man bun to the sweet boy lurking inside.

He swung her around onto the dance floor, and she laughed. She wasn't really surprised that he could dance so well. She was surprised, however, that he was actually as tall as he was. He had a slighter build than Gage and she kept thinking of him as being so much smaller, but he really wasn't.

"All right," she said, "who taught you to dance?"

He looked a little chagrined. "My mother."

Her smile widened. "I love that. Maybe one day I'll be teaching Killy how to dance." Since her father had no reason to attend the wedding or reception, Killy was spending the night with him.

"Think you'll have more? Kids, I mean?"

Her gaze unerringly landed on Gage. He was standing to one side of the buffet tables in conversation with Bart, who had the whole chef thing going on, from white coat buttoned to his neck to tall toque on his head. The only point of color on Bart was the small Angel River logo emblazoned on his lapel.

Gage, on the other hand, was dressed entirely in black. The suit had undoubtedly been custom tailored. For all she knew, the shirt that fit him so perfectly had been, too. The fact that he'd packed a suit when he'd come to Angel River was surprising.

In contrast, Noah wore an ivory cashmere pullover and jeans. The man bun was there, but he'd shaved for the first time since he and Gage had arrived at the ranch, making his resemblance to his brother more pronounced.

"I never thought I'd want kids," Noah said, reminding her that she hadn't gotten around to answering his question. "Turns out they're not so bad."

"They're great," she assured him. Gage was watching them and smiling slightly. "Even when they sometimes drive you a little crazy." She remembered Gage's comment when she'd asked him if he had kids.

Thank God, no.

Had he really meant it?

Or was it just one of those things you said to

someone you didn't know when you got on a subject that you didn't want to discuss?

She was going to make herself crazy.

She dragged her gaze away and focused on Noah. "My mom told me once that you never knew how much you could love someone until you became a parent. Killy is my world. But if I had another child, I'd love him or her just as much."

"My mom used to say something like that. But I know she preferred Gage."

"Oh, Noah. I'm sure that's not true."

"It is." He nodded, so matter-of-fact about it that she hurt for him. "Julian—my old man—he must've proposed to her a dozen times, but she never said yes. She worked for him, but she wouldn't marry him. Not even because of me."

When Gage had said Noah wasn't close to his father, either, she'd assumed that meant he hadn't been involved in his life at all. "That doesn't mean she preferred Gage to you. Did you *want* her to marry your father?"

She felt the vague shrug in his shoulders. "If she had, maybe he'd have acted more like a dad."

She thought about her ex-husband. "Marriage isn't any guarantee of that, Noah. Not with some people. That's not your failing, though. That was his. And it doesn't mean he didn't love you. Maybe it just means he didn't know how to show it."

He gave that faint shrug again. "Doesn't matter now. He's dead."

"It'll always matter if you let it drive—" She broke off when she felt a tap on her shoulder, and she glanced around to find Marni looking unusually determined.

"Mind if I cut in?"

Delighted, Rory stepped back. Marni looked pretty as could be in a dress as bright a pink as her hair. The color in her cheeks was only slightly dimmer. "Thank you for the dance, Noah," Rory said as she surrendered her position.

With no graceful way to get out of it, he took Marni in his arms and continued dancing. He was even smiling about it when Rory chanced a look their way as she made her way around the perimeter of the room to where Gage and Bart stood. "I would say we have a success on our hands."

Bart looked over the rims of his eyeglasses. "You talking about the reception or young Marni over there?"

Rory smiled. "Maybe both."

"Thought it was supposed to be hands-off between staff and guests," Gage murmured close to her ear. Out of sight from everyone, he trailed a meaningful finger down her spine.

"Since the Piths arrived and Frannie got sick, Noah has been more like one of the crew." She sent him a look from beneath her lashes. "Same as you."

The corners of his lips twitched. "Isn't that interesting?"

"Oh, for Lord's sake," Bart said, shooing them

away. "Take it on the dance floor or something. I'm too old for all the pheromones flying between you."

Gage wrapped her hand in his. "An excellent idea." He drew her toward the edge of the crowd and pulled her close even though the beat of the music was fast.

She didn't care. There were enough other people dancing that the two of them were barely noticeable. And she wasn't giving her sore feet a single thought. Not when she could feel his long fingers splayed against the small of her back the way they were.

"Pretty dress," he murmured. "Thought it was bad form to outshine the bride."

"It'd take the sun to outshine Sabrina," Rory returned. The girl was radiant with happiness. "But I appreciate the compliment all the same. You clean up pretty well yourself. I've been meaning to ask all night. Do you always travel with a suit?"

He chuckled. "Regrettably. Old habits die hard. Was talking to Ludo earlier."

"The wedding photographer?"

"Ludovico Bianchi is a master wedding photo-*journalist*, sweetheart. He doesn't pose the shots. He records—"

"—the truth and realism in the moment," she finished, trying not to get too flustered by the *sweetheart*. "I know the gist."

"Then you shouldn't be surprised to hear he wants to do a story on Angel River."

She pulled her head back from the spot against

his jaw where it naturally fit to give him a narrow look. "How do you know that?"

"How do you think? He told me. You should agree and get a tease of his story to push the flash deal. Bitsy Pith might be a pain in your beautiful derriere—" his fingers dipped an inch lower on her spine "—but she didn't stint when it came to hiring him. His work's well-known."

Rory arched back, reaching around to catch his hand before it could drop farther. "Stop," she whispered fiercely. "Someone's going to notice."

"Then let's go where nobody can see."

She was so sorely tempted she was quaking inside. He had no idea of the gift that Megan had slipped into Rory's hand while the reception was gearing up. But Rory did, and she'd been swamped with anticipation of this moment ever since. "I can't just disappear at a function like this," she reminded herself as much as him.

"Then when?"

"After!"

"This thing could go on all night. As Noah keeps telling me, I'm not a young man anymore. I could have a heart attack waiting—"

She laughed, covering his mouth with her hand. "You're a nut." Then she twisted out of his arms. "And it won't last all night, because they only have the band and the bartending team until midnight. But let me get my coat. We'll go out and... I don't know. Take a stroll." She gave him a stern glance. "*Just* a stroll." And maybe the cold air would cool them both off.

The air was cold, for sure. But it didn't cool Gage off all that much.

And it quickly became apparent that they weren't the only ones out for a little "stroll." They even happened upon a couple making out in one of the boats tied near the bridge.

Still, the few kisses Gage did manage to steal were enough to keep him going through the rest of the interminably long wedding reception.

But finally, it was last call. Most of the guests who had kids had called it a night once the bride and groom had cut the cake earlier in the evening. But that still left a good-size crowd cozying up to the bar for that last drink of the night before they climbed into the vans to be shuttled by Megan and Marni back to the Uptown camp. Meanwhile, the band was packing up their equipment and loading it in their truck. Like the bartending team and the couple of servers Rory had hired, they had a longer drive ahead of them than just the few miles to Uptown. They had to return all the way to Wymon.

Gage and Noah helped Bart break down the buffet and pack it all to go back to the lodge while Rory went around collecting flowers and linens and doing pretty much everything else that still needed doing.

He knew she was exhausted, but she kept on going.

He wasn't sure he'd ever met anyone who worked as hard as she did. And coming from him, that was saying a lot.

She'd kicked off the sexy high heels she'd been wearing earlier, and her long, narrow sheath of a dress swished against the wood floor as she walked back and forth collecting this, sorting that. She'd done something with her hair for the wedding, too. She usually wore it loose or pulled back in a pony-tail. But tonight she'd twisted it up in a thick, coiling rope. It emphasized the slender column of her neck.

And he'd been thinking about letting that coil down for nearly eight hours.

He shot Bart a look. Even the chef had let his hair down at this point—at least he'd doffed the toque and loosened a few buttons on his white coat. "You're not doing something obscene like baking bread in a few hours, are you?"

Bart chuckled. "Not this week. It's no-knead bread this week." He snapped a lid down on the last plastic tub. "Plus we have that special post-wedding brunch to deal with tomorrow. Guess that'd be *today*. Fortunately, everything is set to go for that. I'll just be carving beef and making omelets on the fly."

Noah reached for the tub and hefted it up. "Does *every* wedding go like this?"

"Eh." Bart waved his hand. "More or less. Under the skin, you know, it's all pretty much the same stuff." He picked up a big trash bag that Rory had filled with the table linens to be washed and followed Noah out to the UTV he was using.

Rory dropped an armload of ivory flowers on the table in front of him.

"What happens with all of the flowers?"

"Bitsy only wanted these for the reception." She moved her shoulders slightly as she stroked one of the ruffled petals. She gave Gage a wry look. "She has *other* decor in mind for the brunch. That'll be all blues and yellows. Instead of blues and—" she lifted an encompassing arm "—ivory."

"What was up at the lookout?" He hadn't gone over for the ceremony. One, the place had barely enough room for all of the wedding party and guests, and, two, he'd been down here helping Bart transport all the last-minute food from the ovens at the lodge. Because, as nice a setup as the wedding barn was—and Gage had to admit it had a particularly appealing location on the other side of the river away from the lodge—it did not have its own kitchen.

He needed to remember to mention that point to April and Jed. In case they wanted something similar at the Rad.

But right now, his mind kept short-circuiting at the way Rory's fingertip stroked over that velvety flower.

"More peonies like these," she said. "Just none of the blue ribbons." Her arm cut a swath through the air. "That had to be all white. Pure. For the ceremony, of course. The only blue allowed was the programs."

"That you printed and folded."

"Megan and Marni helped." She smiled wearily. "I think I probably bought out all the peonies this side of California just to have enough. Poor Bitsy. She had a spring wedding in her mind that landed squarely in November."

"Poor Bitsy nothing." He'd watched Rory already fill five giant trash bags with just flowers. "Got enough there to make a bed of them." As soon as the words came out, that was the vision that filled his head.

Laying Rory down on a thick white cushion of flowers. Pulling away a shimmering white veil from her head.

He yanked at his tie, loosening it enough to free the button at his neck. He was more tired than he thought if he was imagining *that*.

"I do love them," she said. Then she looked at him, humor lighting her blue eyes. "Compost pile is going to smell really pretty for a while." She shook open another black bag and, with one long sweep across the table, sent flowers tumbling down into it.

Then she propped her hands on her hips and looked around them. "I think that's it."

Sure enough, all of the tables were bare, the chairs tucked in, the decorations gone.

"We don't have anything else going on down here

now, so maybe the floors can wait to be mopped until Frannie is back." She pushed her feet into her shoes with a little groan. "Oh, for a good foot massage."

He dropped her coat around her shoulders. It was a stylish thing. Long and black and fitted. Entirely different from that muddy red one she wore nearly every day. "You need more help."

She sent him a wry smile as they headed for the door. "So I keep hearing."

Then she hit the lights on the way out, plunging the cavernous interior into black.

The UTV with the trailer was gone. Bart and Noah had taken it across to the lodge already. Gage nudged Rory into the last one remaining, stuffed the flower bags in the cargo box as well as he could, then climbed behind the wheel himself. With the cold weather enclosure in place, it seemed smaller inside.

She let out a soft sigh, her shoulder leaning into his as he started driving back. When he crossed the narrow bridge spanning the river, her palm seemed to naturally come to rest on his thigh.

His own tiredness fled. "Do you need to stop at the lodge?"

She made another soft sound. He felt her shake her head.

When he reached the loop road, instead of heading toward the building on the knoll, he kept right on going, and he didn't stop until he reached her cabin.

By then, she was a limp weight against his side. She'd fallen asleep.

He sat there for a moment, staring out at the star-speckled sky while he willed his body to calm the hell down. It probably was just as well. He hadn't had a condom the other morning in the barn. He hadn't had a single opportunity to acquire one in the time since.

He was pretty sure the universe was having a hell of a laugh at his expense.

He carefully slid her over so he could get out of the utility vehicle without disturbing her and went up to check the cabin door. It swung open when he turned the knob, which was convenient for the moment but still made him want to lecture her about common safety. He left the door open and returned to the UTV. He started to reach for her but hesitated.

Suddenly coming to a decision, he worked a couple of the bags free from the cargo box and carried them inside her cabin. She'd left a lamp on by the aquarium being prepared for Nelson, so he had no trouble seeing his way up the stairs. Once he reached the landing, the night-light plugged into the wall helped the rest of the way. The cabin had the same floor plan as where he and his brother were staying. Distinguishing Killy's room from Rory's even in the faint light was a no-brainer.

Feeling a little strange because he'd never once done anything remotely like this, he turned on the small lamp on her nightstand, then folded back the

quilt on her bed and dumped out the flowers on the
sheet, muttering a curse when they tumbled every-
where, including the floor. He scrambled around
for a few minutes tossing them back up onto the
mattress. At the rate he was going, she'd probably
wake up in the UTV and wonder what the hell he
was doing in her cabin.

He balled up the bags in his fist and went back
downstairs, convinced she'd be awake by now. But
she was still asleep, her head lolled over to one side.

He couldn't help smiling at her. "You *really* need
help," he whispered. If he had his way, that help
would include a new manager so she could get back
to doing what she really loved. He tossed the empty
bags in the cargo box and gathered her up in his
arms. She snuffled slightly and turned her nose into
his neck.

He kissed her forehead, then carried her inside
and nudged the cabin door closed with his foot. She
hadn't put her coat on properly so it was easy enough
to work it off her shoulders. It fell on the floor before
he turned sideways to get her up the stairs.

In her bedroom, he leaned over, carefully deposit-
ing her on the mound of white flowers.

He dislodged some when he straightened and
tossed them back on the bed before he started to
leave the room.

"Gage?"

He froze, feeling as guilty as a kid caught with
his hand in the cookie jar. He looked back at her.

Her eyelids were at half-mast. Her hand stretched toward him, fingers softy curled against her palm. And all around her were those velvety, ruffled balls of sweet-smelling flowers. "Where are you going?"

He'd been wanting her from day one. Now that chronic ache had an even sharper edge. But he wasn't certain she was awake enough to even realize she was lying on a bed of flowers. "Sweetheart, I can't stay. If I do—" He broke off. Cleared his throat. "I can't stay," he repeated.

She pushed herself up onto her elbow. "Are you sure?"

She was killing him. "You're not on the pill. I still don't have a condom."

Her hand stretched toward him again. Her fingers uncurling. "But I do," she said softly.

He stared at the shiny square packet in her palm. "Where did you come up with that?" She hadn't moved once he placed her on the bed. He would have sworn to it.

"Megan." Then her hand slid down her side and disappeared into a pocket he hadn't even realized her dress possessed. Her hand emerged again with a second shiny square packet. "Just in case. So…" Her voice lowered as she nuzzled her cheek slightly against a flower, putting an end to any lingering notion that she wasn't entirely awake. "Are you still sure you have to go?"

He shrugged out of his suit coat and yanked off

his tie, putting his knee on the side of the bed before kissing her.

He was hard and she was wet, and the one portion of his mind still capable of thought after he finally buried himself inside her and swallowed her gasping cries was that he owed Megan.

Big-time.

It was a long while later before either one of them had the strength to speak. Rory's fingers were trailing over his bare hip, her silky leg gliding along his. Her uncoiled hair streamed over his chest.

"Have to say—" there was a smile in her soft, husky voice "—when you give a girl flowers, you really give a girl flowers."

Chapter Thirteen

Bliss.

There was no other word to describe what it felt like waking in Gage's arms.

The few flowers they hadn't already dislodged from the bed quickly ended up on the floor when he smiled sleepily and pulled her down to him once more.

By the time they made their way to the lodge to set up for Bitsy Pith's big post-wedding brunch, Rory knew she'd never been so well loved.

From the soles of her feet that he'd rubbed while he kissed his way up her legs, to the tears he'd brushed away from the corners of her eyes when her pleasure grew too great, there wasn't one inch of her that Gage hadn't discovered.

One day, perhaps, she'd tell Megan about waking up on a cushion of flowers.

She owed her that much, at least, for having slid those two packets into Rory's hand during the wedding reception.

But for now, she was going to hold the experience close—because it was in that moment she'd realized she was falling head over heels in love with Gage.

She knew perfectly well that it couldn't last.

How could it, when her life was at Angel River and Gage's wasn't?

He wasn't going to stay there forever. He had a business to run. A life that was entirely separate from hers waited for him.

But until then, Rory was going to savor every moment.

That didn't mean, however, that she wanted to advertise this new development in their relationship to everyone. "I have Killy to consider," she told Gage as they went in through the storeroom of the lodge.

"I get it." He wrapped his arms around her waist, pulling her up tight against him. "I have the kid in my place to consider, too."

"Noah's not a kid," she murmured against his kiss. "And he's been a huge help—" She broke off when his hand slid between her thighs. She frantically pulled at his wrist even though everything inside her yearned to follow the press of his palm. "We *can't*. Not here!"

He laughed softly. "But I love the way you come

so sweet and—" He swiftly released her when the hinges of the door to the kitchen squeaked, and he walked right past Bart with a calm "g'morning" that gave no hint of what the chef had nearly interrupted.

Rory, on the other hand, was left in a flush of wanting that plagued her the rest of the day and bloomed with fresh heat every time Gage's eyes caught hers.

He knew it, too.

Fortunately, the brunch was a raving success. She even caught Bitsy genuinely smiling as she made her way among her guests. Then Rory's dad arrived with Killy in tow as half the guests joined in a game of touch football and the other half headed for the river and the rowboats.

Even though the wedding was finally over, that didn't mean the guest rooms and cabins didn't need tending.

"I'll make you pay for this," she murmured to Gage as she passed him with her arms full of sheets from Uptown.

"I'm looking forward to it," he murmured as he headed the other way with an armload of firewood.

The payment, however, had to wait. Luckily, the rest of the day passed quickly. Then the next morning, after a mass exodus that was far more orderly than the group's premature arrival, all of Uptown was finally quiet once more.

The lodge was empty, too.

The only guest cabin being occupied was the Brown.

The lull wouldn't last forever, not with more guests coming in the following week for the Thanksgiving holiday. But it was enough to give them all a much-needed rest as they regrouped.

And Rory, taking advantage of the fact that Killy was at school, her dad and Bart were in Wymon, and Marni had wrangled Noah and Megan into helping her repaint the kitchen in her cabin, finally had her chance to extract payment.

She picked up Gage in one of the UTVs and could tell by his expression as they headed toward the staff cabins that he figured they were heading to hers. But when she kept driving right on past, his certainty turned to curiosity. "Where are we going?"

She slid him a smile. "You'll see."

She was more nervous than she let on. It had been so long since she'd been up to the studio. She could well find it infested with displaced barn mice.

Hardly ideal for the tryst she had in mind.

But when the UTV made it through the trail overgrown from disuse and she pulled to a stop in front of the small square building, the look in Gage's eyes more than made up for any nervousness she felt.

He helped her pull the riotous shrubs away from the windows and the door. She'd never had a reason to lock it, and when she turned the knob, it opened easily.

Inside, the windows that faced the same view

SOMETHING ABOUT THE SEASON

he'd seen the first time he'd kissed her were caked with dust. Otherwise, the interior looked the same as it always had. Shelves loaded with supplies and tools. Two different kilns. Her wheel still sat near the window, because she'd liked looking out as she'd worked.

Gage's hand curved over her shoulder. "How'd you learn to carve wood with the chain saw?"

"I did some ice carving when I lived in Seattle. Never did much with wood at all." She kissed his hand and moved farther into the studio. "Place is cleaner than I expected." She noticed his expression. "What?"

"You amaze me."

She flushed slightly. "I can't imagine why."

"You created that *wing* without endless practice? Jesus, Rory. What would you be able to create if you could focus on your art?"

"It doesn't really matter." She picked up a wrapped piece of clay. It had gone hard and dry. "I don't have time for all of this anymore, anyway." She dropped it back onto the plaster-topped wedging table. "Not with the ranch."

"Do they have to be mutually exclusive?"

"Yes," she admitted. "I was never good at splitting my concentration when it comes to this." She waved her arm, encompassing the studio and all that it contained. "If I'm running Angel River, I have to run it. I can't be thinking about which clay bodies I prefer and whether I can coax more color from a glaze if I just try one more combination." She didn't even realize she had tears in her eyes until one spilled hot onto her cheek.

She dashed it away and moved to the larger of the kilns. "Can you imagine how much worse things would be for the ranch if I didn't keep my focus where it belonged?" She restlessly lifted the lid. Three honey pots sat inside, still unfinished. She closed the lid again and glanced at him.

His gaze was warm on her face, as if he saw everything that she wasn't saying. Her throat tightened even more.

"The art is not worth the price that keeps coming with it," she admitted huskily.

"Your mom didn't die because you were away living *your life*," he said quietly. "Your dad didn't get sick because you were throwing pots."

She ran her finger around the edge of her potter's wheel. "Megan tell you that, too?"

"Educated guess." He crossed to her and kissed the top of her head, sliding his arms around her. "Hire another manager. Come with me to Denver."

She froze, yet everything inside her was wildly spinning. "What?"

"You and Killy." He turned her around to face him. "He can get the advanced placement he needs without having to go to a school fifty miles away." He smiled slightly. "You can have a studio with all the clay and chain saws you've ever wanted."

She swallowed hard. "I...I don't know what to

say." She wasn't even certain exactly what he was asking.

"Say yes. And I'll take care of the rest." Then he let out an impatient sigh and yanked his cell phone from his jacket pocket. "Archer. My lawyer. Impeccable timing as usual." He silenced the vibrating and tucked the phone away again. "Come to Denver."

He said it so easily. As if it weren't the least bit momentous. "Wh-where would we live?"

His eyes searched hers. "Where do you want to live?"

She could hardly breathe. "Gage—"

"With me." He cupped her face in his hands. "Where did you think I meant?"

"I don't know." She swallowed. "This is all happening too fast. I can't think straight."

"Sometimes thinking is overrated. Sometimes you have to go with your gut. And mine tells me the world needs more beauty, courtesy of Rory McAdams." He brushed his lips over hers. "And I need more of her nights."

"This is not what I came up here for," she said faintly.

Suddenly, his eyes held fresh intent. "What *did* you come up here for?"

Despite the uncertainties and temptation whirling dizzily inside her, heat streaked through her veins. "You know very well what for. To torture you for that business in the storeroom yesterday."

His lips curved. "Torture me?" He reached around

her and picked up the coiled cutoff wire she'd used to slice clay and let it dangle from one of the small wooden end rods. "Not planning to garrote me, are you?"

"I was thinking more along the lines of this." She tossed aside the tool and drew his hand to the juncture of her thighs.

His eyes darkened as his fingers cupped her through her jeans. "Aren't you suddenly the bold one?"

"Yes." Her legs were already going weak.

His head lowered toward hers, his breath whispering over her ear. "If you're really bold, unzip your pants."

Her hands shook. She unzipped her jeans. Then moaned inadvertently when his hand slid beneath her panties.

He inhaled on a hiss when he found her. "How." His fingers slowly delved. Swirled through her wetness. "How is this torturing me?"

She leaned against the wedging table, her head falling back as she watched him from beneath her lashes. Her breath was already coming harder, and she could feel her nerves coiling. Tightening. Her fingers curled against the cold plaster at either side of her. "Because I don't have a third little packet," she breathed shakily. "And I don't think you've all of a sudden conjured one, either."

And for some reason, she'd stupidly thought that particular fact would be harder on him than on her.

The corner of his lips lifted, and his eyes darkened even more. "Then by all means…" His fingers slid farther, pressed deeper and she was suddenly gasping, convulsing. Before the tremors even had a chance to abate, he'd swept her jeans away and lifted her onto the table, his head lowering to join his hands. "Let me be *really* tortured."

She was the one who cried out for mercy, though.

He just laughed softly, exultantly, and "suffered" some more.

Gage didn't say anything more about her moving to Denver, but as the month dwindled—taking Thanksgiving along with it—his words never left her thoughts.

Now it was December, and the end of Gage's stay was drawing even closer.

The flash sale—helped by the spectacular photography of Ludovico Bianchi—turned out to be a wild success.

Even though there was no snow yet, they had more three-night reservations than Rory could recall ever having before.

Noah and Gage helped them haul the enormous white spruce her dad had ordered from a local tree farm into the lodge. It stood almost as tall as the exposed beams in the ceiling, and all of the Angel River staff—even Seth and Toonie—helped decorate it. They fastened fresh boughs of greenery and red ribbons on the staircase banisters. They hung mistletoe in doorways and twirled lights around the railings outside. Holiday carols played on the sound system nearly twenty-four hours a day.

When it came to ambience, Angel River had it in spades. Of course, the food and booze had never been a problem, and while it remained to be seen if the flurry of new business could sustain itself, Rory couldn't help but feel hopeful.

Thankfully, Frannie was fully recuperated from her bout with the chicken pox by the time the first of the holiday guests began checking into the lodge. Rory was so grateful she was back to work, she gave Frannie the promotion to head of housekeeping and told her to hire someone to help her. Maybe, like Noah had with the children from the wedding, Frannie just needed a reason to rise to the occasion.

There was no denying the woman seemed to show a brand-new commitment to the work.

And yet more days dwindled away, giving Gage and Rory precious little time to sneak away when nobody was looking. She knew they hadn't fooled Megan, of course. And not Bart, either. But Killy remained innocently unaware of his mother's secret and so, apparently, was Noah, who'd been spending more and more time with Marni anyway.

By the second weekend in December, nearly every room in the lodge was booked.

Instead of the huge bonfire down by the river, they kept one going in the firepit outside the lodge and served gallons of Rory's hot chocolate at the mahogany bar.

She was refilling the bowls of toppings—marshmallows and caramels were neck and neck when it came to favorites—and watching Noah across the room sitting at the grand piano she'd rented from a place in Montana, when Gage came up next to her. He secretly brushed his hand over hers before he filled a mug with the rich cocoa.

"Did you know Noah played?"

"He took lessons when he was little. But otherwise?" He shook his head.

"What else did he do when he was little? Besides dive for fishies in your aquariums?"

Gage smiled wryly. "He was a holy terror. My mother said he was just like me." His smile turned bittersweet. "Then he got a little older. I was out on my own. Things changed."

She squeezed his hand. "Things can change again."

"Probably not that much." The big door opened, letting in a group of laughing people, and they both automatically glanced that way.

Then Gage let out a surprised grunt, and he suddenly crossed toward the group, his hand outstretched. "Why the hell didn't you say you were coming?"

She watched him clasp hands with a tall blond guy then swing a woman with wildly curling brown hair around in a circle.

Rory couldn't help smiling as he drew the couple toward her.

"—and so we thought, why not," the woman was saying. "It's not that long a drive from Braden. And this is our last free weekend of the year."

"Didn't expect to see this many people here," the man added. "Thought it'd be a good surprise, but the surprise'll be on us if there's no room at the inn."

"There's room," Gage assured him. He briefly dropped his hand on Rory's shoulder. "This is Rory McAdams. She runs the place. Honey, this is my lawyer, Archer Templeton, and his much prettier better half, Nell."

"I'm almost his better half," Nell said with a laugh. "The wedding's still a few weeks off. New Year's Eve." She clasped Rory's hand in both of hers. "It's so nice to meet you. Gage has told us so much about you."

Rory's eyebrows rose as she gave Gage a look. "Has he?"

"Well, about Angel River," the other woman allowed with another laugh. She pulled off her black swing coat, and Rory realized she was pregnant. "It's so beautiful here. The pictures I saw don't do it justice."

Archer took her coat and added it to his own over his arm. He looked from Gage to Rory. "Seriously. *Is* there a room?"

"There's almost always a room at this inn," she answered wryly. "Here. Let me take those." She reached for the coats. "I'll go and get your room key."

He reached into his pocket. "Can I just give you the credit card?"

She waved it away. "Please. You're Gage's friend. Consider it Angel River's pleasure." She swung her arm wide, taking in the festive room all around them. "Make yourselves at home." With coats in hand, she quickly started out of the great room, stopping off to hang the coats on hooks before heading for the office.

Gage watched her go, then slid Archer a look. "What's really going on? You didn't say anything about wanting to come up here last time we talked." Which had been damn near every day about one thing or another, including the wedding from which Gage still hadn't managed to extricate himself. He'd become resigned at this point. Just because he'd be surrounded by a bunch of people named Templeton didn't have to mean anything. Thanks to the fact that his mother had never married his father, his name had always been Stanton.

"I could ask the same question," Archer countered. *"Honey?"*

Gage eyed him blankly.

"Interesting," Archer said, giving Nell a look.

"You gonna keep talking in code or what?"

Archer's smile widened. "We came up here because we wanted to give the news in person." He leaned forward conspiratorially. "All of Rambling

Mountain that you don't own is officially on the fast track to become Wyoming's newest state park. The first one to be named in decades."

Nell was practically bouncing on her toes. "He found out just this morning," she added. "We stopped long enough to tell April and Jed."

Gage couldn't help staring. "A state park. They're actually going for it."

"A press release is going out from the Parks Department sometime next week," Archer told him. "It'll still take time before all is said and done. First thing that'll go up is a ranger station while the access road to the lake is built. Other plans are still in the talking stage. But yeah. They're actually going for it. So congratulations. Once the Rad is up and running as a guest ranch, it'll be bordered by land that people are going to line up to experience. There's no way the Rad could fail."

They'd been working toward this for months, and now that it was happening, it felt strangely surreal. "Guess we should celebrate with something more than hot chocolate." Gage went behind the bar and set up a couple glasses.

Nell patted her small baby bulge. "I'll stick with the hot chocolate. Which—" she peered over the array of accompaniments "—is pretty impressive." She gave Archer a look. "What do you think Vivian would say to having a hot chocolate bar at the wedding?"

Archer laughed. "Since you have my grandmother wrapped around your finger, is that really a question?" He took the shot of bourbon that Gage handed him. He waited until Gage had his own, then tapped his glass to it. "Congrats again, man. The Stanton magic strikes again."

Gage chuckled, aware of Rory heading their way once more, though a portion of his attention was still on the hand Nell was still pressing against her belly.

He felt a little buzzing inside his head.

With only one exception, he and Rory had been scrupulously careful to use protection.

She still hadn't answered him about Denver. If she were to get pregnant, would she then?

"Here." Rory handed Archer a small envelope containing the card key when she reached them. "I've put you in the baron's suite. It has one of the best views on the property."

"Top of the stairs and end of the hall," Gage added. "Helluva bathroom."

Rory's cheeks pinkened. Because he'd cornered her there just a few weeks earlier when she'd been cleaning the vacated suite. They'd had a truly exceptional time together under the shower spray.

The miraculous part was nobody even noticed that she'd spent part of the afternoon with wet hair and a glow on her face.

And now, all he could do was probe that buzzing inside his head. He wanted Rory and Killy with him in Denver.

But was he really ready for all the rest, especially when Gage knew that when it came to life outside of business, his record was anything but magical?

Chapter Fourteen

The brunch that Bart had put on for the Pith group had been so popular they decided to begin regularly offering it on Sundays, at least for as long as the flash deal kept bringing in new people.

Rory's dad and Killy came down and joined her for the first one. It was the first time in a long while that the three of them had a meal together in the lodge. All the other tables scattered throughout the great room were occupied as well. Only a few guests were hearty enough to brave sitting outside on the deck, even with the propane heaters running.

Gage was one of them; he was sitting at a table visiting with a couple who'd come in from Chicago.

His lawyer had left a week ago, staying only the one night even though Rory had assured them they were welcome to stay for the whole weekend in the suite. But Nell had said they needed to get back. Both she and Archer had given her unexpected hugs on the way out. It was so obvious that Gage and Archer were good friends, she'd teased him later about the way he only ever referred to the man as his lawyer.

"He *is* my lawyer," he'd countered lazily and returned his attention to kissing his way to her breasts. They'd had a whole thirty minutes together behind the locked door of her office before duty had called again in the form of new arrivals.

They hadn't had another opportunity for locked doors until last night, when Killy spent his usual Saturday night with her dad.

"Can I have more fruit?" Killy's question dragged her from her thoughts.

"I'll get it for you." He still hadn't learned the art of not touching every piece of fruit whether he intended eating it or not. "Dad, you want anything?"

"I'm good." He was working a crossword puzzle from a three-day-old newspaper and barely glanced up.

She went over to the buffet, where Megan was making a process out of selecting one of Bart's handmade bagels, and picked up a plate.

Her friend gave her an arch look. "Anything new?"

Rory dropped a spoonful of sliced berries on the plate. "I'm not pregnant," she said under her breath.

She'd had to tell Megan about her and Gage's slip. Strangely, she had not told her about Denver. She wasn't sure why.

"Too bad."

"Megan!"

Her friend shrugged unrepentantly. "You make good babies. I was right about the three weeks. I'm right about this."

Rory glanced at the deck beyond the glass-paned doors.

"Right about what?" Noah reached past them to grab a carafe of fresh-squeezed orange juice.

"Nothing," Rory said quickly while Megan muffled a laugh.

He gave them both suspicious looks but walked away again, taking the carafe with him.

"They look cute together, don't they?" Megan nodded toward the table he was aiming for out on the deck, where Marni was sitting. "Man Bun and Pinkie."

"You really need to stop giving everyone nicknames," Rory scolded. Though she had to agree, Noah and Marni together did cut a striking pair. She rotated a tiny ceramic Christmas tree to better show off the even tinier red bulbs on it. "Have you given *them* a three-week timeline?"

Megan just laughed, and Rory brought the plate of fruit over to Killy. She jiggled his wannabe man bun. "We're having Donna cut this next week," she warned.

He shrugged, clearly more interested in the fruit he was shoveling into his mouth. As soon as he finished, he asked if he could go outside.

She saw no reason he couldn't. "Take your coat."

He grabbed it off the spare chair and pulled it on as he ran out to the deck, where Noah and Marni were sitting.

Rory slid onto Killy's vacated chair. "Feeling all right, Dad?"

He looked up at her. "Any reason why I wouldn't be?" Then he sighed and pushed aside his crossword. "Honey, you have to stop worrying about me."

"Might as well ask me to jump in the river." Her gaze strayed toward the deck again. "You should think about taking a vacation," she said. "Go somewhere warm. Play golf."

"What for? I hate golf." He refolded his newspaper and slid it toward her. "New state park is coming."

Faint dismay whisked across her nerves as she pulled the paper closer. A black-and-white photo of the peaks of Rambling Mountain was accompanied by a smaller one of a wizened old man. "Landowner Leaves Mountain for State," the headline read. A few lines of print beneath it comprised the entire article.

"Going to be one of the next hot spots in the state," her dad said. Needlessly.

Gage had to know. The paper was days old. His *attorney* had been there just a week ago.

Yet he hadn't told her.

"Excuse me." She left the table and went out onto the deck. As soon as she did, the chill permeated the knit of her turtleneck. She caught Gage's eye and he followed her when she reentered the lodge, neither of them stopping until they'd reached the office.

She'd barely closed the door when he was reaching for her, and even though she wanted to succumb, she sidled away and moved to sit behind her desk.

His brows jerked together slightly. "What?"

She folded her hands over her desk pad and the doodles there. "Hear there's going to be a new state park. On land surrounding the guest ranch that you're planning."

His dark gaze was steady. "Yes."

"And you didn't say anything about it."

"We've all been pretty busy around here. You most of all."

He was right, but that still didn't soothe the little churning that had started inside her. "You must be pleased about it, though. It's almost a guarantee you'll be successful right out of the gate."

"Yeah, but it's obviously bugging you."

"What's *bugging* me is the fact that you didn't say anything about the land becoming a state park! You know it's bound to have a greater effect on our business here at Angel River!"

"What's affecting Angel River is that you're afraid to get someone in here qualified to run the place and move on with your life!"

She lifted her chin. "Good to know you've gained

all the expertise you need. Not just about Angel River, but about me as well."

"This isn't about the state park," he said flatly. "This is about what's going on between *us*."

"No," she said doggedly, "this is about *your* business competing against *my* business."

He let out an abrupt laugh. "Sweetheart, that is no competition."

He was right. Again. Stanton Development was huge. Even with their surge in business—which she could only attribute to him since it had been his idea—Angel River was just...Angel River. And their hopes of competing against a brand-new property bordering a brand-new, unexplored state park were slim. "Then I'm surprised you wasted so much time here learning the secrets of our success, when it clearly wasn't even necessary!"

"I told you—" He broke off, starting to look annoyed. He took a breath and started fresh. "I told you I needed a place to get Noah away from everything. Angel River was just...convenient." He shoved back his hair. "And getting involved with you—"

"Was what?" She shot out of her chair, and it bounced against the credenza. "Another convenience?" Right about then, she felt as out of control as Bitsy Pith.

"For God's sake, Rory. You know that's not true. When, *when* haven't I been clear that the two of us sleeping together has *nothing* to do with business?" His voice rose, and his hand sliced the air. "You're freaking out because I asked you to come back with me to Denver! And you're either too afraid to admit you want to or too afraid to just tell me no!"

They both jerked at the sound from the doorway.

Noah stood there holding a brightly colored gift bag with tissue sticking out the top. His face was pale, and his blue eyes blazed. "Bastard." He pitched the bag to one side as he advanced, and it hit the coffee table with an ominous sound of glass breaking. "You just had to do it, didn't you? You had to steal the one thing you knew I wanted and—"

Gage swore. "Grow up, Noah. Not everything in this world is about you!"

"No. It's all about Gage Stanton! The perfect son," Noah spat. "The one whose touch turns everything to gold." His curled fist suddenly flew. "Except you don't know sh—"

Rory cried out, dashing out from behind her desk.

Gage, though, had deflected his brother's swing and held a tight, hard grip on his brother's arm. "I know you're still a kid playing at being a man." Looking disgusted, he shoved at Noah, releasing him, and his brother stumbled back.

Noah, though, caught his footing and looked like a bull ready to charge again.

"Stop it!" Heedless, she ran between them, her arms outstretched. "Stop it right now!"

"Dammit, Rory." Gage reached for her, trying to push her to one side. "Get out of the way before you get hurt."

She slapped his hands away. "The only ones who're going to get hurt are the both of you!"

She shoved Noah's shoulder before he could butt Gage. "If you're gonna behave like idiots, you can do it somewhere else!" She pushed at the younger man one more time for good measure. "Now *get* over there," she snarled, pointing behind him. And though he didn't exactly slink away in shame, he did at least back off a foot. "I am very fond of you, Noah, but nobody has *stolen* anything. Especially me." Her hands were shaking when she raked back her hair. "You know I don't feel that way about you, and if you were honest, you'd know you don't feel that way about me! I'm just someone who listens to you! And *you*." She turned her wrath on Gage. "The only thing I am *afraid* of is falling all over again for someone who can't tell the truth!"

His teeth clenched. "I told you. The state park thing has *nothing* to do with us."

"And it never will!" She swatted the air. "*How* can you behave like this with your own brother?"

His head jerked back. "What?"

"Family is everything." She stuck her face close to his. "Ev-er-y-*thing*!"

Noah snorted behind her. "Gage doesn't care about family. He cares about controlling the money Julian left me." He lifted his hands and wriggled his fingers like he was playing with marionettes. "He cares about making sure we're all dancing to his tune." He dropped his hands. "If he cared about family, he'd tell some of them that he actually *exists*!"

She saw the pallor creep into Gage's face. "What's he mean?"

But Gage wasn't listening to her. He was staring at his brother. "What do you know about that?"

Noah sneered. "That you're Thatcher Templeton's son? Vivian Templeton's *grandson*? The old lady's worth ten times what Julian was. I'm just surprised you haven't spoken up so you can get your claws in that particular pot at the end of the rainbow."

Gage sank bank on the edge of the desk. "How'd you know?"

"You're not the only one who had Althea Stanton for a mom," Noah reminded him. "Just 'cause she loved you more didn't mean she never told me about *your* father. *Thatcher.*" He puffed his fingers out in a little explosion. "About how he was estranged from his wealthy, wealthy mama. How she never knew about the two of them. Or about you." His whole body jerked with emphasis. "My mother could work for Julian. Sleep with him and have me. But nobody was ever going to replace *Thatcher*. Father of the sainted Gage." Noah looked at Rory. His eyes gleamed. "Imagine what it would do for that old woman to learn her firstborn had produced a son before he died."

Rory looked at Gage. "Templeton. As in Archer? Your *lawyer*? The one you won't even call a friend? Is he a relative, too?"

His compressed lips were nearly bloodless. His silence was stony.

"I don't know you at all." She turned on her heel and walked out of the office. But the truth was inside her head, mocking her with every step.

Of course she knew him. She just hadn't paid attention. *Relationships don't work for me.* He'd said so himself. Work was the only thing that suited him. He'd never claimed to love her. In asking her to go with him to Denver, he hadn't been offering a lifelong commitment.

She could hear the laughter and voices as she neared the great room, and she stopped. She didn't have the stomach to play her Angel River part just then.

She turned on her heel and went back to her office.

The two men were still there squared off against each other, but at least they didn't look as though they were a breath away from throwing punches. She wrapped her hand around the doorknob. "This is my office." The words sounded as harsh as they tasted. "Get out."

Noah was the first to go, though the look he sent Gage was searing as he brushed past her and left.

She looked to Gage, tightening her hand on the doorknob and ignoring her shakiness inside as she stared him down. If he thought she'd fold first, he had another think coming.

But he didn't make it easy.

Finally though, he pushed away from the edge of the desk and walked out.

She slammed the door shut so hard that one of the framed awards fell off the wall and broke when it landed.

Then she sniffled and sank down on the couch.

She picked up the gift bag that Noah had thrown. It was heavy, and she was half-afraid to read the tag on it. But it wasn't from him. The handwriting was girlish. Looping. "To our Angel River family," the tag said.

It was from Sabrina and Dante.

Remorse joined the rest of the funereal feelings churning inside her. She carefully lifted the tissue, bringing with it a glass figurine of a winged angel.

Broken in two.

"Her mother used to have a temper," Sean said. He set a bottle of whiskey and three short glasses on the table between Gage and Noah and sat down, looking out from the deck toward the glimmering blue river. A group of guests was on foot, clearly heading that way. Closer by, Gage could see Killy and Damon running around, tossing a football between them.

"Fierce," Sean added. "When Eleanor got going, it was always a good idea to just let the storm blow over." He chucked the collar of his coat up his neck before unscrewing the bottle. "She liked to smash a dish now and again." He poured a shot into each glass. "Never around the guests, of course."

Gage looked from the amber liquid to the older man, wondering what he was up to. He knew Noah couldn't—shouldn't—drink. But Sean's gaze was distant. Clearly stuck in his reminiscence.

As for Noah, his expression was stoic.

Though Gage couldn't explain why, for the better part of an hour, they'd both been sitting at opposite sides of the table without throwing a punch. Ever since Rory had thrown them out of her office.

Instead of heading to opposite sides of the earth, there they were.

It made as much sense as anything else.

Sean lifted one of the glasses. "To the women it's our privilege to love and our challenge to understand." He smiled faintly and tossed back the contents.

Then he got up and began heading toward the door.

Noah suddenly stirred. "Who *did* she smash the dishes around, then?" He looked over his shoulder at Sean.

Sean's lips twitched. "Only the people she loved, of course." He went inside. Several minutes later, he emerged below them on the lawn. He called something to Killy and caught the football when his grandson threw it to him.

Noah made a rough sound and reached for the

glass. His eyes met Gage's. He smiled mockingly and lifted it.

The instinct to stop him was automatic. Immediate. "Noah—"

"You expect me to fail, Gage." Noah swirled the glass. "Every single time. You expect it." He turned the glass over and poured the shot harmlessly over the railing. Then he turned the glass upside down and thumped it on the table between them. "I'm not drinking it because you've stopped me. I'm just not drinking so I can prove you wrong."

Then he, too, disappeared inside.

The next morning, Rory knew that Gage was gone.

He didn't show up at the barn to load the spreader.

He wasn't in the office with her dad when she showed up there after mucking the stalls on her own.

He wasn't in the kitchen with Bart.

And the low-slung black car that had been parked for so many weeks now outside the Brown cabin was gone.

She told herself that was fine. That was good. That he could dream on if he thought she would chase after him.

She spent the morning settling bills with departing guests, confirming more reservations for the coming weekend and ordering Christmas gifts online for Killy now that she'd gotten a peek at the letter he'd written to Santa.

The only thing that jarred her carefully modulated equilibrium was discovering that Noah was still there.

She discovered that particular fact when she returned to the lodge with Killy after picking him up from the bus stop. Noah was in the storeroom with Bart, unloading a supply of canned goods, and she stopped cold at the sight of him.

Mostly because at first glance she'd thought he was Gage.

Not that she would ever admit it.

She sent Killy on ahead. "Go and see Grandpa in the office," she told him, and because it was their usual routine, he saw nothing unusual in it at all.

After he was gone, she dangled his backpack from her fingertips. "You're here," she finally said to Noah.

He was still standing there with a giant can of tomatoes in each hand, and his expression was wary. "Is that okay?"

"Gage isn't." Just saying his name made the hollow feeling inside her worsen.

"No."

She wasn't going to ask if he would return. Or where he'd gone. She'd always known his stay at Angel River would come to an end. Now it had.

"Come to the office when you're finished with Bart," she said, heading through the doorway into the kitchen. "You can fill out the paperwork."

"For what?"

She didn't stop. "To get on the payroll." She ignored Bart's raised eyebrows as she walked past him.

In the great room, she threw away a crumpled napkin and stuck a stray glass in the rack of dishes waiting to be washed behind the mahogany bar.

She continued out of the great room and soon heard Killy chattering about his day to her father.

She let the sound of his voice wash over her. She drew in a deep breath and went into the office. Her dad was seated behind the desk.

"Killy," Sean interrupted him. "Bart has a whole batch of Christmas cookies that I think he needs your help with decorating."

Her son dashed past her and disappeared down the hall.

She sat down and began pulling stuff from his backpack in search of his usual worksheets. She pulled out another dinosaur; she wasn't even sure where he'd gotten it. The worksheets were crumpled at the bottom, and she tugged them out, smoothing them on the coffee table.

"I'm selling Angel River," her dad said.

She blinked, certain she hadn't heard right. "What?"

"I'm selling Angel River."

She shot off the couch. Panic filled her. "But why? You can't! Angel River's our home. It means… means everything to you."

"It does," he said quietly.

She whirled around to face him again, fresh alarm making her voice catch. "Is your cancer back?"

He sighed. "No."

"Then…then why?" Tears burned behind her eyes. "Everything's g-getting better." She spread her arms. "Angel River's even a trending topic!"

"I've had an offer for a while," he said. "A long while. And I think it's time I took it. You need to go, Rory."

"What?" She laughed brokenly. Disbelievingly. "You're kicking me out?"

"I'm telling you that it's time for you to start living *your* life."

"This is about Gage, isn't it?" She swiped her nose. "He's the one who talked you into selling."

"He didn't talk me into anything. But in a way, this *is* about him. He asked you to go with him."

She gaped. "He told you?"

"And you picked a fight because it was safer than taking another chance."

It stung harshly because in her heart, she knew it was true. "How can I want to be with a man who doesn't know what family means? He has a grandmother who doesn't even know he exists! Family should never be ignored like that!"

Her father's eyebrows lifted. "The way you've ignored the fact that Killian has a father he's never met?"

"Jon was the one who left us. Why should I give him another opportunity to reject Killian?"

"He hurt you. I'm no fan of the guy. But regardless of Jon's failures, Killian deserves to at least meet the man. Maybe Jon won't care. But then it'll truly be his failing. Not yours. And Killian will survive because he is surrounded by people who love him no matter what." He stood and rounded the desk, catching her chin in his hand. "You are in love with Gage Stanton. Am I wrong?"

When he looked at her that way, she could no more lie now than she could when she'd been a girl. "No."

"Then what the hell are you doing here, Rory?"

"You can't sell Angel River," she whispered.

"I can and I will if you don't get your butt in gear and go after that man," he said with as much vigor as he had in days long past. "And don't worry about Killian. I got you to school when you were his age. I can still do it now."

"B-but…right *now*?"

"You think the world is going to wait on you?"

She wiped the tears from her cheeks. "I don't even know where to find him."

Her dad just gave her a look. "I do."

Rory stared at the tall skyscraper and felt her nerves flagging.

She'd driven half the night to get there. Now it was morning. The street behind her was teeming with buses and cars and pedestrians walking with their heads lowered against the snowflakes swirl-

ing around them. Which fit in with the big snow-
flake decorations affixed to the light posts lining
the street.

Gage didn't merely live in the behemoth tower-
ing in front of her. Stanton Development was head-
quartered there. And Gage owned all of it.

And she felt wholly unequipped to deal with this
Gage Stanton.

She needed the one who'd muck out a horse stall
and set up a simple fish aquarium.

The doorman was still holding the door for her,
waiting patiently despite the weather.

She shook her head at him in silent apology and
backed away, nearly bumping into the woman behind her. She veered around her. She'd go home.
She'd figure out a way to keep her dad from selling Angel River.

Except he'd been pretty plain.

"Rory?" An overly cheery voice followed her.
"Is that you?"

Rory turned and knew she was losing her marbles
for sure. "Willow?"

The other woman giggled. "I *knew* that was you.
What are you doing here? You came to see Gage?"
Before Rory could stop her, she'd slipped her arm
through Rory's and was pulling her out of the snow,
right past the patient doorman and into the lobby
dominated by an enormous Christmas tree. She
flashed some sort of badge as they passed a secu-
rity desk and hit an elevator button while Rory was

still trying to figure out what Tig's flavor of the month was doing at Stanton Tower.

"What are *you* doing here?"

"Didn't Gage tell you?" Willow giggled again and pulled her into the elevator car. "I work here."

Rory's stomach swooped with the bullet-fast ascent. "Since when?"

"Since last month." Willow shrugged her shoulders, slipping out of her coat. She wore a plain brown jacket and trousers, looking nothing like she had when she'd been at the ranch. "Tig and I broke up. He's married, you know."

"I know," Rory said faintly. "But why here?"

"Gage told me if I ever needed a job to call his office. And I did." She smiled brilliantly. "I'm just a receptionist, but a girl has to start somewhere, right?"

Rory's stomach swooped again when the elevator suddenly slowed and eased to a stop. The doors opened smoothly and Willow stepped out. Rory mindlessly followed, her overwhelmed senses barely taking in the sleek industrial decor and the same holiday music that had been piped into the elevator. They passed endless windows and Willow entered another doorway. "Did he offer you a job, too?"

Rory looked away from the massive aquarium wall where brilliantly colored fish as big as her arm darted through the water to yet another Christmas tree with brightly wrapped gifts crammed beneath it. She laughed brokenly. "Honestly, Willow, I don't know what he offered me."

"What did you want me to offer?"

She spun and stared mutely up at Gage.

His jaw was smooth, his espresso hair brushed ruthlessly back from his handsome face. He wore a dark gray suit and tie and a watch that probably cost as much as her pickup truck. Her mouth was dry, and every doubt that had plagued her on the long drive there clamored inside her, just aching to escape. "I... Hi."

With a serious expression on his face, he took her elbow and drew her into an office with a wall of windows and closed the door.

She moistened her lips as she noticed the expansive desk and the rest of the expensive furnishings. The bottom floor of her cabin could have fit inside this office. "I don't know what I'm doing here," she whispered. She nervously walked across the office toward the windows. Snowflakes fell against the glass and slid downward, collecting in slight little drifts at the bottom before even they tumbled out of sight.

It was dizzying.

She turned back around and looked at Gage. He'd moved to lean against his desk, his eyes watchful.

"I shouldn't have said what I did about you and your grandmother." Her jaw worked. "My father pointed that out to me."

His eyes narrowed slightly. And still he said nothing.

She tugged on her ponytail. She felt underdressed in her jeans and red coat and wished she'd taken the time to dress with more care. "I told Noah we were putting him on the payroll." She smiled weakly. "Don't know if that'll last once you've purchased the ranch but—"

"I'm not buying Angel River. I told you that."

"But my dad has an offer. He told me."

"Yeah. From Tig."

She jerked.

"He told me about it when we first got to Angel River. Tig's wanted to buy the place for nearly a year. Every time he visits, he ups the ante." Gage's expression was unreadable. "Might as well know I kept that from you, too."

She winced.

"What did you want me to offer, Rory?"

She tugged at the buttons on her coat. Rocked on her heels. "Everything," she said huskily.

"What if everything I have isn't good enough?"

Her eyes flew to his.

"I don't know how to be anything other than what I am." His voice was low. "Some things I do pretty well." His gaze roved over the office. "And some things—" He looked at her. "The most important things, I've messed up every single time."

And just that easily, she recognized the man he was. The one who made her a bed of flowers. Whose touch made her feel whole. It didn't matter if he had manure on his boots or an expensive watch on his wrist. It was the man inside—the brother who kept trying, the man who kept learning, the one she'd laughed with and cried with. That was the man he was.

The man she was terrified of losing.

"I love you. You didn't mess up *us*. I did that. Because you were right. I was afraid. Afraid of finding everything that I've ever wanted in you and... and losing it."

"Do you think you're alone in that?" His eyes met hers, and she saw in them all her own fears reflecting back at her.

She was quaking inside. "Do you love me?"

His brows drew together. "I asked you to come with me, Rory. You and Killy. I want *you* for my family. I don't say that to other people. I say that to you. If that's not love, I don't know what it is."

She blinked back her tears. "Then is the offer still open?"

His expression softened. "Nothing's changed in the last day, sweetheart, except we're not in your territory. We're in mine."

She took a step closer. Then another. Until she was running into his arms and she could feel his heart hammering just as unevenly as her own. "I don't care about everything you have." She stared into his eyes. "Because everything you are is exactly good enough."

He touched her cheek and she felt the fine tremble in his fingers. "Are you sure?"

She didn't know what exactly the future would hold. But she knew she only wanted it to be with him.

She covered his fingers with her own. "Positive. I just have one question, though."

"What's that?"

"Are we spending Christmas at your place or mine? Because Killy's going to want to tell Santa where we'll be."

Gage's smile was suddenly wide and brilliant. "I think we can figure that one out together."

Together.

She'd never realized before what a beautiful word it was.

* * * * *

MILLS & BOON

Coming next month

AWAKENING HIS SHY CINDERELLA
Sophie Pembroke

"Trust me," Damon said, with feeling, "it's drawing exactly the right amount of attention to your figure. You look incredible." And he really had to stop looking at his big sister's best friend that way. Not least because she'd never given him even the slightest hint that she wanted him to.

There was that one night, his brain reminded him. That one night when you could have kissed her, if you'd wanted to.

But he hadn't. Because she was Celeste's best friend. Because she wasn't the sort of girl you messed around with, and he hadn't known how to do anything else.

Because she'd seen deeper than he liked, and it had scared him.

Her smile turned shy and she went back to studying the creatures on her dress, thankfully oblivious to his thoughts. "It is like my windows, isn't it?"

Somewhere someone clapped their hands again, and bellowed for them to take their places.

"Come on. We're starting." Damon took her arm and led her towards the bar. He needed another drink, and she hadn't even had one yet. "Let's grab a glass of something bubbly, and you can tell me more about your windows and your work until it's time to shout out the countdown, or whatever we need to do."

"You really want to know more about the windows?" She sounded astonished at the prospect.

"As it happens, I really, really do." And not just because of the way she lit up when she spoke about the things that mattered to her. Or because it would give him a chance to listen to her melodious voice. Those things weren't important to him. Or shouldn't be, anyway.

No, he wanted to know more because he had the inklings of an idea that could help both of them get what they needed in life. If he could persuade her to take a chance on him.

It was just business. That was all.

He just needed to keep reminding himself of that.

Continue reading
AWAKENING HIS SHY CINDERELLA
Sophie Pembroke

Available next month
www.millsandboon.co.uk

COMING SOON!

We really hope you enjoyed reading this book.
If you're looking for more romance, be sure to
head to the shops when new books are
available on

Thursday 12th November

To see which titles are coming soon, please visit

millsandboon.co.uk/nextmonth

LET'S TALK
Romance

For exclusive extracts, competitions
and special offers, find us online:

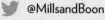 facebook.com/millsandboon

@MillsandBoon

@MillsandBoonUK

Get in touch on 01413 063232

For all the latest titles coming soon, visit
millsandboon.co.uk/nextmonth

JOIN US ON SOCIAL MEDIA!

Stay up to date with our latest releases, author news and gossip, special offers and discounts, and all the behind-the-scenes action from Mills & Boon...

 millsandboon

 millsandboonuk

 millsandboon

It might just be true love...

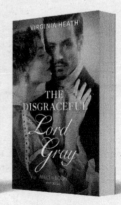

MILLS & BOON
MEDICAL
Pulse-Racing Passion

Set your pulse racing with dedicated, delectable doctors in the high-pressure world of medicine, where emotions run high and passion, comfort and love are the best medicine.